In Every Heartbeat

Books by

Kim Vogel Sawyer

FROM BETHANY HOUSE PUBLISHERS

Waiting for Summer's Return
Where Willows Grow
My Heart Remembers
Where the Heart Leads
A Promise for Spring
Fields of Grace
A Hopeful Heart
In Every Heartbeat
Courting Miss Amsel

IN EVERY HEARTBEAT

Kim Vogel Sawyer

BETHANY HOUSE PUBLISHERS
Minneapolis, Minnesota

In Every Heartbeat
Copyright © 2010
Kim Vogel Sawyer

Cover design by Brand Navigation
Cover photography by Steve Gardner, PixelWorks Studio, Inc.

Scripture quotations are taken from the King James Version of the Bible.

Published by Bethany House Publishers
11400 Hampshire Avenue South
Bloomington, Minnesota 55438

Bethany House Publishers is a division of
Baker Publishing Group, Grand Rapids, Michigan.

Printed in the United States of America

Library of Congress Cataloging-in-Publication Data

Sawyer, Kim Vogel.
    In every heartbeat / Kim Vogel Sawyer.
        p.   cm.
    ISBN 978-0-7642-0816-4 (alk. paper) — ISBN 978-0-7642-0510-1 (pbk.)   1. Friends—Fiction. I Title.
    PS3619.A97I5   2010
    813'.6—dc22

                                                                    2010014686

For my soul-sister, *Sabra*.
In many ways we're different, but God made us friends,
and I, for one, am truly grateful.
Love you muchly!

" . . . *the foolishness of God is wiser than men;*
and the weakness of God is stronger than men."

—1 Cor. 1:25 KJV

CHAPTER ONE

D*on't you dare cry.*

Libby Conley snapped the wardrobe door shut on her scanty belongings and spun to face her mentor and friend. "Well, I guess this is it." Her throat tightened, making her words come out an octave higher than normal. How she would miss Maelle!

She forced her lips into a quavering smile. "Thanks so much for bringing the boys and me to college. It was wonderful to have your company on the train. But . . ." She flipped her hands outward and angled her chin high. "I guess you're rid of me now."

Maelle Harders stepped away from her husband and wrapped Libby in a tight hug. Libby closed her eyes and accepted the hug without contributing to it. If she took hold of Maelle, she might never let go.

"Rid of you? Oh, bosh." Maelle's husky voice carried a hint of humor. "I think we'll be seeing you again." She released her hold and gave Libby's chin a light pinch, an affectionate gesture left over from Libby's childhood. "After all, you, Pete, and Bennett will be coming back to Shay's Ford for Mattie's wedding in less than six weeks. Mattie will need all of his groomsmen in attendance."

Libby nodded. Knowing she would soon return to the orphans' school that had been her home for the past eight years had helped Libby say good-bye to the school's directors, Aaron and Isabelle Rowley, yesterday. Libby could bear temporary good-byes, but she never said the word when she thought the separation might be permanent. She didn't plan to say it to Maelle, her favorite person in the whole world, even if she knew it would be a short separation. She *hated* the word *good-bye*.

"I'll be there for sure. I'm excited about the dance after your brother's wedding." Libby caught hold of her brand-new skirt and quickstepped a jig, making the brown worsted swirl above the tops of her patent leather boots. She planned to dance with Bennett, and with Petey, too, even if he was a little clumsy on his peg leg.

"It'll be a grand time." Maelle's tawny brown eyes crinkled with her smile. She slipped her hand through Jackson's elbow and beamed up at him. "As much fun as our after-wedding party was."

Libby admired the toes of her new shoes as the gaze passing between Maelle and Jackson heated. Although they were far from newlyweds—having married immediately upon Jackson's return from serving in the Missouri legislature five years ago—the pair had eyes only for each other. Libby admitted to some jealousy when Jackson had returned to Shay's Ford. Until he'd shown up, she'd had Maelle's attention to herself. Closing her eyes, she allowed a familiar daydream to surface.

"So you're really going to be my ma?" The happiness exploding through Libby's middle erupted in a joyous giggle.

Maelle smoothed Libby's tangled hair from her face. "Why, of course. I've always wanted a daughter, and I can't imagine a better one than you, Libby."

Libby threw herself into Maelle's arms. "Oh, I'm so happy you're adopting me! Thank you!"

"No, let me thank you, dear one." Maelle's cheek rested on the top of Libby's head, the contact warm and comforting. "You've made me the happiest mother on earth. . . ."

The sound of a clearing throat chased the fanciful musing away. Libby looked up to find both Maelle and Jackson grinning at her. Jackson said, "My apologies, Libby." He tucked his arm around Maelle's waist. "Sometimes I get lost in my beautiful wife's beguiling eyes and forget anyone else exists."

Maelle shook her head, her tumbling auburn locks swaying with the motion. "Goodness, the things you say . . ." But the tender look she gave Jackson contradicted her gentle reproach.

Libby clamped her lips tight as her anger swelled. Why hadn't Maelle and Jackson adopted her? When Libby was ten, she'd asked Maelle to be her mother, and Maelle had lovingly explained she wanted Libby to have the privilege of both a mother and a father. But then Jackson had returned and he and Maelle had married, and even then they hadn't adopted Libby. Now it was too late. No one had wanted Libby at the age of ten; why would anyone—even Maelle, who professed to love her dearly—adopt an eighteen-year-old? She'd never have the joy of calling Maelle *Ma*, the way her heart longed to.

Maelle shifted to face Libby. "Should we go find the boys? I imagine Bennett is hungry by now."

Jackson held his hand toward the door, and Libby scurried past him. As she careened out the door, she nearly collided with two girls in the hallway. Isabelle Rowley's lessons on etiquette rose in her memory, and she automatically excused herself.

The pair looked Libby up and down before they exchanged a quick haughty look. The taller of the two said, "You need to slow down."

"Or at the very least, look before you leave your room," the second one added.

Libby folded her arms over her chest. "I said, 'Excuse me.' And it isn't as if I *tried* to run you down. It was just bad timing."

The taller one opened her mouth, but before she could say anything, Maelle and Jackson stepped into the hallway. The girl snapped her mouth closed, took her companion by the elbow, and hustled toward the stairs.

Girls! She'd never gotten along well with other girls. They were too snooty or too prissy or too giggly. The condescending, scolding tones used by the girls in the hallway had sounded too much like the orphanage's founder. How often had Mrs. Rowley berated Libby for escaping into a daydream or for unladylike tree-climbing or frog-catching? Libby had grown to love Mrs. Rowley, but she'd never felt completely accepted by her. Girls were *no fun*. Except Maelle.

Libby clasped her hands beneath her chin and gave Maelle her best pleading look. "Can't I go back to Shay's Ford with you and Jackson?"

Maelle's brow crunched in confusion. "Why would you want to do that? You were so excited about attending the university."

That was before I met Snoot One and Snoot Two. Libby caught Maelle's arm. "If I'm too old to stay at the orphans' school, I could get a job at the newspaper, or even work for you as your assistant." She knew how to operate Maelle's camera. She'd spent so much time in Maelle's photography studio, it had become as much a home to her as her room in the orphanage dormitory.

"Libby, you know you wouldn't be happy working in my studio." Maelle spoke in a kind yet no-nonsense tone. "You've always wanted to be a writer. God must have opened this door for you, because you're at the perfect place to learn the trade of journalism. Not every college in Missouri allows female students in their journalism programs, but here at the University of Southern Missouri, women can learn right next to men."

Libby already knew she'd been given an amazing opportunity, even though she credited Mrs. Rowley's letter-writing skills rather than God for securing the scholarship. How she'd looked forward to sitting under the tutelage of the fine professors, learning the best ways to put words together to impact readers' emotions! But Maelle had learned photography by practice; surely Libby could learn newspaper writing through practice. "I know, but—"

"When God opens a door, you need to walk through it. Otherwise you'll miss the blessing He has planned for you." Maelle gently disengaged Libby's hands from her arm. "Besides, my sister worked so hard to get these scholarships for you, Pete, and Bennett. Think how disappointed Isabelle would be if you just threw it away."

Libby bit down on her lower lip. Mrs. Rowley had been almost giddy with excitement when a donor agreed to sponsor the orphan home's first graduates—their consolation prize for never having been adopted. She'd lectured the three of them endlessly on making the most of this tremendous opportunity. No, Isabelle Rowley would not be happy to see Libby return to Shay's Ford.

She sighed. "I suppose you're right."

Jackson stepped forward. "It's understandable for you to be apprehensive, Elisabet. This is a big change for you—leaving your home and meeting new people. When I left Shay's Ford to attend law school, I suffered homesickness and wondered if I'd made the right choice. It took some time, but I settled in."

Libby listened, rapt, to Jackson's encouragement. Might a father speak to her in just this way?

He smiled, reaching out to give her upper arm a light squeeze. "So you wait and see. I wager in a month's time, you'll love being here so much you won't want to leave even for a weekend visit."

Libby's mouth went dry. Not want to return, even for a visit?

Might college make such a change in her? She swallowed. "Y-you really think so?"

Maelle gave a gentle tug on one of Libby's loose curls. "You should never squander the chance for an education. Not everyone has that chance."

Libby knew Maelle regretted her lack of schooling. She'd spent her childhood traveling from state to state in a photographer's wagon, learning the trade. Even though she'd built a good life for herself, she had always encouraged Libby to study hard and take advantage of the education offered through the orphans' school. Even more than pleasing Mrs. Rowley, Libby wanted to avoid disappointing Maelle.

"All right. I'll give it a chance."

"Good." Maelle smiled, warming Libby with her approval. "And you'll find out there's no reason to be afraid."

Libby lifted her chin. "I'm not *afraid.*"

Maelle's smile never dimmed. "I know, Libby." She slung her arm around Libby's shoulders. "C'mon, let's go find the boys so we can say our good-byes. Jackson and I will miss our train if we don't skedaddle."

As Libby, Maelle, and Jackson walked across the thick, grassy carpet toward the ornate rock building that housed the dining hall, Libby breathed a sigh of relief that at least she wouldn't be alone here in Chambers. Her longtime pals Petey Leidig and Bennett Martin were right here on the University of Southern Missouri campus, too. Those familiar faces from the Reginald Standler Home for Orphaned and Destitute Children would help her battle the feelings of homesickness that tied her stomach into knots. Even so, they were boys and their fields of study were different, which meant they all lived in different dormitories. It wouldn't be the same as it had been at the orphans' home, where they resided on different floors under one roof.

They neared the dining hall, and Jackson pointed. "Is that Pete on the porch?"

Petey must have spotted them at the same time, because he lifted his hand in a wave and began stumping toward them. The breeze lifted the fresh-cut strands of his thick blond hair. The recent haircut and brand new pin-striped suit made him appear as dignified as Jackson the lawyer. Libby's heart swelled with pride for her friend. His peg leg—the result of a childhood accident—gave him a permanent limp, but the limp didn't bother Libby. He didn't feel sorry for himself, so she'd never felt the need to feel sorry for him. He was just Petey, her best friend and confidant.

When they met in a patch of sunshine in the middle of the yard, Libby asked, "Where's Bennett?"

"He went on in." Petey quirked one eyebrow. "You know how he is when it comes to food . . . he said he couldn't wait."

Jackson laughed, the corners of his dark eyes crinkling in amusement. "It's all right. You can tell him good-bye for us." He snaked out his hand and caught Petey around the neck. The two men hugged and thumped each other on the back. "You take care of yourself, Pete." Jackson pulled loose and sent a teasing smirk in Libby's direction. "Keep an eye on our girl, too."

Libby's heart swelled at his reference to "our girl." Oh, if only she were *their* girl!

"Make sure she stays out of mischief," Jackson added.

Petey chuckled. "As if I could! Nobody can tame Libby."

Libby snorted and glowered at the pair. "Honestly! As if anyone needs to *tame* me." She shook her head and turned to Maelle. A huge lump filled her throat. She didn't want Maelle to go. Her lips quivered, but she managed to form a small smile. "You have a safe trip h-home."

Tears sparkled in Maelle's eyes, but she blinked them away. "And you study hard. Make us all proud."

"I will. I promise."

Maelle hugged Libby fiercely, and this time Libby hugged back. Maelle's shoulders shuddered—was she crying? Maelle didn't cry; she was tough, just like Libby. Then Libby heard a sniffle near her ear. Maelle *was* crying. Tears burned like fire behind Libby's nose, and she crunched her eyes tight to hold them at bay. She wouldn't cry. *She wouldn't!*

"Maelle, we need to go," Jackson's voice intruded.

Maelle gave Libby one more tight squeeze and then stepped back. Libby hugged herself, blinking rapidly. Maelle opened her mouth, but before she could say good-bye, Libby blurted, "I'll see you in six weeks for the wedding." She grabbed Petey's elbow. "Let's go eat. I'm hungry."

CHAPTER TWO

P ete pressed his elbow against his ribcage, resisting Libby's tug on his arm. "Hold on. I want to give Jackson and Maelle a decent farewell."

Libby let out a little huff of displeasure, but Pete ignored it. He was used to Libby's huffs. It was the only girlish thing she did, and it was harmless. He stood watching until Jackson and Maelle reached the tall rock walls that lined the campus's entrance. As he had suspected they might, they paused and turned back. Both waved.

Petey waved with his hand held high. A vivid memory filled his mind: standing outside his family's tenement building, staring at the window, waiting for someone to look out and wave good-bye. He'd stood for hours, but no wave ever came.

He nodded toward Libby. "See there? How would they have felt to look back and find no one watching?"

"Sad." Libby's tone reflected the one-word answer and seemed to pluck the emotion from his heart. She gave a feeble wave and pulled again at his arm. "All right, you've given them a proper send-off. Now let's go eat."

Pete laughed as he turned toward the dining hall. He had to hop-skip on his wooden peg leg to match her swift pace. "I've never seen you so eager for a meal. You must have built up an appetite putting your things away. But slow down. You're going to send me tumbling."

She stopped so abruptly he almost fell forward. He looked down at her, ready to complain, but the tears winking in her velvet brown eyes stopped him. He'd never seen Libby cry—not when she'd fallen out of a tree and cut her chin, not when Bennett had accidentally smacked her with a homemade baseball, not even when she'd earned a licking for climbing the rose trellis on the side of the school dormitory.

Concerned, he cupped his hand over hers. "Libby, what's wrong?"

Instead of answering, she spun away from him and faced the campus. "I changed my mind. I . . . I don't think I could eat a bite. I'm going to take a walk instead." She started off in a determined gait, her arms pumping.

"Wait!" Pete trotted after her, hopping twice on his good leg for every one time on his peg leg. Even after years of using the wooden replacement for flesh and bone, it still jolted his hip when he moved too fast. He grimaced, but he caught up to her. Taking hold of her arm, he brought her to a halt. "What's the matter? Tell me." Over the years, he'd been privy to her secrets, her worries, her frustrations. He waited expectantly for a reply. But to his surprise, she turned stubborn.

"Nothing's wrong. I just want to take a walk. Go eat." She gave him a little push. "Bennett's probably holding a spot for you. So go on."

Even though his stomach murmured in desire, Pete shook his head. "Nah. You know when Bennett's got food in front of him, nothing else matters. He won't even miss me. I'll walk with you instead."

She pursed her lips, and for a moment Pete thought she'd send him away. But then she released another little huff. "Very well. Let's go. That way." Arms folded over her ribs and head low, Libby moved in the opposite direction of the path Jackson and Maelle had taken earlier. Occasionally, she kicked at a stone. Her movements seemed jerky, almost uncontrolled, so different from her usual grace. Although Pete wondered what had her in such a dither, he didn't ask. He'd learned sometimes it was best to let Libby stew. Eventually, she'd let the steam out and he'd know what was wrong.

They walked down a tree-lined path that ended in a field of uncut grass dotted with patches of wild flowers. She stopped and looked right and left, as if deciding which way to go. He waited patiently for her to make up her mind, refusing to fidget even though standing still intensified the ache in his hip. Whichever direction she chose, he'd follow.

Her brow puckered, and she tipped her head, frowning. "What is that?" She moved forward, her feet crushing the foot-high grass. Pete followed, his gaze on the shining locks of black hair that flowed almost to her waist. She stopped so suddenly he almost collided with her.

She clasped her hands beneath her chin and released a delighted laugh. "We found it!"

He glanced around, noting nothing of significance. "What did we find?"

"The foundation." Libby skipped forward and then crouched, skimming her hand over a rough rock wall only inches high. The free-growing grass and abundance of wild flowers had masked it from view. Pete propped his hands on his thighs and examined the gray weather-worn stones that formed a large rectangle.

"Remember what Mrs. Rowley said?" Libby's voice held excitement. "The original academic building burned to the ground in the late 1870s, and they chose to build a new one closer to the road rather than rebuild on the old foundation." Her gaze followed the line of the stones, her full lips forming a soft smile of wonder. "But it's still here, hunkering down low like a secret fortress for chipmunks or squirrels." Her voice took on a whimsical quality, and Petey knew she was drifting into one of her make-believe worlds.

With a little giggle, she stepped onto the foundation and extended her arms. Pete automatically caught one of her hands, and her dimples flashed with her smile. Holding the tips of his fingers, she put one foot in front of the other and walked the length of the little wall, her chin high and expression serious. Watching her, Pete couldn't help smiling. Libby had a way of making ordinary moments seem special.

She reached the corner and leapt off, landing in an exaggerated curtsy. She laughed, then spun to face the foundation again. Sobering, she tapped her chin with one finger. "It's kind of sad, isn't it, to think of such a grand building all burnt up and gone, only these few stones remaining? I wish I could have seen it when it was still here." Her gaze lifted slowly upward, and Petey knew she was trying to picture the building in her mind. He remained silent, allowing her the moments of silent introspection. When she'd had her fill of whimsy, she'd move on, and he'd tag along. Like always.

After several long seconds, she released a deep sigh and turned to face the opposite direction. Her eyes flew wide, and she let out a gasp. "Petey!" She ran to the opening between the trees.

"What?" He limped up beside her and peered into her astonished face.

"Oh . . . look." She pointed down the lane they'd taken. Her eyes seemed to dart everywhere. "The trees, the way they form a canopy over the walkway. See how the sun sneaks between the leaves and dapples the path? Why, it's simply laden with splashes of sunshine and shadow. How enchanting!" She laughed, clapping her hands once. "Doesn't it look like a fairy road?"

Pete tapped his peg leg against the ground, his means of battling the feeling of numbness in his missing limb. "A fairy road?"

She bopped his shoulder, just the way she had when they were younger and he irritated her. But she grinned at him. "Don't make fun."

He held up both hands. "I'm not making fun. You're right. It's . . . enchanting." But he kept his eyes glued to her face. Fingers of sunlight crept through the tree branches overhead, bringing a sheen to her dark hair and making her eyes shimmer. At least the tears had disappeared from her eyes.

He frowned. "Libby? You were ready to cry earlier. Why?"

The delight immediately faded from her expression. "I don't cry."

"I know you don't. That's why you have me worried."

She gave him a puzzled look "You really worry about me?"

He shrugged. "Sure I do. We're . . . we're friends, aren't we?" Lately, he'd found it hard to be just friends with Libby. A part of him—the larger part, he realized—longed to protect her, to shower her with little gifts and words of devotion, to tell her he thought she was the most intriguing female God had ever placed on the earth. But he held those words inside. Libby was so independent, with such lofty plans for success. He couldn't begin to compete with her dreams of traveling to big cities and writing stories that would capture the attention of a major newspaper publisher. He'd been saved to serve God. Why should she give up the chance for accolades to become the wife of a one-legged minister?

She placed her hand on his sleeve. "You don't need to worry about me. I had a momentary attack of melancholy. I wasn't ready for Maelle to leave." Her chin quivered briefly, but she set her jaw, and her brown eyes snapped with determination. "I'm fine now, as you can see, and we should probably return to our dormitories. Being late for curfew our very first day on campus won't bode well with the teachers."

Pete held out his elbow. With a little giggle, Libby caught hold, and he escorted her down the tree-lined walkway back toward the main part of campus. They walked in silence, which didn't bother Pete. Unlike many of the other girls at the orphans' school, Libby didn't seem to need to chatter constantly to be happy. He appreciated that about her. A fellow could just *be* and not worry about impressing her.

He swallowed a chuckle when he thought about how he'd once viewed her as just one of the boys. Isabelle Rowley, the most prim and proper woman he knew, had never allowed Libby to don boy's trousers, no matter how often she begged. But even wearing a dress, and even carrying a grace no boy could master, Libby had never seemed girlish. Her thick black braids flying, she'd kept up step-for-step in races, climbed just as high in trees, and nailed her target in mumblety-peg with amazing accuracy.

And then one day, shortly after their sixteenth birthdays, he'd looked at her and realized she was beautiful. He'd told her so, too. His arm had ached for two days where she'd punched him. He wouldn't tell her again. But she couldn't keep him from thinking it.

"Well, look at this, Claude. We've caught us a couple of lovebirds."

Pete instinctively tucked his arm hard to his side, trapping

Libby's hand between his elbow and ribcage. He hoped the pressure would keep her silent. Two young men swaggered toward them, cocky grins on their faces. Pete knew they were college students by their matching fraternity jackets. His stomach tightened in apprehension. Jackson had warned him about freshman hazing. He had no plans to join a fraternity, so he'd hoped to avoid the tradition, but he surmised from the looks on the men's faces that they were determined to make sport with him.

The pair stopped directly in Pete's path, fists on hips and feet widespread, trapping him and Libby in place. "So am I right?" the taller of the pair drawled. "Are you two lovebirds?"

Libby bristled. "Certainly not! We're—"

Pete jerked his arm, and to his relief she hushed. "I'm escorting Miss Conley to her dormitory so she doesn't miss curfew. If you'll excuse us."

"Miss Conley, huh?" The one who'd done the talking so far stepped forward, leaning close to Libby. She pressed her cheek to Pete's shoulder, puckering her face in distaste. The man laughed and slapped his leg. "You've got time yet for curfew. I'd like to get a better look at this little darlin'. She's quite the looker, huh, Claude?"

"That she is, Roy." Claude waggled his eyebrows, leering at Libby. "I like a girl with some color in her face. And all that loose black hair. Reminds me of the picture on a calendar my pop had hidden in the back of his workshop where Ma wouldn't see."

Fury rose from Pete's gut at the man's brazenness. Upper classmen or not, they had no right to insult Libby. "Gentlemen," Pete said through clenched teeth, "you've had your fun. Now let us pass."

"Oh, our fun's just beginning, sonny boy." The one named Roy gave Pete's shoulder a smack with the butt of his hand.

Pete planted his peg leg and managed to keep his balance despite the other's man's rough treatment.

"You're new, aren'tcha?"

With a quick glance at Libby, Pete offered a hesitant nod.

"Thought so. That means we've got seniority. And that means you've gotta do what we say. Huh, Claude?"

Claude grinned. "That's right, Roy."

"So for starters . . ." Roy took a menacing step forward, stopping mere inches in front of Pete. "Let go of this sweet little thing's hand."

Libby sucked in a sharp breath. Pete shook his head. "No, sir."

Roy's thick eyebrows rose. "Did you say no to me?"

Lord, help me. I don't want this to turn ugly. Libby could be hurt. Pete sucked in a lungful of air and looked directly into the face of his tormenter. "Yes, I did. I'm not going to release my friend's hand, and I'm not going to allow you to harass her any further. Now, step aside and let us pass."

Roy stared at Pete in open-mouthed amazement before hooting in laughter. He grabbed Claude's arm and shook it. "Did you hear him, Claude? The pretty boy here just said he wouldn't *allow* me to bother his little lovebird." The laughter ended, and Roy's eyes narrowed into slits. "I'm curious, pretty boy, how you plan to keep me from bothering her?"

Aaron Rowley, Pete's foster father for most of his life, had taught him to use his head instead of his fists in disagreements. Aaron's advice made sense—violence rarely provided a permanent solution; and with his peg leg, Pete had the disadvantage in any physical altercation. So he'd followed Aaron's instruction. But from the look on Roy's face, Pete sensed talking wouldn't diffuse this situation. To rid himself of this man's company, he'd have to use his fists. He took hold of Libby's shoulders and set her aside.

Her eyes grew huge as realization dawned. "Petey, no!"

"Petey?" Roy blasted another laugh. "Oh, Claude, did'ja hear that? His name is Petey!"

Libby whirled on the men. "You stop laughing at him!" She plunked her fists on her hips, and fire sparked from her eyes. Pete cringed, recognizing the signs of Libby gearing up for a fight.

"Oh, how brave you are—two against one," she continued. "But look at him standing up to you! He's twice the man either of you are!" Her face blazed red with indignation, and her volume increased with the color in her face. Other students, milling outside the dining hall, turned in their direction.

Pete sent Libby a pleading look, but she waved her fists. "You get away! How dare you attack a woman and a crippled man!"

Shame washed over Pete. She thought of him as crippled? "Libby, enough."

But she cupped her hands beside her mouth and yelled to the approaching students. "Everyone look at the big men! Harassing a woman and a man with a peg leg. Will any of you stand up to them?"

Suddenly one man broke free of the crowd and charged across the grounds. Pete groaned when he recognized Bennett's fiery red hair. Hadn't he been humiliated enough by Libby's shouts? Now his childhood buddy had to come rescue him?

"Bennett, stay out of this," Pete growled as soon as Bennett reached them.

But Bennett grinned. "Don't you worry, Pete. I'll take 'em down a notch or two. I got no bum leg holdin' *me* back." Bennett raised his fists and went into a fighter's crouch. "All right, fellas, all I ask is you come at me one at a time. That's only fair, right?"

"Sure, that's fair," Roy agreed, waving his arm. A half dozen young men, all attired in dark blue jackets with a gold emblem on the left shoulder, trotted across the lawn and joined Roy and

Claude. "We'll even let you decide which one of us you want to take first."

Bennett rubbed his thumb on the side of his nose and swept his gaze across the circle of men. Before he could point at any of them as his first contender, Pete jolted forward.

"This is ridiculous!" On his second step, Pete's peg leg slid in the grass. He flailed.

Bennett caught Pete's arm, preventing him from falling. "Get back, buddy. I'll handle this."

"But it isn't necessary." Pete grabbed for Bennett's elbow, but his friend danced sideways, evading his grasp.

Bennett rotated his fists, drawing small circles in the air. "Come on. I'm ready. Who wants to start?"

The crowd grew, made up of men and women both. By their curious gawks and eager grins, it appeared all were keen to witness a melee. Pete looked around in frustration. Wasn't it enough that the newspaper headlines were filled with stories about the war waging in Europe? There was no need for a scrape right here on the University of Southern Missouri campus.

"Bennett, stop showing off. Let me handle this on my own." Pete managed to grab Bennett's arm, but his friend shook loose.

"I can take 'em." Bennett's narrowed eyes bounced from one adversary to another. "Just get out of my way."

Two of Roy's friends tugged off their jackets and stomped up to within a few feet of Bennett. One pointed at Pete. "Let's go."

Bennett bolted upright. "Wait a minute. Pete's not fighting."

"He started it," Roy called from the sidelines, "so he's gonna help finish it."

The man who'd pointed at Pete advanced.

Libby flew across the grass and flung herself in front of Pete. "Don't you dare touch him!"

24

The man came to a startled halt. Laughter broke out across the crowd.

Pete groaned. Less than an hour ago, Jackson had chided him to keep Libby from mischief. And look at what he'd done—inspired a riot with her at the very center. He curled his hand over her shoulder. "Libby, please . . ."

"No!" She batted his hand away, her hair swinging wildly around her face. She held her arms out and blocked Pete with her body. "If you think you have to fight someone, you're going to have to fight me."

The man looked past Libby to Pete. Disdain curled his lips. "You're gonna let this girl fight your battle for you?"

"No." Pete grabbed Libby around the waist and lifted her. She squawked, slapping at his hands. Pain shot from his stump to his hip, and it took every ounce of effort he possessed to keep his footing, but to his relief he remained upright and set her aside.

But the moment he released her, she darted back in front of him. She shot him a furious look before whirling on the other man. "If you want to fight, you'll fight me. You won't lay a finger on Petey."

Pete wished the ground would rise up and swallow him whole.

CHAPTER THREE

Bennett eyed the tall, curly-haired man at the front of the crowd. Arms folded over his chest, laughing. He was enjoying Libby's exhibition. Good ol' Lib, always in the middle of a fracas. Her antics were buying him the time he needed to size up the situation.

Running wild on the streets of Shay's Ford, Missouri, he'd learned a thing or two about survival, and one of the most important lessons was recognizing the leader of packs. All Bennett had to do was take down the leader, and the pack would scatter. Worked every time.

"Hey! You there!" Bennett took one step toward the curly-haired man laughing at Libby.

The man swung his face in Bennett's direction, his smile changing to a sneer.

Bennett bounced, his knees loose. "You said I could choose who I wanted to fight first, right?" Bennett aimed his trigger finger directly at the man's nose. "I choose you." Out of the corner of his eye, he saw Pete whisk Libby away from the action. Good. Now he'd be able to focus on his target instead of worrying about one of his pals getting hurt.

Bennett crouched again, his fists ready. "So c'mon."

For a moment, the man looked uncertain. Bennett didn't bother to hide his smirk. He wouldn't be at all surprised to see the bully turn and run now that he'd been confronted. But then the man yanked off his coat. He handed it to one of his friends and began rolling up his sleeves with slow, deliberate movements. His buddies shouted encouragement.

Elation zinged through Bennett's frame, powerful as a lightning bolt. So the man would fight! Besting him would be even better than seeing him run. Bennett danced in place, waiting for the taller man to finish readying himself. "C'mon, man, hurry up. You're as slow as my grandmaw." Bennett didn't even know his grandmother, but the taunt hit its mark.

The man's face blazed red. His friends called, "Let 'im have it, Roy. Show him who's boss."

"That's right, Roy. Show me." *Or better yet, be prepared to let me show you no one bests Bennett Martin.*

Bennett tensed as the man approached. Although a good six inches shorter, Bennett figured he outweighed the other man by at least twenty pounds. Ever since the Rowleys had pulled him off the streets, he'd taken advantage of the free meals. The abundance of food, combined with Bennett's ceaseless activities, had resulted in a thick, muscular build. All he had to do was get this fellow pinned, and the fight would be over in no time.

For several seconds Roy stood motionless, one leg braced in front of the other, his fists in position, eying Bennett. Bennett watched the man's face, anticipating the first lunge. A slight tensing of jaw muscles gave a warning, and Bennett easily sidestepped the first punch. While Roy was off-balance, Bennett brought his right fist upward and caught Roy under the chin. Roy staggered, his arms flailing, and Bennett swung with his left. He connected firmly with Roy's nose.

"Ohhh! Ohhh!" Roy grabbed his face and bent over. "My nose! You broke my nose!"

"That can happen in a fight, my friend." Bennett rubbed his stinging knuckles.

Blood dripped between Roy's fingers. He slinked to the side, still holding his nose.

Bennett looked across the group of Roy's friends. "Who's next?"

The gang of men murmured and backed away. Roy, hunkered over like an old man, headed for the men's dormitory. The crowd dispersed, muttering and shaking their heads.

Bennett waited until everyone had gone before turning to Pete and Libby. He grinned. "Leave you two alone for one hour and look what happens. You all right?" His gaze flicked past Pete to Libby and lingered. How could anyone so pretty be so tough? "Honestly, Lib, one of these days you're going to have to start acting like a girl."

Libby tossed her head. Her long hair waved like a horse's mane. "Those men made me so mad! They had no reason to attack us. Just because we're new around here, they—"

"Get used to it," Bennett said without sympathy. "We're first-year students, and first-year students are nothin'. Hazing is just part of a freshman's college life. But—" He gave her a warning look. "With Pete over in Landry Hall in the Bible College, you in the journalism classes, and me in the School of Engineering, I won't always be around. So be careful when you're pickin' fights."

Libby glared at him. "*I* didn't pick that fight! That . . . that Roy brought it to us!"

"All right, all right, don't start fighting with *me* now."

Libby slipped her hand through Pete's arm and smiled up at him. "But all's well that ends well, right, Petey?"

Pete didn't smile in return.

Bennett socked him on the shoulder then flexed his fist. That Roy had a hard head. "C'mon, buddy, don't look so glum. Nobody got hurt. Except Roy." He waited for Pete to laugh. But he didn't.

Pete turned Libby toward the women's hall and began limping in that direction. "Come on, Libby. We need to get you to Rhodes Hall and then return to our own dormitories before curfew."

Bennett sauntered along on the other side of Libby, his usual spot. When it was the three of them, he and Pete always flanked Libby. And no matter what he did to gain her attention, she always looked to Pete first.

He bumped her lightly with his elbow. "Hey, I didn't see either of you in the dining hall. Food's pretty good—not as good as ol' Cookie Ramona's grub at the school, but there's plenty of it." Bennett patted his belly. "I got filled up with no trouble at all. I put some rolls in my pocket. Want one?" He reached into his jacket pocket and encountered a jumble of crumbs. "Aw, Roy must've crushed 'em when he plowed into me. Sorry."

Libby flashed him a quick grin. "Don't worry. We weren't hungry anyway, were we, Petey?"

Pete pointed to the arched double doors of the women's hall. "Go on in, Libby. We'll see you tomorrow morning at breakfast."

"All right. Good night, Petey. Good night, Bennett."

Bennett bristled. He'd just fought to protect her. Couldn't she at least tell him good night first? But of course Pete would always be first where Lib was concerned; he had the sympathy factor going for him with his bum leg. "Night, Lib."

He and Pete stood on the sidewalk and waited until Libby closed

29

herself behind the doors. Then they turned toward Franklin Hall, where Bennett's room was located. Bennett slowed his steps to match Pete's stride. Pete could run when he wanted to on that peg leg. It was a clumsy way of running—kind of a double hop on his good leg followed by a skip on his peg—but he could move pretty fast. Even so, most of the time he kept to a sedate pace. Bennett tried not to get impatient with him over it.

"So how's your room in Landry?" Bennett asked. His own room was small and smelled a little bit like the cave he and Pete had stumbled upon when they were children, but he'd slept in a lot worse places.

"Small," Pete said, "and it smells kind of like bat dung."

Bennett grinned. Funny how the two of them thought alike. Bennett supposed that was bound to happen, as much time as they'd spent together. He and Pete had latched on to each other from the first day Bennett had arrived at the Reginald Standler Home, rescued by Aaron Rowley. Being the oldest boys in the school, they'd ruled the roost, although Pete seemed to look out for the younger kids while Bennett preferred to boss them around.

Bennett snorted. "I told Libby to get used to it, but it's not gonna be easy, being low man around here." He bumped Pete with his elbow. "But we survived the streets and we'll survive being lowly college freshmen, huh? We got through tonight just fine."

Pete came to a stop and frowned at Bennett. "Listen, about tonight . . ."

Bennett pushed his jacket flaps aside to slip his hands into his pants pockets. "Don't bother to thank me, Pete. You know I can never pass up a good fight. Didn't bother me at all to come to your rescue."

The furrows in Pete's forehead deepened. "That's just it. I didn't want you coming to my rescue. I could have handled the situation fine. There might not have even been a fight if you hadn't come charging over there with your fists in the air. The Bible says—"

Bennett held up both palms. "Hold it right there. I know you're planning to be a preacher. You want to spend your days praying and sermonizing? Go ahead if that's what makes you happy. But you aren't *my* preacher. So don't sermonize at *me*."

Pete dropped his head back and sighed. "All right." He met Bennett's gaze again. "I tell you what: I won't fling sermons at you if you won't fling your fists around for me. Pact?" He held out his hand.

Bennett frowned at Pete's hand for a moment. He wasn't sure he liked the tone Pete used. His pal sounded sore about something, but what? Thanks to Bennett, Pete'd kept his nose clean . . . and unpunched. He ought to be grateful that Bennett had stepped in when he did. But if Pete wanted to fight for himself next time, so be it. Bennett wouldn't deny him the pleasure.

He grasped Pete's hand and gave it a firm shake. "Pact, buddy. From now on, your battles are your own."

❧

"Your battles are your own." Pete replayed Bennett's parting comment as he limped toward Landry Hall. The big rock building loomed ahead, its many-windowed roof peaks reminding Pete of eyes peering across the campus. The first time he'd seen the Bible college building, he'd liked it. Built of stone—sturdy, immovable. Unlike some of the other buildings, no towering trees shaded Landry, and the stones glowed like gold in the waning sunlight. The building seemed a sanctuary. Pete liked the idea of having a place of refuge.

"Your battles are your own." The words continued to niggle at Pete's mind as he made his way through the corridor to the

staircase. He was able to hop up the stairs using only his good leg to support himself, but tonight he took them with two feet on every step. Trudging progress. Left, right; left, right. One riser at a time. *Click* with the peg leg and *clunk* with his boot sole. Slow going, but quiet.

He reached his room and closed himself inside. The soft snap of the door latch echoed, and despite the warmth of the room, Pete shivered. He'd never had a room all to himself. Before his folks kicked him out, he'd shared a three-room apartment with his parents and five younger siblings. At the orphans' home, he and Bennett roomed with six other orphaned boys. Before that, he'd slept at the Rowleys' market in a storeroom with an ever-changing population of street boys. Even when he'd spent nights on the street, there'd been other homeless kids around.

He wished he could room with Bennett, but they were in different programs. Besides, everyone enrolled in the Bible college had a private room. The professors said it would give them the privacy they needed to study, pray, and meditate. Pete supposed he'd get used to the silence eventually.

He removed his new store-bought jacket and hung it on the back of the desk chair, then sat on the edge of the squeaky little bed in the corner. He looked out the window at the grounds, now shadowed as the sun slipped behind the trees. Heaving a sigh, he spoke aloud in the empty room. "Your battles are your own, Pete." A rueful laugh left his lips. "That is, if you can keep Libby from fighting them for you."

Humiliation washed over him, making him break out in a sweat. What must those who watched the evening's squabble on the lawn think of him? A grown man, being defended by a slip of a girl. He'd seen the smirks, heard the disparaging comments. Libby, unwittingly, had branded him a coward. And a cripple. He hated that word. He hated that Libby had used it to define him.

He unstrapped his wooden leg and tossed it aside, then pushed to a standing position. He found his balance quickly after years of standing on one foot and hopped to the window. Bracing his palms on the smooth, cool stone ledge that formed the sill, he peered across the campus, but the memory of Libby's fierce expression as she defended him filled his vision.

Libby was feisty—she'd always been. Just as he was. And Bennett, too. They'd had to be feisty to survive. Libby had lost her parents in a carriage accident; Bennett didn't even remember his folks; and Pete's pa and ma had kicked him out to fend for himself when he was only seven years old. If he, Libby, and Bennett hadn't been aggressive, they might have rolled over and died.

Even though they'd each eventually found their way to the orphans' home and the loving attention of Aaron and Isabelle Rowley, they still carried that childhood feistiness into adulthood. The only difference between him and his friends was his missing leg. He looked down at the empty pant leg dangling a few inches above the floor, and anger rose up, hot and all-consuming. He'd have two good legs had it not been for his parents, Gunter and Berta Leidig.

Aaron Rowley had told Pete he needed to forgive his parents, and Pete agreed, but he didn't know how to let loose of the resentment. He wouldn't have been on that trolley, carrying an armload of newspapers to sell on a corner, if they hadn't sent him out into the cold. He'd never forget the shock and pain of the trolley wheel rolling across his leg. Three brief seconds of time had changed his life forever. And he'd never forget the parents who'd allowed it to happen through their lack of responsibility toward their child.

Pete slapped the window frame and hopped back to the bed. The mattress complained when he plopped down, but he ignored the squeak and undressed, laying his pants and shirt neatly across the seat of the chair to wear again tomorrow. Then he stretched out and put his linked hands beneath his head. He stared at the ceiling, eager to sleep but disturbed by that simple statement: *"Your battles are your own."*

The truth was, from the time he'd been a very small boy, his battles had been his own. And he had one big battle he was now ready to face. One he'd been gathering courage for years to face. He intended to find Gunter and Berta Leidig and tell them, very honestly, exactly what he thought of them. Then maybe this ever-present cloud of resentment would fade away.

CHAPTER FOUR

Y ou aren't going to pledge to a sorority?"

Libby turned from the washstand, a towel pressed to her chin, and looked at her roommate. The girl's aghast expression made her want to laugh. She placed the soggy towel over her lips and cleared her throat, chasing away the bubble of laughter. "Actually, no. I don't see the point."

"But . . . but . . ." Her roommate, Alice-Marie Daley from Clayton—in St. Louis County, didn't Libby know—rose from her perch on the edge of her bed and held out her hands in supplication. Her ruffly nightgown billowed around her ankles in an explosion of shimmering pink. "Everyone, but just *everyone*, pledges to a sorority or fraternity!"

Libby turned back to the round mirror hanging above the washstand and continued drying her face. Alice-Marie walked up behind Libby and talked to her reflection in the mirror.

"I intend to pledge Kappa Kappa Gamma. They're one of the

oldest sororities, which Mother says is very important—it's all about the *history* of a thing, you know." She giggled, nudging Libby's shoulder. "But what I like about them is their flower. The fleur-de-lis. I just love the way it sounds. *Fleur-de-lis.*" She emphasized each syllable, rounding the vowels.

Libby resisted rolling her eyes. "Uh-huh." Damp tendrils of hair stuck to her temples, and she rubbed at the fine strands with the towel.

Alice-Marie fluffed the long tresses falling down Libby's back. "Your hair is very, very long. Do you always wear it down? Mother says the Grecian style is now all the rage. That's why I brush mine back into a tight roll. For the hairstyle to hold, I have to keep my hair at a manageable length. But with my natural curl, it's still very difficult to control. Maybe I should let mine grow longer and hang loose, too."

Libby shifted sideways a bit, removing herself from Alice-Marie's fingers. "I like mine long." Maelle wore her hair long. Most of the girls at the orphans' school wore their hair shoulder-length for easy care, but Libby had pitched a fit each time Mrs. Rowley approached with a scissors. Mrs. Rowley had finally given up. If long hair was good enough for Maelle, it was good enough for Libby.

"Well, you have pretty hair anyway," Alice-Marie said. "So very, very soft, but dark, almost like an Indian's." She released a nervous-sounding giggle. "You *aren't* an Indian, are you? Even your skin is browned . . . but that *is* from the sun?" She smoothed her own creamy cheek with her fingertips, her gaze fixed on her reflection in the mirror. "Mother says white skin is the sign of a true lady. I always wear a hat or carry a parasol if I must be out in the sun too long."

Libby draped the sodden cloth over a little wooden rod and turned to step past Alice-Marie.

But Alice-Marie moved directly into Libby's path and clasped her hands beneath her chin, flattening the abundance of ruffles on her nightgown's neckline. "Elisabet, you simply must pledge a sorority. Pledge to Kappa Kappa Gamma with me, please? You'll be completely friendless if you don't pledge!"

Swishing her palms together, Libby gave Alice-Marie a grim look. "Then I suppose I'll just have to be friendless."

Alice-Marie's mouth fell open in a perfect O. She stared at Libby as if she'd seen an apparition.

Libby flounced past her roommate to the wardrobe and tugged her simple white cotton gown over her head. "Alice-Marie, please don't think me unsociable, but I'm not here to join clubs and make friends. I came to learn journalism. I intend to find a job in town, which will probably take up a great deal of my time. Between a job and studying, I don't see how I'll have time to spare for clubs and such."

Alice-Marie crawled into her bed and nestled against the pillows. She puckered her lips into a pout. "Oh . . . poor dear. You have to work to pay for your own schooling? Won't your father pay the bill?"

Libby couldn't decide if Alice-Marie was sympathetic or appalled. But she answered honestly. "I'm here on scholarship. My schooling is paid for by a benefactor to the orphans' school where I've lived since I was a little girl. I do need to earn spending money, but I want a job not so much for the money as the experience."

"Ooooooh!" The single word ran up the scale and down. Alice-Marie fussed with her blankets, her eyes zinging everywhere around the room except directly at Libby. "You—you're an orphan?"

Libby'd heard that tone before, and she'd never liked it. Why did people react so negatively when they discovered her parentless state? She'd done nothing to create it, so why should people act as though it meant there was something wrong with her? But then again, maybe there *was* something wrong with her. No one had seemed to want her after her parents died. "Yes. I am."

"I see." Alice-Marie pulled the covers to her chin and wriggled lower on the mattress. "Well, that's sad. Hmm. Well, as I said, I plan to pledge Kappa Kappa Gamma, and I'd like to run for a position on the Women's Council. I also hope to be accepted to the Women's Pan Hellenic Council. As long as it doesn't interfere with playing tennis. I'm so glad they have a court right here on campus. I adore a good game of tennis."

Libby imagined Alice-Marie playing with a racquet in one hand and a parasol in the other. She released a little snort. "Are you here for entertainment or education?"

Alice-Marie lifted her head. "What did you say?"

"Nothing. Just that I hope you enjoy all the . . . activities."

"Oh, I intend to. Mother says the most interesting women are those who are well-rounded, so I need lots of experiences to . . . well . . . round me out!"

A high-pitched giggle carried across the room and pierced Libby's ears. She pulled the covers over her head. "Good night, Alice-Marie."

"Oh? Are you ready to sleep?" She sounded more puzzled than miffed. "All right, then. Do you want me to turn out the light?"

"Unless you plan to sleep with it on."

The covers must have muffled her sarcastic words because Alice-Marie said, "What was that?"

Libby flapped the covers down and spoke loudly. "Yes, please turn it off."

"Very well. Good night, Elisabet. Sleep well. Mother says a proper night's sleep is very important."

Libby buried her face once more. *Mother says* . . . Envy nearly turned Libby's chest inside out. How she wished she could tell someone, "Mother says . . ." But she didn't have a mother. Not even an adopted mother. She could say, "Mrs. Rowley says . . ." or "Maelle says . . ." But then people would ask, "Who's Mrs. Rowley? Who's Maelle?" No one ever had to ask, "Who's Mother?"

Libby rolled to her side and squeezed her eyes tight. She was eighteen already—a woman herself. And she was going to be a well-known journalist. Someday, people on the street would say to one another, "Did you read today's *Gazette*? Elisabet Conley says . . ." Then they'd quote directly from her articles. Alice-Marie's mother was only known to Alice-Marie; Libby would be known to thousands. And when that day came, it wouldn't matter one bit that she was an orphan.

When Libby awakened the next morning, she discovered Alice-Marie had already dressed and gone. She squinted at the round wind-up clock on her roommate's bureau and released a squawk of surprise. Almost eight-thirty! Breakfast would end in another thirty minutes. After she'd skipped supper last night, her stomach pinched painfully. She planned to visit the various newspaper offices in town today to seek employment; she needed food to keep up her strength.

She jumped out of bed, slipped into the brown worsted skirt and weskit she'd worn yesterday, and tied her uncombed hair into a ponytail at the base of her skull with an unpretentious piece of brown ribbon. Her fingers trembling, she groped in the bottom of the dark wardrobe and located the black leather satchel Maelle and Jackson had given her to keep her writings organized. For a moment she held the satchel on her open palms, like a servant bearing a crown on a pillow, and held her breath. Within the leather case rested her hope for the future.

Please, oh please, let them be good enough!

She usually allowed Petey to do the praying, but this plea formed in the deepest parts of her being.

Hugging the satchel to her heart, she flung the door open and started to charge into the hallway. She barely remembered to look first. To her relief, the hall was empty. She ran to the staircase and clattered downstairs, her shoes making a terrible racket.

Her feet never slowed as she dashed across the grassy courtyard. Expertly she dodged other students, ignoring their laughs or warnings to be careful, and careened into the dining hall, where she skidded to a stop just inside the door. There she paused to straighten her skirts and smooth the stray wisps of hair around her face before stepping into the room with a decorum that would have made Isabelle Rowley proud.

Most of the tables were empty; only a few students still sat in small groups to finish eating or to chat. She scanned the room for Petey or Bennett but didn't find them. Disappointed, she picked up a tray. With her satchel tucked under her elbow for safekeeping, she crossed to a long wooden table near the kitchen, where bowls and platters waited. Most of the offerings had been picked over—only a dab of scrambled eggs, a withered apple, and a few dry-looking pieces of toast remaining. With a sigh, she scooped the eggs onto her plate and took a piece of toast.

Looking down at the unappetizing items, she thought about the wonderful waffles and fried sausages Cookie Ramona prepared for breakfast at the orphans' school. Her mouth watered. If only she were in Shay's Ford right now!

"Elisabet!" A lilting voice carried across the room.

Libby turned and spotted Alice-Marie with three other girls at a far table.

Alice-Marie waved her hand. "Join us, Elisabet!"

Libby stifled a sigh. She preferred to sit with Petey and Bennett or by herself, but she couldn't think of a way to gracefully refuse the invitation. So she carried her tray to the table and sat down next to her roommate. "You were up early."

Alice-Marie simpered. "Yes. I had a meeting with"—she pointed to each girl as she stated their names—"Margaret Harris, Kate Dunn, and Myra Child." Tipping close to Libby, she whispered, "They're sophomores, and they're all members of Kappa Kappa Gamma." Sitting upright, she beamed at the others. "This is Elisabet Conley. She's from Shay's Ford, and she's my roommate."

Libby nodded at each of the girls in turn, then dug in to her plate. The eggs were cold and flavorless, the toast dry and hard, but she ate every bite, unwilling to waste it. The others went on talking while she ate, seemingly oblivious to her presence. But as soon as she started to rise with her empty tray in hand, the girl sitting directly across from her—Kate Dunn—grabbed Libby's wrist.

"Stay for just a bit longer, Elisabet."

Libby hovered half standing, half sitting. "Actually, I have some errands to run."

"But we haven't even had a chance to chat. Surely your errands can wait for another few minutes."

Alice-Marie turned an imploring look at Libby. Becoming a part of these girls' sorority was important to Alice-Marie. Even though Libby thought her roommate was somewhat empty-headed, she didn't want to sabotage her chances for getting into Kappa Kappa Gamma. With a strained smile, she sat down.

Kate sent a quick look around the circle of girls before returning her attention to Libby. "All right, Elisabet, we're all dying to know . . . aren't you the girl who was involved in the fisticuffs last night on the lawn?"

The others leaned in like cats around a cornered mouse. Apprehension made Libby's scalp tingle. It appeared they'd been planning this moment of attack, which was another reason she didn't like girls. They could be so conniving. She was tempted to tell them they were all mistaken, but her conscience wouldn't allow her to lie. So she squared her shoulders, looked directly into Kate Dunn's sparkling eyes, and said simply, "Yes."

Two of them gasped and covered their mouths with their hands. Libby almost rolled her eyes. They'd already known the answer— there was no need for melodramatics.

"So who was that man you were protecting?" Margaret asked. Three freckles stood in a row across her upturned nose, bold as pennies on a sheet of white paper. "Is he your boyfriend?"

"He's my *friend*," Libby snapped. "And he'd done nothing to provoke an attack. That Roy"—she spat the name—"came at us for no reason at all. I'm glad Bennett put him in his place."

"But, Elisabet, didn't you know Roy is the captain of the basketball team?" Kate's face and voice reflected astonishment. "He's a senior member of Beta Theta Pi. Roy is a very important man on campus."

"Roy is a bully," Libby said.

Alice-Marie's face flushed bright red. Margaret gasped, "Elisabet!" The others shook their heads and stared at each other in dismay.

Libby rose and tucked her satchel under her arm. "I'm just speaking the truth. I hope Roy will stay out of our way from now on, because I know Bennett won't be afraid to punch him again if he needs it." *And neither will I!*

Another round of gasps came from the gathered girls. Libby ignored their reaction and headed for the kitchen to dispose of her tray. She heard one of them say, "Alice-Marie, how can you possibly room with such an undignified girl?"

Alice-Marie's answer carried to Libby's ears. "Oh, you have to excuse Elisabet. She's an orphan, you see—she doesn't know any better. She might even be an Indian."

Libby whirled around. "I'm not an Indian!" She wanted to yell, also, that she wasn't an orphan, but she couldn't. So she slammed her tray onto the nearest table and escaped.

CHAPTER FIVE

Libby dashed out of the dining hall and ran smack into a solid chest. The impact shocked the air out of her lungs and knocked the satchel from her hand. Little lights danced in front of her eyes. Strong hands grabbed her upper arms, holding her upright when she might have collapsed. And then a familiar, husky laugh rang.

"Good ol' Lib, always in a rush and never looking where she's going."

Libby recognized Bennett's voice, but she had to blink several times before her vision cleared enough to bring his square-jawed face into focus. Restored, she tugged loose from his grasp and scooped up her satchel. She clutched it with two hands like a shield. "Sometimes a person needs to hurry."

Bennett laughed, a few of his freckles disappearing into eye crinkles. "Hoo boy, you're all fired up. What's got you in such a lather?"

A huff exploded from Libby's lips. "Last night we discovered some of the men on this campus are complete barbarians. Today I'm finding some of the women to be unbearable!" She sent a withering look over her shoulder. "Calling me an Indian . . ." She whirled to face Bennett and snapped, "If someone offered me a train ticket right now, I'd go home!"

Bennett stuck his finger in his ear and rotated his hand, as if reaming out his ear. "Did I hear you right? Someone called you an Indian?"

Libby huffed again. "It doesn't matter. It's just—" She slapped her leg with the satchel. "Girls! Why must they be so . . . girlish?"

Bennett threw back his head and guffawed. Irritation puckered Libby's lips. She wished she could clop him over the head with her leather case. But his hard head would probably damage the satchel. "Stop that! It isn't funny."

He sobered, although his gray-blue eyes twinkled with suppressed laughter. "Sorry, Lib. But sometimes I think you forget you *are* a girl."

"How can I forget?" Being a girl had been a problem for years. Her uncle had turned her over to an orphanage after her parents' deaths, unwilling to raise a girl on his own; prospective adoptive parents passed her by because they wanted sturdy boys to help with chores. Even Maelle, the one Libby loved most of all, had initially been uncertain about spending too much time with her because she feared her unconventional behavior would hinder Libby from becoming the kind of lady of which Mrs. Rowley approved.

She squeezed the satchel, the soft leather warm and pliable beneath her fingers. Being a girl might have robbed her of some opportunities in the past, but she wouldn't allow a misfortune of birth to stand in the way of her working for a reputable newspaper.

She gave a little jolt. She needed to get to town! "I have to go,

Bennett. Are you meeting Petey for lunch?" She inched backward as she spoke.

Bennett shrugged, the suit jacket's buttons straining with the movement. "Not sure of Pete's schedule today—he had a meeting or something this morning. Seems to be a lot of those before classes start tomorrow. But I'll be in the dining hall at eleven-thirty. Wanna join me?"

Libby wrinkled her nose. That wouldn't give her much time in town. "I'll try, but no promises." She lifted her hand in a wave. "See you later! Wish me luck!" She whirled and took off running for the walkway that led to the street.

"Luck? Luck for what?"

Bennett's voice followed her, but she ignored him and continued on her pell-mell dash. Before coming to Chambers, she'd written to the town's Association of Commerce and requested the names and addresses of every newspaper in town. She intended to inquire at all three for a position.

Certainly with everything heating up across the ocean, there would be a need for journalists to record the events as they unfolded. Libby had heard Aaron Rowley and Jackson Harders praise President Wilson's calm demeanor in light of Germany's aggression—the men seemed certain the president would work to keep America out of the conflict. Thankfully, Petey and Bennett were enrolled in college and were therefore safe from fighting in a war. But if she had her way, she'd be in the thick of it, pad of paper and pencil in hand, reporting every detail of the skirmish. To do that, she had to have a job with a newspaper.

She stopped first at the *Chambers Courier.* To her delight, she was ushered in to the editor's office, but her elation quickly dimmed when the man openly laughed at her desire to write news stories.

"You're too cute, honey," the man said, giving a brazen wink.

"Better suited for a drugstore clerk. Why don't you check next door—they might be hiring."

Libby marched right past the drugstore and made her way to the second paper on her list, the *Weekly Dispatch*. The editor took the time to glance at a few of her writing samples before telling her he didn't need any other reporters—but was she any good at mopping? He could use a reliable cleaning woman.

Libby reined in her frustration and replied in an even voice. "Sir, I have no desire to clean for your newspaper. I wish to write."

"Sorry." He pushed her stack of sample stories across the desk. "I don't think I'll ever hire a female to do reporting. As a whole, females are too moody."

Libby almost proved him right by flying into a temper, but she bit down on the end of her tongue. She gathered her stories, tucked them neatly into her satchel, and charged outside before the angry thoughts filling her head found their way out of her mouth.

On the sidewalk, she looked at the final name on the list and muttered, "My last hope . . ." Sucking in a breath of fortification, she turned on her heel and headed for the red brick building on the corner of Second and Ash. When she reached the glass doors, she raised her chin and marched in, her satchel held in the crook of her arm. She moved directly to the receptionist's desk and spoke with as much confidence as she could muster. "I'd like a few minutes with the editor-in-chief, please."

The woman peered at her from behind thick round spectacles. "Do you have an appointment with Mr. Houghton?"

Libby didn't bat an eye. "No, ma'am, but I promise not to take a great deal of his time. Would you please tell him Miss Elisabet Conley from the University of Southern Missouri is here to see him?"

The eyes behind the spectacles narrowed. "You aren't here to sell him an ad for the yearbook, are you? He already purchased all his ads for this year."

"Oh no, ma'am." Libby released a soft laugh, giving the woman a smile. "I assure you, I'm not here to sell him anything." *Except myself* . . .

"Well . . ." The woman tapped her pencil against a pad of paper on her desk, scowling. "I suppose it won't hurt to ask. You stay here." She screeched her chair legs against the wooden floor, unfolded herself from the seat, and waddled around a corner. Libby waited, battling the urge to tap her toe in impatience. Moments later, the woman returned, followed by a tall, gray-haired man with his shirt sleeves rolled above his elbows. Black ink stained the tips of the fingers on his left hand.

"Miss Conley, I'm Fenton Houghton. How may I help you?"

Libby flashed her brightest smile. "Actually, sir, I'm here to help you. Could we possibly retire to your office for a few minutes?"

His lips quirked briefly. "As long as it is just a few minutes."

Although he maintained a friendly expression, Libby caught the subtle warning in his words. She tipped her head. "Five at most?"

"That I can spare." He gestured toward the hallway, and Libby clipped behind him. The clack of typewriter keys rang over the mumble of voices, making Libby's pulse race in curiosity. What stories were being created by the fingers tapping those keys right now? She breathed in the enticing scents of ink and paper, the combination more heady than perfume. *This is where I belong!*

Mr. Houghton ushered her in to a large cluttered office and pointed to a ladder-back chair. "Have a seat." He sank into the leather chair behind the desk and leaned back, linking his hands over his stomach. "Don't tell me—you want to be a reporter."

Libby's jaw dropped. "How did you know?"

He waved his hand as if shooing a fly. "I get at least a dozen prospective reporters a year through here. Most of them are . . ." He cleared his throat. "Of the male persuasion, however."

Of course. "Well, I have no intention of letting my gender interfere with my becoming a top-notch reporter." Libby flopped her satchel open and withdrew a few neatly written pages. "As you can see from my work, I—"

Again, Mr. Houghton put a hand in the air. "Hold it right there, young lady." He leaned forward, resting his elbows on the edge of the desk. "How old are you?"

Too stunned to do otherwise, Libby answered automatically. "Eighteen, sir."

"Have any training?"

"No, but I am enrolled in the university."

"First-year student?"

"Yes."

"In the journalism program?"

"Yes, sir."

"Mm-hmm." He stroked his upper lip with his finger. "Enrolling more females all the time . . ." He lowered his hand and gazed seriously across the desk. "Miss Conley, let me give you some advice. I can see you're a determined young woman. I even admire your desire to become—as you put it—a top-notch reporter. But it takes more than drive and determination. It takes experience. And that's something you don't have."

Libby, remembering the morning's many rejections, blew out an aggravated breath. This man couldn't reject her, too! "And how am I to get experience if no one gives me a chance?"

Mr. Houghton laughed. "Miss Conley, you'll have your chance at the university. The journalism program publishes two newspapers right there on campus. You'll be involved in the production of those publications. There's your opportunity to build experience."

But Libby didn't want her name in a college newspaper; she aspired to greater things. She scooted to the edge of the seat and rested her fingertips on the editor's desk. "But what if I want something more? Won't you just look at my writings? My teacher from Shay's Ford assured me I had a gift."

"Writers with a gift are a dime a dozen," the man said with a wave of his hand. "What counts is can—you—do—the—job." He punched out each word with as much force as a boxer. He pointed at her. "And that assurance comes from building a résumé of writings with an established, recognized publication, such as the newspapers on campus." He started to rise. "So—"

Libby grabbed the seat of the chair with both hands, holding herself in place. "Mr. Houghton?"

He paused, his lips twitching. "Yes, Miss Conley?"

"I would very much like to build a résumé, but not with a college newspaper. I prefer a more well-read publication. If you aren't willing to hire me as a part of your staff, do you have any recommendations?"

The man plopped back into his chair. He rocked for a few seconds, scowling across the desk at Libby. Then he sighed. "Try magazines. From the looks of you, I would imagine you have the makings of a fine romance novelist. Maybe you could write some serials—build a résumé that way."

Romance novels? Libby wanted to do serious reporting! Stung by his cavalier attitude toward her dream, Libby ducked her head. "I . . . I see."

"Best I can do for you, I'm afraid." His chair squeaked as he pushed to his feet. "But in a couple of years, when you've built that résumé, come back and see me again."

Slowly, Libby raised her head to meet his gaze. "Really?"

"Sure. If I like your samples, and if you've proved you can handle meeting deadlines, I might be willing to give you a chance."

He smiled. "The newspaper can always use a good homemaking or gossip column."

Libby nearly leapt out of the chair. She grabbed up her satchel and whirled toward the door. She would most definitely *not* return to this office. Gritting her teeth, she forced herself to remember the manners Isabelle Rowley had taught her. Turning back, she said stiffly, "I thank you for your time, Mr. Houghton. Have a good day."

She fled, not even glancing at the receptionist on her way out. She charged down the sidewalk, her feet clip-clipping in angry little stomps. Homemaking? Gossip column? Romances? Mr. Houghton would never have made those suggestions to a man seeking employment.

How unfair to be seen as less than able just because she wore a dress rather than trousers. Little wonder Maelle had worn trousers for so many years. Perhaps Libby would throw convention aside and purchase a few pairs of britches for herself! She kicked viciously at an empty can lying in the gutter. It clattered and bounced ahead several feet, coming to rest next to a small, dingy, flat disk. Curious, Libby bent over and pinched the disk between her thumb and finger. Her heart leapt in delight. A nickel! She looked around at the other people traveling the sidewalk; no one seemed to be seeking a lost coin.

The unexpected windfall lifted her spirits. She could use this nickel a dozen different ways. The drugstore waited just ahead. With a little skip, she darted forward and entered the store. A long, high counter ran along the right-hand side of the store, but all of the black iron stools were filled with customers enjoying a soda or a sandwich.

Libby's mouth watered as the smell of grilled onions reached her nose, bringing a memory to the surface. Her parents had taken her to St. Louis to the World's Fair two years before their death.

They'd eaten a delicious sandwich—a hamburger, they'd called it—of cooked beef on toast with pickles and grilled onions. After her sad breakfast and unsuccessful job search, she deserved a special treat. Might she be able to buy a hamburger with her nickel?

She inched forward, peeking between shoulders to read the sandwich list and prices listed on a cardboard placard behind the counter. To her disappointment, the only offerings listed were egg salad on white, ham and cheese on rye, or a frankfurter on a roll. Fingering the nickel, she looked for something else. A milk shake, a bowl of ice cream, a large dill pickle . . . After having her taste buds set for a hamburger, nothing else appealed. With a sigh, she turned toward the doors to leave, but a display in the corner caught her attention.

Magazines.

Mr. Houghton had suggested she build a résumé by writing magazine stories. Although the thought of writing romance serials didn't appeal to her, maybe the magazine editor would allow her to write articles instead. She inched her way to the display of magazines and pulled a volume of *Carter's Home Journal* from the shelf. She flipped through it. No articles of a serious nature—mostly recipes and gardening or homemaking tips. She put it back.

Looking down the line of options, her gaze settled on a copy of *Modern Woman's World.* A sarcastic thought filled her mind: Maybe the magazine would show her how to fit in as a woman in this world. She removed the magazine from its spot and let it flop open in her hand. A brazen headline—"A Kiss at Midnight"—leapt off the page and made her stomach flutter in an unfamiliar way. After flicking a glance over her shoulder, she began reading.

The opening paragraphs left no question in Libby's mind that this was one of the romance stories Mr. Houghton had referenced. By the end of the first column, she knew she could write something just as good. Or even better. Mrs. Rowley had often chided

Libby for her overactive imagination, encouraging her to stay in the present rather than escaping to make-believe worlds in her head. But for the first time, Libby wondered if her imagination might be able to work for her instead of against her.

Mr. Houghton indicated she needed to build a writing résumé. Without question, she would be able to concoct stories such as this one. If a magazine purchased her stories, she could build a résumé quickly, proving her ability to meet deadlines, and then she could turn to more serious writing.

She flipped the magazine closed. The price stared up her, and she nearly laughed out loud. *Five cents.* Surely it was providential that she'd found the nickel immediately after her meeting with the newspaper editor. Magazine in hand, she hurried to the counter and held up her nickel.

The soda jerk bustled over and pocketed her nickel. He tipped his funny little paper hat and grinned. "Happy reading."

Libby grinned back. "You mean, happy writing!"

CHAPTER SIX

Bennett glanced at his pocket watch—a special gift from the staff at the orphans' home—and let out a little growl of aggravation. Five after twelve and still no Libby. He grabbed up his plate, sauntered to the serving line, and filled the white ceramic plate for the third time. Would he ever feel as if he got enough food? Those early days of hunger, although long past, still haunted him. He plopped two slices of bread on the plate and pocketed two more for later, then chose a seat facing the doors so he could watch for Libby.

He sprinkled salt and pepper over the meatloaf, boiled potatoes, and corn before stabbing the meat with his fork. Conversations buzzed around him, and he listened, always aware of his surroundings.

"Yes, well, I still say America can't stay out of it," a male voice barked from behind Bennett, "and it's a fool who thinks otherwise. Too much commerce goes on between the different countries.

If there's money at stake, we can't ignore what's happening over there."

The reply was buried under raucous laughter blasting from Bennett's left. He scowled in the direction of the merrymakers, but he didn't need to hear the answer. He agreed with whomever made the comment. Things had been cooking overseas for months, with Germany declaring war on nearly every European country. Bennett released a soft snort. Maybe the U.S. ought to declare war on Germany and see how they liked having the tables turned. His aggressive spirit rose to the fore with the thought. The minute the U.S. was ready, he'd be ready. Wasn't he always up for a good brawl?

A flurry of activity at the dining hall doors captured his attention, and his fork paused between his plate and his mouth. But when he didn't see Libby in the cluster of students entering the room, he jabbed the bite into his mouth and chewed with a vengeance. Where was she?

Two young men stopped across the table from Bennett and pointed at the empty chairs. "Taken?"

Bennett considered telling them to go away—they'd block his view of the door and he might miss seeing Libby. But what difference would it make? Obviously she wasn't coming. He shrugged. "Have a seat." They slid out the chairs, metal legs screeching in unison against the floor, and they sat.

One of them bowed his head to pray, reminding Bennett that he hadn't offered thanks for his meal before eating. Guilt whispered at the back of his mind, but he pushed it away. So what if they'd always prayed before eating at the orphans' home? As much as he'd appreciated the good meals and the warm bed, he'd never taken to all of the rules. Now that he was on his own again, he could do as he pleased. And he preferred to leave the praying to Pete.

As soon as the man raised his head, he said, "I'm Jim." He pointed at his buddy. "This's Ted."

"Bennett Martin." Bennett forked up another monstrous bite and pointed at the jackets the pair wore. "You two in one of those fraternity groups?"

Jim grinned. "That's right. Delta Tau Delta. You planning to pledge? Ours is a good one."

Bennett mopped at the grease on his plate with a folded slice of bread. "Probably. But not sure which one. Gotta do some thinking on it."

"Don't think too long," Ted advised. "The fraternities only accept so many pledges. If you put it off, you might miss getting the one you really want."

Bennett shrugged again even though the idea of being in one of the groups appealed to him. He'd been alone until Aaron Rowley convinced him to leave the streets and live at the orphans' school. There, he'd formed a friendship with Pete and Libby, but even with them, he sometimes felt as if he didn't quite fit. What would it be like to join a fraternity and really belong?

The two fraternity members put their heads together and talked quietly while Bennett continued to eat. He gulped the last bite, patted his stomach, and rose. "Well, fellas, I'm done, so—"

The pair leapt up. "Hold on there."

Bennett curled his hands around his tray. "Why?"

A sly grin crept up Ted's cheek. "Wondered if you'd made up your mind yet about pledging. You gonna consider Delta Tau Delta?"

"Maybe." Out of the corner of his eye, Bennett observed Jim inching around the table.

"Well, since you're thinking about it, we need to find out a few things." Ted folded his arms over his chest. "We like singers in our fraternity. Can you sing, Martin?"

Chairs squeaked as people turned to watch. The noisy banter of moments ago hushed as whispers and muffled laughter rolled across the dining hall. The hair on the back of Bennett's neck prickled. He hadn't minded being the center of attention on the lawn because he'd been playing offense. But he didn't care for defense. "I'm not much of a singer. So I probably wouldn't be a good fit for the Delta Tau Delta."

"Let us decide that." Jim took the tray from Bennett's hands. "Climb on the table there and give us a little concert." He swung around, grinning at the others in the room. "How 'bout some encouragement? Martin here's gonna sing for us."

A cheer rose. Bennett stood stiff-legged, his hands clenched into fists. He had two choices: let them control him or take control. His cheeks twitched as he fought a grin. Had anyone ever forced him to do anything he didn't want to do? He leapt onto the table. It wobbled, and he made a show of catching his balance, earning a round of laughter. Then, his balance restored, he held his arms wide.

"All right, I'll sing a song. But first, is there a Caroline in the dining hall?"

High-pitched giggles erupted from a corner table. Two girls pointed to a third girl—timid-looking with straggly wisps of brown hair hanging around her thin face. She covered her cheeks with both hands. Bennett grinned and crooked his finger at the girl. "C'mon over, honey. Can't sing this song without you."

The girl's dining mates pulled her from her chair. Pink-faced, she resisted, digging in her heels and shaking her head wildly. But the other two propelled her across the floor to the edge of Bennett's table.

He crouched down and gave her his most disarming grin. "So you're Caroline, huh?"

"Y-yes." The girl strained against her friends' hold, her brown eyes wide.

Bennett nearly rolled his eyes. Silly girl—she wasn't being dragged to the gallows. He placed his hand on her skinny shoulder. "I'm not out to hurt you. I just need a pretty Caroline to serenade. Will you help me?"

Truthfully, Bennett had seen prettier girls than this one. But his words had the desired effect. Her pink cheeks deepened to a blazing red, and she stopped trying to escape. She offered a timorous nod. Her friends fell back, and Bennett gave her shoulder a quick squeeze. "That's a good sport." He winked. "Now just stand right there and keep smilin' at me, honey—that'll give me the encouragement I need to get these fellas off my back."

He stretched to his feet. With his eyes pinned to Caroline's face, he belted out the words to "Can't You Hear Me Callin', Caroline?" Bennett had been told he couldn't carry a tune in a bucket, but he didn't let it stop him. He sang at full lung. While he sang, he gestured broadly, occasionally going down on one knee to brush Caroline's cheek with his knuckles or smooth his hand over her frizzy brown hair. The red in her cheeks spread until her face was mottled with color from neck to hairline, yet she stayed pressed to the edge of the table, her face upturned.

He couldn't remember all the words—he'd only heard the song a few times on the radio—but he substituted with *la-la-la* where needed. Laughter and cheers rang throughout the entire performance, and by the time he finished, Caroline was gazing at him in rapture, completely besotted.

When the song reached the last line, he jumped to the floor, cupped Caroline's cheeks with both hands, and held the final syllable on "Caroline . . ." until he ran out of breath. He faked a cough, winning more laughter and a spatter of applause. Then he lifted Caroline's bony hand and pressed a kiss to its back. Finally, he bowed to the cheering audience. Jim and Ted pounded him on the back as wild clapping and foot stomping made his ears ring. Bennett stepped away from the two men and slipped his arm around Caroline's waist.

"C'mon, honey, let's get you back to your lunch."

Caroline hunched her shoulders, holding her clasped hands to her heart. "Yes. Please."

Accustomed to Libby's boldness, Bennett found himself impatient with this girl's bashfulness. But he played the gentleman and escorted her to her table, where she melted into her seat, her doleful eyes still glued to his face. "Thanks for your help, Caroline." He hummed a couple of bars from the song, grinning as Caroline fanned her still-red cheeks with both hands. Then he winked at her friends, who giggled hysterically, before he swaggered back to his own table.

Just as he lifted his tray, Libby and Pete entered the dining hall. He scowled at them as they approached. "*Now* you show up. Where've you been?" He bounced his empty tray. "I'm all done." He didn't mention his impromptu concert. He also didn't ask why Libby was with Pete when he'd invited her to have lunch with him.

"Sorry I'm late." Libby stuck out her lower lip and blew, lifting the fine strands of hair along her forehead. "It took longer than I thought it would to get to the newspaper offices in town."

Bennett frowned. "Newspaper offices?"

"I was seeking employment."

They'd all need to find jobs to help with spending money. Their scholarships covered school expenses but nothing else. And they didn't have parents to send them a monthly allowance. Pete was lucky—Mrs. Rowley had arranged for him to be a student assistant for the biblical professors. But of course the Rowleys hadn't bothered to set anything up for him or Libby; they were on their own. He wished he'd known that's what Libby'd been doing all morning—he could've gone with her and done some job-seeking himself. "Find anything?"

A secretive smile creased her cheek. "Yes. Something completely unexpected." Before Bennett could ask her what she meant, she turned to Pete. "Well, I'm glad we ran into each other. Since Bennett's finished, I'll just eat with you. Assuming there's anything left."

Pete looked at Bennett. "Do you want to stay and visit with us while we eat?"

Bennett snorted. "Nah. I've been here long enough." If he'd left sooner, he might have been able to avoid giving the concert. Of course, that hadn't been without its benefits. He glanced over his shoulder. Caroline and her friends continued to gawk at him, all looking moon-eyed. He couldn't resist waggling his eyebrows at the trio, which created another round of giggles, before turning back to Pete and Libby. "I'm heading to my room—gonna enjoy my last afternoon of freedom before classes start tomorrow."

"All right. We'll see you at supper?"

Bennett nodded. "I'll be here." He dumped his tray in the bin and headed for the doors. He encountered Jim and Ted heading out at the same time. He clapped Jim on the shoulder. "Hey, thanks for giving me the chance to sing." He raised one eyebrow. "The ladies sure like it when a fella sings to 'em. You did me a real favor."

Ted cleared his throat. "You're about the worst singer I've ever heard."

Bennett laughed. "Does that mean you don't want me to pledge . . . what was it again? Delta Cow Delta?"

Ted scowled. "That's Delta *Tau* Delta."

Bennett feigned embarrassment. "Oh. That's right." He rubbed the underside of his nose with his finger, hiding his smile. "Sorry, fellas."

Jim said, "You're welcome to pledge, but we're only taking three new members this year. So . . ."

Bennett knew what the man was intimating—his chances weren't good. Nothing new there. When had Bennett ever received a break? The two started to walk away, but Bennett dove into their pathway. "Hey, before you go, can I ask you a question?"

Jim shrugged. "Sure."

"Do you know a tall guy . . . curly hair. Name's Roy?"

The two gaped at him. Jim said, "Hey, you're the one who . . ." He grabbed Ted's arm.

Ted grunted and pulled away.

Jim gave Ted's arm a whack and grinned from ear to ear. "You know who we've got here? This's the guy who socked Roy in the nose last night. Am I right? Wasn't that you?"

The admiration in the man's eyes almost made Bennett blush. Almost. He puffed out his chest. "Yep, that was me."

Jim shook his head. "I've never seen anybody stand up to Roy like that." He leaned forward and added conspiratorially, "He's a big man around here, you know."

Bennett snickered. "He didn't look so big all bent over, holding his nose."

The other two laughed, although they glanced around as if afraid someone might overhear them.

"So are you friends of his?" Bennett withdrew a slice of bread from his pocket. He munched while he waited for an answer.

"Oh, not friends exactly . . ." Jim scratched his head. "But we know him."

"You mean, know *of* him," Ted added. "He's in Beta Theta Pi, like most of the athletes. We, um . . ." He cleared his throat, looking at the ground. "We don't mix much with that group."

Bennett swallowed a smirk. "Oh. Well, thanks." He stepped off the porch.

"Wait!" Jim stumbled after Bennett, Ted on his heels. "Are you going to pledge Delta Tau Delta? You can even bring your friend—you know, the one Roy was pestering. His wooden leg's no problem for us."

Bennett's fist formed without effort. So Pete's wooden leg wouldn't bother them, huh? For reasons he didn't understand, the statement rankled. He pressed his fist against his thigh to keep from popping Jim right in the mouth. "As I said, I don't know if I'm going to pledge. I'll let you know."

Without waiting for a reply, Bennett turned and headed for his dormitory. By the time he reached the rock building, he'd made a decision. He would pledge to a fraternity. But it wouldn't be Delta Tau Delta. He had his sights set on Beta Theta Pi. And he intended to bring Pete in with him.

Chapter Seven

His fingertips grazed her cheek. She gasped. "Oh please, sir, how forward you're being! You mustn't . . . mustn't . . ." *She gulped as his firm, cool hand curved along her jaw.*

"I cannot resist," he whispered. His breath stirred the errant curls falling across her forehead. "Your exquisite beauty, my darling, is"—

"Hello, Elisabet!"

The cheerful greeting sent the imaginary characters in Libby's head scrambling for cover. Libby slapped down her pencil, whirled on her seat, and glared at her roommate.

Alice-Marie's bright smile faded. She dashed to the desk and perched on its edge. "Why, what's the matter? You look so cross." Her focus flitted to the pad of paper on Libby's desk.

Libby smacked the pad of paper facedown and rested her linked hands on it. "I was . . . busy. You startled me." She nudged Alice-Marie's leg lightly with her elbow.

Alice-Marie missed the hint. She folded her hands in her lap and beamed at Libby. "Oh, I do apologize most sincerely. Mother says I really must stop rushing into rooms and calling out, but I can't seem to stop myself!" She hunched her shoulders and tittered. "I'll try, though, so I don't keep you from . . ." Once more, she turned a curious look toward the pages.

Libby scooped the pad off the desk and dropped it into the desk drawer. She closed the drawer with a firm snap. "What time is it?"

Alice-Marie glanced at her dainty wristwatch. "A quarter to six."

Libby jumped up. "I'm meeting my friends for supper." After missing lunch with Bennett, she shouldn't keep him waiting.

Folding her arms over her chest, Alice-Marie affected a pout. "Oh, but I hoped you might eat with me. That's why I came up here before going to the dining hall."

"You're not eating with Kate and Myra and . . . ?" Libby couldn't remember the name of the third girl from breakfast.

"Margaret," Alice-Marie supplied. Her lip poked out farther. "I've made no plans with anyone . . . except you."

Libby nibbled her lower lip. She and Alice-Marie were roommates, but she didn't fancy forming a friendship with the girl. Yet, looking into her disappointed pale blue eyes, Libby couldn't refuse. She knew how it felt to be rejected.

"Well then," she said through gritted teeth, "why don't you join my friends and me?"

Alice-Marie's bright smile returned. She bounced up and slipped her hand through Libby's elbow. "Oh good! I hoped you might introduce me to your *friends*." Her giggle rang as they headed down the hall to the stairway. "So which one is your beau? I wouldn't want to accidentally flirt with the one you've already claimed."

Was it possible to flirt accidentally? Libby gently disengaged her arm from Alice-Marie's hold. "Neither Petey nor Bennett is my beau. We're all just good friends. Since childhood."

Alice-Marie caught Libby's arm and drew her to a halt in the dormitory lobby. "Since childhood? They're orphans, too?"

Knowing whatever she said would be repeated, Libby chose her response carefully. "One is. One isn't." Sometimes Libby thought Petey carried deeper scars from being abandoned than she did from losing her parents. But Alice-Marie didn't need to know the details. "If we don't hurry, we'll miss supper. Let's go."

Petey and Bennett were waiting on the lawn outside the dining hall. The pleasant aromas wafting out the open doors stirred Libby's hunger. She skipped the last few steps to join her friends and jammed her thumb at Alice-Marie. "This is my roommate, Alice-Marie. She's eating with us." Then she gestured to the men by turn. "Alice-Marie, this is Bennett Martin and Petey Leidig."

"Pete," Petey corrected.

"Pete," Libby repeated, offering him a grin, which he returned. He'd been pestering her for two years to drop the childish nickname, but to her, he'd always be Petey.

Alice-Marie bustled forward and shook Petey's hand. Then she reached for Bennett and clung. "Oh, it's so nice to meet Elisabet's good friends from childhood. I hope you won't find my presence an unwelcome intrusion. I wanted to have supper with Elisabet, but she said she already had plans to meet you. I was so very, very disappointed that she relented and said I could come, too." She giggled, covering her lips with her fingertips. "And I must say, it isn't often a girl gets to dine with two such dashing men. I feel so very honored."

Libby shook her head. Would Alice-Marie stop talking long enough for them to eat? She grabbed Alice-Marie's elbow and gave her a little push toward the door. "Let's go." She sent an apologetic look over her shoulder as Petey and Bennett fell into step behind them. They joined the line that snaked along the wall from the serving table all the way to the door. The line moved slowly, but they chatted about their chosen courses of study—to Libby's surprise, Alice-Marie hoped to become a nurse one day—and filled the time.

When they reached the serving table, Bennett zipped around the girls and handed them each a tray. "Here you are, ladies."

"Oooh." Alice-Marie tipped her head and fluttered her thick lashes at Bennett. "Aren't you the gentleman?"

Libby rolled her eyes. If Alice-Marie only knew. Instead of gesturing the ladies forward, Bennett retained his spot ahead of them and began filling his plate. Libby looked at Petey, and they exchanged a grin. In his blue eyes, she read her own thought: *Bennett just wanted to be first.*

When they'd all made their selections, Bennett led them to a table along the south wall. He pulled out Alice-Marie's chair for her, earning another simpering look, and then quickly sat down beside her. Libby plunked down her tray and reached for her chair, but to her surprise Petey pulled it out and held it for her. Embarrassed yet pleased, she slid into her seat.

Petey started to sit, but his peg leg slipped on the smooth tile floor. He tilted sideways, banging his elbow into Libby's shoulder.

"Petey!" she cried in alarm and grabbed his arm with both hands.

He caught the table edge and lowered himself into the chair. "Whew." He flashed a grin around at the others. "I'm all right. Just clumsy." He looked at Libby's hands. "You can let go—I'm safe now." Although his tone was mild, she sensed irritation in the firm set of his jaw.

Rebuffed, she jerked her hands back. Her fingers trembled slightly as she needlessly lined up her cutlery next to her plate like soldiers at attention. "W-would you bless the food for us, Petey?"

Immediately, Alice-Marie bowed her head. Bennett released the salt shaker he'd just picked up. Petey folded his hands and closed

65

his eyes. Libby did likewise. Petey's low voice was nearly swallowed by rowdy conversations, clanking silverware, and squeaking chairs in the crowded dining hall. But by leaning sideways slightly, Libby was able to hear his simple prayer of thanks for the food.

He said amen and Libby straightened. Her shoulder lightly bumped against his arm, and he sent her a quick smile. Whatever had irritated him earlier seemed to have fled. Relieved, she grinned back and then turned her attention to her food.

While they ate, Alice-Marie plied them with questions. Before long, she directed every question to Bennett, ignoring Petey and Libby. She seemed particularly enamored with Bennett's tales of caring for himself on the streets. The girl had seemed dismayed— even repulsed—by Libby's orphan status, yet she offered only admiration and sympathy to Bennett. Libby jabbed her fork into the mound of mashed potatoes on her plate and tried not to seethe.

Bennett scraped up every last crumb on his plate and headed for seconds. Alice-Marie watched him go, her expression rapt. Then she leaned forward and fixed Libby with a scolding look. "Elisabet Conley, I could throttle you!"

Libby jolted, her spine connecting with the back of the chair. "What on earth for?"

"You didn't warn me what a charmer Bennett is. Had I been warned, I would have prepared myself. I must look a mess in the same dress I wore *all day*. And I didn't take the time to apply rouge or brush my hair . . ." She pinched her cheeks and then smoothed her wavy blond hair behind her ears, her gaze seeking Bennett across the room.

Libby held back a huff of annoyance. "You look fine, Alice-Marie."

Alice-Marie heaved a deep, dramatic sigh. "Oh, I'm so relieved you haven't laid claim to him. I should hate to have a man come between us, but I'm positively smitten!"

Smitten? With Bennett? Libby almost laughed. She looked over her shoulder at Bennett, who was busily loading his plate with slices of roast beef. Turning back to Alice-Marie, she asked, "But why?"

Alice-Marie stared at Libby. "Why? Oh my!" She fanned herself with one fluttering hand, her lips forming an O of astonishment. "That unruly red hair; those boyish freckles; his broad shoulders and dimpled chin . . . Elisabet, my dear, he's simply *darling!*"

Bennett . . . darling? Libby opened her mouth to protest, but Petey interrupted.

"I'm going to get some dessert." He pushed against the table with both palms, rising. "I saw apple pie and a white cake. Do you want something?" He looked back and forth between the girls.

"No thank you," Libby said.

Alice-Marie shook her head. Petey ambled away in his hitch-legged gait. Libby turned to Alice-Marie again. "I suppose one might consider Bennett . . ." She couldn't quite bring herself to use the word *darling.* "Appealing," she finished.

Alice-Marie sighed dreamily, resting her chin in her hand. Then she sat upright. "And how wonderful it would be, Elisabet, if he and I were to begin . . . well, keeping company." She giggled. "Especially if you and Pete did the same."

Libby dropped her fork. "What?"

"Oh, silly girl, if you could only see your face! Don't look so shocked." Alice-Marie released another scale-running giggle.

Libby carefully closed her mouth and flicked a glance over her shoulder. Had Petey heard? To her relief, he was already several tables away.

Alice-Marie continued, "You and Pete would make a striking couple—you so petite and him so tall; you with your spirit and him with his calm demeanor; you with such dark hair and him with hair as pale as moonlight . . ."

Hair as pale as moonlight? Maybe she could use that line in her romance story.

"You and Pete seem opposites in every way." Alice-Marie yanked Libby back to reality. She toyed with a lock of hair coiling along her neck. "But Mother says opposites attract."

To Libby's relief, Bennett returned. "Sorry it took me so long. Ran into a couple of fellas from Beta Theta Pi. I'm thinking about pledging to their fraternity."

"Oh really?" Alice-Marie beamed up at him. "The sorority I plan to pledge is the sister group to Beta Theta Pi."

Bennett plunked into his chair and picked up his fork. "Well, that'd be something if we both got in, wouldn't it?"

"Indeed." Alice-Marie could melt butter with the sultry look she offered Bennett. Libby wanted to throw her roll at the flirtatious girl.

Bennett pointed at Libby with his fork. "If you want seconds, Lib, you better hurry. They didn't make nearly enough potatoes tonight." Bennett grinned. "So what did you ladies discuss in my absence?"

Motioning toward Petey's empty chair, Alice-Marie laughed. "I've been doing my utmost to convince Libby that she and Pete would make a darling couple."

Bennett covered his mouth with his napkin and coughed. Then he dropped the napkin, yanked up his glass, and took a noisy drink. He snickered. "Libby and Pete?" He threw his head back and laughed, holding his stomach.

Alice-Marie's brow puckered. "What is so funny?"

More irritated than she could understand, Libby snapped, "Yes. Why is that so funny?"

Bennett cleared his throat several times, bringing the laughter under control, but his eyes continued to sparkle with suppressed humor. "Sorry, ladies. I wasn't laughing at you. I was just trying to imagine Lib and Pete as a couple." He laid his arm on the back of Alice-Marie's chair but looked toward Libby. "You and Pete are great friends—always have been—but it could never go beyond that."

Alice-Marie tipped closer to Bennett. "Why not?"

"Yes. Why not?" Libby folded her arms over her chest and glared at Bennett.

"Come on, Lib. Think about it. Pete's gonna be a preacher. He'll need a wife who's . . . docile. One who's willing to stay home and cook soup for sick people and things like that. Libby couldn't do it. She hates cooking. And when it comes to being docile . . ." He chuckled, shaking his finger at Alice-Marie. "You're wrong on this one. Libby with Pete would never work."

Libby wanted to argue with Bennett, but she couldn't. She could never be a good wife to a minister for the reasons he'd listed and so many more. To her surprise, it pained her to acknowledge it. "You're right, Bennett. Petey and I could never be anything more than friends. To expect more would be ludicrous."

Bennett suddenly looked somewhere behind her shoulder. The sheepish look on his face sent a tingle of awareness down Libby's spine. She turned to peek, but even before she looked, she knew what she'd find. Petey was standing behind her. The sadness in his eyes turned her heart upside-down.

❧

Pete took an awkward side step and held tight to his dessert as Libby jumped from her seat. She captured his hands, which curled around the plate bearing a large wedge of apple pie. He'd been looking forward to the cinnamon-laden treat, but with Libby's comment, his appetite fled.

"Petey, I didn't know—"

"—that I was here?" Pete forced a chuckle. He swallowed the

lump of anguish her words had created. "It doesn't matter, Libby. You didn't say anything dishonest, did you?"

"No, but . . ."

He took one shuffling step forward and placed the plate in the center of the table. "Bennett, I hope you're still hungry. I brought the biggest piece of pie left in the pan." He sensed Libby's troubled gaze following him, but he managed to keep his tone light. "The cake looked dry, so—"

"Petey, please." Libby tugged at his arm, as she'd done dozens of times over the years. In an instant, they were eleven years old again and she was begging him to join her in a game of marbles or to push her on the wooden swing that hung from the tallest tree behind the orphans' school. But whatever she wanted this time, he couldn't offer it. His heart felt so bruised, he was amazed it continued beating.

Very gently, Pete disengaged Libby's hands from his arm. He looked at Alice-Marie, who didn't quite meet his gaze. "I enjoyed meeting you, Alice-Marie. I'm sure there will be other chances for us to have a meal together since you're Libby's roommate and Libby and I are . . . such good friends." He even managed to smile. "I hate to rush off, but my first class is at eight tomorrow morning, and I'd like to do a little reading before I turn in. So . . ." He moved backward a few inches, cautious that his peg leg didn't slide.

Libby gripped the back of her chair, looking directly into his face. "I'll see you tomorrow?" Her eyes begged forgiveness.

"Sure. Tomorrow." He nodded good-bye and made his way out of the dining hall. Slowly. Aware that one misstep could send him toppling. If only he could run. His body strained against the restriction of his wooden appendage. If he could break into a run on the expansive grassy lawn between the dining hall and his dormitory, maybe he could expend this overwhelming frustration.

"To expect more would be ludicrous."

Yes, ludicrous. How could she possibly see him as anything other than Petey, her childhood buddy? How could any woman—especially one as bright and beautiful and alive as Libby—see a crippled man as whole and desirable?

He reached Landry Hall and, unconcerned about disturbing any other students in the building, hopped up the stairs on his good leg as quickly as possible. Ignoring the handrail, he put every bit of effort into launching himself, one step at a time, to the second floor. His muscles burning and lungs heaving, he reached the landing. Without a pause, loath to use the despised peg leg, he continued hopping until he arrived at the door to his room. With a vicious twist on the crystal knob, he threw the door open and stumbled inside, finally allowing his artificial leg to touch the floor.

Sinking onto his cot, he rolled up his pant leg and wrenched the form from its leather bracing. For a moment, he considered throwing it out the window. But he hated using crutches even more than he hated the wooden leg. Releasing an agonized groan, he pummeled the mattress with the turned length of wood, swinging it with all of his strength again and again and again.

Finally, exhausted, he flopped sideways on the mattress with the peg leg still gripped in his trembling hand. He stared at the empty pant leg dangling over the edge of the bed. Odd how his body still believed a foot was there. A dull, never-ending ache did its best to convince him he had two feet instead of just one. But the drooping fabric exposed the truth—he was a cripple.

Closing his eyes, he whispered a halting prayer. "God, I know I can't grow another leg, but please . . . please . . . won't You help me feel complete?"

CHAPTER EIGHT

Alice-Marie slipped her hand through Libby's elbow as they neared the women's dormitory. "Elisabet, may I call you Libby, the way Bennett and Pete do?"

Libby, only half listening, shrugged.

"Very well. Libby from now on." She drew back on Libby's arm, bringing her to a halt. "Libby, please don't be sad. This is an exciting time! Just think"—she leaned close, her blue eyes sparkling—"tomorrow our classes start, we can begin pledging to Kappa Kappa Gamma and make many friends, the college campus is swarming with handsome men, there are no parents with watchful eyes keeping us from having fun . . ." Alice-Marie's voice rose in enthusiasm with each addition to her list of reasons to celebrate.

Libby heaved a huge sigh.

Alice-Marie shook her head. ". . . and yet you sigh and frown." She took hold of Libby's hands. "Tell me—why are you so downhearted?"

With a little huff of impatience, Libby pulled free of Alice-Marie's light grasp. "Didn't you see Petey's face when he left the dining hall? I . . . I hurt him." She swallowed, regret a bitter taste on her tongue. "He's been my best friend for . . . well, forever, it seems. He's the only one who's always accepted me just the way I am. And I've always accepted him."

"You mean his wooden leg?"

Is that all Alice-Marie saw when she looked at Petey—a peg leg where a foot should be? Libby shook her head. "Petey's special. He's not like other boys."

She'd never forgotten her first conversation with Petey, less than an hour after being deposited at the orphans' school. She had climbed a tree and refused to come down, proclaiming the people at that dumb school didn't really want her and she didn't want them, either! While Aaron Rowley and his hired hand pleaded and cajoled and finally threatened, Petey calmly limped to the storage shed, dragged a ladder across the scraggly grass, and shocked her by hopping up the rungs to join her.

There, perched beside her on a sturdy branch, Petey had asked why she thought no one wanted her. Even after all these years, she remembered her angry response: "My parents died an' left me, my uncle sent me away, an' all those people who came to meet the orphans on the train . . . none of 'em wanted me. All they wanted was a *boy*. So why should these people want me? I'm never gonna be a boy."

She also remembered Petey's calm reply: "But your folks didn't *want* to leave you, not like mine who told me to get out 'cause they couldn't afford to feed me no more. As for all those others . . ." He scratched his head, leaving his thick blond strands standing in tufts like little shocks of wheat. "Seems to me that's their problem, not yours, if they turned away a fine girl who can climb trees faster'n any boy I know." Sticking out his peg leg, he'd added, "Don'tcha think that if the folks here would take in a one-legged boy an' give him a good home, they'd be more'n pleased to have a girl like you?"

Remembering the feeling of acceptance that had filled her in those moments, tears stung Libby's eyes. He'd made her feel wanted, something she'd desperately needed. And tonight she'd made him feel unwanted. Unworthy. Unloved.

But Petey wasn't the unworthy one, and somehow she had to find a way to tell him. Maybe she could write him a note. She always expressed her thoughts better on paper. Eager to make things right with Petey, she turned toward the dormitory. "I don't want to talk anymore. Let's just go in." But before she took a step, three girls rushed across the lawn and blocked her path. One of them grabbed Alice-Marie's hand.

"Alice-Marie! Did I see you eating with Bennett Martin?"

Alice-Marie lifted her chin, a haughty smile curving her lips. "Why yes. He's a good friend of my roommate. Have you met Libby?"

"Elisabet," Libby said quickly. Her nickname, bestowed by Maelle and adopted by everyone at the orphans' school, was too intimate for everyone's use.

Alice-Marie gave her a funny look. "Oh yes, excuse me. Elisabet Conley. She and Bennett have been friends since they were children."

To Libby's relief, Alice-Marie left out the part about Libby being raised in an orphanage.

The trio of girls tittered, ignoring Libby. The one holding Alice-Marie's hand nearly bounced in place. "We met him at lunch. Isn't he charming? I adore his red hair and freckles. And do you know what he did? He sang to Caroline! Right there in the dining hall!"

"What?" Alice-Marie slapped her hand over her heart. "He did no such thing!"

Libby surmised the middle girl with frizzy brown hair and plain features must be Caroline by the way her face flooded with color. She nodded so hard the bun on the back of her head flopped. "He did. Oh yes, he did. Sang to me, and then . . ." She held out her hand and gazed dreamily at it. "He kissed me."

The other girls practically swooned, but Alice-Marie stomped her foot. She whirled on Libby. "Is Bennett a masher? Because if he's one to toy with a woman's affections, you should have warned me."

Libby gave Alice-Marie a firm look. "I am not Bennett's keeper. Whatever he does, he does on his own. If he wants to kiss Caroline at lunchtime"—she ignored Alice-Marie's gasp—"and then flirt with you at suppertime, that's his doing. Don't hold me responsible."

Libby stormed through the doors of the dormitory, shaking her head. Girls! She had no patience with their histrionics. Caroline, or Alice-Marie, or even Queen Mary of England was welcome to Bennett! Libby had more important things to do than giggling over some boy, such as writing Petey a note that would set things right again.

She charged to her desk and sat down hard enough to bounce the chair. She yanked out a pencil, slapped the notepad onto the desk, and started to riffle through for a clean sheet. But she glimpsed the story she'd begun that afternoon. The characters—Arthur and Arabella—called out to have their story completed.

Tapping her lips with the pencil, she waged a battle with herself. Finish the story so she could get it sent off to the magazine editor first thing in the morning, or set the story aside and write to Petey? Her gaze fell on the lines of print; they enticed her into reading. Within a few seconds, she was absorbed in another world.

Her pencil flew across the page, the story flowing almost without conscious thought.

At some point during the next hour, she was dimly aware of Alice-Marie entering the room and dressing for bed, but she steered clear of Libby. Lost in her make-believe world of a wealthy gentleman wooing a lowly chambermaid, Libby continued to write until she drew the story to a close.

"Oh, my darling Arthur, you've given up all for me." Tears rained down Arabella's creamy cheeks as she lifted her lover's hand and bestowed kisses on his knuckles. His skin was smooth as silk beneath her lips.

"Nothing I've left is as dear to me as you, precious Arabella," he vowed.

"But won't you one day regret living in this tenement rather than in your fine mansion, toiling every day as a common laborer instead of receiving the inheritance of your ancestors?" she asked him. Fear filled Arabella's heart. She gasped between salty tears, "Won't you, one day, resent me for all you've had to leave behind?"

Arthur drew her to his breast. His heart beat reassuringly beneath her ear. He promised rapturously, "Never, Arabella. The gilded trappings of my past are but dust when compared to my love for you. I shall cherish you—only you—until my dying day."

Secure in his statement of devotion, Arabella melted into his embrace. She lifted her face to his as she whispered breathlessly, "And I you, my dearest."

Their lips met in an expression of joy and promise that would last through all the morrows.

THE END.

With a little giggle, Libby dropped her pencil and massaged her aching fingers. Finished! Tomorrow, first thing, she'd purchase an envelope at the college postal window and send her story to the editor of *Modern Woman's World*.

Impulsively, she lifted the neat stack of pages and planted a kiss right in the middle of the top page. Then, embarrassed, she peeked over her shoulder to be certain Alice-Marie hadn't witnessed her ridiculous act. To her surprise, the room was dark—save the little lamp burning on the corner of her desk. Alice-Marie slept soundly in her narrow bed across the room. What time was it?

She squinted at the little clock on Alice-Marie's bureau and jumped from the desk. Eleven thirty-five? She'd completely lost track of time! She scrambled into her nightgown, clicked off the lamp, and dove into her bed. Classes started in the morning—she must be fully rested and alert tomorrow.

Scrunching her eyes closed, she willed sleep to claim her quickly. Then her eyes flew open. Petey! She needed to write him a note of apology. She started to throw back the covers, but she looked at the stars winking outside the window. No, she didn't dare stay up any longer for fear she'd oversleep and miss her very first class.

Petey's note would have to wait.

Libby's first days as a college student passed in a blur, and time and time again something came along to delay her note to Petey. At the close of each day, she raced to the mail cubbies, eager for a reply from *Modern Woman's World*. But she found letters from Shay's Ford instead. She appreciated the short missives sent by Maelle, Mrs. Rowley, and some of the children at the orphans' school, but impatience plagued her when she didn't receive a response concerning her story. What could possibly take so long?

She longed to pour out her frustration to Petey, but their different courses of study and subsequently varying schedules kept their paths from crossing during the day. Not until suppertime, when classes were over, did they have an opportunity to meet. But even then, to her disappointment, she usually did not get to spend time with Petey.

He sat with the other men enrolled in biblical studies, and she felt the need to keep her distance when Petey was with his fellow Bible scholars. Although she'd gone to church services every Sunday with the other orphans, her mind often wandered into fantasy worlds. She hadn't retained the lesson from even one sermon, so what could she contribute to their conversation? She and Bennett often ate together, but visiting with Bennett wasn't the same as visiting with Petey. Bennett, although funny and never short of something to say, took nothing seriously.

When she expressed concern about her fading friendship with Petey, he waved away her worries as if they were unfounded. Because he treated her heartache over that loss so casually, she didn't even consider discussing the magazine submission. How he would laugh if she confessed she'd submitted a romance story to a magazine! But Petey wouldn't laugh—Libby just knew he would encourage her to not lose hope.

Her journalism teacher advised the class to establish a habit of writing every day; then they would be prepared to meet deadlines when they were writing for pay rather than merely for learning. In response to the teacher's instruction, and to help take her mind off of missing Petey, she started a second story. It seemed wise to have a second one ready to go in case the magazine editor wanted to purchase more than one story from her.

Between attending classes, completing her assignments, writing an article for one of the school's newspapers on the merits of dormitory living—an assignment that stretched her to the very bounds of her abilities—and working on the second story, September slipped away, lost beneath a frenetic schedule that should have robbed her of time to think about Petey. Yet he crept into her thoughts at odd moments, stealing her concentration.

Did he think of her and miss her, as well?

On October first, three weeks to the day after she'd mailed her story, "Unlikely Lovers," to the editor of *Modern Woman's World*, she opened her mail cubby to find a long, narrow envelope with her name and address typed on the front. Even before she looked at the return address, her hands began to shake. This was it! The response she'd been anticipating!

Hugging the envelope to her chest, she raced up the stairs and closed herself in the room. After a moment's pause, she turned the lock on the door. She and Alice-Marie never locked their door, but Alice-Marie wouldn't knock before entering, and Libby didn't want her roommate surprising her. Especially if the envelope contained a rejection. She feared she might break her self-imposed edict about crying if the editor declined her story.

Please, please let them have said yes!

Sitting on the edge of the bed, she placed the envelope face-down in her lap. Very carefully, she slid her finger beneath the flap, loosening the glue. Then, with fingers that turned clumsy, she removed the letter. Slowly, holding her breath, she unfolded it. A slim piece of paper fell from the fold and glided across the floor, where it came to a halt next to the baseboard. Libby started to reach for it, but there didn't appear to be anything written on it. Puzzled, she turned back to the letter in her hand.

The salutation—*Dear Miss Conley*—seemed to pulse on the page. She crushed the letter to her bodice and sat bolt upright, gathering her courage while her pounding heartbeat ticked off seconds one by one. A full minute passed, anticipation building until finally, unable to abide the tension any longer, she jammed the letter to arm's length and forced herself to read the opening lines.

Her eyes widened. Her pulse raced. She leapt off the bed, tossed the letter in the air, and squealed with joy. They wanted it! They wanted her story! They wanted *her*! She danced in circles, laughing out loud and then covering her mouth to hold back the sound in case someone knocked on the door and asked what she thought she was doing in there. Scooping up the letter, she paced the room and read it in its entirety, her lips forming the words without sound.

Her story would be printed in the December edition—only two months away! They had enclosed a check as compensation at the rate of one-fifth cent per word. Libby jolted. A check? She peeked in the envelope—where was it? Then she remembered the discarded slip of paper on the floor. With a little cry, she grabbed it up, turned it over, and read the amount. Five dollars! Why, that would keep her in spending money for a month! Another gleeful laugh poured from her lips. But then the laughter abruptly stopped, her spine straightening with a sudden thought.

"Oh, but . . ." For a moment, she chewed her lower lip, silently berating herself. She hadn't bothered to count the words before submitting the story. She would have to trust their count this time, but she'd be certain to do a count before sending in her second story. "Lesson learned," she told herself and slid the check into her desk drawer, where Alice-Marie wouldn't see it. Then she read the final paragraph in the letter:

In what manner should the story be credited? Do you prefer "By Elisabet Conley"?

Libby clapped a hand to her cheek and sank down on the cot. A part of her wanted to use her given name—to have others know it was her story. But what would be best? A war took place in her mind, two conflicting opinions sparring like contenders in a tennis match.

Use your name—don't you want the recognition?

But do you want to be recognized for story writing or news articles?

But recognition is recognition! And think how wonderful it would be to have people stop you and tell you they read your work and enjoyed it. That can't happen if you use a made-up name.

But if you use your name for fictional works, will it carry credibility when you begin reporting real-life happenings?

After a few minutes of reflection, she decided the purpose in writing the stories was to prove she could meet deadlines, not to see her name in bold print on a magazine page. "I won't use Elisabet Conley," she whispered, tapping her pointer finger on her chin. "Instead I'll use . . ." Imaginary names—literary in tone—paraded through her mind: Lavinia Courtland, Cordelia Tremaine, Rosalie Hart . . . She hurried to her desk and wrote them on a piece of paper. Then, tracing little curlicues beneath each, she contemplated which one she liked best.

Suddenly, other names—not imaginary, but real—reared from the past: Leonard and Bette Conley. *Papa and Mama.* Libby gasped. Should she? With her neatest script, Libby combined her parents' first names. *Bette Leonard.* While not as flowery as those from her imagination, she liked the way the name looked on paper. And using her parents' names would be a way of immortalizing them.

With a giggle that sounded frighteningly girlish, Libby tore a clean sheet of paper from the pad and dug in the drawer for an ink pen. Looking at the letter of acceptance from the magazine, she copied the name from the signature and began a reply.

Dear Mr. Price,

It is with appreciation I write to thank you for purchasing my story. Please use the pseudonym Bette Leonard as the author's name for "Unlikely Lovers" and for any other stories you may purchase from me in the future.

Chapter Nine

P ete set aside the latest letter from Aaron and Isabelle Rowley. Every other day since his arrival at the University of Southern Missouri, he'd received a short note from Aaron or a long letter from Isabelle. He had bound all of the envelopes with a piece of string and displayed them on his bureau top, where he could see them or place his hand over them when he started feeling lonely for his surrogate parents.

This last one was the longest yet—a joint letter, with both Aaron and Isabelle contributing by turn, and they'd included train tickets for him, Libby, and Bennett to journey back to Shay's Ford in two more weeks. He glanced at the neatly written pages again before folding them and returning them to the envelope. Warmth flooded his frame when he glimpsed the warning penned in Isabelle's precise hand: *Be careful you don't lose the tickets. Put them in a safe place.*

It was the kind of admonition a parent would give. He

supposed some young men would resent such a statement, but he welcomed it. The motherly reminder was proof that Aaron and Isabelle looked at him as theirs.

At least someone wants me. . . .

He pushed the disparaging thought aside as he added the most recent letter to the stack on the bureau, then tucked the tickets into the corner of his desk drawer for safekeeping. He needed to tell both Libby and Bennett that he had their tickets when he saw them next.

His stomach clenched at the thought of seeing Libby. Had it really been more than three weeks since he'd left the dining hall, heartsore and offended? Not since he was ten years old had he gone an entire day without talking to Libby. He missed listening to her describe everything she saw in her unique, eloquent way. He missed seeing the fire spark in her eyes when someone got her dander up. He even missed the way she wrinkled her nose when she was thinking. He missed *her*, and he wasn't sure how he'd make it the rest of the year on this campus, knowing she was there but out of his reach.

Voices, loud and masculine, carried through the window, which he'd opened a crack to let in the crisp evening air. He hobbled to the window and peered out. Several students were playing baseball in the side yard, and it appeared the older ones had swiped hats from first-year students to use as bases. Apparently Bennett's was being used for home plate, because he was engaged in a lively argument with the catcher, his red hair glowing in the fading sunlight.

For a moment Pete considered going out and joining the game. He'd done nothing but study since his first day on campus when he and Libby had taken a short walk. If he went down, would they put him on a team? At the orphans' school it hadn't mattered that he had a peg leg. Everyone was used to it, so he felt comfortable romping and climbing and playing just like all the other boys.

But here the wooden appendage set him apart. Girls sidestepped him; guys never asked if he wanted to play catch or go hiking around the lake at the edge of the campus. In the classroom he could keep up, pace for pace, with the others. But only in the classroom. Maybe if he gave the ball a whack and made it around the bases, the students would look beyond his peg leg to Pete, the person.

He turned toward the door, but a stack of books on the corner of his desk seemed to cry out for attention. He didn't have time to play. With a grunt, he pushed the window casing down until it met the sill, sealing out the sounds of the game. Then he limped to his desk and sat, determined to begin the latest assignment from Pastor Hines.

Pete greatly admired the man. His wealth of biblical knowledge and studious manner set him apart from the other instructors. Pete aspired to be just as wise and stately as Pastor Hines when he graduated from the Bible school. He wanted to please the man, and so far he believed he'd succeeded. All of his essays had been returned with high marks. His professor had even stopped him twice in the hallway to discuss Scripture.

This most recent assignment, however, was more challenging than any of the others thus far. It required a great deal of thought, so he hunched over the assignment sheet and read the directions again, underlining the words with his index finger to help himself focus.

As a minister of the gospel, there will be times you must stand firm against forces that would pull your flock from a life of holiness. Look at the world around you. What forces are currently at work to bring about a moral or spiritual decline? You will choose a known force and go to battle, just as the men of Israel fought against the Philistines. However, you will not fight with sword or sling, but with the Word of God.

Pete kneaded his forehead. His professor had lectured for nearly an hour today on being holy—set apart. He'd banged his fist on his desk, expounding on the importance of righteous living. "Temptation will plague you," Pastor Hines had warned, his green eyes narrowed to slits and his gray brows knit in concern, "so you must resist temptation. One slip, just one time of allowing immoral thoughts or actions to seize you, and you can fall into a pit of ruin."

Replaying the professor's words, Pete wondered what he could choose to fight that would best garner the man's approval and do the most good. He sat, thinking, for several minutes, but nothing came to mind. Frustrated, he rose and tugged on his suit jacket. Maybe a walk in the evening air would awaken ideas.

He headed across the campus, past the makeshift baseball diamond. Bennett spotted him and waved, and Pete slowed his steps. Maybe his friend would ask him to join the game. Bennett knew Pete was a decent baseball player in spite of his peg leg. But after Pete lifted his hand in reply, Bennett turned his back and returned to cheering for his teammates. Head low, Pete continued on. He reached the tree-lined path that led to the open field and angled his steps to walk beneath the tree-branch canopy, smiling as he remembered Libby calling it a fairy path.

He stopped. Loneliness created an ache in the middle of his chest. Bennett didn't have time for him right now, but what about Libby? He gnawed his lower lip, gathering the courage to face her after their lengthy separation. Libby had said *anything more* than friendship with him would be ludicrous, but did that mean they couldn't still be friends? How he longed to restore his friendship with Libby.

At the very least, he needed to tell her he had the train tickets. Maybe he should go to the women's dormitory and ask the house matron for permission to speak to Libby. If she wasn't too busy, maybe after he told her about the ticket, they could sit for a while. Talk. Or just sit and not talk. The way they used to. If she had time.

Please let her have time . . .

The decision made, he headed for the women's dormitory. If the house matron told him Libby was too busy to talk, he'd just go back to his own room and, as he'd been doing for the past weeks, lose himself in his studies. At least his bum leg didn't interfere with his ability to think.

❧

"Elisabet?" One of the girls from Libby's floor stuck her head in the room. "Miss Banks sent me up for you—you have a visitor downstairs."

Libby pushed off her bed, where she'd been sitting cross-legged while editing an article for the college newspaper. She wouldn't mind a break—the person who wrote the article possessed a dismal grasp of proper grammar. And the spelling errors . . . *erroneus*, indeed! "Who is it?" She hoped it wasn't Roy. For some reason, he'd requested a visit with her twice in the past week, but she'd refused to meet him.

The girl shrugged. "I don't know his name. The new student with the wooden foot."

Petey! Libby's heart turned over with joy. "Tell Miss Banks to tell him I'll be right down." The girl left, and Libby quickly pulled on her shoes and buttoned them. She would run downstairs in her stocking feet were it not for the strict house matron. Miss Banks didn't approve of bare feet or of running, as Libby had quickly learned. Miss Banks and Mrs. Rowley would no doubt be good friends.

Her feet covered, Libby hurried down the stairs. Her gaze swept the cozy common room, which bustled with activity this evening. Four girls were sitting in a row on a settee in front of the window, their focus on a magazine held by one of the center girls.

As if choreographed, the quartet shot Libby a quick look over the top of the magazine when she entered the room, then returned their attention to whatever they were reading.

A little buzz of awareness wiggled down Libby's spine. Might these same girls read her words in the magazine in another two months?

She turned toward Miss Banks's desk near the front doors and spotted Petey. His gaze met hers, but he didn't move a muscle. The house matron's stern glare had apparently pinned him in place. But how wonderful to see him!

Swallowing a delighted laugh, she forgot the rule to move sedately. She skipped to the desk, linked her hands behind her back, and smiled up into Petey's dear, familiar face. "Good evening, Mr. Leidig. So good of you to come calling." She glanced at the house matron. The woman's sour expression didn't soften one whit.

"Yes." Petey cleared his throat. "I had a letter from Aaron and Isabelle today, and . . ." His brows high, he shifted his eyes briefly to indicate Miss Banks, then he tipped his head toward the door. "Could we go outside? It's a pleasant evening with a nice breeze."

"That sounds wonderful." Libby caught his arm and aimed him toward the doors. "And maybe we could take a short stroll around the grounds?" Her heart felt lighter than it had for weeks, just walking by his side. "We can take the path past the old stone foundation at the far edge of campus—it always makes me feel a little glum, but I love to stand beside it and try to imagine the grand building it supported before fire brought it down."

As soon as they stepped off the porch, Petey jiggled his elbow. Libby released him and stepped aside, looking at him in confusion. "Was I holding too tight?"

"No." His focus darted to her left. "But you're being watched by the house matron and several girls who are at the common room windows. I didn't think you'd want to give them the idea that you and I are . . ."

Heat attacked Libby's face. Why hadn't she ever composed that letter? But at least now she had the chance to apologize. "Petey, about what I said—"

"You don't need to explain yourself." His gentle voice increased the ache in her heart. She could bear his anger; his kindness nearly killed her. "I understand."

"Then you know it isn't you who's at fault? You know it . . . it's me?" She held her breath. If he truly understood that she wasn't the right match for him because of her inadequacies, then their friendship could resume unchanged.

"Yes." He lowered his head and tapped the tip of the peg leg against the walkway, a habit left over from his childhood. "I understand completely."

"Oh, Petey." Libby nearly collapsed, the relief was so great. "Then we can still be friends? Just as we've always been?"

A lopsided, somehow sad smile creased his face. "Yes, Libby. As we've always been. Now—" He drew in a breath. "I came to tell you I have our train tickets to go home on the sixteenth. Bennett and I will come by for you in the morning. We'll walk to town and hire a cab to take us to the station. Be sure you talk to all of your instructors so they know you'll be gone that Friday."

"I already have. I'm so eager to see Maelle and the Rowleys."

"Me too."

"And I can't believe Matt's getting married! He and Lorna are such a sweet couple." The children at the orphans' school had witnessed friendship blooming to love between the cook's daughter and Mrs. Rowley and Maelle's brother, Matt, who served as a part-time groundskeeper at the school. Although Libby held the impression Mrs. Rowley didn't approve of the match, she thought

Matt Tucker and Lorna Jensen were perfectly suited to one another.

She lightly swatted Petey's arm, her lips twitching with a teasing grin. "And lucky you—getting to stand up with Matt. You'll be very handsome in your suit, with a rosebud tucked in your lapel."

Petey chuckled and scratched his head. "Oh, I don't know about that."

They stood in silence for several seconds. A comfortable, settling-in kind of silence that brought a hint of healing to Libby's aching soul. In the distance, a firm clack indicated someone's bat connected with a baseball, and cheers erupted. In response, a bird scolded from a nearby tree. Libby lifted her chin to seek out the bird, and she smiled as two dry leaves broke free of their branch and swirled to the ground. The leaves' graceful descent through the air reminded her of the dance scene she'd written in her latest story. Eagerly, she turned to Petey.

"Petey, I—" she started.

"Libby, I—" he said at the same time.

She flapped her hands at him, laughing. "Go ahead."

"I have an assignment I need to finish tonight, so I'm going to head back to Landry Hall."

Her shoulders sagged. "So soon? But we've hardly had any time to talk."

He pulled his lips to the side in an expression of regret. "I'm sorry, but I really need to work. I'll see you . . . at dinner tomorrow?"

She wanted to tell him about the story she'd sold—to have him be happy for her—but she wouldn't interfere with his studies. Becoming a minister was so important to him. Just as important as becoming a journalist was to her. If only their goals weren't so very, very different . . .

"Yes, that would be splendid." She reached out and brushed his sleeve with her fingertips. "I've missed you, Petey."

That odd smile returned—an upturning of lips with no answering light in his blue eyes. "I've missed you, too. But we'll talk more tomorrow at dinner. Good night now, Libby."

She watched him go, his hitching gait as familiar as her own reflection in a mirror. But something in the way he carried himself seemed different. He'd always appeared older than his years, a result of having to care for himself at such a young age, but tonight there was an oldness about him that went beyond maturity to . . . Libby sought an appropriate word to describe his appearance and finally settled on *tiredness*.

Yes, Petey looked tired. His studies must be wearing him down, she decided with a rush of sympathy. Perhaps it was good that they'd be returning to Shay's Ford soon. There, Mrs. Rowley would make sure he rested, and Cookie Ramona would spoil him with his favorite foods—Petey was everyone's favorite at the orphanage. Time with Mr. and Mrs. Rowley and Matt, a fun time at the wedding, and being home would surely brighten Petey's outlook.

And at some point during their time away from school, away from all the busyness and all the—she flicked a glance at the dormitory and spotted several girls peering out from a common room window—nosy people, she'd show him the letter from Mr. Price. How proud he'd be!

A wide smile on her face, Libby twirled in a circle right there in the open. And she didn't even care when the girls behind the window giggled.

CHAPTER TEN

Bennett tossed the ball in the air with one hand and caught it with the other while he waited outside Landry Hall. Toss, catch. Toss, catch. Back and forth. Monotonous, but at least it was something to do.

Where was Pete? Bennett wouldn't be able to stick around there much longer—crazy curfew rules. He tossed the ball with a little more force, sending it in a high arc above his head. Weren't they all adults on this campus? A fellow ought to be able to decide for himself when he wanted to turn in.

He peered across the grounds, seeking a glimpse of his old pal. When Pete had walked past earlier, Bennett had wanted to ask him to join the game. But he wasn't sure he carried enough clout yet with the fellows to bring in Pete. Oh, he'd been talking him up—his best buddy from way back, smart as a whip, a real good egg. Of course, he hadn't mentioned Pete by name. That would come when he had the others all convinced his pal was *the person* to know on campus. Bennett figured he only needed another couple of days, and then he could draw Pete into the action.

He smacked the ball from one palm to the other. Finally he spotted Pete coming up the walk. Jamming the worn baseball into his pocket, he trotted to meet him. "Hey, Pete, out for your evening constitutional?" He affected a British accent and grinned at his own joke.

Pete offered a weak laugh in reply. "I walked over and saw Libby. I needed to let her know the Rowleys sent me the train tickets for our trip back home."

Bennett stifled a growl of irritation. Of course the Rowleys would send the tickets to Pete—good ol' trustworthy Pete. "I saw you heading off earlier, but I couldn't holler in the middle of the game." He experienced a twinge of conscience with his little white lie and hurried on. "And phew . . . my team didn't do so great tonight—lost by seven runs!" He made a sour face. "But Sunday afternoon we're planning a rematch, and we need a decent pitcher. Wanna play?"

Pete's eyebrows lowered a fraction of an inch. "Me? Pitch?"

Bennett laughed. "Didn't you pitch for us back at the school? You've got a good arm." Pete couldn't play catcher—it required squatting, something not easily done on his artificial leg. And he wasn't the greatest baseman or fielder with that peg making him clumsy. But he'd proved he could plant the tip of his peg leg in the dirt and throw a ball hard and fast right over the smashed tin can that served as home plate.

Bennett smacked Pete's shoulder. " 'Course, Libby could pitch better than the numskull who pitched for us tonight." Bennett never would understand why Libby had such trouble throwing a ball; she could hit a tree dead center with a penknife.

Pete rubbed his lips together. "Sure, Bennett. I'd be willing to pitch for you, if the others won't mind."

"They won't mind." Between now and Sunday he'd talk Pete up so much they wouldn't even flinch when he limped out to the mound. And as soon as the other fellows saw Pete in action, they'd realize he wasn't so different. Then they'd be willing to let him pledge the fraternity. Bennett grinned, thinking how flabbergasted ol' Roy would be to see Pete and him showing up for meetings.

Pete shifted his weight to his good leg, grimacing a bit. Bennett frowned—Pete better not do that during the game. "We're planning to play right after lunch." He pulled the baseball from his pocket and bounced it in his palm. "One o'clock."

"I'll be there."

Bennett plopped the ball into Pete's hand and then scuttled backward several feet. He hunkered into the catcher's position and cupped his hands. "Put 'er in here, pal."

Pete examined the seams, laid his finger precisely between them, and fired the ball back to Bennett. Bennett rose, grinning, and shook his right hand. "Good one!" He hissed through his teeth. "That stung! You'll be ready Sunday."

With a short laugh, Pete closed the distance between them. "I've been walking to the chapel around the corner from the campus for services on Sunday mornings. Do you want to meet for breakfast and go over together before the game?"

Bennett shoved the ball back into his pocket. Trust Pete to bring up church. "Nah. You go on without me. I like to sleep in on Sunday mornings."

"You sure?" Pete's face twisted into the same look Aaron Rowley had always worn when Bennett tried to play sick on Sunday mornings. Bennett disliked the expression even more coming from his friend. "Now that we're settled in here on campus, it would do us good to go—to feel like we're part of a church family."

"Libby going?"

Pete shrugged. "I haven't asked her yet, but I'm sure she will. I don't know why she wouldn't."

"Well . . ." Bennett stuck out his jaw and folded his arms over his chest. "I'd rather sleep. Gotta get up early for my classes all week long, and gotta get up early Saturday to get to my job." He'd been hired by the school's groundskeeper to help with yard maintenance. After the man found out Bennett had done similar chores at the orphans' school, he'd hired him on the spot. Apparently a lot of the students at the college had never lifted a shovel or weeded a garden—spoiled namby-pambies. "I don't wanna get up early my only day off."

Pete didn't look happy, but he didn't argue. "All right, but when we go home for Matt's wedding, Aaron and Isabelle will expect you to go to church with them before we head back Sunday afternoon."

"Yeah, yeah, I know."

"It'll be good to see them." Pete seemed to drift off somewhere; he didn't react to Bennett's derisive tone. "I'm looking forward to a weekend at home."

Both Pete and Libby called the orphans' school *home*, but Bennett never used the term. He said, *the school* or *where I live*, but not *home*. Someday—when he settled down, got married, maybe had a kid or two—he'd call the place he shared with his family "home." But he wouldn't squander a word like that on anything less than a place of his choosing.

"Well, the wedding's still two weeks away, and we've got plenty to do before then . . . including whomping those Beta Theta Pi guys in Sunday's baseball game!" Bennett squinted one eye at Pete. "Sun's not quite down. Wanna try a few more throws? Just to make sure you're good and limbered up for a full game?"

"I'd like to, but I've got an assignment I—"

"Never mind." Bennett drew the words out into a groan, but he grinned while he said it. "I figure you'll do just fine in the game. In case I don't see you beforehand, meet us right here in the side yard at one on Sunday. We'll skunk 'em this time. Night, Pete!"

Bennett took off at a trot toward the men's dormitory. He hoped a couple of the guys were still lounging in the common room. He wanted to let them know he'd found their team a dandy pitcher.

❧

Pete hop-skipped, adding a little jump on his good leg between steps, down the hallway that led to the classrooms. He needed a few minutes alone with his professor. Pastor Hines always came in early in case one of his students had questions or concerns, so Pete wasn't worried he'd miss the teacher. But he did want to beat all of the other Bible students to the room.

In the back of his mind, he replayed the scene he'd witnessed when he'd entered the common room of Libby's dormitory yesterday evening. A group of young ladies sat in a row in front of the window, holding a magazine to catch the light. By their pink cheeks and occasional bursts of laughter, which they quickly muffled with their hands over their mouths, it was obvious something in the magazine had piqued their interest. Their intrigue appeared to go beyond curiosity or entertainment to an embarrassed excitement, which led him to believe whatever they were viewing was not wholesome. He'd seen Bennett and a couple other fellows at the orphans' school act in the same snickering, flush-faced way when viewing the pages advertising women's undergarments in the Sears catalog.

When he'd returned to Landry Hall, he'd dug through the basket of magazines their resident director left in the common room for the students' use. In the very bottom, beneath *Harper's Magazine*, *Top-Notch Magazine*, and three copies of various issues of

The Windsor, he'd located a publication that looked similar to the one the girls had been reading. He'd taken it to his room and laid it flat on the bed to read. Between the covers, he'd found what he surmised the girls had seemed so enamored with—a rather risqué story about a young movie starlet and her older, caddish director.

The description of pounding hearts, feverish desires, and furtive meetings in dark corners where the man and woman allowed their lips to explore one another's mouths left Pete feeling uncomfortable. Twice, while reading, he'd been compelled to glance around the room to be certain no one knew what he was doing. Would he have felt so uneasy if the reading material were wholesome? Surely stories like that could turn young women toward impure thought.

By the time he'd returned the magazine to the basket—once again, clear at the bottom, but upside-down—he believed he'd found the subject for his assignment in Pastor Hines's class.

Of course, Pastor Hines had to approve it. So before he went any further, he wanted the man's opinion.

The classroom door stood open, and Pete glimpsed the silver-haired professor seated at his desk. The man's wire spectacles rested on the end of his nose, and he frowned at a stack of papers. Pete tapped lightly on the doorframe. The man looked up, and a smile immediately cleared the scowl from his face. He removed his glasses with one hand and gestured Pete forward with the other.

"Mr. Leidig." Pastor Hines pointed to a front-row desk. "Come in and sit."

Pete limped forward and slid into the seat. He gave his teacher an apologetic look. "Am I disturbing you?"

The man shook his head. "No, no, I don't mind setting these aside." With a grimace, he slapped the stack of pages to the corner of his desk. "Obviously I didn't do a sufficient job in my lecture on following the Ten Commandments. These essays—" He shook his head and blew out a noisy breath. "Appalling." Then he leaned back in his chair. "But that isn't your concern. With what can I assist you, Mr. Leidig?"

Pete rested his elbows on the desk and briefly described the scene he'd witnessed in the women's common room. "I located a similar magazine and looked inside, and there was a rather unsavory story. . . ." Pastor Hines's eyebrows drew down until they formed a distinct V between his eyes. Pete's face felt hot. He stammered on. "I thought perhaps the story would make a suitable subject for our assignment on moral decline since it included—"

The teacher waved his hand. "Don't bother."

Pete sagged in the chair. "This isn't something worth pursuing?"

"On the contrary, there's no need for you to explain. I already know the type of story you reference, and it's certainly unsuitable." Pastor Hines pursed his lips in distaste. "Disgraceful, is what it is. Stories written for the sole purpose of inducing titillation."

So Petey's initial instincts when he'd seen the girls' actions had been right. The realization increased his confidence in his abilities to be a good spiritual leader.

Pastor Hines continued in a disparaging tone. "The stories are, unfortunately, quite popular with women of all ages, but most particularly with the younger set." He sighed. "I can't help but believe it leads impressionable young women into impure thought, not to mention gives them an unrealistic expectation of the relationship between a man and a woman."

Shaking his head, the professor clicked his tongue on his teeth. "This is precisely the kind of battle that must be warred—and won! Young women caught up in these romanticized tales could very well begin seeking a relationship based on only . . . er . . . physical attraction—" the man's jowls mottled red—"rather than seeking a God-centered, well-grounded man who will be a moral leader for his household."

Pete sat up eagerly. "So this would meet the requirements for the assignment?"

"Yes, Mr. Leidig. Most certainly." Pastor Hines rose and rounded the desk. "And I wish you much success in your attempts to dissuade magazine editors from printing such filth." His brow crinkled for a moment, his piercing eyes pinned on Pete's face. "Mr. Leidig, in addition to reasoning with magazine editors, do you have other plans to help bring an end to these types of writings?"

Pete pushed to his feet and stood beside the desk with one hand braced on the smooth top. "Not yet, sir. I wanted to get your approval before I began planning."

"That's fine," the man replied. "Knowing what you'll tackle is enough for today. But keep in mind that when it comes to winning a war, success is more certain with multiple directions of attack."

Pete nodded slowly. Although he'd read many newspaper accounts about the battles going on overseas, he hadn't paid attention to military strategy. But his teacher's words made sense. If the attack came solely from one direction, then the enemy would have many directions in which to flee. He'd need to plan attacks from several different directions to make the greatest impact.

"I'll be in thought and prayer concerning the best way to end the printing of these stories." Pete stuck out his hand, and Pastor Hines took it. "Thank you, sir. You can trust I'll do my very best on this assignment."

His teacher smiled, giving Pete's hand a strong shake. "I wouldn't expect anything less from you, Mr. Leidig."

CHAPTER ELEVEN

"Ooh, isn't it exciting?"

Alice-Marie was going to cut off the circulation to Libby's hand if she didn't let loose. She moved even closer to Libby on the blanket, making room for another girl to join them on the square of green-and-red-plaid wool thrown over the grass. "I just love watching a sporting event! I hope the Beta Theta Pi boys win!"

One could hardly call this an official sporting event, considering it took place on the grassy side yard of the Bible school rather than at a real baseball diamond. There were no bleachers on which to sit, so a few students, including Alice-Marie, had dragged out blankets and spread them on the lawn. Most spectators, however, formed a jagged line along the east side of the playing field. Already some of them were shifting restlessly, apparently tired of standing. Libby decided the players had been wise to settle on a short game of three innings only—a rematch, Bennett had called it, for his team to regain its dignity.

Libby peeled Alice-Marie's fingers from her arm. "Beta Theta Pi? Is that the team Pete and Bennett are on?"

For a moment, Alice-Marie's lips puckered into a pout. "No. They're playing with a group of Delta Tau Delta boys." With a little expulsion of breath, she snatched up her parasol and snapped it open. "And I just don't understand. If Bennett intends to pledge Beta Theta Pi, why would he choose to play against them? Surely that will not soften them toward him. . . ."

Libby shrugged. She'd long ago given up trying to figure out Bennett's motivations. He did whatever pleased him, regardless of another's opinion. At times, his self-serving actions annoyed her, but other times she envied him. Bennett was the most carefree person she knew.

Alice-Marie rested the parasol handle against her left shoulder, shielding both her and Libby's faces from the sun. "Regardless of his reasoning, I'm eager to see him play. I just *know* he'll be the best on either team."

Libby rolled her eyes. Alice-Marie's fascination with Bennett was growing more tiresome by the hour, but she knew nothing she could say would dissuade her roommate from seeing Bennett as a knight in shining armor. However, Alice-Marie's infatuation provided Libby with fodder for the stories she worked on between classes and late at night. She discovered writing at night, her page illuminated only by a thin band of moonlight, was the most productive time. The stories flowed so easily, they almost wrote themselves.

One group of players—attired in trousers, suspenders, and shirts with their sleeves rolled above their elbows rather than baseball uniforms—darted out onto the grass. A cheer rose as they positioned themselves at bases or out in the field. Libby scanned their faces.

Few were familiar, except the pitcher, who wore a strip of white tape across the bridge of his nose. She pursed her lips in disgust. That detestable Roy.

Even without the telltale bandage marking his healing nose, she'd have known him by his curly brown hair that fell across his forehead in a roguish way. She supposed he had the looks of a storybook hero, but she'd never use him in her stories—unless she had need of a true lout.

Roy held the ball toward the audience, his grin wide. Alice-Marie patted her palms together, bouncing on her seat. Her parasol slipped sideways and bopped Libby on the temple. With a little grunt, Libby shifted to the edge of the blanket. The sun hit her full in the face, but she shielded her eyes with her hand and watched Roy throw three perfect pitches across home plate. The first batter went down without once swinging his bat.

The cheers set Libby's teeth on edge. What did these people see in that arrogant oaf? If Bennett and Petey weren't playing, she'd return to the dormitory where she could write in peace—it seemed the entire student body had come out to watch the game—but Petey had indicated he would be pitching. She hoped he would make Roy look like an inept bumbler.

The second batter got a hit, but it bounced right to the first baseman, who scooped it up and touched the base long before the runner reached it. More cheers chased the defeated fellow back to his team. Then Bennett stepped up to bat. Alice-Marie let out a squeal that nearly pierced Libby's eardrum.

Libby frowned at her. "I thought you were rooting for Beta Theta Pi?"

Alice-Marie hunched her shoulders. "I couldn't resist. Look at him, so handsome and muscular, with his hair shining like rich red satin." She released a deep sigh.

With a soft snort, Libby turned her attention to Bennett. Alice-

Marie was right about Bennett being muscular. His biceps bulged as he angled the bat over his shoulder. Bending his knees, he faced the pitcher with a look of concentration on his face.

Roy's lips twisted into a sneer. He smacked the ball into his mitt and planted his weight on one hip. "Well, well, well, look who's up. It's gonna give me great pleasure to strike you out, Martin."

"Give it a try." Bennett held his position, his lips barely moving as he spoke.

Roy spat on the grass and went into an elaborate windup. The onlookers broke into hoots and cheers as the ball zinged straight and true toward the plate. Bennett swung—and caught air. He stumbled and almost fell. Laughter broke across the crowd. Roy bowed to his audience, his grin cocky.

Libby wanted to run out on the field and give him a good kick in the shin. She turned to Alice-Marie. "Why do people egg him on? He's the most obnoxious person I've ever seen!"

Alice-Marie twirled her parasol and hummed to herself as if Libby hadn't spoken.

The girl on the other side of Alice-Marie leaned forward and answered. "Roy has led the basketball team to a winning season three years in a row. Even as a freshman, he scored more points than any other player in the conference."

"So that makes him immune from acting like a decent human being?"

The girl shrugged. "I suppose he believes he's earned the right to behave however he pleases." She glanced around, indicating the supportive throng. "Everyone else seems to feel that way, too. Or they just don't want to be considered his enemy. He has the power to make your life miserable if he doesn't like you."

Libby shook her head. No one person should have that much power. She intended to pen a strongly worded editorial on that very topic at the earliest opportunity.

Bennett returned to the batting position. Sweat glistened on his forehead. "Knock off the theatrics and play ball!"

With an insolent swagger, Roy returned to the pitcher's spot and went into another windup. This time when Bennett swung, he connected. The *crack!* echoed across the field, and the ball sailed over Roy's head. Libby let out a cry of elation, but no one else cheered. Her voice hung in the silence as everyone's faces followed the ball like a field of sunflowers trailing the course of the sun.

The orb of white flew high, high, high against the backdrop of blue sky. Bennett dropped the bat and bounded toward first base with his focus upward, watching the ball's progress. The center fielder scuttled in reverse, his face aimed at the sky, his mitt raised. And just as Bennett rounded second base, the ball fell directly into the center fielder's glove. He held it over his head and jumped up and down.

The crowd went wild. Roy waved to the audience and then sauntered off the field with a grin on his face. His teammates pounded his back, leaping around as if they'd won a championship match. When Roy's team cleared the field, the team made up of Delta Tau Delta men scurried into position. Libby's heart skipped a beat when she spotted Petey moving toward the center of the makeshift diamond, a baseball in hand.

The loud babble of voices changed to startled gasps, whispers, and soft titters. Libby knew the spectators were looking at Petey—at his wooden leg. And making judgments about him. Alice-Marie tapped Libby's arm. "Is this some of kind of ploy to destroy the Beta Theta Pi team's concentration? Surely he can't . . . can't *throw* with that peg leg!"

Libby shot her roommate a stern look. "He *throws* with his hand."

Someone muttered, "Is this a joke?" And another voice answered, "It's gotta be. They're wantin' to get the Betas to feel sorry for him so they won't even try to get a hit." Someone far to Libby's left let out a low, "Boooo!" Several others took up the cry. "Boo! Booooo!" The jeers continued, underscored by bursts of laughter.

Protectiveness welled up in Libby's chest, and it took every bit of self-control she possessed to stay seated rather than jump up and give the whole lot of them a tongue-lashing. But Petey seemed unaware of the crowd's derisive reaction. He put his peg leg behind him, pressing its tip into the dirt. Then, bending forward slightly, he rested his weight on his good leg. He positioned his hands in front of him. His face wore an expression of concentration. He was ready.

Watching him, Libby felt a smile twitch her cheeks. She knew what Petey could do. Very soon, those hecklers would be silenced.

❧

Pete shifted his eyes as one of the Beta Theta Pi men separated from the tight cluster of players and ambled toward home plate. He swung his bat, nonchalant, a slight grin on his lips. His teammates laughed, calling out, "You go, Chester! Home run, buddy, home run! Easy hit!"

Pete remembered the player from his first night on campus— one of Roy's friends who'd come running when Roy quirked his fingers for reinforcements. He swallowed. Bennett had already played these guys; he knew the team was made up of Roy and his cohorts. So why had Bennett dragged Pete into a rematch with them? He didn't want to suspect his friend of using him to cause trouble, but his mind swerved in that direction anyway.

Bennett, at third base, cupped his hands and yelled, "Get 'im, Pete! Easy out!" A few of his teammates echoed the cry, but their voices lacked real confidence. Pete supposed he couldn't blame them. After being—as Bennett had put it—stomped by Roy's team the other evening, they'd been hoping for a champion pitcher to save the day. And what they got was a peg-legged cripple instead.

Suddenly, from the spectators, a familiar voice rang out. "Strike him out, Petey! One, two, three . . . out!"

A few outright snickers followed the comment, but Pete didn't mind. Having Libby offer her support gave him the boost in confidence he needed. He straightened his shoulders and locked eyes with Chester, who settled into position at home plate. Pete looked the batter up and down, silently measuring his height, and chose the best place to aim the ball based on the distance between the man's waist and knees. Drawing his arm back, he prepared to throw.

"Hey!" a voice blasted.

Startled, Pete jerked, throwing himself off balance. He regained his footing and then turned toward the voice.

Roy stood in front of his team with his hands on his hips. "Aren't you gonna take a practice pitch?"

Bennett stepped off the base, his face twisted into an angry scowl. "That's interfering with a play, Ump—automatic strike!" He glared at the umpire, daring him to call it.

But the umpire raised his skinny shoulders in a shrug. "Fair question." He called to Pete, "You want to practice? We'll give you two throws." Chester bounced in place on the balls of his feet, looking from the umpire to Pete.

It had been a while since he'd pitched, but Pete didn't want to risk wearing out his arm before the game ended. He set his jaw. The fewer throws, the better. And he'd better make each one count. Pete shook his head. "I'm ready. Let's go."

Chester hunched into position. The crowd began a low-pitched mutter: "Home run, home run, home run . . ." Pete closed his ears to the taunting hum and drew his arm back. With a snap, he released the ball. It smacked into the catcher's mitt. Chester jerked upright, his jaw dropping. He hadn't even swung.

"Chester!" Roy screeched from the sidelines. "You dimwit, watch the ball!"

Chester threw his arms wide. "Watch it? It came so fast, I didn't even see it!"

Roy ran both hands through his hair. "Watch closer this time!"

Bennett called, "That's the way, Pete! One down! Two to go!"

Pete's teammates echoed the cry, surprise underscoring their voices. Pete tried not to smile. He waited until Chester settled into position, then snapped off a second pitch. Chester swung, but too late.

"Strike two!" the umpire bellowed, then sent a hesitant look toward Roy. Pete chose not to look at Roy. He sensed the man's irritation from a distance of forty feet.

"One more!" Bennett nearly crowed, bouncing on his heels beside the base. "Just one more, Pete—c'mon, buddy, you can do it!"

An unearthly hush fell as Pete pulled his arm back for the third pitch. He cocked his elbow and snapped the ball toward home plate. The ball zipped directly over the unpainted slab of wood and into the catcher's glove.

The umpire jammed his thumb toward Chester. "You're out!"

Chester stood for a few stunned seconds, staring at Pete as if he couldn't believe what had just happened. Then he dropped the bat and rejoined his team, skirting around Roy. Roy clenched his fists for a moment, glaring at Pete, then he grabbed another teammate. He threw the man forward, hissing, "You better get a hit."

But the second batter didn't get a hit, either, nor did the third.

By the ninth straight strike, Pete's team was wild with excitement. Even the spectators, who'd remained unhervingly silent through the final six pitches of the first inning, broke into uncertain applause when Pete came off the field.

Roy stormed out to the pitcher's mound. His first pitch was wild, hitting the batter on the leg. "Take your base, Jim," the umpire said, then offered a mild reprimand. "It's supposed to be a friendly game, Roy. Take it easy, huh?"

Roy didn't respond.

Bennett bumped Pete's shoulder. "Let's hope Melvin sends Jim home—we could use a point." But Jim remained stuck at first base when Roy threw six straight strikes and brought down Melvin and then Ted, earning cheers from the crowd.

Pete noted that the cheers and applause for Roy possessed greater enthusiasm than what had been offered him, but he chose not to be offended. Roy was well-known; Pete was new. Roy was a bully who could exact revenge; Pete was a ministry student who would turn the other cheek. He understood the reason for the exuberant response. Even though a small part of him wished it might be different, that once—just once—the rousing cries would be for him. Then again, he doubted his future congregation would ever stand in the pews and applaud at the close of a sermon.

By the bottom half of the third and final inning, Roy's team had two runs to the Delta Tau Delta's zero. Bennett's frustration grew, evidenced by his red face and tightened jaw muscles. "You never should've let 'em hit off you," he said to Pete when the team gathered to line up for batting.

Pete tried not to bristle. Had Bennett expected him to throw nine straight strikes each inning? Not even professional pitchers managed that feat.

Bennett went on. "We gotta make it up."

"So who's up?" Jim asked.

Ted consulted his list. "Lanny, then Stanley, then Bennett, then . . ." He swallowed. "Pete."

Bennett's lip pinched into a grim line. "All right, listen." He looked at Lanny and Stanley. "All you gotta do is get on base. Bunt if you have to, but get on base. I know I can hit him. I got the rhythm now. You two get on, and I'll hit you home."

Lanny and Stanley exchanged quick looks. "You sure?"

"I'm sure. Now go!" He slapped a bat into Lanny's hands and gave him a push. Pete watched the man shuffle to home plate and take his position. Just as Bennett had instructed, he bunted toward third and barely made it to first ahead of the ball. Bennett's team cheered, and a few spectators, including Libby and Alice-Marie, joined in.

"See there? See there?" Bennett clapped Stanley on the back. "Now it's your turn!"

But Roy's team must have suspected Stanley would mimic Lanny's play, because the third baseman inched forward. He easily snagged the ball and shot it across the field to the first baseman, who tapped the base before Stanley crossed it. Lanny, on his way to second base, paused momentarily, as if confused as to what he needed to do. Then he darted toward second base as the first baseman shot the ball to the player at second base. Lanny tried to dive between the second baseman's legs to avoid being tagged, but the baseman whacked him on the shoulder just before his fingers connected with the short plank of wood serving as a base.

"Out, and out!" roared the umpire, pointing first at Stanley then Lanny.

Defeated, the pair returned to their team. They looked at Bennett with sad eyes. "We tried," Stanley said.

Bennett didn't answer. Snagging a bat, he stomped to home plate. Pete held his breath. He'd seen Bennett in moods like this before, and it wouldn't take much to send him into a rage. He hoped Roy wouldn't do something stupid.

Roy, smirking, bounced the ball in his hand. "You gonna bunt, too, Martin?"

Bennett whacked the ground with the end of the bat. "Just pitch it."

Without preamble, Roy pitched a fastball. Bennett braced, swung. A resounding *crack!* signaled a solid hit. Roy jumped aside as the ball zinged past his knees, hit the ground, and bounced between the second baseman and shortstop. Bennett took off running, arms pumping, lips set in a determined sneer.

The ball continued its pell-mell course toward the outfield. The center fielder called it and ran forward, swooping his glove to scoop it up—but he came up empty. The surprised look on his face sent the spectators into gales of laughter. Both the left and right fieldsmen raced toward the ball, which finally came to a stop near a stand of trees at the edge of the grassy area. The left fielder got to it first and threw it to third, but it went wild, and Bennett crossed third base before the baseman could recover the ball.

The crowd erupted. The whoops and whistles sent Roy into a tantrum. He stomped his feet, waved his fists in the air, and hollered vulgar threats at his teammates. Eventually, the umpire brought everyone under control. He looked toward the group of Delta Tau Deltas. "Who's up?"

Pete gulped. His turn.

Chapter Twelve

Bennett leaned forward and braced his palm on his knee, ready to sprint. Just a tap—that's all Pete needed. A tap. Hard enough to give Bennett time to cross home plate. They'd agreed to a shortened game of three innings, given they were playing on the Sabbath, and they'd reached what could very well be the finishing play. He could take losing if only they scored a run.

He watched Pete limp to the batter's box. Still hunkered low, he hollered, "Good eye, now, Petey ol' pal—you can do it! Give 'er a clop!" *Just a tap. That's all you need.*

Roy stood with his arm hanging limply, the ball caught between his thumb and two fingers. "Ump, are you gonna allow this? He can't bat. How's he gonna run the bases?"

Pete didn't so much as flinch, making Bennett grin. Ol' Roy wouldn't rattle Pete. The umpire scratched his head, staring at the wooden peg sticking out from Pete's pant leg. "We let him pitch. I guess that means we have to let him bat."

Roy snorted and sent a warning look across the Delta Tau Delta team members. "Don't any of you come crying later that this wasn't a fair game. I tried to give the gimp a break." Then he reared back, raising his knee and angling his elbows high, and released the ball. It whizzed toward the plate, and Bennett held his breath, inching forward, as Pete scowled at the approaching ball. At the very last minute, Pete swung.

The bat caught the ball and sent it high in the air, sailing toward the left fielder. Bennett feared the player would catch the ball, but he dashed toward home plate anyway. If the man caught it, he'd try to return to third before the ball made it in.

Pete tossed the bat and took off toward first base with his funny double hop-skip way of running. Bennett crossed home plate before Pete made it halfway to first. "Run, Pete, run!" Bennett waved his hands at Pete while their teammates hollered encouragement. "All the way—keep going!"

Roy stood in the center of the diamond, one hand cupped over his eyes, watching the ball. The outfielder danced back and forth, his face aimed toward the sky. But every other member of the opposing team watched Pete. And every other member openly laughed. Some held their stomachs; others doubled over and slapped their knees. The sound of their mirth topped the roar of Pete's teammates. And, uncaring, Pete kept running. Hop-hop, skip, hop-hop, skip, faster and faster.

Bennett stared at the outfielder, holding his breath. If the man caught Pete's fly ball, it was all over. The ball arced and began its descent, seeming to fall straight toward the waiting glove. And then the outfielder jerked. His jaw dropped, and he stared at Pete, who turned on his peg at first base and aimed himself toward second. The ball hit the ground behind the outfielder, and he didn't even try to retrieve it.

Roy jumped up and down and screamed, "The ball! Get the ball!"

But the man stood there, mouth open, and watched Pete chug along, now midway between second and third. Roy took off running for the outfield. He pushed the fielder out of his way and retrieved the ball, but by the time he gave it a heave toward home, Pete was only a few feet from home plate. Pete's peg leg thudded on the plate a few seconds ahead of the ball. The catcher didn't even try to snag it—just stood grinning at Pete and shaking his head.

"Two to two!" Bennett grabbed Pete around the middle and lifted him in the air. "Two to two, Pete! We're tied! We're tied! And we've still got one more out to go!" Their teammates raced forward, surrounding them. Everyone patted Pete's back, congratulating him.

The umpire shooed them away from home plate. "Get your next batter up here. Game's not over yet."

Roy stomped around, smacking his players on the arm and bringing everyone under control. Then he stormed to the pitcher's mound. A furious gleam lit his eyes.

Bennett, gesturing toward Roy, whistled through his teeth. "I don't envy the poor sap who bats next. Roy's out for blood. Who's up, Ted?"

Ted pointed at a skinny, pimple-faced youth named Parker Potts. "Him."

Bennett stifled a groan. The young man didn't look strong enough to heft a bat, let alone swing it. But Bennett grinned and threw his arm around Potts's shoulders. "Get on up there. Doesn't even matter if you strike out. Game's gonna end at three innings no matter the score, just like we agreed, and we're already tied. So they can't say they skunked us. That's all that matters. So swing away, Parker—swing away!"

Parker took Bennett at his word and swung away, missing the

ball three times in a row and bringing the game to an end. Bennett turned, expecting his teammates to congratulate him for bringing Pete into the game, but to his surprise, everyone crowded around Pete instead. The Delta Tau Delta men, half of the Beta Theta Pi team, and at least a dozen spectators surrounded him, asking how he learned to pitch like that. Didn't it hurt to run on his peg leg? If they got a game together next Saturday, would he be able to pitch for them?

Bennett stood back, his jaw slack, while Pete received the attention and Bennett was ignored. He spun around in disgust and came nose to nose with Roy, who scowled into his face.

"Think you're pretty smart, turnin' that cripple into a hero?" Roy hissed the words, his voice raised only enough to reach Bennett's ears. "Well, I saw the pledge list. Saw your name—and his." Roy sent a disparaging look past Bennett in Pete's direction. "As president of Beta Theta Pi, *I* decide who pledges and who doesn't. And if you think you're gonna sneak into my fraternity, you better think again."

Roy stalked off, waving his hand as a silent command for his teammates to follow. Most of them scuttled after him, but three stayed behind, worming their way in front of the Delta Tau Delta men. They leaned in close to Pete, gesturing and talking excitedly.

Bennett propped one fist on his hip, shaking his head in disgust. He'd carefully plotted to bring Pete into the group, but he hadn't anticipated being bumped by him! Exactly how had the tables been turned? He yanked the hat from his head and smacked his leg.

"Bennett?"

The puzzled female voice came from behind Bennett. He turned and found Alice-Marie watching him, her head tipped to the side. She held a small pink parasol over her head, the ruffled brim shading her face from the sun. Even so, her nose glistened with perspiration, and curls stuck to her forehead and cheeks. He grunted, "Yeah?"

Her rosy lips formed a pout. "My, you're so grumpy. And after such an incredible display of athletic prowess. Why, do you realize you were competing with some of the school's very finest athletes? And you met them run for run." She shook her finger at him. "I would never have taken you for a sore winner."

Bennett heaved a sigh. "I'm not sure I won anything today, Alice-Marie."

She glided forward two steps, bringing her skirts into contact with his pant leg. She smiled, twirling the little parasol. "The day isn't over yet . . ."

Only a fool would have missed the implication, and Bennett was no fool. But for once, he wasn't in the mood for flirtation. There were bigger battles to be won—namely, finding a way to get in to the most prestigious fraternity on campus. He stepped away from Alice-Marie. "I'm hot and tired. I'm gonna go to my room and cool off."

She gave the grass a stomp. "Bennett Martin, I never would have guessed you'd be as ill-tempered as my buffoon cousin. Why, Mother says we shouldn't even claim that part of the family—they all behave like such bohemians."

How did Libby tolerate this girl's senseless prattle? "What are you talking about?"

"He's always been insufferable. He simply can't bear to be bested in anything—not even a simple game of checkers! So I wasn't at all surprised to see him stomp away like a spoiled little brat. But I expected you to—"

Bennett caught Alice-Marie's hand. "Roy's your cousin?"

She huffed. "Isn't that what I just said? On my father's side, second cousin twice removed. Or something equally ridiculous.

But it doesn't matter. I don't care for his boorish behavior, and right now I certainly don't care for yours! So—"

"I'm sorry."

She stopped and gave him a skeptical look.

He ducked his head and peeked at her, attempting to appear sheepish. "I'm hot and tired, and you're right—I got cranky. It won't happen again."

"Well . . ." Alice-Marie swayed slightly, making her skirts dance. "I suppose I understand, seeing as how you've been playing hard under the hot sun. But"—once again, she pointed her finger at him—"don't expect me to always be so forgiving. I don't care for being barked at."

Bennett held up his hand, as if making a pledge. "No more barking." He offered an impish grin, and Alice-Marie giggled. "Now . . . I do need to cool off, so how about you and me walking to town for a dish of ice cream or a soda?"

Alice-Marie's eyes flew wide. "On Sunday? The drugstore won't be open."

Bennett groaned. His parched throat begged for something cold. "Well then, the dining hall. They've always got the lemonade crock ready." She still seemed uncertain, so he added, "After that, maybe we could take a walk . . . get to know each other better?" He tipped his head, offering another grin.

Finally she laughed and waved her hand at him. "Lemonade does sound wonderful after sitting in the sun."

He offered his elbow, and she took it. He curled his hand over hers and turned her toward the dining hall. "Now, Miss Alice-Marie, I want to hear all about your family. Let's start with your father's side—second cousin, twice-removed. . . ."

There were times, during the week following the baseball game, Bennett actually wanted to punch his best friend in the nose. But he didn't. Deep down, he knew it wasn't Pete's fault that everyone was suddenly enamored with him. But Bennett couldn't help but be jealous. His plan to establish himself as an important man on campus by besting Roy and his buddies had only succeeded in turning Pete into the campus hero. "Peg leg Pete" they called him—and without an ounce of hostility or sarcasm.

Everywhere Bennett went—in the dining hall, in the classrooms, out in the courtyards—Pete's name came up. He supposed, seeing as how he was Pete's buddy, the others assumed he wanted to hear them sing Pete's praise. But they were wrong. By the end of classes on Thursday, Bennett was ready to escape. So when he charged out of the engineering building and spotted Alice-Marie on the lawn with a couple of other girls, he trotted over and slipped his arm around her waist.

"Hey, sugar. You done with classes for today?"

The other two girls giggled and ducked their heads, sending moon-eyed glances at Bennett through their lashes. At least the ladies still seemed to fancy him. That was flattering, but it could end up bringing resentment from some of the fellas. He needed to watch himself. Except with Alice-Marie. She had the potential for getting him in with the Beta Theta Pi crowd.

Alice-Marie flashed a haughty grin at her friends. "Why yes, I am finished for the day." She fluttered her lashes.

"Good." He patted his pocket, where coins won in a crapshoot behind the dormitory a couple of nights ago jingled. "We never got that soda on Sunday—let's get one now."

She crinkled her nose. "But it's nearly dinnertime. Won't a soda spoil your appetite? Perhaps we should wait until after we've visited the dining hall."

Bennett had no desire to enter the dining hall and listen to another round of Pete-praise. Besides, he didn't care for Alice-Marie acting like she was his mother. He almost told her to forget it, he'd just go on his own, but he remembered in time that he might need his relationship with her to ensure a spot on the pledge list for the Betas. According to Chester, Roy hadn't scratched it off yet, but that could change.

He forced a grin. "Aw, c'mon, sugar. The drugstore sells other stuff, too. I'll even buy you a frankfurter—two, if you're really hungry. That'll be dinner."

The other girls giggled again, and Bennett was certain if he asked either of them to eat a frankfurter with him, they'd jump at the chance. Alice-Marie initially grimaced, but when she saw her friends' reaction, she tipped her head and offered a coy smile. "Very well, Bennett, tonight we shall feast on greasy frankfurters with mustard and onions."

He didn't miss the touch of sarcasm, but he chose to ignore it. "Good." He grabbed her hand and tugged. "Let's go."

"My books!" she cried, attempting to pull loose.

He groaned and turned to the other girls. "Would one of you take Alice-Marie's books to her room for her?"

Both girls immediately reached for the books. Alice-Marie plunked the stack into the closest pair of hands and then laughingly turned to Bennett. "My, you are eager!"

He didn't bother with a reply, just grabbed her hand again and took off at a trot. She caught her skirts with her free hand and trotted alongside him. When they reached the street, Alice-Marie gasped out, "Please, Bennett! Can't we *walk*?"

Bennett obliged, but he made no effort to shorten his wide strides, forcing Alice-Marie to take two steps to his every one. She panted beside him, one strand of hair trailing down her cheek. At least the pace prevented her from talking. Bennett had never met a more yakky girl.

When they reached the drugstore, he remembered his manners in time and opened the door for her. She nearly fell through the opening. Fanning herself with both hands, she sagged into the nearest booth and stared up him with her mouth slightly open. "Gracious, Bennett, after that rigorous walk, I shall require a long rest."

"Suits me." Bennett pointed to the counter, where two businessmen and one young boy sat on stools. "So . . . one frankfurter or two?"

Wearily, she lifted one finger. "And a cherry phosphate, please."

As he stepped up to the counter to order, the cowbell above the drugstore door clanged, and two young men sauntered into the store. Bennett recognized them from the campus. He gave a nod of greeting, which both returned, and then they plopped into the booth directly behind Alice-Marie. Bennett idly counted his money, waiting for the soda jerk to take his order, and the voices of the pair in the booth carried to Bennett's ears.

"You think they'll get another game going this coming Sunday? I wouldn't mind playing this time."

"Me neither, as long as I don't have to hit against Roy or that other guy—you know, Peg leg Pete."

The first man laughed. "Yeah, never saw a straighter pitch—and fast! Why, you hardly saw the ball go, it went so fast! I think he's even better than Roy. . . ."

Not even here could Bennett escape having to listen to Pete's amazing abilities extolled. Slapping the counter, he spun toward Alice-Marie. He grabbed her arm and pulled her from the booth. "Let's go."

"Bennett!" She jerked her arm loose, a scowl marring her face. "Kindly do not be so rough!" She rubbed her arm. "I thought you wanted a frankfurter."

"Changed my mind is all. Why pay for dinner when we eat free at the dining hall?"

She huffed. "Isn't that what I said before we came?"

The two young men in the booth leaned around the tall wooden back to grin at Bennett and Alice-Marie. One of them muttered, "Must be a lovers' spat."

Bennett started to reach for Alice-Marie's arm again, but she flinched away. Remorse smacked him. He leaned close and whispered, "Did I really hurt you?"

Tears shimmered in her blue eyes. Her chin quivered.

"I'm sorry, Alice-Marie. I didn't mean to—honest. I just . . ." But he couldn't complete the sentence. He had no excuse for taking his frustration out on her. With a sigh, he repeated himself. "I'm really sorry. Let me walk you back to the dining hall. I'll go slow this time."

After a few moments of hesitation, she gave a slight nod. He placed his hand on the small of her back and guided her out of the drugstore. They walked in silence to the campus, and after he escorted her to the dining hall, he jogged to Franklin Hall and flopped onto his bed. He couldn't ever recall deliberately skipping a meal, but he had no appetite tonight.

Who would've thought he'd be eager to return to Shay's Ford? At least nobody there had seen that stupid baseball game. Tomorrow couldn't come fast enough.

Chapter Thirteen

"Look, Petey, Bennett!" Libby pointed out the window as the train chugged slowly toward the small depot on the outskirts of Shay's Ford. "They've all come to meet us. There's Maelle and Jackson, Matt and Lorna, Mr. and Mrs. Rowley and their children . . . even Cookie Ramona!" She squealed and clapped her hands. "Oh, what a wonderful surprise to have them all waiting!"

Petey pressed his face to the window and waved, but Bennett remained slouched in his seat, a surly expression on his face. Libby poked him on the shoulder. "Sit up, Bennett. Don't you want to wave to our welcoming party?"

He grunted and turned his face away. "They aren't out there to welcome me." He mumbled something else, but Libby didn't catch it.

She clicked her tongue on her teeth. "Bennett, you've been grouchier than a sleep-starved bear. Can't you improve your attitude? We're here for a wedding."

Bennett didn't even glance at her.

The train screeched to a stop, and Libby dashed for the platform, calling over her shoulder, "Would you be a dear and get my bag, Petey? Thank you!" Without waiting for a reply, she bounded off the platform and ran straight for Maelle. She threw herself into Maelle's open arms, laughter trickling from her throat. "Oh, it's so good to be home!"

After receiving a tight squeeze from Maelle, she hugged everyone by turn. By the time she returned to Maelle for a second hug, both Bennett and Petey were off the train with the luggage. Mr. and Mrs. Rowley flanked Petey, who held the Rowleys' one-year-old son, Reggie, while their daughters, five-year-old Constance and eight-year-old Rebecca, circled his waist with their arms. Cookie Ramona held Bennett in her embrace. Libby giggled at the sight of the gray-haired cook rocking Bennett from side-to-side as a mother might rock her infant. Bennett, with his enjoyment of eating, had always been Cookie's favorite.

"I can't believe all of you came." Libby's gaze bounced down the line of smiling faces. "Who's at home with the schoolchildren?"

Mr. Rowley chuckled, taking Reggie from Petey's arms. "Clancy." He referred to the grizzled ranch hand who oversaw the sheep on Jackson's family's ranch. "Who else could single-handedly corral twenty-two children?"

"He's more than reliable. But even so," Mrs. Rowley said, "we shouldn't impose upon him indefinitely. Now that our college students are home"—pride beamed from her emerald eyes—"we should head back. Come along." She took Rebecca by the hand and led the group toward the orphan school's old familiar wagon, which waited in a slash of shade beside the depot.

How many times had Libby ridden in the bed of that wagon on a mound of prickly hay, heading to Saturday shopping excursions or Sunday church services? A feeling of security wrapped itself around her when she spotted the worn high-sided wagon, and her feet sped on their own volition the final yards. Turning backward, she braced her palms on the edge of the bed and prepared to heave herself into the back. However, Maelle caught her arm and stopped her.

"Jackson and I wondered if you'd like to spend the weekend with us." Maelle flicked a smiling glance at her sister. "Isabelle has already given permission, but if you'd rather go out to the school, you won't hurt our feelings. Either way, we'll see you tomorrow for Mattie's wedding and again Sunday in church."

Libby crinkled her nose and considered what would be best. She had intended to help Mrs. Rowley set up for the wedding, but how could she refuse the opportunity to spend extra time with Maelle? She looked at Mrs. Rowley. "Are you sure you don't mind? You won't need my help this evening?"

Mrs. Rowley offered a smile. "There are plenty of hands at home, and now that Bennett and Pete are here, they can help, too. You go on with Maelle, if you'd like. I know you two enjoy your time together."

"Thank you!" Libby took her bag from Petey, and Jackson immediately plucked it from her hand. She grinned at him and then turned to the others. "Bye, everyone! I'll see you tomorrow for the wedding!" As a chorus of farewells came in reply, Libby linked arms with Maelle. "I'm all yours."

As they walked across town to Maelle and Jackson's pleasant home in the center of the town's residential district, Maelle plied Libby with questions about school. Libby told her about her classes, about Alice-Marie and the other girls in the women's dormitory, about the articles she'd written for the school's newspapers, and even about Roy. But she didn't mention the romance stories she'd written—and the second one she'd sold just that week—even though she longed to. The news was too special to blurt out in the midst of other things. When she and Maelle had a private moment, then she would share about her upcoming publishing credits.

When they reached the white-painted picket fence that surrounded Maelle and Jackson's bungalow, Libby came to a halt at the gate. She rested her fingertips on the pointed tips of the pickets and let her gaze drift across the wraparound porch generously bedecked with white-and-green painted gingerbread. The front door with its oval leaded-glass window stood slightly ajar, as if inviting her to enter.

Although she'd never lived in the house, she'd spent many weekends there with Maelle prior to Jackson's return from serving time in the Missouri legislature, and then, less frequently, with both Maelle and Jackson after their wedding. In her daydreams, she'd imagined coming home to this very house, with Maelle waiting on the porch, smiling the way mothers did when their children returned. She closed her eyes and allowed the childish daydream to briefly surface.

Turning to Maelle, she clasped her hands beneath her chin. "May we have lemonade and cookies out on the porch swing like we did for my eleventh birthday? Do you remember?"

Maelle chuckled. "How could I forget? You ended up with crumbs smeared across your face and lemonade splotches on the new apron Isabelle had sewn for you . . . and I took your photograph anyway. It's still one of my favorites."

Jackson swung the gate open. "I'll put Libby's bag in the guest room. There aren't any cookies in the house, but we do have some lemons. I'll mix up a pitcher of lemonade and bring it out to you. You ladies enjoy a few minutes of being lazy."

"Thank you," Libby and Maelle chorused.

They ambled arm in arm up the rock-paved sidewalk and perched on the hanging swing in the back corner of the porch. Libby wriggled into the seat, smiling when the chains squeaked, just as they always had. She released a sigh of contentment. She loved this porch and its white wicker swing. Shielded by massive spirea bushes, the corner was always shaded, so it was the perfect spot on a hot summer afternoon.

As a youngster, she'd pretended this part of the porch was a hideaway. In some ways, coming to this house had been her way of hiding from the reality of being orphaned. Countless times, she'd leaned over the porch railing as evening fell, watching the sky for the first glittering star. The moment one appeared, she'd throw out her dearest wish: *Let Maelle be my mother.*

Maelle interrupted Libby's reflections with a light pat on her knee. "I gather from everything you said on the walk over that you're glad you decided to stay and be a college student."

Libby nodded. "Yes. You and Jackson were right. I like it very much—more than I even imagined." A light breeze whisked around the corner and tossed a few curls of hair over her shoulder. She ran her fingers through the tangled locks. "Sometimes I grow frustrated, though. I want to learn the craft of writing faster so I can do more and more. I'm already weary of being assigned to write silly articles about class schedule issues and whether or not the dining hall should provide three different meats at dinner instead of two." She wrinkled her nose, recalling some of her least favorite topics from class. "It's all so unimportant!"

"Not at all, Libby," Maelle countered. "In everything of life, we have to start at the beginning. You wouldn't put a newborn on his feet and tell him to run, would you?"

Libby laughed at the idea.

Maelle grinned. "Babies first roll over, then scoot, then crawl. Finally they take those first stumbling steps, and then—only when they've mastered walking—do they learn to run. But all of those preliminary movements, seemingly unimportant to the casual observer, serve a purpose in gaining strength and balance for the eventual running."

She took hold of a strand of Libby's hair and tickled her chin with it. "These 'unimportant' articles, as you put it, will teach you to create meaningful sentences and to communicate in powerful ways to your future readers. Consider these articles your means of rolling over or crawling. You'll get to your feet in time, and you'll be a much stronger, more able runner because you took the time to do the 'unimportant' things first."

Libby considered the stories she'd sold to magazines. She'd written them as a way to prepare for serious journalism, yet she received payment for them. Would Maelle consider them "rolling over" or "running"? She opened her mouth to ask, but the slam of the screen door intruded.

Jackson came around the corner with a tray in his hand. "I wasn't sure how much sugar to add. I hope it'll be all right." He handed each of them a glass and took the last one for himself. Setting the tray on the floor, he perched on the porch railing and took a cautious sip. "Hmm." He smacked his lips then took a deeper draw. "Not bad for a first attempt. What do you think?"

Libby sipped. The lemonade was tart, and her lips quivered with the desire to pucker. But she managed to smile instead. "It's fine, Jackson. But . . ." She smirked at Maelle. "I think this particular batch of lemonade would be considered a *crawl*."

Maelle had just raised her glass to her lips, and at Libby's comment she snorted, spewing lemonade down her chin. She mopped at herself with her hand, and both women snickered.

Jackson made a wry face. "I believe I'm safer not asking what that means."

The snickers turned to outright laughter.

Jackson sent them a scowl so fierce Libby knew it was fabricated, which added to the gaiety. Soon Jackson was laughing right along with them, even though he couldn't know what was funny.

As the laughter faded, Libby closed her eyes and—as she had so many times in the past—pretended they were a family.

❦

Pete sat in the corner of the wagon and watched Aaron Rowley and Bennett each brace one hand on the wagon's side and leap over the edge. Their feet hit the ground with a solid thud, and dust rose. Aaron swung his children to the ground one at a time, then held his hands out to his wife while Bennett sauntered to the back of the wagon and released the hatch. "There you go, folks," Bennett said with a cocky grin. Cookie Ramona and her daughter, Lorna, climbed out. Then Bennett reached over the edge and snatched up his bag. Giving Pete a quick wave, he swaggered toward the orphans' school, completely unaware of the envy tangled around Pete's middle.

Pete painstakingly climbed out, using his good leg and his hands to scoot himself across the wagon's bed. Like an old man would do. He wished he could jump over the side and land two-footed. The last time he'd done that he was a boy of seven, and it had been out of a trolley with his arms full of newspapers. He tapped his peg against the hard ground, willing away the persistent tingle that felt like a sleeping limb. But his foot wasn't asleep. It was gone. Forever.

Matt peered down from the seat and grinned at Pete. "You gonna grab your bag outta there now, or do you want me to get it for you after I put the horses away?"

"I'll get it." Pete hadn't meant to snarl, but the words came out on a harsh note that made Matt's eyebrows rise. Pete apologized.

Matt shrugged. "No offense taken. I just figured you're tired after your train ride, and I'd be glad to tote it in for you."

"I can do it, but thanks." Pete reached into the back for his bag, but his arm wasn't long enough to reach. He tried to go up on tiptoe, but he lost his balance. Slapping the side of the wagon, he grunted in frustration.

"Pete, seems to me you got a bee in your bonnet." Matt held loosely to the traces, his head angled to meet Pete's eyes. "Wanna let it loose?"

Pete rubbed his finger under his nose and considered Matt's offer to let him talk. Pete admired this man who'd been kind enough to bring him to Shay's Ford almost a dozen years ago, saving him from squandering his childhood working for an uncaring employer. If he were to trust anyone with his resentment about his missing leg—and the people responsible for it—it would be Matt. Pete loved Aaron Rowley, who had raised him, but Aaron wouldn't be able to understand how it felt to grow up parentless and unwanted. Matt had been orphaned at a young age and lived a hard life as a child. He'd know exactly how Pete felt.

Curling his hands over the edge of the wagon, Pete gave a nod. "I need to let it loose, Matt. And I know what'll get it done. I've known for a long time. I'm just not sure how to go about it."

Matt tipped sideways, the brim of his ever-present cowboy hat throwing a shadow across his face. "An' what is it that needs doin'?"

Pete sucked in a deep breath. "I need to find my folks."

"Hmm." Matt scratched his head, sending his hat askew on his head. He jerked the brim back into position. "Well, seems to me you've got people right at hand who could help with that. Aaron an' Isabelle; Jackson an' Maelle. Have you asked any of 'em for help?"

Pete shook his head.

"Talk to 'em while you're home this weekend. As important as family is to all of them, they'd be more'n willing to help you meet up again with your parents."

Matt apparently misunderstood Pete's reason for wanting to find his folks, but he decided not to divulge his intentions. Matt was amiable and valued family, having been separated from his sisters for most of his growing-up years. He was an even-tempered, kind-hearted man, but he'd surely chide Pete for holding on to a grudge. And he'd be right to do so. Pete wanted to cast off the ugly feelings—and surely spewing his anger at the emotion's source would finally bring freedom. He nodded. "You're probably right."

Matt reached into the back and gave Pete's bag a push that sent it to the hatch. "There you go now."

Pete easily swung his bag from the back of the wagon and fastened the hatch. "Thanks, Matt."

"You're welcome, partner." Matt slapped the leather traces down. The horse lurched forward, and Matt called over his shoulder, "Good luck to you, Pete! I'll be prayin' you find 'em soon!"

Me too.

Chapter Fourteen

Wake up, Libby. There's lots to do if we're to be ready for my brother's wedding at six this evening."

Libby bounced out of bed and rubbed her eyes. Although the room was shadowed, she could see Maelle wore trousers rather than a skirt. She pointed. "Can I borrow a pair and wear some, too?"

Maelle gave Libby a little push toward the hall. "Isabelle would have my hide. Hurry now."

Thirty minutes later, she and Maelle joined Jackson in his two-seat buggy for the drive to the orphans' school. Sitting three abreast in the narrow seat made for a tight fit, but Libby didn't complain. They watched the sun sneak from its hiding spot beyond the horizon and chase away the gray and pink of dawn, revealing a clear, blue mid-October sky—a perfect backdrop for Mattie and Lorna's special day. And they talked. First about the town's ferry operators' continued opposition to the railroad coming to Shay's

Ford, and then about the possibility of Libby returning to work for the town's newspaper when she graduated from college.

The opportunity to spend the rest of her life in Shay's Ford should have filled her with glee—she'd have the chance to stay close to Maelle if she made Shay's Ford her permanent home—but for some reason excitement didn't build at the thought. How could she become world-renowned if she settled in a little-known town like Shay's Ford?

When they reached the school, they discovered Mrs. Rowley in the yard, pacing and watching for them. Even before they alighted from the buggy, she began giving orders. "Jackson, go to the barn and help Pete, Bennett, and Clancy build benches." The sound of pounding hammers indicated the others had already started. "Would you please make sure there will be adequate seating for two hundred guests? I trust you to estimate accurately."

Jackson gave a mock salute. "Yes, ma'am." He hitched his sorrel horse to the post outside the large school building and trotted for the barn.

"Maelle, you—" Mrs. Rowley broke off and scowled as her sister rounded the buggy. "Oh, you wore those detestable britches! You *will* change before the wedding."

Maelle winked at Libby. " 'Course I will. These are my workin' clothes."

Mrs. Rowley shook her head, as if clearing it, then went on. "Cookie Ramona needs your assistance with the wedding dinner preparations."

Maelle's face reflected uncertainty. "You want me to help with the cooking? Isabelle, you know I'm not a good cook."

"No, you aren't," Mrs. Rowley agreed, "but Cookie Ramona is, and she'll tell you everything you need to know. Hurry now—she has mounds of potatoes that must be peeled."

Maelle scuffed off, muttering.

"And Libby, come with me." Mrs. Rowley caught Libby's elbow and propelled her across the dusty ground to the barn. The din of pounding hammers was nearly deafening inside the sturdy building. "I know it's dreadfully loud, but if this is where Mattie's wedding is to take place, this is where we must decorate the trellis."

Libby knew Mrs. Rowley wished her brother had chosen to be married in the chapel where she and her husband had exchanged vows ten years earlier—the same chapel in which Maelle and Jackson had united their lives. But Matt insisted he wanted his ceremony at the place where he and Lorna had met. While several buildings comprised the orphans' school, only the barn had a space large enough to accommodate a sizable gathering.

Mrs. Rowley pointed out an arched wooden trellis at the front of the barn. She skimmed her fingers across the chipped white paint and made a sour face. "It's a sorry-looking canopy for the bride and groom as it is, but I purchased crepe paper in a variety of soft colors for rosettes. I've already made one—" she reached into a box and withdrew a pale pink rosette as big around as a grapefruit and placed it in Libby's hands—"and I should like to see the entire structure laden with flowers and draped with white tulle. Do you think you can figure out how to twist the paper into rosettes and fasten them with wire to the lattice?"

Libby examined the paper rose. Her head was already beginning to throb as a result of the off-beat percussion concert provided by hammer, nails, and enthusiastic builders. But the rosette didn't appear to be too complicated. She could complete the task. "Yes, ma'am."

"Very well. I trust your creative abilities will turn this decrepit lattice structure into a thing of beauty. There's little we can do to hide the fact that Mattie and Lorna are marrying in a stable, but at the very least they should have a lovely place to stand." Sadness tinged Mrs. Rowley's voice.

Sympathy swelled in Libby's breast. She touched Mrs. Rowley's arm. "Ma'am?"

"Yes, Libby?"

"I was just going to say . . . Jesus was born in a stable. I suppose if a barn was good enough for His birth, it'll make a fine place for Matt and Lorna to become man and wife."

Mrs. Rowley looked at Libby in surprise. Then her lips curved into a soft smile. "You're very right, dear. Thank you for the reminder." She gave Libby's hand a quick squeeze. Releasing it, she stepped back. "I'll send out some help. You'll need it to get this done in time." She turned and scurried out of the barn.

Moments later, two girls, one of whom held a thick bolt of white netted fabric, entered the barn and looked around as if confused. Libby waved them over. As they neared, she realized she'd never seen these girls before. "Are you new?"

The pair nodded in unison, and one said, "Come on the train two weeks ago. I'm Hannah. She's Hester. We're twins."

Libby needed no clarification. If they hadn't been dressed in different colors, she wouldn't have been able to tell one from the other—their unsmiling faces were identical in every way. Remembering how out of place she felt her first days at the orphans' school, she offered the girls a warm smile. "Well, I'm very relieved you're here, Hannah and Hester. I need your help." She quickly explained the process of creating rosettes and set them to work. Although they were young—probably no more than twelve—they proved amazingly adept. She praised their ability, and Hester shrugged.

"Nothin' to flower twistin'. Could do it already by the time we was four."

"Four?" Libby paused in attaching a lavender flower to the trellis and stared at the girl. "Do you mean four years of age?"

"Yes'm." Hannah sat cross-legged on the ground and quickly formed a perfectly shaped rosette out of yellow crepe paper. "Me an' Hester helped Mama make little poppies to sell on the corner. Got two pennies a dozen for 'em. It helped pay the rent."

Libby shook her head in amazement. "I'm sure your mother was very grateful to have your help."

Hester went on working without looking up. "Oh, not so much, but then she was sick. Hard to be grateful when you ain't feelin' good. Now she's dead."

Libby's chest tightened at the girl's blithe recital, and she paused to touch Hester's tangled blond hair before reaching for another flower. Here she thought she had suffered immeasurably by losing her parents. But at least she'd not been forced to work from a very young age. In some ways, perhaps she'd been fortunate.

By noon, with the twins' help, the trellis wore a lovely swag of tulle coiling amongst a bevy of pastel rosettes. The arch bore little resemblance to the scarred trellis that once supported vines in the school's flower garden. Libby sighed in satisfaction. The canopy would certainly earn Mrs. Rowley's approval. She thanked the girls for their assistance, and the pair shuffled off without so much as a smile in return.

Watching them go, a rare prayer formed in Libby's heart: *God, let someone come along to adopt Hannah and Hester and teach them to be carefree little girls before they grow up all the way.*

She gathered the remaining scraps of paper, dropped them in the box, and tucked the box in the tack room in the far corner of the barn. Then she headed for the house to ask what Mrs. Rowley would like her to do next. Halfway across the yard, she heard someone call her name. She turned to spot Lorna, Matt's fiancée, racing toward her.

Lorna came to a panting halt in front of Libby, grabbed her hands, and gasped, "Oh, Libby, something awful's happened. I'm gonna need your help."

Chapter Fifteen

Libby held a cluster of wild pink foxglove and faced Reverend Shankle. Although she was a last-minute replacement for Lorna's chosen bridesmaid—the poor girl had contracted a fever and been ordered to bed by the doctor—she couldn't deny a sense of pride in playing an important part in the wedding ceremony.

From the front bench, Cookie Ramona cried copiously into an embroidered handkerchief while the reverend solemnly advised the bride and groom of the sanctities of marriage. Libby's gaze drifted across the row of faces at the front of the barn. Maelle and Isabelle, serving as the bride's attendants, each wore expressions of introspection. Libby wondered if they were reliving their own wedding ceremonies in their minds.

On the other side of Lorna and Matt, Clancy—the weathered sheepherder—repeatedly cleared his throat and shifted from foot to foot, as if eager to be finished with the ceremony. Next to Clancy, Aaron Rowley seemed to be examining his wife, and the tenderness in his face made Libby's heart skip a beat. She tried to memorize Mr. Rowley's expression—it would be the perfect look for one of her story heroes to offer his beloved.

Her gaze shifted to Petey, on the far right. And her heart swelled. How handsome he looked today in his finest suit, his thick blond hair combed straight back and glistening with macassar oil, his chin high and shoulders square. The solemn set of his lips told her how seriously he held the privilege of standing up with the man who had brought him to Shay's Ford.

Countless times, Petey had talked about the day Matt Tucker rescued him from the hands of a cruel employer. He held Matt in high esteem, and Libby's admiration for Matt grew in those moments that she witnessed Petey's pride at being in the wedding ceremony. Matt could easily have chosen Jackson Harders instead—his standing in the community would certainly be elevated by having a lawyer serve as one of his groomsmen—but instead he'd chosen Petey, a cast-aside, unwanted boy.

Today, however, Libby realized with a start, Petey bore little resemblance to the boy she'd met ten years ago. When, she wondered, had he grown from adolescent awkwardness into this handsome, self-assured man? While she stared at him, awed by the transformation that seemed to have taken place before her eyes, his face shifted. His gaze collided with hers and held. For several seconds they stared at one another across the swept dirt floor while the minister's voice continued, paper fans stirred the air, and Cookie Ramona softly sobbed.

Libby's breath caught in her lungs as Petey's lips curved ever so slightly and tenderness set his blue eyes aglow. She saw in his face the same expression of rapture Aaron Rowley offered to his wife—the same look she'd frequently seen pass between Jackson and Maelle. Pleasant chills climbed her spine and wriggled down her arms to her hands, where her fingers trembled, causing the wild flowers to quiver. Uncertain and overwhelmed, she glanced away, and looked instead at Matt. She gasped. Petey's expression while looking at her had mimicked the one Matt was—at this very moment—bestowing upon his bride.

Unbidden, her focus returned to Petey, and disappointment sagged her shoulders. He'd shifted his attention to the minister, who lifted his hands and announced, "I now present Mr. and Mrs. Matthew Tucker." His eyes crinkled as he smiled. "Matt, you may kiss your bride."

The barn exploded in wild applause as Matt leaned forward and touched his lips to Lorna's. Tears rained down Lorna's face, and she dashed to her mother's arms for a hug before returning to Matt with a joyous giggle that echoed from the rafters. Matt and Lorna exited the barn amidst applause and congratulations. Clancy offered his bony elbow to Maelle, and they followed the newly married bride and groom down the aisle. Mr. and Mrs. Rowley trailed behind them, and only Libby and Petey remained.

With a crooked grin, Petey offered Libby his arm. Odd feelings coursed through her middle, making her hesitant to place her hand in his elbow. But why? Hadn't she clung to Petey's arm hundreds of times over the years? Yet suddenly everything had changed, and she didn't know why.

Reverend Shankle cleared his throat, bobbing his chin at them. Libby recognized his silent command for them to leave. Drawing in a shaky breath, she gingerly slid her hand into the curve of Petey's elbow. The same chills that had swept her frame earlier returned, and her fingers tightened. They walked together, Petey's slight limp causing his arm to bump against her ribs as they moved up the aisle. With each brush of his sleeve against her side, her awareness of him grew.

They entered the sunny yard, and Petey stepped away from her. He flashed one more smile before moving to the tables set up with food, where Bennett clapped him on the back. The wedding guests streamed from the barn, forcing Libby to dart to the side. But even then, puzzled yet captivated, she continued to seek Petey. For reasons beyond her understanding, she had a need to hold him in her sights. Or perhaps, more accurately, she longed to hold him in her heart.

&

Pete accepted a cup of punch from the little girl at the serving table and limped toward the corral fence, moving slowly to avoid sloshing the pale pink liquid over the rim. His leg ached from the lengthy time of standing still. Standing was always worse than moving, although he didn't understand why. His stump throbbed, but the discomfort gradually lessened as he walked across the hard-packed earth.

He reached the corral fence and rested his elbow on the top rail, using the sturdy wood rail to help him balance while he gently tapped the tip of the peg on the ground to take his mind off the persistent subtle ache. He lifted the cup and downed its fruity contents without pause. The cool liquid felt good on his dry throat, and he loosened his tie and sucked in a relieved breath. As a minister, he'd be expected to wear a suit every day, so he'd have to get used to the tight collar and formal tie. But for now it felt good to give himself some breathing room.

His heart was still thudding like the hooves of a runaway horse. It had started when he'd caught Libby looking at him during the wedding ceremony. He drew a lungful of air and released it slowly in an attempt to bring the rapid beat under control. But the extended breath didn't slow his pulse any more than the tapping erased the discomfort in his missing foot. If she'd stop staring at him from her spot beside the barn, maybe at least his heart would settle down. He turned his back on her and forced himself to look elsewhere.

People swarmed the yard, laughing, talking, helping themselves to the platters of food that covered every inch of the cloth-draped plank tables forming a neat line across the middle of the open schoolyard. He examined the food offerings. Cookie Ramona had outdone herself in preparing for her daughter's wedding. Oven-baked chickens, smoked hams, and beef roasts competed for prominence among a bevy of vegetables, salads, and desserts. No one should go away hungry today. He chuckled as he watched Bennett fill his plate to overflowing. His friend's face wore a grin for the first time in days. Pete was glad to see the change.

But the change he'd seen in Libby during the wedding . . . He gulped. Slowly, almost against his own will, he angled himself to look toward the barn where he'd last seen her. She remained in the same spot, hands behind her back, a wistful look on her face. He spun away again, heat rising from his neck to flood his cheeks. A groan left his throat.

He wished he could gather enough courage to march over there, plant his palms on the barn on either side of her shoulders, and demand why she'd pinned him with such a reflective look during the wedding. Didn't she know she'd turned his world upside-down with that expression? Because he knew something had risen to life within her in those moments of examination. He knew, because he'd experienced the same change toward her two years ago.

He'd sent many pleas heavenward, asking God to awaken in Libby the ability to love him the way he loved her, if it was God's will for him. Now he suspected Libby's feelings were moving from friendship to something more, but how could it be God's will? Their life goals were so different. . . .

"Hey, buddy, aren't you gonna eat?" Bennett bumped Pete with his elbow. He lifted a chicken leg and took a huge bite.

"Yes. Soon," Pete answered absently, still trapped beneath Libby's unwavering observation.

Bennett took another bite. He glanced across the grounds, and he chuckled. "Why's Lib still over there?" He waved the chicken bone in the air. "Hey, Lib! Come get something to eat!"

Pete swung on Bennett. "What'd you do that for?"

Bennett gaped at him in surprise. "Do what? Tell Libby to eat? Why shouldn't she—" Then his jaw dropped. He looked from Pete to Libby to Pete again. He burst out laughing.

Pete whacked Bennett's shoulder. A few green beans tumbled over the edge of his well-filled plate. "Stop it."

Bennett took a firmer hold on his plate and stepped away from Pete. "*Me* stop it?" Humor bubbled under his words. "How about you and Lib, going all cow-eyed over each other. If anybody ought to stop something . . ." His voice trailed off, but the implication hit its mark.

Pete blew out a mighty breath. "I know. As Libby so eloquently pointed out, it's ludicrous." He swallowed, forcing down the bitter taste that filled his mouth. He tried to sound glib. "I think it's just the wedding. Seeing Matt and Lorna together . . . It's put ideas in her head."

"Yeah." Bennett munched a roll. "She is, after all, a girl. And girls have peculiar romantic notions. Always wanting some fella to fawn over them." He raised one eyebrow. "So you gonna give her what she wants?"

"I can't. You know why."

"Uh-huh. 'Cause you're planning to be a preacher." Chewing thoughtfully, Bennett looked at Libby again. "And Libby doesn't want to be a preacher's wife. So you might wanna go over there and remind her of it. Before she lets her wild ideas get out of control."

Pete nodded. Rarely did he follow Bennett's advice. As much

as he liked Bennett, his friend generally acted without much fore-thought. This time, however, Bennett made sense. It was only the romance of the moment that had brought out this attentive side of Libby. It was best if they both recognized that fact.

His stomach churned as he wove between other guests, creating a meandering path to the spot against the barn where Libby seemed to have taken root. *Lord, give me strength.* As much as it had hurt to hear her claim anything beyond friendship would be ludicrous, he knew it would be infinitely more painful to say the words himself.

He stopped a few feet in front of her. Her eyes had grown wider the closer he'd drawn, and she stared at him, unblinking, her lips parted slightly. The bodice of her rose-colored church dress visibly rose and fell with her rapid breaths. She reminded him of a scared rabbit. But was she frightened of him or of her own feelings?

He drew a fortifying breath. "Libby, I—" Before he could say anything more, she grabbed his hand and pulled him through the barn's open doorway. Stumbling behind her, his focus turned to staying upright. She dragged him up the aisle to the spot where she had taken his elbow before leaving the ceremony. Finally she released his hand and whirled to face him.

The change from full sun to shadow forced him to squint to make out her features, but he glimpsed the same adoring warmth he'd seen earlier. He shook his head. "Libby, stop."

She tipped her head, the innocent bewilderment in her eyes nearly breaking his heart.

"Don't look at me that way."

Stepping forward, she rested her palms on his chest. A soft smile lit her face, and he suspected she felt his pounding heartbeat beneath her hands. "But why?"

"Because." He caught her wrists and pushed her hands down. Hurt flashed in her eyes. "Petey?"

"Don't you remember what you said in the dining hall? Ludicrous—that's what you said. And you were right." He forced the words past his closed, aching throat. His tone turned harsh. "You and I are friends, and you'll ruin everything if you start—"

"If I start loving you?" She matched his tone in severity, but her chin quivered. "I'm afraid it might be too late for that." She took several gulping breaths. Clasping her hands at her waist, she fixed him with a pensive look. "Petey, today when I looked at you . . . it's as if I saw you for the first time. I saw not the boy who's always been my friend and playmate, but someone new. Someone . . . completely desirable." Her hands rose and she placed them flat against her heart. "Inside of me, something changed. A *good* change, Petey. And I—"

"You're willing to give up your plans of travel? Of writing about world events?" He searched her face, praying she might say yes. But to his distress, she flinched. He sighed. "You see, Libby? It *is* ludicrous. I can't travel the world with you—not with this . . ." He glared down at his ever-aching leg. "This piece of wood holding me back." Raising his chin, he added, "And I wouldn't even if I had two good legs. Because that isn't what God's called me to do. I have to become a preacher, Libby, don't you see? And you have to be what you've been called to be."

Tears glimmered in her eyes. She never cried. To do so now spoke of how deeply his words affected her. But they had to face the truth. Cupping her shoulders with both hands, he lowered his voice to a whisper. "I do love you, Libby. I have for a long time. I probably always will." He swallowed again, fighting the desire to crush her to his chest. He tightened his hands into a gentle squeeze. "But I can't ask you to love me back. Not if it means asking you to abandon the task God's given you."

"But . . ." She fell silent and hung her head.

Pete dropped his hands and took an awkward step backward.

He gestured weakly toward the open barn doors. Sounds of the after-wedding celebration drifted in, the happiness in the guests' voices a direct contrast to the sadness hanging like a storm cloud in the barn. "We better go. You need to get something to eat, and the dance'll be starting soon. People will wonder where we are."

She nodded, the movement so slight he almost thought he'd imagined it. "Y-you go ahead. I need to sit and . . ." Her throat convulsed, but then she lifted her chin, taking on a regal stance. "I need a few minutes alone."

"All right." Pete turned and took a few slow steps toward the doors. Then he paused and looked back. "Libby?"

She stared straight ahead. "Yes?"

"Can I have the first dance?"

For long seconds she sat so still it appeared she'd turned to stone. Then she shifted her face slightly to meet his gaze. She gave him the saddest smile he'd ever seen. "Of course. The very first."

"Then I'll watch for you."

She looked away without replying. Pete shuffled out of the barn, his steps labored. He'd done the right thing. It wouldn't be fair to hold Libby back. A wild spirit like hers deserved free rein. Letting her go was the best thing. For both of them.

So why did he feel as though he carried the weight of the world on his back?

Chapter Sixteen

When Pete stepped from the barn, he nearly collided with Jackson Harders. The man caught Pete's arm and laughed. "Whoa. You're in a hurry. Eager to get to the dance, huh?"

The only person Pete wanted as a dance partner was Libby, and even though she'd promised him the first dance, he suspected she'd try to avoid him. "Not really. But I'm glad I ran into you. I have something important to ask you."

Jackson slipped his hands into his trouser pockets and rocked back on his heels, his expression attentive. "Certainly, Pete."

"Do you think you could help me locate my parents?"

Jackson seemed to study Pete's face. Pete fidgeted, glad for the heavy shadow cast by the barn. Perhaps the lawyer wouldn't be able to see beneath his surface to the lurking resentment.

Jackson's eyebrows rose. "I assume you mean your birth parents, since Aaron and Isabelle are right there."

"Yes." Pete nodded. "Gunter and Berta Leidig. I . . . I need to see them." *I need to purge myself of this fury, which has no place in my life.*

"I can certainly try." Jackson's calm voice contrasted with the wild emotions churning through Pete's middle. "But are you sure? It's a big step, trying to reunite with your parents. Could go one of two ways." He lifted his hand and flicked his fingers upward to count. "They could welcome you back into the fold, or they could refuse to see you." His hand curled into a fist, and he lowered it to his side. "Either way, you'll be changed permanently. So . . . are you sure you want me to open that door for you?"

Pete set his jaw. He knew he'd carry this bitter anger until he laid it at his parents' feet. He had to see them, regardless of the costs involved. "I'm sure."

"All right, then." Jackson gave Pete's shoulder a clap. "I'll send out inquiries on Monday. Now let's go join the party."

❧

Libby sat, staring at the flower-laden trellis where Matt and Lorna had stood and committed themselves to love, honor, and cherish each other for the remainder of their lives. She'd stared so long, unblinking, that her eyes hurt. Finally she let them fall closed, but behind her lids she saw an image of Petey standing straight and tall and proud beside Matt. At last, her stiff spine collapsed. She slumped over her lap, burying her face in her hands.

How foolish she'd been to throw herself at Petey that way. Hadn't she already realized she didn't possess the necessary traits to be a preacher's wife? Petey was right—they had to be what they were each called to be.

She sat upright again, her breath catching. Petey had said God had called him to become a preacher, and he'd intimated she'd received a similar call to be a writer. But she couldn't honestly say

God had prompted her to take up paper and pen. It was something she'd chosen herself. In fact, she couldn't recall ever feeling as though God had communicated anything to her. She'd prayed to God—the Rowleys made sure the children in the orphans' school attended Sunday services, prayed before meals and at bedtime, and they'd encouraged each of the children to develop a relationship with God by accepting His Son Jesus as their Savior. Yes, Libby had frequently talked to God over the years, but not once had she heard Him so much as whisper in reply.

Once, soon after she'd come to the orphans' school, Libby had asked Maelle about receiving answers to prayers. But Maelle's reply had been less than satisfying. *"God doesn't always speak to us in an audible voice, Libby. Sometimes He speaks directly to our hearts. We just have to know how to listen."* Even now, years later, Libby could make little sense of God speaking into her heart.

Crunching her brow, she puzzled over the difference between desire and a distinct calling. Might it be God had planted this overwhelming desire to write within her as a way of calling her? Calls were intended for the better good—that much she understood. And writing articles that informed people of happenings in the world that affected them personally would certainly do a service. But . . .

She bit down on her lower lip, facing the truth. Her desire to write world-impacting stories was rooted in the recognition it could bring her rather than the good it might do for others.

Frustrated, she bounced from the bench and paced the short aisle. A faded shaft of sunlight, allowed in through one of the windows facing west, angled across Libby's path. She stopped and let her eyes follow the soft beam from its beginning to its end. Dust motes danced in the yellow light, reminding her of stars glittering in the sky. A longing rose from her middle—to speak to God and ask Him what she should do. Her heart pounding, she licked her lips and whispered, "God?"

"Libby?"

She let out a little shriek.

A familiar chuckle rolled—Maelle's. Libby turned toward the barn doors, where Maelle and Jackson stood. They stepped fully into the barn as Jackson said, "Did I frighten you?"

"Yes. For a moment I thought— Oh, never mind what I thought." Disappointment created an ache in the center of her heart. As if the almighty God would take time to speak to someone as unimportant as she . . .

Maelle brushed a strand of hair from Libby's cheek. "What are you doing in here all by yourself?"

She shrugged, uncertain how to answer.

Maelle smiled. "Oh, it doesn't matter. I'm glad we found you, though. There's something important we need to discuss with you." She and Jackson exchanged a secretive look.

Libby's spine tingled with awareness. "S-something important?"

"Life-changing," Jackson added with a serious nod.

Libby found it difficult to breathe. Could God finally have decided to answer her dearest prayer? Her legs began to tremble. "W-well then, let's sit down and y-you can tell me."

She sank onto a bench, and Maelle and Jackson sat on either side of her. Maelle took her hand. "Libby, before we share our important news, I want you to know how much I've always loved you."

"I know you do," Libby said quickly. "I've always loved you, too."

Maelle squeezed her hand. "And you also know why I didn't adopt you when you were a little girl."

Libby nodded, her hair swinging in her face. She tossed the strands over her shoulder with an impatient flick of her wrist. "Yes.

You didn't think it would be fair since you were unmarried. You wanted me to have a mother *and* a father." She sent a quick shy smile to Jackson before turning back to Maelle.

"That's right." Maelle leaned forward slightly, looking at Jackson.

He cleared his throat, and Libby turned her head to face him. "Maelle and I were forced to wait until I finished my legislative work before we could get married." He released a rueful sigh, rubbing his finger under his nose. "It turned into a longer wait than either of us anticipated. While we've enjoyed these years together, we've also longed to begin building a family."

"Of course, we hoped to have children of our own . . ." Sadness flashed through Maelle's eyes. "But for whatever reason, God hasn't chosen to allow it."

Jackson leaned across Libby to give Maelle's hand a brief squeeze. "So God has opened our hearts to forming a family by less traditional means."

Libby's heart pounded so hard she feared it might bounce into her throat and choke her. She gasped out a single word. "Y-yes?" At last she'd be able to call Maelle Ma! It might take her a while to feel comfortable enough to call Jackson Pa, but—

"And that's why," Maelle said, her smile serene, "Jackson and I have asked permission of Isabelle to adopt Hannah and Hester."

For a moment, Libby thought she'd been kicked, because the air seemed forced from her lungs. She could scarcely draw a breath. "Hannah and . . . and H-Hester?"

"That's right. They're the sweetest girls, but so sad." Maelle shook her head. "The first time we met them, our hearts just went out to them. We know they need us as much as we need them." Maelle reached past Libby to clasp Jackson's hand. "We're so happy to become parents. And we wanted you to share our happiness, Libby. You're the first person we've told. Well—" she laughed lightly—"besides Isabelle and Aaron, of course. So are you happy for us?"

Resentment and anger coiled through Libby's frame, so intense she couldn't remain seated. She jumped up, forcing Maelle's arm aside. Stomping forward several feet, she clenched her fists and pinched her eyes closed. *How dare You, God? How dare You give the mother I wanted to someone else?* Then a sardonic thought flitted through her mind. Earlier that day, when Hannah and Hester had finished helping her make the crepe paper flowers, Libby had asked God to provide the girls with loving parents. God had certainly answered. . . .

She covered her face with her hands and groaned, "But I didn't mean Maelle."

"Libby?" Warm hands curled over her shoulders and tried to turn her around. But Libby couldn't face Maelle. Not now. She jerked loose and ran from the barn. Just as she careened into the yard, a fiddle's merry tune filled the air. The dance was beginning.

How she'd looked forward to this weekend at home. To celebrating with Matt and Lorna, to dancing with Petey and Bennett, to spending time with Maelle. All of that happy anticipation now stung like salt in a wound. She'd promised Petey the first dance, but she couldn't face him.

Maelle and Jackson stepped out of the barn. Maelle called, "Libby?"

Libby held up both hands like a shield. She spoke through gritted teeth. "Leave me alone." Then she turned and ran.

❦

Bennett slinked behind the crowd, working his way closer to Mr. and Mrs. Rowley. Moments ago, Maelle Harders had taken the couple aside. Judging by the worried looks on their faces, something bad had happened. And Bennett wanted to know what it was. He edged sideways, keeping his back to the three while pretending to tap his foot to the music. But his ears were tuned to their conversation.

". . . just took off. I haven't seen her that upset since she was a little girl." Maelle sounded confused.

"Well, you know Libby . . ." Mrs. Rowley clicked her tongue on her teeth. "I love the girl, but she can be given to theatrical displays."

Bennett stifled a chuckle. Mrs. Rowley knew Libby pretty well.

"I think this is more than a childish tantrum" came Maelle's insistent voice. "You didn't see her. Aaron, I'm going to take a lantern from the barn and go—"

"Let her be, Maelle." Mr. Rowley sounded kind but firm.

"I can't just—"

Mr. Rowley spoke over Maelle's protest. "This is your brother's wedding party. You need to be here, celebrating with Matt and Lorna, not chasing after Libby. When she calms down, she'll return. In the meantime, why don't you . . ."

Bennett had heard enough. Apparently Pete's conversation with Libby had rattled her good. He worked his way to the opposite side of the dance circle, seeking Pete's head of thick blond hair. If Pete was in the crowd, he probably didn't know Libby was miffed enough to take off. After a few minutes of searching, Bennett located Pete leaning against the hitching rail in front of the dormitory. Which meant Libby was out there, somewhere, alone.

Bennett scratched his head, weighing his options. He could do what Mr. Rowley had advised Maelle—just let her be. Or he could tell Pete. Pete would have a good idea of where Libby would hole up, and Bennett knew Pete'd go after her no matter what the Rowleys thought. *And the Rowleys would think it was fine, just 'cause he's Pete.*

No, he wouldn't tell Pete. And he wouldn't leave Libby out there upset and alone, either. He'd go find her himself. He had a good idea of where to look. When they were kids and Libby got her nose out of joint, she always went down to the creek and climbed a tree. Although he couldn't imagine her climbing a tree in her best dress, she could be at the creek. He'd start there.

Hands in his pockets, he assumed a nonchalant air and sauntered past the crowd surrounding the dancers and headed behind the barn. Once out of sight, he took off at a trot. Bonfires and lanterns lit the area where the wedding party continued, hiding the fact that dusk had fallen. Evening shadows masked the landscape, and Bennett tripped over a small mound of dirt and almost fell. Why hadn't he thought to grab a lantern? If Libby wasn't at the creek, he'd be out of luck. Before long, it'd be too dark to look anywhere else.

He slowed his steps but continued across the gray countryside, his ears tuned to pick up the thrashing of critters in the brush. He heard the creek before he saw it, the trickling water taking him back to boyhood fishing trips with Pete and Aaron Rowley or Matt. Good memories . . .

He crested the rise leading to the creek and scanned the bank. And there she sat, curled up with her arms around her knees, facing the water. He made sure he set his feet down hard enough to be heard as he closed the distance between them. After his third step, she dropped her hands to the ground and whirled to face him. Her face looked pale in the meager light. "Who's there?"

"Me—Bennett." Bennett took two more wide strides and plopped down beside her. "Glad you're here. I didn't cotton to keep searching, as dark as it's gotten. Sun sure dropped fast tonight."

She hugged her knees again, staring forward. "Why'd you come anyway?"

Shrugging, he plucked a piece of dry grass and twirled it. "Dunno," he lied. He did know. He did it because he knew Mrs. Rowley would disapprove. "But if you want me to go, I'll . . ." He made as if to rise.

"You can stay." She sounded more irritated than welcoming. "Just don't talk. I've heard more than enough *talk* this evening."

Bennett broke the piece of grass into tiny pieces and dropped them, one by one, into the gently rolling creek. How many of those pieces, he wondered, would make it all the way to the Mississippi? One of them could even get carried all the way to the Gulf, and then to the ocean. That'd be something . . .

"Wonder what it's like to go across the ocean." He hadn't intended to share his thoughts out loud.

Libby's chin jerked, and she shot him a glare. "I thought I told you not to talk."

"Not talking. Thinkin' out loud is all."

"It's the same thing."

"No it's not. Talking is a back-and-forth exchange. Thinkin' out loud is just that—saying something out loud only meant for yourself." He raised one eyebrow at her. "You didn't have to answer."

She huffed and hunched forward. For long seconds they sat in silence. An owl hooted from the nearby tree, and a coyote answered. Libby shivered, and he started to suggest they head back to the school. But then she said, "I intend to find out."

He shook his head, confused. "Find out . . . what?"

"What it's like across the ocean." She sounded determined.

He bit the insides of his cheeks to keep from chortling. She wasn't trying to be funny, but for some reason her tone tickled him. "Oh yeah? How?"

"I'll be reporting on the war. And I'm not going to wait until I graduate, either. I intend to have a position with a newspaper by this time next year. Everyone knows wars last a long time, so I'm sure it'll still be going." Her voice rose with passion. She sat straighter, her chin jutting out stubbornly. "I'll get on a ship and sail to Europe, where I can write about what's happening over there. Every article will have 'by Elisabet Conley' printed underneath the title, and then people, including Maelle and Petey, will finally see me as—" She clamped her lips together.

Bennett didn't ask what she'd planned to say. Her business was her business, and the less he knew the better when it came to females and their messes. He sometimes enjoyed having a pretty girl on his arm, but he sure didn't want to get too deeply tangled. Took all the fun out of things. He gave a brusque nod. "I'll look for you over there, 'cause I'll be goin', too. With a gun in my hand."

She swung to face him, her jaw dropping. "You mean to fight?"

Bennett pictured himself in a uniform, side by side with other men in uniforms. He'd fit right in—and he'd fight harder than any of them, proving his mettle to his commanders, too. He puffed his chest. "Sure, to fight."

"But the United States is remaining neutral. We aren't sending soldiers."

He snorted. "For how long? You think we can keep ignoring the scuffle over there? And do you think I could stay out of it? I'll be the first to sign up the minute Uncle Sam gives the call." There was no way Pete could step up and replace him as a soldier. Man with a peg leg on the battlefield? Laughable.

"The ship can't leave soon enough to please me." Libby's tone turned reflective, as if she'd forgotten he was there. "There's nothing here holding me back."

"Or me." He chuckled. "Looks to me, Lib, like you and I have more in common than you knew, huh?"

She didn't answer, but he didn't let that bother him. He could tell by the look on her face he'd given her something to think about. Maybe, just maybe, Pete wouldn't end up winning everything after all.

Chapter Seventeen

Are you *still* sitting at that desk?"

Libby jerked at the sound of Alice-Marie's cranky voice and pushed the pencil point hard against the page. The freshly sharpened point snapped. With a little huff of annoyance, she glanced up. Her roommate stood in the doorway of their room with her hands on her hips and a scowl on her face. "I need to finish this, Alice-Marie." Another page—maybe two—and her most recent story would be complete. In the three weeks since Matt and Lorna's wedding, she'd written and mailed out three romance stories. Some of her homework had gone undone, but she didn't care. The homework wouldn't earn her a list of writing credits. The homework wouldn't make her known to thousands of readers.

"One would think you were chained to that chair." Alice-Marie approached, her curious gaze aimed at the pad of paper. Libby covered the lines of print with her palms when Alice-Marie

perched on the edge of her desk. "I've never seen anyone so dili-
gent, and it's quite admirable. But you must do more than complete
assignments, Libby."

Alice-Marie put her hand on Libby's arm. "You didn't join a
sorority; you've shunned every club on campus. All you do is write,
write, write. I talked to Mother about you when I spoke with her
over the telephone yesterday, and she said to remind you that all
work and no play makes Jack a dull boy."

The reference to "Mother" pierced Libby's heart. Might Maelle,
right now, be encouraging Hannah and Hester to throw off their
somber countenance, to play games and laugh? She yanked her arm
free of Alice-Marie's hand and gave the girl's hip a sharp jab with
her elbow. Alice-Marie squawked and jumped up.

"I'm not a boy named Jack," Libby said through clenched teeth,
"and how I spend my time is not your mother's concern." She
grabbed the little penknife she used to sharpen her pencils and
flicked tiny shavings onto the floor.

Alice-Marie's chin began to quiver. "Why are you being so
mean?"

Libby closed her eyes and stilled her hands. It wasn't her roommate's fault that Maelle and Petey had both rejected her. Drawing
in a deep breath, she tipped her face to meet Alice-Marie's gaze.
"I'm sorry. I'm just very overwhelmed right now, trying to finish
this . . . assignment. Would you please let me be? When I'm finished, I'll get up and do something fun." She resumed sharpening
the pencil.

"You promise?"

Libby resisted rolling her eyes. "I promise."

Alice-Marie immediately brightened. "Oh, I hoped you'd say
that. Because I'd like you to come home with me this weekend.
Mother is having several of her society ladies over, and it would
be ever so much fun to join them."

Spending a weekend with Alice-Marie's mother and her society friends sounded like as much fun as a toothache. She dropped the penknife into her desk drawer and fiddled with the drawer handle. "I don't know, Alice-Marie . . ."

"Please come. Mother's hosting a lady author from the East, and the lady will be sharing her experiences in publishing with Mother's group." Alice-Marie affected a little pout. "I felt certain you'd be interested in hearing her, since you're in the journalism program."

Libby's heart skipped a beat. She slammed the desk drawer shut and spun to face Alice-Marie. "I would find that very interesting."

"Then you'll come?"

Libby nodded. "Yes. I'd love to. Thank you for inviting me."

"It's my pleasure. Now . . ." Alice-Marie backed toward the door. "I'll let you finish your work in peace. Meet me for dinner?"

Although Libby preferred to eat alone so she could finish quickly and return to her writing, she gave a quick nod. "Yes. At six." She nibbled the end of the pencil as she contemplated the unique opportunity Alice-Marie had just offered. To be able to talk to a real published writer! Might this woman be willing to look at some of Libby's writings and advise her?

She'd already sent off her other stories, but she had this one. Although she'd intended to mail it out the moment she finished it, she changed her mind. She would take this story along to Alice-Marie's house. And, somehow, she would find a way to steal a few minutes of time with the visiting lady author.

❧

Pete dropped his pencil and leaned back, releasing a sigh. He kneaded the back of his neck with one hand. The muscles were as tight as knots in wet rope, but that shouldn't have surprised him, considering how long he'd been sitting at his desk.

He looked down at the neat stack of letters ready to be mailed. Although he'd never written a letter to an editor of a newspaper before, he had no apprehension about doing so now. His strategy to bring an end to the morally degenerative practice of publishing and reading titillating stories was ready for dispatch, and these letters to each of the area editors was one part of his intensive battle plan.

Pastor Hines had acquired the addresses of each newspaper within a hundred-mile radius for Pete. He dutifully picked up his pencil again to address more envelopes. His pulse sped as he thought about his letter appearing in the newspapers. People would read his opinion. Maybe their opinions would change as a result of reading his carefully worded letter, which his instructor had wholeheartedly approved. Pete's chest had expanded when Pastor Hines praised his use of Scripture—"Excellent, Mr. Leidig. It is always best to quote God's words rather than depending your own; His carry the power."

Pete had drawn from the book of Acts, in which Luke had admonished followers to abstain from things polluted by sexual immorality. His face had grown hot while he penned the words, but he hadn't sugarcoated his view of the damage that could be caused by reading inappropriate material.

He finished addressing the last of the envelopes, slid one of the neatly written letters inside each, and then glued the flaps shut. He glanced at his watch. He had time to purchase stamps and get the letters in the post box before dinner. By Monday, his letters would be on editors' desks.

After donning his jacket, he left Landry Hall and headed for the main building, where the campus post office was located. A cool breeze, scented of rain, slapped his face. He slipped the letters into his jacket pocket as he headed down the sidewalk past the women's hall, and his heart skipped a beat when he spotted Libby charging out the dormitory doors. Since they'd returned from Matt's wedding, their paths had crossed numerous times, but they hadn't spoken a word to each other. Pete sensed Libby was embarrassed by her admission after the wedding and was deliberately keeping her distance.

He'd prayed repeatedly for a way to put her at ease again so they could maintain the comfortable friendship of their childhoods. His fingers curled over the letters in his pocket. Libby was a writer. Perhaps his efforts to have his letters printed in the paper would give them a reason to talk a bit. He waved the envelopes over his head and called, "Libby!"

She paused in her pell-mell dash across the grass and turned to face him. The tip of her tongue sneaked out to lick her lips, and she watched him unsmilingly as he closed the gap between them. "Yes?"

She sounded so formal. So unlike the Libby he'd always known. His chest ached. He and Libby were changing. Growing up. But did growing up have to mean growing apart? "I . . . I just wanted to say hello. Are you going to dinner now?"

She nodded. "Alice-Marie is waiting."

He caught the implication, but he chose to ignore it. "I'll be going to the dining hall in a few minutes, too. After I mail my letters to the editors of the area newspapers." He waited for an answering spark of interest in her eyes. He wasn't disappointed.

"You're writing to the editors?" Her gaze dropped to the envelopes in his hand. "About what?"

Encouraged by her interest, he took another forward step. "I have a special assignment from one of my professors." He briefly explained the project. "I've chosen magazine stories that present an improper view of the relationship between men and women. I hope to prevent young women, such as yourself, from being unduly influenced by the morally obstructive stories being printed in—"

"Why?"

He jolted at her angry, defensive query. "Why . . . what?"

"Why did you choose magazine stories?" Libby folded her arms over her chest and glared at him.

Pete hesitated. She reminded him of a cornered alley cat. "Because . . . because I believe it's something that needs to change. The Bible is very clear in instructing us to think about things that are pure, noble, and right. How can stories intended to—" he swallowed, his face heating—"physically arouse be considered pure?"

Libby laughed, but it sounded brittle. "What difference does it make to you if people want to entertain themselves by reading a story in a magazine? The last I knew, our country still includes freedom of the press in the Bill of Rights. Why should you decide what kind of reading material is appropriate for me, or for her, or for him?" She pointed at other students who passed by.

Pete fidgeted as her voice rose with fervor and people glanced inquisitively in their direction. "I didn't mean to upset you. I just wanted to tell you—"

"I'm not upset!" Her flushed face and high pitch belied the statement.

He chuckled softly. "I must have been mistaken about you yelling at me. Excuse my confusion."

For the first time he could remember, his gentle teasing did nothing to appease her. She continued to glare at him, her lips set in an angry line. He tried for a low, reasonable tone. "Libby, I believe, as a minister of the gospel, my responsibility is to prevent people from making mistakes that could impact their spiritual lives.

That's why I want people to consider how reading overly descriptive stories could lead to immoral thoughts. Do you understand?"

He held his breath, waiting and hoping her expression would soften. That she would smile and agree that he should continue this fight. He needed support and encouragement from this young woman he considered his best friend.

But Libby tossed her head, making her hair flow in a wild wave. "I don't understand, Petey. If you don't want to read passionate stories, then fine—that's your choice. But trying to encourage others to avoid them is hurtful to those who write the stories, and I—" She bit down on her lower lip. "I need to go. Alice-Marie is waiting." She turned and ran across the grass.

Pete watched her go, confused and heartsore. He'd intended to patch things up between Libby and himself, but somehow he'd made things worse. Her refusal to understand his point of view reminded him of Bennett's refusal to listen to anything that smacked of spirituality. If he couldn't convince his two best friends of what was right according to the Word of God, how could he expect to successfully minister to a congregation?

His head low, he continued his progress toward the post boxes. The chill wind reached beneath his jacket, and he shivered. His traitorous leg, always sensitive to the cold, set up a fierce ache. He tapped his peg against the floor while he purchased two-cent stamps, affixed them to the envelopes, and dropped the envelopes in the mailing tray. He started to turn toward the dining hall, but then he paused. He hadn't retrieved his mail for a couple of days. He should check his box while he was there.

To his delight, two letters awaited him, one from Aaron and Isabelle, and one from Jackson Harders. Pete frowned, puzzled. Jackson had never written to him before. Then a sizzle shot through Pete's chest, as if a falling star had zinged from the sky and struck him. Could it be . . . ?

His hands shaking, he pocketed the letter from Aaron and Isabelle and ripped open the envelope from Jackson. He pulled out a single sheet of paper and unfolded it. The brief message made Pete's temples pound. Jackson had located Gunter and Berta Leidig.

Chapter Eighteen

Libby held the fine china saucer on her palm, lifted the teacup to her lips, and sipped daintily. Although she'd balked against Mrs. Rowley's etiquette lessons at the orphans' school, she now appreciated the woman's insistence that she learn proper manners. She knew how to conduct herself appropriately in Alice-Marie's family parlor. And after meeting Alice-Marie's mother, she was certain she'd have been put in the kitchen with the servants if she'd proven incapable of following the dictates of polite society.

Throughout the ostentatiously decorated parlor, women, all topped by oversized feathered, flowered, and beribboned millinery, perched straight-spined on the edges of chairs. They sipped tea, pinky fingers high, and engaged in quiet conversation. Alice-Marie had been put to work refilling cups from a silver footed teapot, so Libby sat alone in the corner, waiting for the author to speak. On her right, two women discussed the memorial fountain being erected at the United States Barge Office in New York. She listened, trying not to giggle, as the conversation became heated.

"I simply think the money could have been put to better use. Perhaps as educational funds for the children of the operators," the one with an ostrich-plumed hat said. The feather bobbed, nearly dipping into the woman's teacup.

"I'm sure the owners of the *Titanic* are providing for any survivors of those lost at sea," the second responded, her lips pursed so tightly Libby was amazed any sound managed to squeeze out. "But this fountain's funding was provided by wireless operators to recognize one of their own. I see it as quite a complimentary gesture."

"A *gesture*? Gracious, Myrtle, they're erecting a twelve-ton white granite fountain!" The ostrich plume quivered indignantly as the woman tsk-tsked. "Isn't that a bit . . . well, excessive?"

"I hardly see that it's your concern. Did you contribute to the funding?" The second woman's tone became severe, and the ostrich-plumed woman squirmed. "I personally think it's lovely that a memorial is being established. The loss of the *Titanic* was such a tragedy." Suddenly she leaned forward and pinned Libby with a penetrating look. "What do you think, young woman? I'm certain you heard every word of our exchange."

Heat flooded Libby's face. Had she been so obvious in her eavesdropping? "I . . . um . . ."

The woman with the ostrich-feather hat put her glove-covered hand on Libby's knee. "Oh, ignore Myrtle. She's a rabble-rouser. Always has been." She bobbed her head up and down, tickling Libby's cheek with the tips of the feather.

The purse-lipped woman leaned in, her eyes sparking. "And just ignore Stella. Everyone knows her entire family pinches a penny until Lincoln howls. Besides that, she'd argue with a table leg."

Libby decided she preferred to ignore both of them. "Excuse

me, please." She rose and weaved her way through the room, searching for another empty seat. The only open chair sat beside a tall, thin woman with a very long, thin nose. Her features might have appeared less austere had she not parted her hair down the center and combed it smooth over her ears to the nape of her neck, where a tightly twisted bun stuck out like a doorknob. The austerity ended at her neck, however, where the high ruffled collar of her suit touched the underside of her pointy chin.

Libby couldn't help staring at the woman's suit; she'd never seen so many ruffles. Layers of ruffles marched from the woman's chin past her narrow shoulders to her hips. The suit gave way to an expanse of smooth fabric that fit closely to her thighs and then exploded in a second abundance of wider ruffles from knee to ankle. If the ruffles weren't enough to call attention, the color—bold turquoise—seemed to pulsate. A peacock would have been less noticeable.

Even though Libby wanted to sit rather than stand in the midst of the group, she hesitated at joining the flamboyantly dressed, dour-faced woman. While she stood, contemplating what to do, the woman in the peacock suit raised her hand and quirked her fingers at Libby.

Libby placed her hand against her chest, raising her eyebrows in silent query. The woman smiled and nodded, then patted the empty seat beside her. To refuse now would be rude, which would certainly displease her hostess. She crossed the room and sat gingerly on the edge of the embroidered chair seat.

"I don't believe we've met." The woman held out a startlingly slender hand. Libby hardly dared take it, the fingers looked so fragile. "I'm Catherine Whitford. And you are . . . ?"

Libby gasped, jerking her hand free. She nearly tipped her teacup. Carefully, she set the cup and saucer on the closest table and stared into the woman's plain, impassive face. "You're the author!"

Catherine Whitford laughed, showing small, straight teeth. "Yes, I am. And I must also be a pariah." Her gaze swept the room, and she released a soft, throaty laugh. "You're the first person who's had enough courage to approach me since I arrived and Mrs. Daley placed me in this inconspicuous corner."

Libby gulped. Had she known this woman was the author invited to share her experiences with Mrs. Daley's society friends, she would have waited for Mrs. Daley to introduce her. She searched her memory for the etiquette rules concerning introducing oneself to a celebrity, but she couldn't recall Mrs. Rowley covering the topic. She gulped and scrambled for a way to appear self-assured. "It's very nice to meet you, Mrs. Whitford."

"Miss." The woman raised her chin. "I've never had the pleasure of matrimony, and at my age it's unlikely."

Libby studied the woman's face and tried to determine how old she might be. Silvery strands lay amongst her otherwise brown hair, and fine lines feathered from her eyes; Libby believed Miss Whitford might have been anywhere from forty to sixty. She almost seemed ageless with her Spartan hairstyle and outlandish suit. Uncertain how to respond, Libby offered, "Perhaps you'll still marry one day."

Miss Whitford raised one shoulder in a nonchalant shrug. "Oh, it hardly matters. I have my career, and I find it very satisfying."

Libby licked her lips and let her excitement surface. "Truly?"

"Truly." Miss Whitford's eyes crinkled at the corners. "But you haven't yet told me your name, young woman."

"Oh!" Libby swiped her palm along her skirt and offered her hand. "I'm Lib—Elisabet Conley. And . . ." Her breath caught in her throat. "I'm a writer, too."

Miss Whitford tipped her head, her gaze penetrating. "What is it you write, Miss Conley?"

"Stories. For magazines. I've sold two so far."

"Really? That's quite an accomplishment for one so young."

The compliment filled Libby with pleasure. "Thank you."

"I assume you're referring to fictional stories involving love affairs between unlikely partners?"

Libby, recalling the title of her first story, nearly gasped at the woman's astute assessment. She nodded in reply.

Miss Whitford examined Libby by inches, her deep-set brown eyes drifting from Libby's hair all the way to her toes and then up again. "And have you drawn from your own experiences to aid you in the construction of these stories?"

"W-what do you mean?"

The woman laughed. "Oh, come now, Miss Conley. A young woman as beautiful as yourself must have been the recipient of male attention. They say to write what one knows. Do you know of love affairs . . . personally?"

Libby thought her nose might catch fire, her face burned so hot. "No, ma'am! I've used my imagination . . . honestly."

Another laugh trickled. "Now, don't be offended. Writers are an obnoxious lot, as you'll discover if you continue in this ridiculous occupation." She smoothed the ruffles that fluttered across her bodice and arched one sparse eyebrow. "So tell me, Miss Conley, do you intend to continue writing love stories for magazines, or do you aspire to novels one day?"

"Actually . . ." Libby paused, half afraid of what the woman would say. "I hope to become a journalist. I'd like to record world events rather than make up stories. I'm using the magazine stories to establish my name as a writer."

Miss Whitford flipped her hand outward and made a little *pffft* sound with her lips. "Journalism . . . a complete waste of time."

Libby jerked backward. "Excuse me?"

"Can you recall for me, Miss Conley, the name of a popular author?"

Although Libby believed she might be walking into a trap, she swallowed and offered a short list of authors. "Frances Hodgson Burnett, Edgar Rice Burroughs, Zane Grey . . ." Petey was particularly fond of Zane Grey. She pushed that errant thought aside.

A smile curved Miss Whitford's thin lips. "Excellent choices. And I'm quite positive those names will be recognized by readers twenty, thirty, even fifty years from now." The smile turned conniving. "Now give me the name of the writer of the headline story for today's edition of the *Missouri Courier.*"

Libby stared at the woman in silence.

Miss Whitford nodded, her expression smug. "Precisely what I presumed."

Libby surprised herself by arguing with the author. "I might not know the man who wrote today's headline, but I do know the names of several renowned journalists. William Stead, for example."

"Yes, and look what happened to him," Miss Whitford countered evenly. "I won't deny he was a more-than-decent reporter, but part of the reason he's well-known is because of his untimely demise in such an unusual manner. How many ships sink on their maiden voyage? The situation lent itself to infamy."

Libby was beginning to feel like a passenger on the *Titanic,* going down with no hope of survival. "But—"

"Miss Conley, if you want to make a name for yourself, you need to become a novelist. Considering the success you've already experienced, I would say your chances are quite good."

Libby held out her hands in supplication. "But I want to write serious stories. *Real* stories." She'd already had to give up her dream of becoming the daughter of Maelle Watts Harders. She wouldn't allow her dream of becoming a journalist to die without a fight. "I want to change the world!"

Libby nearly cringed at her own emotional outburst, but to Miss Whitford's credit, she didn't even blink. Instead, she leaned forward slightly and took Libby's hand. "My dear, if you want to discover your place in the writing world, then you must explore. You're a college student?"

She nodded. "At the University of Southern Missouri."

"In the journalism program, I presume?"

She nodded again.

"And you're finding it agreeable?"

Libby held her breath. Very slowly, she shook her head from side to side.

Miss Whitford's lips twitched. "And why is it not agreeable?"

"Because I'm rolling over and crawling instead of running." The author's forehead furrowed, and Libby rushed to explain her cryptic answer. "So far, the articles I've written aren't terribly important on a large scale. I want to write something bigger, something important. But I haven't yet had the chance."

"Then seize the chance!" Miss Whitford's eyes sparkled with intensity, her plain face taking on a liveliness that made her look more attractive. "You're writing love stories on your own. So write an article on your own. Continue in your coursework—you've paid for it, and the instructors will provide important guidance. But don't limit yourself to their instruction. Do more. Choose a topic that interests you or adopt a cause that makes your blood boil. Write something of *meaning*. It's the only way you'll know for sure that this dream you're harboring is worth pursuing."

She leaned so close, her breath brushed Libby's face. "Writers must write. You've discovered that by venturing outside the bounds of journalism to create fictional stories. But where does your true passion lie? Do some seeking, Elisabet Conley, and discover your passion—fictional stories or real-life events?" She sat upright, her face relaxing into the unperturbed, almost bored expression she'd been wearing before Libby came to sit beside her. "Some dreams are meant to be that—only dreams, dissipating with the morning light. But you won't know for sure until you've tasted them."

Libby nodded thoughtfully. She started to thank Miss Whitford for her advice, but Mrs. Daley bustled over and caught Libby's hand. "Elisabet, go sit with Alice-Marie now. The program is about to begin."

Libby rose and scurried to the far side of the room, where Alice-Marie had pulled two chairs close together near the parlor doorway. She listened to the author's presentation, but nothing the woman said during her prepared talk on the world of publishing held as much intrigue as what she had shared privately.

The moment Miss Whitford finished, Libby slipped out of the parlor and headed for the study, where she'd seen the Daleys' maid lay the morning paper for Alice-Marie's father's use. Eagerness to put the author's advice into action propelled her down the hallway.

Closing the raised-panel pocket doors behind her, she bustled to the carved oak desk in front of the heavily draped windows on the far side of the study. Feeling like an intruder, she sat at the desk and opened the newspaper. She scanned the headings, exploring, as Miss Whitford had recommended, waiting for something to capture her attention so thoroughly it made her blood boil.

And on the seventh page—nearly the very end of the newspaper—a tiny block of print on the lower right-hand side sent her pulse racing.

Sixteen-year-old convicted of robbery and murder of drugstore clerk. Sentencing took place October 16, 1914, by the honorable Judge Merlin Simmons. The youth will be hanged by the neck on the 18th of December in the basement of the courthouse. The judge said, "Perhaps his death will serve as an example to other street ruffians to abandon their lives of crime."

Libby dropped the paper and stared straight ahead, her heart beating so hard and fast her ears rang. Sentenced to hang—and only sixteen years old. What kind of boy committed murder? Suddenly she had to know more. These simple lines couldn't possibly tell the entire story.

On tiptoe, she left the study, then dashed up the stairs to Alice-Marie's room. She retrieved her coat and then crept back down, holding her breath as she passed the parlor doorway. But she needn't have worried. A question-and-answer session, with Miss Whitford at the center, held everyone's attention. No one even looked up as she unlatched the front door and slipped outside.

She intended to visit the office of the newspaper that had printed the brief article and discover where this youth was being held. Then she would find a way to visit him. She would uncover his story and tell it in its entirety. Once she'd written a real story, she'd know where her passions lay—in the telling of imaginary tales or in reporting real-life events.

Chapter Nineteen

Bennett paced his small room, his hands balled into fists and his shoulders tense. Would this rain never cease? It had started early that morning, right after Alice-Marie and Libby left for Alice-Marie's house, and continued all day. He'd planned to spend the morning working on the grounds—earning a little pocket money—and then get several guys together for a baseball game in the afternoon before it got too cold to play. But now evening neared, and he'd spent the entire day cooped up in his room with a roommate who never took his nose out of his books.

Bennett slammed his fist against the window frame and growled. "Dry up, huh?"

His roommate—a short, bespectacled kid named Winston—looked up from his book and frowned. "Are you speaking to me?"

"Talking to the rain."

Winston sat in thoughtful silence for several seconds. Then

he said, "I think that would be a singularly dissatisfying pastime, considering the rain is incapable of response."

Bennett had no answer for a comment like that, so he turned back to the window and tried counting the raindrops that ran down the square panes. If Alice-Marie were here, he'd go over and sit with her in Rhodes Hall's common room. The house matron was always right there, keeping an eye on everything they did, but if they held a magazine high enough, he could sneak a kiss before the nosy old woman cleared her throat and they were forced to lower the cover. So far Alice-Marie had let him kiss her three times. And the kisses had left him hungering for more.

Alice-Marie had invited him to go home with her this weekend, along with Libby. He'd been tempted, but he feared acceptance would give Alice-Marie the wrong idea. He didn't want her around forever. He just wanted to have some fun with her right now.

Thunder rolled in the distance, letting Bennett know the rain intended to stay for a while longer. He snorted. Maybe he should've gone to St. Louis County with Alice-Marie. Giving her the wrong idea and having to backtrack later would have been better than being stuck in this room with Winston.

Stomping to the door, Bennett yanked his jacket from a hook. Winston set his book aside and offered a disapproving look. "Are you going out?"

Bennett jammed his hands into his coat sleeves. "Sure am."

"But it's raining."

"Nothing gets past you, does it, Winnie?"

Winston's scowl deepened. "Would you like the use of an umbrella?"

Bennett paused, his hand on the doorknob. "You have one?"

"I do."

"I would like to use it, if you don't mind."

Winston carefully set his book aside and then knelt on the floor.

His rear in the air, he pawed around under the bed, withdrawing several books, two pairs of socks, and finally a black umbrella. He held it out to Bennett. "My father gave it to me for my seventeenth birthday."

Bennett plucked it from Winston's hand and swung it around by its curved wooden handle. "Great gift."

Winston ducked to avoid being bopped. "Please take care with it. He purchased it on one of his visits to England."

Why'd they stick him with this boring kid, anyway? He and Winston had nothing in common. Next year Bennett planned to reside in a fraternity house instead of in the dorms. If he came back at all.

"I'll be careful. See you later." He hurried downstairs, but once he reached the ground floor, he couldn't decide where to go. He couldn't visit Alice-Marie or Libby—they were both gone. Pete would probably be studying—he was getting as boring as ol' Winston.

He tapped the tip of the umbrella against the floor, and the tapping reminded him of Pete's habit of tapping his peg leg. Even though he figured Pete would be studying, he'd go see him anyway. It would do Pete good to close the books and have some fun for a change. Maybe they'd play a game of gin rummy. He still had a pack of cards in his jacket pocket from the last time he'd played. Pete wouldn't gamble, but they could play for pleasure.

After a few moments of fumbling, Bennett figured out how to raise the umbrella, and he darted across the slick grass to Landry Hall. He shook the raindrops from the umbrella before setting it in the corner of the foyer and clattering up the stairs. His wet shoes left footprints behind, but the floor would dry in time. Without bothering to knock, he twisted the knob on Pete's door and swung it wide. As he'd suspected, Pete was at his desk, bent over a sheet of paper with a pencil in his hand.

"Hey, buddy, working on anything important?"

Pete jerked upright. "Bennett . . . you startled me."

"Sorry." Bennett kicked off his wet shoes and flopped across Pete's cot. The springs creaked loudly in protest. "I came over to see if you wanted to play a game of cards or something. Some of the guys taught me a game called gin rummy—it's pretty fun." He patted his pocket where the deck of cards created a lump. "Want to?"

Pete sighed and massaged his temples. "I'd like to, Bennett, but I need to—"

"—work," Bennett finished for him. He bounced up from the bed and crossed to the window. Bracing one hand on the window frame, he frowned at his friend. "Honestly, Pete, you're turning into a real spoilsport. When's the last time you did anything fun?"

"When I pitched for your baseball game."

Bennett turned quickly to look out the window so Pete wouldn't see his face pinch with anger. The campus chatter about Pete's surprising performance had finally died down, but half the students still called him Peg leg Pete. They hadn't given Bennett any special nickname to set him apart.

"That was weeks ago, buddy." It took real effort, but Bennett kept his voice even. "I'd say it's time for something again."

"Too wet to play baseball," Pete mused. He shifted his attention back to the papers on his desk.

"So who says baseball's the only way to have a good time?" Bennett took two long strides that brought him to the edge of Pete's desk. "Aw, c'mon, Pete. Take a break. Play a round of gin rummy with me. I'm about to go out of my mind with boredom."

Pete's pencil continued scratching across the page. "Read a good book. Work on next week's assignments. There's got to be something you can do."

"I don't feel like reading, and I save Sunday afternoon for homework. This is Saturday. Fellas ought to have fun on Saturdays."

Pete rubbed the back of his neck, yawning. "Tell you what, let me finish this and then I'll try my hand at . . . what did you call that game?"

"Gin rummy."

Pete made a face. "Sounds like an alcoholic drink."

At Pete's tone, Bennett experienced a flash of irritation. "Quit being so stodgy." He sat on the bed again and threw his arms wide. "Just because you're studying to become a minister, does it mean you have to act like one now? Can't you be a regular guy now and then?"

Pete put his pencil down and turned in his chair to face Bennett. "You want an honest answer? No, Bennett, I can't just be a regular guy. I haven't been a 'regular guy' since that trolley rolled over my leg eleven years ago."

Without meaning to, Bennett glanced at the empty pant leg dangling from the edge of the chair. Pete hadn't strapped on his peg leg today—he must not have been out at all. Bennett lifted his gaze to Pete's face. "But having a peg leg doesn't mean you have to be so . . . *right* all the time. Honestly, Pete, it'd do you some good to relax now and then. Even at the orphans' school, you were always everybody's perfect little angel—never did anything wrong."

And Bennett had never been able to compete with Pete in the good-boy department. Maybe that's part of the reason he'd become such a hellion. At least the title got him attention. "You aren't a preacher yet. Stop acting like one."

Pete's face took on that fervent older-than-his-years look Bennett had come to detest. "No matter what I'm doing—whether it's throwing a baseball or working on my assignments or sitting here talking to you—God's Spirit is with me. I represent Him. And I want to represent Him well. When people look at me, I want them to see God's love played out before their eyes."

Bennett made a derisive face. "That's all fine and good. But you want to know what I think, Pete? I think you're doing everything for Him, and He's doing nothing for you."

Pete stared at Bennett as if he'd lost his mind. And maybe he had, because once he started talking, he couldn't seem to stop. "If He's so good and loves you so much, why'd He let you get hurt in the first place?" *Why'd He let me be abandoned?* "Where was He that day you slipped getting off the trolley?" *Or the years I spent scrabbling to take care of myself on the street?*

Pete's face turned red. "God didn't make me fall. It was an accident."

"Yeah." Bennett twisted his lips into a scowl. "An accident that turned you into a cripple."

"He saved my life! I could've died, but God saved me."

"So you're gonna spend the rest of your life preaching the Bible to thank Him?"

Pete gawked at Bennett. "I owe Him."

"You owe Him." Bennett snorted. "Seems to me you already paid Him well. He got a foot and part of a leg out of the deal."

"Bennett!"

Pete sounded angrier than Bennett had ever heard him, but instead of being put off by it, he found it exhilarating. At least they weren't sitting there counting raindrops. Bennett propped his elbow on his knee and gave Pete a cynical look. "God might not've made you fall, but He sure didn't keep it from happening, did He?" Just like He hadn't kept Bennett from living on the streets, fighting for a scrap of bread.

"It wasn't God's fault!" Pete thumped his fist on the desk. "It was—" His voice stopped abruptly, like someone had slammed a door and cut off the sound. He fingered the paper on his desk, crinkling its corner. Finally, so softly Bennett almost didn't hear him, he said, "It was my folks' fault. If they hadn't kicked me out, none of it would've happened. God didn't hurt me, Bennett. My own pa and ma did."

Try as he might, Bennett couldn't conjure up much sympathy. "Least you know who your folks are." He hunched forward, staring at his own feet. "I don't know anything about my parents, except that they didn't want me—dumping me like they did on the doorstep of the children's home. Not even a note pinned to me to let anybody know who I was or where I came from. The sisters had to give me a name. At least your folks kept you. For a while. That's better than some people get."

Rain pattered against the window and thunder growled softly, echoing against the rock walls of the hall. When he'd come over to see Pete, he sure hadn't intended to think about his past. Bennett didn't live in the past—he lived in the now. That's the only thing that counted. Having fun now.

He slapped his knee and rose. "You gonna clear that desk off so we can play a game, or not?" He sounded belligerent, but he didn't care. Pete needed to quit with the God-talk. God had never done anything for Bennett Martin—or whoever he was—and he didn't intend to start trusting Him now.

"Yes, we can play, just as soon as I finish this." He bent over his paper.

Bennett sat on the floor and tugged on his shoes. Then he stomped to the door. "Forget it, Pete. There's always something more important than me. Pleasing God. Pleasing your professors. Well, go ahead and do what you need to do. I won't bother you again."

He heard Pete call his name, but he ignored him and took the stairs two at a time. No way Pete could hop after him fast enough to catch him. He grabbed up Winston's English umbrella, snapped it open, and stepped out into the rain.

Chapter Twenty

If only he had two good legs! Pete slapped the banister at the top of the stairs. He wanted to run after Bennett and assure him he didn't want their friendship to dissolve. Why did it seem he was losing the people who meant the most to him? First Libby, and now Bennett.

He blew out a mighty breath and hopped back to his room, where the assignment lay on his desk, awaiting completion. He'd specifically requested all of the week's assignments in advance, and his instructors had been happy to oblige when he'd explained why he wanted to work ahead.

If he had everything finished by Wednesday, as he hoped, he planned to board a train on Thursday morning and journey to the place of his birth. He could hardly believe his parents were still living in Clayton, although no longer in the apartment they'd rented when Pete was young. But his pa still worked at the brewery, the noon-to-eight shift, according to the information Jackson had uncovered. Pete still remembered the yeasty smell on his pa's clothes when he returned from work. And the sick stench of his breath when he'd spent too much of his paycheck on his employer's product. If Pa had spent his paycheck on groceries instead of liquor, would he still have sent Pete out on his own?

Pete picked up his pencil to continue working on his essay, but his hand trembled, making legibility an impossible feat. He put down the pencil and closed his eyes. How he anticipated the moment when he'd be able to look at his parents, face-to-face, and tell them how much he loathed them for the pain they'd inflicted on him.

A Bible verse they'd studied in Pastor Hines's class winged through his mind: *"God is love; and he that dwelleth in love dwelleth in God, and God in him."* A twinge in his gut accompanied the remembrance. He'd just told Bennett that he wanted to serve God well, to be an instrument of God's love to those he met. How did finding his parents for the sole purpose of verbally attacking them fit with being an instrument of God's love?

But his parents didn't deserve his love. They'd rejected him— thrown him out the way people threw away garbage. God could love them if He wanted to, but Pete had no use for Gunter and Berta Leidig. Once he'd had his say, he intended to talk to Jackson about something else.

He had no desire to hear congregants call him Pastor Leidig. The reference would be a constant reminder of his uncaring parents. He'd given it a lot of thought, and the best way to rid him of his worthless birthright was to throw off all the trappings of his former life. He wanted to be Pastor Rowley. Aaron and Isabelle wouldn't mind, and Aaron's parents—who'd become his surrogate grandparents—would be delighted to have Pete share their name.

Only a few more days of being Peter Leidig. He could hardly wait to make the change. But first, he needed to finish his work.

Thoughts of his disagreement with Bennett fled as he focused once again on the waiting assignment.

❧

Alice-Marie's father cranked a lever and the Model T's engine changed from a steady *chug-chug* to a sputtering, persistent cough. "Here you are, ladies. Back again."

Libby fought against the vehicle's vibrations and wrenched the back door open, eager to clamber out. Although she'd initially thought riding in a motorcar sounded exhilarating, the bouncing motion had churned her stomach. Or maybe it was the secret she now carried that had made her sick. Regardless, she sighed with relief when her feet found solid, steady ground.

Alice-Marie sat in the front seat, silent and ramrod straight, until her father rounded the car and opened the door for her. Even after she stepped off the running board, she kept her lips tightly clamped. Libby hadn't known Alice-Marie was capable of prolonged silence. The girl even talked in her sleep. But during the entire three-hour drive from her home to the school, Alice-Marie had sat close-mouthed with her arms folded over her chest. The cold wind whisking into the car hadn't chilled Libby as thoroughly as Alice-Marie's disapproval.

Mr. Daley moved to the rear of the Model T and opened the small trunk area. He lifted out Alice-Marie's bag. "Here, punkin. Do you want me to carry it in for you?"

"No, thank you." Alice-Marie's words came out stilted, as if her tongue were relearning how to talk. "I can manage quite nicely." She leaned forward and planted a peck on her father's mutton-chop-whiskered cheek. "You'll come for me again Thanksgiving weekend?"

"You know I will." Mr. Daley lifted Libby's bag and held it out to her. "Elisabet, are you going home for Thanksgiving?"

His innocent question nearly suffocated her. She clung to her bag's handle with both hands and bounced the bag with her knees. "N-no, sir. I don't believe so." How could she go to Shay's Ford and watch Maelle and Jackson fawn over their new daughters? "I'll probably stay here and do some writing."

A loud huff exploded from Alice-Marie's lips, and she stuck her nose in the air.

Mr. Daley scratched his chin. "Well, I better head home. It's a long drive, and dark will catch me if I'm not careful. Good-bye, Elisabet. It was . . . nice . . . meeting you." He offered Libby a brief impersonal smile, then turned to Alice-Marie. The father and daughter shared a few whispered comments that didn't reach Libby's ears, but her face burned at their furtive glances.

Alice-Marie gave her father's cheek another kiss. "Good-bye, Daddy." Mr. Daley climbed into the driver's seat, and Alice-Marie and Libby stood beside the road until the Model T spluttered around the corner. Then, without a word, Alice-Marie spun on her heel and began marching toward the dormitory with her bag banging against her leg. Libby trotted along behind her.

Alice-Marie threw a stormy look over her shoulder. "Don't even think of apologizing. I won't accept it."

Libby bristled at Alice-Marie's superior tone. "I wasn't going to offer."

Alice-Marie came to a halt and whirled to face Libby. Fire sparked from her eyes. "You should be ashamed of yourself, leaving the house the way you did. And then refusing to tell my parents where you'd been. Why, you behaved abominably! But then what should I expect from an *orphan*? I should have listened to Mother. She tried to tell me not to waste my efforts on a girl raised with no parental influence, but I foolishly believed I could have a positive impact on you. Now it's clear to me your behavioral patterns have already been well established, and I shall never—"

Anger coursed through Libby, carried on a wave of embarrassed hurt. "You were trying to make an *impact* on me? There's nothing you could teach me worth knowing!"

"Oh no?" Alice-Marie threw her bag on the ground and angled her chin high. Her eyes snapped with fury. "What about how not to be a misfit? If it weren't for me including you, no girl on this campus would give you a moment of time."

Libby's jaw dropped. "That's not true."

"For heaven's sake, Elisabet, how can you be so obtuse? As if any decent girl would befriend you after you involved yourself in fisticuffs right in the middle of the campus on your very first day here. Were it not for my excusing you, you would have been shunned from the very beginning."

Libby started to defend herself, but Alice-Marie continued railing without a moment's pause.

"And then you hide away in our room, refusing to join any of the clubs or groups on campus." She swept a disparaging look over Libby from head to toe. "You leave your hair hanging down your back like a curtain instead of putting it up, the way any self-respecting woman would do. Your shoes, if you bother to wear them, are always half unbuttoned. Your fingertips are covered in ink stains, your nails are chipped. . . . I've never met a girl so unconcerned about her personal appearance." She made a sour face. "You might be exceptionally beautiful, as my cousin Roy is so fond of pointing out, but you do not *fit*, Elisabet Conley. And it's become abundantly clear to me that you never will, because you don't care enough to try to fit. To fit would require reaching out to others, and apparently you are too self-centered to do so."

Alice-Marie balled her hands into fists and tapped one toe furiously. "I took you to my home as a favor to you. To give you an opportunity to see how civilized people live and socialize with one another. To show you what your life could be like if you would only cast aside your uncultured ways and behave like a refined human being. But how do you choose to repay me? By sneaking off in the middle of an important meeting!"

"But I was only trying to—"

"Mother was mortified; Daddy was shocked." Alice-Marie's shrill voice covered Libby's explanation. "And because of your poor behavior, I was forced to bear a lengthy scolding for exposing our family and Mother's friends to such outlandish conduct. Well!" She tossed her head, holding her palms out. "I have washed my hands of you and your strange behaviors. I will *not* offer excuses for you. I will *not* be your friend anymore. You are now completely on your own—just the way you like it."

She snatched up her bag and marched off toward their dormitory, her nose in the air.

Libby stared after Alice-Marie, too stunned to speak. As much as she wished to deny it, the view she'd been given of herself through her roommate's eyes wasn't pretty. The word *misfit* had hurt, but the other descriptions inflicted a deeper pain. Alice-Marie intimated she was someone uncaring toward others, someone who flouted convention and shunned companionship. Libby had always wanted to be like Maelle, a person comfortable being herself. But while Maelle certainly flouted convention, she was a deeply caring woman who reached out to others.

Within her soul, Libby cared. At this moment, she carried a burden bigger than she knew how to hold. But she'd been unable to tell the Daleys where she'd been and what she'd learned. She couldn't find appropriate words to describe the worry, revulsion, and dread her errand had created.

So she'd remained silent in the face of their questioning. And in doing so, she'd put a huge gap between herself and Alice-Marie.

Not until that moment had Libby realized how much she'd come to depend on her roommate's companionship.

The wind picked up as the sun slunk slowly toward the treetops, and Libby shivered. She scooped up her bag and hugged it to her aching chest. Oh, if only she hadn't left Alice-Marie's house. If only she'd ignored Miss Whitford's advice. If only she hadn't seen that newspaper article. . . .

Discover where your true passions lie, the author had instructed Libby. For years Libby had dreamed of becoming a reporter. But for the first time, she realized reporting the truth—telling the whole story—could prove difficult. Heartbreaking. For her, and for some of those reading the truth.

Libby impulsively lifted her face to the sky. Might she find an early evening star so she could wish this newly discovered knowledge away? She sighed, dispelling the childish thought. Wishing changed nothing. She'd uncovered the truth behind the short lines of print in Mr. Daley's newspaper. And somehow she must find a way to tell Petey about the youth sentenced to hang in the basement of the St. Louis County courthouse. Because that boy was Petey's brother.

CHAPTER TWENTY-ONE

H ow do you know he's Pete's brother?"

Libby toyed with the straw in her tall soda glass, giving Bennett only a brief, impatient look. She hunched farther into the high-backed booth in the corner of the drugstore and hissed, "Didn't you hear anything I just said? The man at the newspaper office said the boy's name was Oscar Leidig."

"And?" Bennett slurped a bite of ice cream.

Libby wished she could yank the dish and spoon away from him. She'd consumed very little of her vanilla phosphate, too tense to enjoy the treat Bennett had purchased. His appetite, however, appeared to be intact. He'd already finished one ice cream sundae and started on a second. "And what? His last name is Leidig!"

Bennett laughed. "Lib, you always let your imagination get away from you. You hear a name and right away you think—"

"What else am I supposed to think? The man who covered the trial said the boy is tall, with blond hair—he showed me sketches made during the trial. He looks exactly like Petey." Libby had spent the past three days mulling over the few facts she'd gleaned from the newspaper reporter when she'd sneaked away from Alice-Marie's house. The knowledge had eaten at her until she could no longer hold it inside. So she'd asked Bennett to accompany her to the drugstore for a private chat. Libby hugged herself, remembering the artist's renditions of the trial lawyers, judge, and defendant. The emptiness in the defendant's eyes—eyes so much like Petey's—continued to haunt her.

"There are lots of tall, blond-haired men in the world, you know. They aren't all Pete's family members." Bennett swirled his spoon through the etched glass bowl, turning the remaining chocolate sauce and melting ice cream into a mushy brown mess. "There's probably more than one Leidig family in a town the size of Clayton. It's possible the kid is related to Pete—maybe a cousin or something—but he doesn't have to be Pete's brother. Has Pete ever mentioned a brother named Oscar?"

Libby shook her head. "But that doesn't mean anything. He could have a brother named Oscar and we wouldn't know it, because Petey never talks about his family. He thinks of Mr. and Mrs. Rowley as his parents now."

Bennett took one last bite and then pushed the dish away and clanked the spoon onto the table. "Yeah. They always treated *him* like a son, but—"

Libby waited for him to finish, but he clamped his lips shut and stared to the side. She asked, "So what do I do, Bennett? How do I tell him?" Ordinarily, Libby wouldn't ask Bennett for advice. His cavalier attitude usually made him respond flippantly rather than seriously. Yet she hoped the seriousness of the situation would elicit sympathy and cooperation from Bennett.

Bennett rested his elbows on the edge of the table. "All right,

Lib, let's pretend for a minute that this kid—this Oscar Leidig—*is* Pete's brother. He's committed a crime—"

Libby grimaced, remembering what the newspaper reporter had told her. "A *terrible* crime."

"A terrible crime," he repeated. "And he's going to pay for it with his life."

The imagination Bennett had mentioned earlier painted ugly pictures in Libby's mind. She shuddered. "That's right."

"So that means he's going to be dead."

Libby wished Bennett wouldn't speak so matter-of-factly about something so distressing. "You're far too indifferent about this, Bennett!"

He flipped his palms toward her. "I'm just stating the facts. Isn't that what you wanted to do—uncover the truth? Well, there it is. If this kid's already condemned to die, what difference does it make if he's Pete's brother? The judge has already given the sentence. How will telling Pete change anything?"

Libby stared at Bennett in silence, digesting what he'd said. Although she didn't care for his apathetic tone, his statement made sense. Might it be better to keep the information to herself? Telling Petey would only bring him pain—especially since there was no hope of saving his brother.

"But if you really think he needs to know," Bennett continued, "you better find out for sure whether this boy is Pete's brother. Get all the information before you go running to Pete and telling him his kid brother has been convicted of murder. Did that newspaper man tell you who the kid's parents were?"

"He only told me what he'd gleaned from sitting in on the trial—the boy's name, what crime he'd committed, and the sentence." Libby slumped in the seat. "I got the impression no one really cares much about this boy. He's just one of any number of young troublemakers running wild, wreaking havoc. The newspaper man even seemed relieved to have one less ruffian on the streets." She sighed. "Maybe I should tell Petey just so someone else cares about this boy. Everyone else seems completely indifferent."

Bennett reached into his pants pocket and withdrew some coins. He flipped a nickel onto the table next to his ice cream dish and slid out of the booth. A humorless laugh left his throat. "His brother or not, Preacher Pete would hurry right to the jail to talk to the kid."

Libby nodded solemnly. Yes, Petey would care. Even if the boy sitting in that basement cell was no relation at all, he'd care—because Petey had a heart of gold. Even with all the difficulties he'd been forced to bear—being abandoned by his parents, mistreated by people, and losing his leg—he chose to pour himself into others rather than feel sorry for himself. He'd make a wonderful minister. Her heart panged as she realized, once again, how his becoming a minister would separate them one day.

Libby rose, and Bennett draped his arm across her shoulders as he led her toward the door. They walked in silence to the campus, their breath sending little clouds of condensation into the cool evening air. When they reached Rhodes Hall, Bennett turned Libby to face him. "Can't tell you what to do, Lib. But I wouldn't say anything to Pete unless I had all the facts. If you really think he should know, find out for sure whether this Oscar Leidig is really his brother or not."

"But how can I do that?"

Bennett chuckled and brushed his knuckles along her jaw. "Seems simple enough to me. Ask Pete."

"If I ask Petey, he'll want to know why I'm asking, and there will be no way to avoid telling him what his brother has done."

Bennett shrugged and turned to head down the sidewalk toward his dorm. He called over his shoulder, "Then go ask the kid."

❧

On Thursday morning, Pete plopped his suitcase open on his bed. He stood staring into the empty case, gnawing his lower lip in indecision. What did a person wear when seeing his parents for the first time in almost a dozen years?

He decided to wear work trousers and a soft chambray shirt for travel; he would don the suit Aaron and Isabelle had given him as a graduation gift when he went to his parents' apartment. Pa and Ma wouldn't expect him to look like a gentleman. He smiled, anticipating the surprise he'd certainly witness in their eyes. He hoped to glimpse pride, too—a displaced pride, since they'd had nothing to do with the man he'd grown to be. Would that pride change to shame by the time he'd finished speaking his piece?

He hopped to the wardrobe on his good leg and withdrew his suit. Turning awkwardly, he made his way back to the bed. Every jarring step drove deeper his angry resentment toward Gunter and Berta. *Once I've said what needs saying, the anger'll be gone.* He prayed that would prove true.

His hands shook as he meticulously folded his pants, jacket, and shirt. Sweat beaded on his upper lip and broke out across his back, making him feel sticky. Nausea attacked, and he sank onto the edge of the bed. Holding his stomach, he willed the feeling to pass. Nerves . . . just nerves. But he had to gain control before he boarded the train or the motion would surely make him sick. Gritting his teeth, he finished packing and strapped on his peg leg. He glanced at his pocket watch.

The train was scheduled to leave at ten o'clock. He'd eat breakfast, let his stomach settle, and then head to the station. *And by tomorrow I'll be rid of Gunter and Berta—and their hold on me—for good.*

With that thought hovering in his mind, he walked across

189

the grounds toward the dining hall. Halfway there, pounding footsteps sounded behind him, and he braced himself in case the runner accidentally bumped him when passing. But to his surprise, the steps halted and someone threw an arm around his shoulders. His surprise grew when he looked into the grinning face of Roy Daley.

"Morning, Peg leg."

Roy's firm grip on Pete's shoulder combined with his swaggering gait made Pete feel off-balance. His muscles tensed as he fought to keep his footing. "Good morning."

"Mind if I join you for breakfast? Somethin' I'd like to discuss with you."

Puzzled, Pete shrugged. What could Roy want? The other man had ceased harassing Pete and Bennett, to Pete's relief, after the Sunday baseball game. In fact, Roy had kept his distance, ignoring them so thoroughly Pete believed he'd forgotten they existed. His sudden friendliness put Pete on his guard.

They entered the dining hall side-by-side, with Roy keeping a grip on Pete's shoulder as if afraid he might bolt. Roy waved at a table of friends, smirking and raising one eyebrow in a way that seemed to communicate a secret message. Pete's apprehension grew more intense by the minute. Roy pointed to an empty table and gave Pete a little push toward it.

"Have a seat, Peg leg, ol' buddy. I'll get us both some breakfast and be back in a minute."

Uncertain but unwilling to cause conflict, Pete pulled out a chair and sat. He watched Roy amble to the front of the line. Two students voiced mild protests when he butted in front of them, but Roy laughed and plopped two plates on his tray. Pete looked over to the table where Roy's friends sat. They each wore a smirking grin, their eyes darting from Roy to Pete. A cold chill raised the fine hairs on the back of Pete's neck. What was Roy up to?

Roy came to the table and slid a plate of food in front of Pete. "There you go. Waffles today—they look good. Eat up." Roy began sawing off a large chunk of waffle.

Pete kept his hands in his lap. "Do you mind if I say grace?"

Roy's fork paused midway between his plate and his mouth. Then he let the fork clatter onto his plate and held his hands wide. "Be my guest."

Pete bowed his head and offered a brief prayer of blessing. When he finished, Roy cleared his throat and plucked up his fork once more. He took the first bite without saying a word. As soon as Pete lifted a bite to his mouth, Roy drawled, "So, tell me about Miss Conley."

Pete nearly choked on the bite. He chewed, swallowed, and took a sip of milk. "Tell you . . . what?"

Roy snickered. "Everything." He popped another bite in his mouth and talked around it. "I already know from her roommate she's an orphan—doesn't bother me. I know she wants to be a journalist—that'll probably pass. Women and careers . . ." He snorted softly, then grinned. "But what I don't know is how she's connected to you and Martin. You all were thick as thieves at the beginning of the year, but now you've kind of . . . I don't know . . . split up, I guess." He forked up another bite of waffle. "So . . . is she your girlfriend?"

Pain stabbed Pete's chest. How he wished he could say yes. But he shook his head.

"Martin's, then?"

"No." Pete pushed the remaining waffle back and forth on his plate with the fork's tines. "We all went to school together. So we're . . . friends." Or *were* friends. With all that had happened since they'd come to college, Pete wasn't sure he could define his relationship with Libby or Bennett anymore. The thought saddened him.

"Then she's available?"

The eagerness in the man's voice raised Pete's hackles. He dropped his fork, his appetite gone. "Why are you asking me?"

Roy shoved his tray to the side. He rested both arms on the table and leaned close to Pete. "Because I think she's the prettiest girl on campus, and I'd like to get to know her better. I've tried. She resists me. And I'm not one to back off from a challenge."

Pete shook his head, baffled. "I still don't know why you're asking me."

"Because I think you can get me what I want."

Pete laughed. He hadn't intended to, but the sound rose up without effort. "How?"

"You just said you went to school together. That you're friends."

"Yes, but—"

"And I've got something you want. You help me, and I'll help you."

"What do you have that I want?"

Roy's grin turned conniving. "A place in Beta Theta Pi."

Pete chuckled. "I'm afraid you're mistaken, Roy. I'm not pledging Beta Theta Pi."

"Sure you are. Your name's on the list. Right below that buddy of yours, Bennett Martin."

Pete frowned. "I didn't ask to pledge a fraternity."

"But your buddy did. And it looks to me like he wants both of you to get in. Well, here's the thing." Roy cocked his head to the side, his eyes narrowed. "Right now I'm seein' the two of you as a matched set. What one gets, you both get; what one loses, you both lose. If I don't take you, I don't take Martin." He waggled his hands in the air. "Is any of this makin' sense to you, pal?"

Roy was making perfect sense. And Pete didn't like it at all. "Listen, Roy, if you think you can blackmail—"

"Now, let's not use ugly words." Roy sat back, his expression so friendly anyone looking on would assume they were best friends enjoying a chat. "Let's just call it a trade-off. You know what Martin wants—to be a member of Beta Theta Pi. Poor sap—growing up in an orphanage, never having a family." Roy clicked his tongue on his teeth, his brow puckering. "Understandable why becoming a member of the fraternity is so important to him. But that'll only happen if you choose to join, too. And I'll only invite you if you help me get what I want: Miss Elisabet Conley on my arm."

Roy's grin turned smug. "You pitch a mean baseball, Peg leg. Are you as skilled when it comes to pitchin' woo?"

CHAPTER TWENTY-TWO

Why hadn't he gone straight to the train station and skipped breakfast? Pete could have avoided—or at least postponed—being placed in an impossible position by Roy. Already uptight at the prospect of seeing his parents, he didn't need another worry added to the list. "Roy, I—"

Roy threw his hand in the air. "Don't answer now. I expect you to think about it. Take a day. Or the weekend." His gaze shot somewhere behind Pete's shoulder, and his smile grew. "Or if you'd rather not put it off, you've got a chance right now . . ." As he spoke, he pushed away from the table and lurched into the aisle. "Miss Conley, good morning."

Pete jerked his head to find Libby standing at the end of the table, blocked from passage by Roy's body. Her eyes darted back and forth between Pete and Roy, confusion reflected in their velvety depths.

"Good morning," she said without smiling.

"Peg leg and me were just talking about you." Roy flicked a grin at Pete then tipped toward Libby. "But I think we're done. I'll leave you two alone to . . ." He twirled his pointer finger in circles at Pete then ambled off with his hands in his pockets.

Libby watched him go, her face marred by a scowl of displeasure. She spun back to face Pete. "What are you doing, talking with him about *me*?"

She sounded hurt. Betrayed. Heat rose from Pete's middle and filled his face. "Libby, I . . ." He swallowed. How could he explain?

Sinking into the chair across from him, she searched his face. "He was just trying to get under my skin, wasn't he? You weren't really discussing me." She blew out a big breath, nodding as if assuring herself. Sending a venomous look at Roy's retreating back, she pursed her lips. "Just like Roy, trying to create problems where none exist." Then she licked her lips, a pained expression creasing her brow. "At least . . . I wish no problems existed between us, Petey."

Without thinking, Pete reached out and took her hand. He squeezed. "None that can't be fixed."

Relief broke over her face. The beauty of her innocent smile nearly tied his heart in a knot. How he wished he had the freedom to openly profess his love for her. But he couldn't—not without taking something precious away from her. He quickly released her hand and stumbled to his feet. "I . . . I have to go. I have a train to catch."

She rose, too. "A train? Where are you going?"

Out of the corner of his eye, he observed Roy in the far corner of the dining hall, watching them. The man no doubt would assume Pete was convincing Libby to consider him as a potential beau, so he probably should end the conversation quickly. Yet he didn't want to leave Libby's presence just yet. "To Clayton."

Her eyes flew wide. "You are? Why?"

"To see my . . . to visit the Leidigs."

❧

Libby gasped. Did Petey already know about Oscar Leidig sitting in a jail cell, awaiting execution? "You're going to see your brother?"

Petey looked confused. "My parents. I . . . hadn't thought about seeing my brothers or sisters."

So he didn't know. But maybe his parents intended to tell him. "Did they summon you?"

"It's my idea. Something I've needed to do for a long time." Petey sighed, and his gaze drifted away.

She darted around the table and touched his arm. He gave a start and looked down at her. Peering into his sad, haunted eyes, Libby felt as though she were looking once more at the artist's drawing of the courtroom scene. She couldn't let him go by himself. If Oscar Leidig was Petey's brother, then his parents would certainly tell Petey. She couldn't allow him to receive this news from people who cared so little for him they'd cast him aside when he was just a child.

"I'm going with you."

Petey shook his head. "You can't do that, Libby."

"Why not?"

"Several reasons." He flicked one finger upward. "I only have one train ticket."

"I can buy my own."

He put a second finger in the air. "You have assignments to do."

"I can work on them away from the campus."

Shaking his head, he held up three fingers. "It would be

unseemly for us to travel together, unchaperoned. I won't sully your reputation."

Libby suspected, based on Alice-Marie's scathing diatribe from a few days ago, that Libby's reputation was already in question by a few people on campus. But she didn't want to damage Petey's. Especially when he intended to become a minister. She bit down on her lower lip.

He put his hand on her shoulder. "I appreciate your willingness to go with me, but—"

An idea struck. "What if Alice-Marie came, too? Could she serve as chaperone? After all, you and Bennett and I all traveled together and no one questioned it. If there was a third person, it would eliminate ill conjecture, wouldn't it?"

Petey scratched his head. "Libby, I—"

"Her family lives in Clayton, too, and last weekend I . . . I offended them." The idea grew in merit the more she thought about it. Not only would she be where Petey needed her to be, she could set things right with Alice-Marie's family, which would end the uncomfortable icy silence between the girls. "If I returned with Alice-Marie, I'd be able to apologize to them and restore myself in their good graces. Please, Petey? Will you wait long enough for me to ask her? If she says no, then I'll—" She broke off, unwilling to finish the sentence. She wouldn't let him go alone. She'd follow on a later train, if she had to, but she wouldn't let him go alone.

He heaved a sigh. "Hurry and ask her. My train leaves at ten, and it's already past eight."

Joy filled Libby's heart. "I'll be right back." She dashed across the dining hall to where Alice-Marie sat with several girls from Kappa Kappa Gamma. They all sent unsmiling looks in her direction, but she ignored them and went straight to Alice-Marie. "Alice-Marie, I have a favor to ask."

The girl sniffed. "I'm quite certain the answer will be no, but go ahead and ask."

A part of her wanted to blast Alice-Marie for her self-important behavior, but Petey needed her. She could swallow her pride for Petey's sake. "Would you allow me to purchase train tickets for the two of us to travel to Clayton so I can apologize . . . in person . . . to your parents?"

Alice-Marie's haughty expression softened a smidgen. "Apologize?"

Libby nodded. "I was wrong to sneak away and then hide what I'd been doing." A flurry of whispers carried around the table. Libby remained focused on Alice-Marie rather than allowing the gossipy girls to distract her. "I would feel much better if I could make things right."

Alice-Marie raised one shoulder in a slow shrug. "I . . . suppose we could do that. I'm free this weekend."

"I want to go today."

Alice-Marie gawked at Libby. "Today? But it's Thursday. I have classes."

"We could make them up. This is important, Alice-Marie. It can't wait." She held her breath, her heart pounding, while she waited for Alice-Marie to decide. If they didn't leave until Saturday, it might be too late. Petey would gain the information another way.

"Well, you *do* owe my parents an apology, and I suppose I could make up my classes when I return. . . ."

Libby's breath whooshed out. "Thank you!" She grabbed her roommate's arm. "Hurry now. We need to pack. The train leaves at ten!"

While Libby tossed necessary items into a suitcase, Alice-Marie made up for her days of silence. Libby's ears rang from the girl's nonstop commentary on everything Libby had done wrong since the very first day of classes. Libby pretended to listen, nodding and agreeing, while rushing Alice-Marie across campus to meet Petey. Alice-Marie's tongue never stilled the entire cab ride, but her voice came to an abrupt halt when they reached the train station and found Bennett waiting on the steps of the depot with a suitcase dangling from his hand.

Libby bounded toward him. "What are you doing here?"

"Goin' to Clayton, of course. Didn't think you'd leave me out of the fun, did you?"

Alice-Marie fluttered her lashes. "Why Bennett Martin, you rascal. Libby didn't tell me you were accompanying us."

"Because I didn't know," Libby said. She suspected if she'd mentioned it, Alice-Marie wouldn't have hesitated to miss her classes.

Petey hitched forward. "How did you know we were going to Clayton? I didn't say anything to you."

Bennett shrugged. "Came by your room this morning to drop off the pen I borrowed, and—"

"Is that where my pen went?" Petey released a little grunt. "I didn't know you borrowed it."

"Now you do." Bennett laughed, clopping Petey on the arm. "I saw your suitcase on the bed, peeked in it, and found the train ticket."

"Bennett!" Alice-Marie looked scandalized. "You're a common snoop!"

"No, I'm an exceptional snoop," Bennett replied without an ounce of remorse. "I figured, why let Pete have all the fun? If he could skip out on classes, so could I. So I packed my bag and bought a ticket." He waved a rectangle of stiff paper. "I'm ready to go."

Libby squealed. "Tickets! I still need to buy mine and Alice-Marie's!"

"Better hurry." Bennett gave Libby a little push toward the

ticket window. "There's a long line, and the train'll board in less than half an hour."

Libby dashed to the window. As Bennett had indicated, several other travelers were already in line. She bit her nails and danced in place, watching the round clock on the wall while praying the train wouldn't leave without her. At last her turn arrived, and she handed the money to the tired-looking man behind the counter. Alice-Marie hovered at her shoulder, watching the transaction. The moment Libby had tickets in hand, Alice-Marie snatched one and hustled to the lobby.

Alice-Marie sank down beside Bennett on a long wooden bench, scooting close. She fanned herself with the ticket and grinned at Bennett. Libby could hardly believe this was the same girl who'd been giving her the cold shoulder all week. Being around Bennett had melted her frostiness completely.

Alice-Marie hunched her shoulders and giggled. "Isn't this exciting? It's like an adventure."

Sitting beside Alice-Marie, Libby decided she wouldn't have defined the trip as exciting. Perhaps nerve-racking. Or even heart-rending. But Alice-Marie didn't know the true purpose for this excursion.

"You must be certain to come by my house," Alice-Marie nearly purred, adjusting Bennett's lapel. "I'd adore the opportunity to introduce you to Mother and Daddy."

"Alice-Marie," Libby said, a sudden worry striking, "your parents won't be angry at us, will they, for arriving without any warning?" If Alice-Marie's parents wouldn't allow the girls to stay at their home, this trip might turn out to be a bigger adventure than Libby had imagined.

Alice-Marie placed her hand against her bodice and stared at Libby with wide eyes and open mouth. "Mother and Daddy would *never* turn me away, expected or not. And of course you'll be welcome to stay there, too, once they've accepted your apology." She assumed a pout. "But the boys will need to find other accommodations. My parents are welcoming but very traditional. They'd never allow someone of the male persuasion to reside under their roof while I'm there."

Bennett sent Libby an amused look, but she ignored it and turned to Petey. "How long do you think you'll need to stay in Clayton?"

Petey grimaced. "I'm not sure. Maybe just a day. It . . . depends."

"On what?" Alice-Marie chirped the question, seemingly unaware of Petey's pale, pinched face.

"On how things go," he answered so softly Libby almost didn't hear him over the voices of other waiting passengers and the hiss of steam engines outside on the track. But her heart wrenched at the anguish in his tone.

She started to rise, intending to sit beside him and offer a few words of encouragement, but before she could speak a blue-suited conductor stepped inside the waiting room and swung a brass bell. The room hushed as the man cupped his hand beside his mouth. "Boarding the ten-o'clock train for Clayton! Let's go, folks—time to board!"

CHAPTER TWENTY-THREE

P ete stood on the curb and looked again at the letter Jackson had sent. The words were smudged from being carried in his jacket pocket, but he could make them out. The address on the page matched the one etched into a flat stone on the front of the tall brick building across the street.

Although he'd itched to come straight to his parents' apartment building upon arriving in Clayton yesterday, he'd carefully chosen today's mid-morning arrival. Since his pa worked from noon to eight, he'd be home in the morning. Plus, if he came during school hours, he could avoid subjecting his younger siblings to an altercation. No sense in getting innocent children involved in his differences with their folks.

After depositing Alice-Marie and Libby at Alice-Marie's parents' fine home yesterday afternoon, he and Bennett had rented a room in a cheap, run-down hotel on the riverfront. Bennett had slept soundly, his snore rattling the windows, but Pete lay awake far into the night, too nervous and restless to sleep. Anticipation for the moment when he would confront his parents had robbed him of his sleep, but oddly he didn't feel tired this morning. He was ready.

Pete's pulse sped as he imagined his father slumped in a chair, drowsing away the hours prior to leaving for work, unaware that his oldest child planned to step back—albeit briefly—into his life. These last few hours of waiting had been the hardest.

Drawing in a fortifying breath, he stepped off the curb and crossed the street, his eyes traveling from the flat roof of the building to the cracked foundation. A slab of chipped concrete served as a porch. Two little boys with matching mops of blond hair sat on the edge of the slab, poking at a dead beetle with a stick. Frowning, Pete peeked at his pocket watch. Nine thirty. Why weren't these boys in school?

Uncertainty made him pause at the edge of the sidewalk. He'd counted on his parents being alone, no younger siblings underfoot tempting him to soften his words. Hardening his heart, he determined to proceed with his plan. He'd come too far to back out now. He'd ask his parents to send the youngsters outside for a while. If they refused, then he'd just have to shame Gunter and Berta in front of their other children.

Pete pushed the letter back into his pocket, smoothed the front of his suit jacket, and approached the concrete slab. Both boys looked up, fixing him with wary stares. Pete smiled at them. "Hello. Is there a school holiday today?"

For several seconds, neither boy spoke. Then the older one, who appeared to be nine or ten, set his chin at a challenging angle and peered at Pete through a fringe of heavy, unevenly cut bangs. "You a copper?"

Pete chuckled. "Me? No. Just a university student."

"Didn't think so. Never saw a one-legged copper."

The younger boy licked his chapped lips, his eyes pinned on Pete's peg leg. With his thick shock of blond hair and dirty face, he reminded Pete of himself at that age. The boy pointed at Pete's leg. "That hurt?"

The phantom pain that never completely disappeared stabbed Pete with its presence, but he forced a smile. "Not anymore." The little boy's shoulders heaved in apparent relief, and Pete warmed toward the child. He repeated his earlier question. "Did your school close for the day?"

The older boy crunched his lips to the side, as if determining whether or not to answer. Finally he gave his shaggy head a quick shake. "No. Just didn't go."

"How come?"

The boy used the tip of the stick to flip the beetle onto its back. "Didn't wanna."

"Don't your folks send you?"

The younger one continued to stare at Pete with round, unblinking eyes. He wrapped his scrawny arms around himself. Although they were well into autumn, the child was barefoot and had no jacket. Pete swallowed. Memories from the past—of being thrust into the cold without the protection of warm clothes or a full belly or even a tearful good-bye—stung. He rested his hand on his good knee and bent forward, smiling at the little boy. "You cold?"

The boy nodded wordlessly.

"Why don't you go inside? Get warmed up?"

The child's eyes flitted to his brother. The older one replied. "Ma told us to get. Pa's fractious today. Too much drinkin' last night. She'll call us when it's safe to come in." The detached recital pierced Pete deep in his soul. Children shouldn't live like this.

Pete jerked upright. "Well, your brother here needs a jacket and something on his feet. Don't you think you could go in and—"

"You sure you ain't a copper?" The older boy glared at Pete.

Pete looked directly into the boy's hostile face. "I'm not a copper. My name is Pete Leidig."

Both boys jolted, and the younger one's eyes flew wide. He grabbed his brother's arm and the stick went flying. "Dennis! You hear him? His name's the same as ours. Marta used to say we had a brother named Pete, but I never believed her." The child bounded to his feet, his hand curled over his brother's shoulder. He stared, awestruck, at Pete. "Mister, are you *really* Pete Leidig?"

The older boy—Dennis—brushed the young one's hand from his shoulder and rose. He pressed protectively in front of the smaller boy, his skinny shoulders squared. "Stay back, Lorenzo." He growled the warning, and Lorenzo remained behind his brother, but he tipped sideways and peeked out with curious blue eyes. Dennis crossed his arms over his chest. "If you're really Pete Leidig, then what's our folks' names?"

"My folks are Gunter and Berta. Who're yours?"

Lorenzo danced in place, tugging at Dennis's shirt. "That's our folks, too! See? He is our brother, Dennis! He is!"

"Shut up, Lorenzo." Dennis jabbed Lorenzo in the ribs with his elbow. The smaller boy yelped and fell silent. Dennis's eyes squinted into sullen slits. "Why're you here? You never come before—not in our whole lives."

Pete's chest ached. Anger, resentment, and an underlying fear shimmered in Dennis's eyes—emotions Pete understood all too well. A hardscrabble life had ingrained those emotions into the core of the boy's being, but none of those feeling belonged in a child's life. Why hadn't he sought out his siblings sooner? He might have been able to help . . . somehow.

Swallowing the bitter taste of regret, he said, "I didn't come because I didn't live in Clayton. I lived in a town called Shay's Ford."

Lorenzo rose up on tiptoe to peer over Dennis's shoulder. "Why din'cha live with us?"

Dennis didn't hush his brother this time but looked at Pete expectantly.

Should Pete tell these boys how their father had sent him out to fend for himself? Knowing would only add to their insecurity. He didn't want to lie, but he couldn't tell the truth. Instead, he asked a question. "Are your other brothers and sisters here, too?"

Lorenzo answered. "Marta ain't—she's married. An' Oscar, he's gone, too. Ma don't know where. But Wendell an' Orel an' Elma live here. They went on to school, though."

Pete figured Marta must be seventeen now. He only had vague memories of Oscar, Wendell, and Orel as runny-nosed toddlers. Elma had been just a newborn when he'd left. He tried to picture what they might look like now, but no images would form. The thought saddened him. He had siblings—seven of them—and they were all strangers to him. All because of Gunter and Berta Leidig's hardheartedness.

Lord, give me strength. Despite the fury stirring his middle, Pete managed to speak kindly. "I need to talk to your folks. Can you take me to your apartment?"

Lorenzo turned and darted for the doors, but Dennis reached out and grabbed for Lorenzo's shirt. "We have to stay outside!"

A soft *rip* sounded. Lorenzo cried out, "Oh no!" He examined his shirt, and tears filled his eyes. "Look what you done, Dennis! Pa's gonna be so mad—he'll give me a whippin'!"

"Stop sniveling," Dennis ordered, but he bit on the corner of his lips, his eyes reflecting fear.

Pete moved toward the younger boy. "Let me see that, Lorenzo." Pete examined the shirt and smiled. "It's just a tear in the seam. This can be fixed easily. Don't worry."

But neither boy looked reassured. One plump tear rolled down

Lorenzo's face, leaving a clean track on his dusty cheek. "Pa'll whip me for sure."

Pete glanced toward the building. He had to visit his parents today; he needed to return to Chambers tomorrow.

But how could he leave the boys to face their father's wrath? He felt partially responsible for the damage done to Lorenzo's shirt. With a sigh, he curled his hand over Lorenzo's shoulder.

"Tell you what, partner. I know how to fix that shirt."

Dennis squinted one eye. "Men don't do stitchin'."

Pete laughed. "Haven't you ever seen a tailor?"

The boys stared at him blankly. Their clothes were probably hand-me-downs from older brothers. Why would they ever have visited a tailor's shop? He told them, "The lady I lived with taught me to stitch so I could sew on my own buttons and fix things like rips." For the first time, he appreciated Isabelle's insistence that he learn to wield a needle and thread. "Come with me to my hotel, and we'll get your shirt fixed. Then I'll come back here to visit your folks, all right?"

Without a moment's hesitation, Lorenzo slipped his grubby hand into Pete's. Pleased more than he could understand by the child's trust, Pete turned to Dennis. He sensed Dennis wouldn't be so easily won. "You coming?"

Dennis drew in his lips and stood unmoving for several seconds. Then he kicked at a stone on the ground. "Ain't gonna let you take off with Lorenzo without makin' sure you bring 'im back. Yeah, I'm comin'."

Pete held out his free hand, but Dennis ignored it and crowded on the other side of Lorenzo. With his little brothers scuffing along beside him, Pete headed for the corner to hail a cab.

"Unless you're that boy's court-appointed representative or a family member, you ain't gonna visit him." The scowling guard folded his arms over his portly belly. His jowls quivered as he added, "Now scoot on outta here, missy, before I arrest you for bein' a public nuisance."

Libby twisted her lips to the side, knowing such a charge would be dismissed without a second glance. The basement of the courthouse was hardly a public gathering spot. Besides, she'd come a long way to see Oscar Leidig, and one overweight jail guard was not going to best her. Lifting her pad of paper and pencil, she smiled sweetly over its top edge. "Very well. Your name, please?"

The man's forehead puckered into a series of deep furrows. "Why?"

"I'll need it for the article."

"Article?"

"Why yes, sir." Libby aimed the pencil tip at the paper. "I'm sure my readers will be very interested in the name of the man responsible for guarding such a vicious felon as Oscar Leidig."

The guard scratched his flubbery cheek. "You say you got readers?"

She nodded. "Yes. I'm a journalist." *At least, I will be.* "And I'm here to document this case. Of course, the article will be dreadfully short and no doubt relegated to the last page of the paper unless I have the opportunity to interview the prisoner, but . . ." She dangled her bait, watching to see if the man would pounce.

The guard looked her up and down, his lips curled in skepticism. "You're awful young to be a reporter."

Libby drew herself as tall as possible and pinned the man with a regal look. "I can assure you I am very qualified. As a student from the University of Southern Missouri, my publishing credits are quite expansive." She'd stretched the truth, but how else would she convince this bulbous-nosed dunderhead to let her talk to Oscar Leidig? "So . . . your name?"

Her heart pounded. Would vanity reign supreme or would he send her away? *Please, please. I must speak to this boy.* She thought her lungs might explode while she waited for the man to make up his mind.

"It's Holloway. Wallace Holloway."

Hiding her smile, Libby dutifully recorded his name. "Wallace Holloway. And you've been employed with the Clayton justice system for how long?"

His chest puffed. "Seven years." Leaning forward, he added in a whisper, "But this is the youngest murderer I ever seen come through. He's a bad'un, I tell you. A real bad'un."

Libby's mouth went dry at the man's statement. Did she dare proceed? Yes, she must gather every fact she could.

She assumed a friendly yet professional air. "I know my readers will be most interested in your bravery in protecting society from this dangerous criminal." She tapped her chin with the pencil. "Of course, the article would hold much more interest if we could determine how this young man became so hardened at such an early age. Perhaps the information I uncover today might assist those who work with our youth, even provide ideas for preventing another young man from making a similar mistake."

Pacing back and forth in the dank concrete-block hallway, Libby hugged the pad and crunched her forehead as if deep in thought. "Just think, Mr. Holloway . . . someday, there could be a criminal-prevention program named in honor of the man who guarded Oscar Leidig. The Holloway Plan." She scrawled the title in the air with her pencil, then swung a beaming smile at the man. "Why, you could become famous!"

"The Holloway Plan?" The man's eyes glazed. Then he shook

his head. "But I don't have no ideas on how to keep these young mutts from performin' crimes."

"That's where Oscar Leidig comes in." Libby scurried to the man's side. "He certainly knows why he was in the drugstore with a gun. He knows what led him to that point in time. He can tell me . . . er, us . . . everything we need to know." She pointed at the guard with her pencil. "But we can't name the prevention plan for *him*. It would be indecent to credit him—after all, he's a criminal. You're a respected lawman . . ."

Defining a jail guard as a lawman took liberties with accuracy, but her words had found their target. The man threw back his shoulders and patted the gun at his hip. "You betcha, missy."

"So of course we'll give the plan your name," Libby finished. "Now—" she inched toward the barred cell door—"all that's left is to ask questions of Mr. Leidig."

Mr. Holloway lurched into her path. "You ain't goin' in that cell."

"But, Mr. Holloway, how can I possibly—"

"You ain't goin' in alone." He pulled a ring of keys from his pocket. "Boy like that . . . who knows what he'd do if he had you all to hisself in there. Nope. I'm goin' in with you!"

CHAPTER TWENTY-FOUR

Bennett roused and sat up in the lumpy hotel bed when the doorknob squeaked, signaling Pete's return. Yawning, he greeted, "Hey, Pete, that didn't take long. I figured—" Frowning, he pointed at Pete's scruffy young companions. "Who're they?"

Pete put his hand on the head of the smaller boy and gave the other one a gentle push into the room. "Dennis and Lorenzo. Boys, this is my friend Bennett."

The boys stared at him, wide-eyed.

"What're they doing here?"

Pete looked at the pair, a funny smile on his lips. "They're . . . my brothers."

Bennett shot off the bed as if fired from a cannon. "Brothers?" Why had Pete brought them to the hotel room? Surely he didn't intend to *keep* them!

Pete guided the smallest boy to the table and chair in the corner, sat down, and stood the boy between his knees. "Lorenzo's shirt has a tear. We're going to repair it." He turned to the older boy, who was standing next to the door with a sullen look on his face. "Dennis, bring me the bag, please. I need the needle and thread we bought."

Dennis shuffled forward, dropped the little paper bag within Pete's reach, and then returned to lean against the door. The kid looked ready to bolt at any minute. If he did, Bennett wouldn't stop him.

Bennett inched closer to the table. "You brought him here to fix his shirt?" Had Pete gone completely batty?

"That's right." Pete nipped off a length of thread and squinted at the needle. He jabbed the thread through the eye and then tied a knot at the dangling end. "All right, Lorenzo, off with that shirt."

Lorenzo backed away, shaking his head wildly. "Huh-uh."

Pete chuckled softly. "I can't fix it while you're wearing it." He held out his hand. "Come here."

But again, the little boy shook his head. "No."

Bennett rolled his eyes. "For pete's sake . . ." The sooner that shirt was fixed, the sooner Pete would get these kids out of there. The last thing they needed was a couple of dirty-faced urchins underfoot. He reached for the kid. "Gimme your shirt so Pete can—"

"No!" The boy raced to his brother.

Dennis shot Bennett a murderous glare. "Leave 'im alone."

Bennett folded his arms and laughed. "Well, well, aren't you the feisty one?"

Pete clumsily rose and stepped in front of Bennett, but he didn't advance on the boys. "Lorenzo, I don't want to hurt you. I might poke you with the needle if you don't take off your shirt."

"He ain't takin' it off." Dennis's eyes snapped, daring Pete to argue.

Bennett had never seen such a stubborn kid. Reminded him of himself at that age.

The boy stuck out his jaw. "It's the only shirt he's got. You don't give it back, what's he s'posed to do? Run around without?"

"He's running around without shoes," Bennett muttered, "so what difference does it make?" The boy's feet were chapped, the toenails rimmed with dirt. He'd been going shoeless for quite a while.

"Can go to school without shoes. Can't go without a shirt." Dennis plunked his fists on his hips. "So you either fix it with him in it or we're goin' home."

Another wail left Lorenzo's lips. "I can't go home, Dennis! Pa'll skin me for tearin' my shirt!"

Pete limped forward a couple of steps, keeping a distance between himself and the boys. Bennett wished he'd just grab the kid and take the shirt, but instead Pete spoke in a soft voice, the way he might talk to a spooked horse. "Lorenzo, all I want to do is fix your shirt for you. I promise I won't keep it. What would I do with it?" He held his arms outward. "It wouldn't fit me."

A grin twitched Lorenzo's lips. "You're too big for it."

Pete laughed as if the kid had said something clever. "That's right." He returned to the table. "So come on over here. You can watch me. Then the next time your shirt gets a tear, you'll know how to fix it yourself."

"But I don't got a needle and thread." The boy slowly scuffed his way to Pete and began unbuttoning the ragged shirt.

"Once I'm done, I'll give you the needle and thread."

The little boy's mouth dropped. "For real? For me to keep?"

"To keep." Pete took the shirt and turned it inside-out.

"My own needle . . ."

Bennett couldn't hold back a snort. Pete wasn't offering the

213

kid anything of value, like an erector set or a pair of roller skates. Why would he get all excited over a needle and thread?

Lorenzo rested his palms on the table and leaned close, watching Pete push the needle in and out, in and out. The boy's ribs showed, and some strange pale marks on his back—fading welts?—captured Bennett's attention. A chill went down his spine when the little boy said, "Nobody never gave me nothin' before . . . not for keeps."

Bennett glanced at Dennis, who stared unsmilingly in Pete's direction, seeming to guard his little brother with his eyes. Sinking onto the mattress, Bennett considered for the first time that there could be worse things than growing up without knowing who his parents were.

᯼

An hour after entering the jail cell, Libby thanked Mr. Holloway for his time and scampered up the dimly lit staircase leading from the basement. The jail area of the rock building had been cool and damp, carrying the musty odors of mold and something that reminded her of an outhouse on a hot summer day. She burst onto the street, sucking in great drafts of fresh, crisp air to clear her nostrils of the unpleasant odors.

Her chest ached. She could escape the dreariness of that underground cell, but Oscar couldn't. "Oh, that poor boy . . ." The back of her nose stung as an image of Oscar Leidig's hopeless face filled her memory. She wasn't sure which haunted her more—Oscar's despair or Mr. Holloway's apathy toward the young man. While she'd carefully recorded Oscar's version of the events leading up to the death of the drugstore clerk, the guard had sat with his hands linked on his belly, his expression stoic or—worse—bored. The man's only concern was that she spell his name correctly.

"No one cares." She whispered the words to the passing

pedestrians, their mindless busyness seeming to prove her thoughts correct. Well, now that she was armed with the facts, *somebody* was going to care! She would not let Petey's brother die without a fight.

She hailed a passing cab and gave the driver Alice-Marie's address. She needed to find Petey and share her findings—but Petey didn't have the power to set his brother free. Alice-Marie's father, however, might. He was a respected businessman and a pillar of his church; his voice would count when raised against injustice. Libby hugged her notebook to her chest and willed the afternoon to hurry by. She'd speak to Mr. Daley when he returned home for lunch. There was no time to lose—Oscar's hanging was scheduled to take place on December 18, only a month away.

The cab pulled up in front of Alice-Marie's stately home. Libby handed the cab driver a quarter and hopped out. She took the steps two at a time. Just as she reached for the brass door handle, she heard Alice-Marie's voice.

"Elisabet Conley, there you are running again. Will you ever learn to behave like a lady?"

Libby spun toward the sound and located Alice-Marie sitting on a wicker chair in the porch's attached gazebo. She hurried over and dropped into a matching chair. A half-empty teacup painted with delicate blue forget-me-nots sat on a wooden tray on a wicker table between the chairs. The vast difference between the horror of Oscar's jail cell and Alice-Marie's pristine world almost made Libby dizzy.

"Did you get the information you needed to finish your article?"

Libby felt a twinge of guilt. She'd led Alice-Marie and her parents to believe she'd left their home to gather information for a school assignment. Mrs. Daley had erroneously assumed Libby's silence when questioned about her whereabouts resulted from embarrassment of her social faux pas. After all, what girl of breeding would leave a social event prior to bidding a polite farewell to the special guest?

Maelle would be disappointed to know Libby had engaged in falsehoods, but allowing the Daleys to hold to their assumptions had made it easy to continue the charade when leaving the house that morning. In answer to Alice-Marie's question, she said, "I have the information, but there's still much work to do."

"So you'll be writing this afternoon?"

"That depends."

"On what?"

Libby took a deep breath. "Whether or not I can secure your father's assistance."

Alice-Marie took a sip of tea, her eyebrows high. "How can Daddy help?"

Instead of answering that question, Libby posed one of her own. "Will he be home soon?"

"Around twelve-thirty, Mother said. We'll have luncheon at one."

Libby groaned. She might burst if she had to wait that long!

Alice-Marie nibbled the edge of a round, crisp cookie. She pushed the little plate holding three more cookies closer to Libby. "Have one—they're wonderful. Lemon butter cookies, the last of the season, since Cook won't be able to get lemons again until next spring."

Libby shook her head. She couldn't eat. Not until she'd unburdened herself. "Alice-Marie, do you read the newspaper?"

She wrinkled her nose. "What on earth for?" She took another dainty bite and brushed crumbs from her skirt.

"To find out what's going on in the world." Libby leaned forward. "Did you know, right here in Clayton, a sixteen-year-old—a mere boy!—is jailed and awaiting execution for a murder he didn't commit?"

Alice-Marie's mouth dropped open. "Truly? But that's despicable!"

Libby nodded wholeheartedly. "It is. The story I was working on when I left your house last weekend involves him." She couldn't bring herself to mention the boy was Petey's brother. "I'm hoping your father might be able to help me find a way to prove this boy's innocence."

"Libby, dear, Daddy isn't a lawyer."

Her patronizing tone irritated Libby, but she swallowed a sharp retort. She needed Alice-Marie's cooperation right now. "But he is a businessman, so he's certainly acquainted with lawyers."

"Of course he is." Alice-Marie broke off a crumbly bit of cookie then carried the morsel to her mouth. "Daddy owns four different businesses in town. He has two lawyers on his payroll who make certain everything is handled appropriately." She giggled. "To be honest, I know very little about what he does. Daddy never discusses business at home. He says it's gauche. And that's fine. I don't need to know about his business dealings . . . as long as I continue to receive my allowance." She popped the last of the cookie into her mouth.

Alice-Marie's superficiality was becoming more glaring by the moment. What made some people so unaware, so uncaring? She hoped Alice-Marie's father possessed more sensitivity.

At that moment, a rattling *chug-chug-chug* carried to her ears. She sat up in eagerness, looking toward the street. Alice-Marie sent a smile in Libby's direction. "Here's Daddy now. I guess he decided to come home early."

Libby joined Alice-Marie at the top of the stairs while Mr. Daley parked the Model T at the curb. He came up the walk whistling and broke into a smile when he spotted the girls. "Hello, Alice-Marie . . . Elisabet. Enjoying the fresh air?"

Alice-Marie slipped her hand through her father's elbow when he reached the porch. "Daddy, Libby was hoping you'd come home early. She has something important to discuss with you."

"Oh?" He fixed Libby with an attentive look.

"Yes, sir. You see—" Libby paused, memories of her time with Oscar Leidig crowding her mind. Where should she start? She opened her mouth and blurted, "Today I talked to a boy named Oscar Leidig, and—"

Mr. Daley's face contorted into an angry mask. He threw his hand upward, bringing Libby's sentence to a halt. "Kindly do not mention that name."

"S-sir?" Libby pressed her hand to her bodice. Her heart pounded beneath her palm.

The man's face mottled with red, and he growled through gritted teeth. "He is a lowdown, worthless excuse for a human being."

Alice-Marie gasped. "Daddy!"

Mr. Daley wiped his hand over his face. "Excuse me for being so harsh. But that young man's actions had an ill effect on every business owner in Clayton. Why, what if he'd chosen to barge into one of my businesses instead? It could be one of my employees dead by his gun."

He drew in a shuddering breath, and the high color in his cheeks slowly returned to normal. He patted Alice-Marie's hand. "Don't you worry, Alice-Marie. The boy will pay and pay dearly for taking the life of that drugstore clerk." Under his breath, he added, "As far as I'm concerned, hanging's too good for Oscar Leidig."

Chapter Twenty-five

Standing in the hallway outside the apartment where his parents lived, dressed in his fine suit with his hair neatly brushed and his one shoe buffed to new-penny shine, Pete felt as though he'd rushed backward through time. He was once again seven years old with a teacher-starred arithmetic paper in his hand, hoping Pa would beam with pride. He shook his head, dispelling the long-ago image. He wasn't there to make his parents proud; he was there to shame them.

"Pete? We goin' in?" Lorenzo tugged at Pete's jacket. His fingers—freshly washed in the sink at the hotel—held tight to the brown paper bag containing the needle and spool of gray thread.

Pete managed to give the little boy a wobbly smile. "Maybe you should go in without me, Lorenzo. Suppertime's coming, and your . . . our ma isn't expecting me. She might feel obligated to ask me to stay and eat, and then there won't be enough for everybody."

Dennis huffed. "*Never* enough."

Pete's conscience panged at his brother's comment. He'd taken the boys to a little diner for lunch, and they'd wolfed down fried egg sandwiches and thick vegetable soup. Then they'd eyed a tall chocolate cake under a glass dome, but Pete had worried his limited budget wouldn't stretch far enough to cover cake and another train ticket, so he'd ignored their pleading looks. Now he wished he'd treated them to cake, even if it meant limping all the way back to Chambers on his peg leg.

"You two go on in," Pete encouraged, giving Lorenzo a gentle push toward the door.

"But I thought you wanted to visit." Confusion puckered Lorenzo's boyish face.

"I do want to visit, but I need to see both Pa and Ma." The names slipped out easily, catching Pete by surprise. "But Pa's not home right now, is he?"

The pair shook their heads in unison. "Reckon he's workin' at the brewery," Lorenzo chirped.

"So I'll have to come back later."

Dennis cast a furtive glance at Pete. "But . . . you're comin' back . . . right?"

Pete wished he could wrap Dennis in a hug that would heal all the insecurity and hurt of his brief life. But he sensed if he reached out, the boy would retreat. Instead, he leaned down to look eye-to-eye with his brother. "I promise, Dennis. I'll come back." He'd keep that promise no matter what it took.

For long seconds, Dennis peered unsmilingly into Pete's eyes. Then, without a word, he grabbed Lorenzo's arm and hauled him inside. Pete waited until the door closed behind his brothers before heading out to the street. He paused on the slab where he'd met the boys that morning, trying to decide what to do. He could go to the hotel and relax until his pa got off work, then come back; or he could sit on the bench outside the little market across the street and wait. If he waited, he'd spare himself the cost of a cab ride. He decided to wait. Only three hours until the end of Pa's shift.

The sun had slipped downward, and Pete buttoned his jacket to protect himself from the cool, city-scented breeze. He settled onto the wood-slatted bench and observed people passing. Some scurried, some slogged. Most sent curious glances in his direction, but few smiled and none stopped to talk. As the supper hour came and went, the scent of ripening fruit from the boxes in front of the market made his stomach growl. So he purchased a rosy apple and a small wedge of cheese from the kind-faced older lady behind the counter inside then returned to the bench to eat his simple supper.

The activity on the street slowed as evening fell. Pete checked his watch—seven-thirty. Only another half hour before Pa got off work. Would he come straight home, or would he stop off at a tavern? With it being Friday, it could be payday. Pete pinched the crisply ironed crease in his pant leg. Was he wasting his time sitting there watching for Pa?

A tall, rail-thin man in a stained white bib apron stepped out onto the shadowed sidewalk, broom in hand, and began busily sweeping dust and dried leaves toward the curb. The straw bristles came within inches of Pete's foot. Pete tucked his legs backward to avoid having dust tossed across his shoe. His wooden leg scraped against the cracked sidewalk, making his stump tingle. Automatically, he reached to massage his leg.

The broom ceased its motion, and Pete's gaze followed the broom handle to the man's face. The man offered a sympathetic grimace. "Did I hurt'cha? Didn't mean to."

"No, you didn't hurt me." Pete cupped his knee, ignoring the persistent distant ache in his stump. "I can move if I'm in your way."

The man waved a callused hand. "Nah. Never sweep under the bench anyway, no matter how much my wife chides me about it. What difference does it make? Nobody sits under there." He chuckled briefly, and then his eyes narrowed. "You new around here?"

Pete nodded.

"Thought so. Don't get too many gentlemen like yourself in this part o' the city." His eyes took in Pete's suit. "Mostly workin' class. A few bums." He snorted. "Too many bums." Then he tipped his head, his gray eyebrows forming a V. "Wasn't for them fancy duds, though, I might mistake you for one of 'em. Lowest of the low lives right over there with his wife an' a whole pack o' young'uns." He pointed to the apartment building where Pete's family lived. "You look quite a bit like him."

Pete's mouth went dry. "That right?"

"Yup. But you wouldn't wanna be associated with that lot. Sends his kids over here to steal from the stands." Shaking his head, the man put the broom to work again. "'Course, I don't turn 'em in to the coppers. As my Norma keeps tellin' me, they're just kids doin' what their old man tells 'em to do. 'Sides that, we don't feel right lettin' a kid go hungry. . . ."

Pete swallowed, his belly twisting at the thought of little Lorenzo sneaking over to snatch an apple or peach out of hunger— or for fear of Pa. "That's kind of you."

The man shrugged, stacking both hands on the rounded top of the broom handle. "Least I can do." He swiped his hand down the front of his grimy apron and then stuck it out to Pete. "By the way, I'm Keith—Keith Branson."

Pete pushed to his feet and shook the man's hand. "Peter . . . Rowley." His conscience pinched, but he reasoned that after this weekend he *would* be Pete Rowley. Surely it didn't hurt to try out his new name? "It's nice to meet you, Mr. Branson."

"Thank ya, Peter. An' call me Keith—everybody does. So what brings you down here?" He set his broom to work again.

Pete licked his lips. While chatting would make the time pass more quickly, he didn't want to tell this stranger the purpose of his visit. He chose a vague response. "Taking care of some long-overdue business."

"Does it have anything to do with the Leidig youngsters?"

Pete pulled out his handkerchief and coughed into it. "Why do you ask?"

Pausing in his work, Keith flashed a grin. "Saw you headin' off earlier with the two littlest boys. Kinda hard to miss, you in that fine suit an' all." He gripped his whiskery chin between his thumb and pointer finger. "Might I be hopin' somebody's finally gonna do somethin' to help them kids?"

Stepping near the man, Pete dropped his voice to a near whisper. Even though the sidewalk was deserted, he felt the need for secrecy. "What kind of help do they need?"

"What kind?" Keith blasted a humorless laugh. "Every kind! They're always dressed in rags, always lookin' hungry . . . Half the time them little ones spend their day playin' in the street 'stead o' goin' to school. My Norma worries herself sick over 'em. Only a matter o' time an' they'll *all* be in big trouble with the law."

He jabbed his finger at Pete. "I seen purple marks on them kids, too. More'n once. Haven't said nothin' to Norma about it. She'd prob'ly march on over there an' apply a fryin' pan to the side o' that man's head, an' then she'd be in trouble." He scuffed the worn toe of his boot on the sidewalk. " 'Sides, a man's got a right to discipline his own kids like he sees fit. Even the Good Book says 'spare the rod and spoil the child.' Folks'd say we shouldn't be interferin', an' most times I'd say they're right."

Shaking his head, he wrapped his hands tight around the broom handle. Pete got the impression he wished the broom were Gunter

Leidig's neck. "But to tell you the truth, Peter Rowley, I don't think them bruises are teachin' bruises. They're left by a mean drunk who takes his mad at the world out on his young'uns. An' whatever anybody else says, I say that ain't right. So—" Keith squared his shoulders and looked Pete straight in the face—"you gonna do anything?"

Pete's knees went weak as helplessness washed over him. "Keith, I'd like to help, but I'm not what you think. I'm just a university student, not a welfare officer or a policeman. I don't know what I can do."

"Oh." Keith's face sagged with disappointment. "Well . . ." Turning, he gave the broom's bristles a final half-hearted push across the pavement. "Sorry I bothered ya then. Just thought since you took off with them boys earlier today, you might know . . ." His voice trailed off as he seemed to focus on something in the distance. He stepped to the curb, his gaze narrowing.

Pete limped over beside him. "What is it?"

Keith's lips pursed as if he'd tasted something sour. "Speak o' the devil, there he comes." He balled one fist on his hip. "Gunter Leidig himself. But praise be, he ain't staggerin', which means he's sober. Maybe them kids'll have some peace tonight." Propping the broom on his shoulder, Keith bid Pete good-bye and stepped inside the market.

Pete's heartbeat thudded in his ears. His father strode up the sidewalk, his head low and shoulders slumped. The streetlamp exposed the lank, thinning hair and sallow complexion of a tired old man. The years hadn't been kind to Gunter Leidig.

While Pete watched, his pa grabbed the rickety railing and heaved himself onto the cement stoop. After eleven long years, Pete finally could confront his father. Face-to-face. Man-to-man.

But he didn't move.

Go! Catch up to him! The inner prodding stirred him to action.

Pete stumbled onto the cobblestone street, opening his mouth to call out. But before any sound left his lips, a horse-drawn cab clattered around the corner and halted in front of the apartment, blocking his way. Grunting in annoyance, he stepped around the cab in time to see a young woman alight. She dropped a coin in the cab driver's hand and then turned. The streetlamp illuminated her features. Pete's jaw dropped.

"Libby! What are you doing here?"

"Petey!" Libby dashed forward and grasped his lapels. "I found you. Thank goodness. Bennett said you'd be here, and he gave me the address, but he wasn't sure he remembered it correctly."

Pete glanced up. His father had disappeared inside the apartment building. He released a groan of frustration. Taking Libby by the shoulders, he led her to the corner of the building, out of the sight of anyone who might peek from an upstairs window. "Why aren't you at Alice-Marie's?"

Even in the shadows, he saw color flood her cheeks. "I . . . I sneaked out."

"Libby!"

"I needed to talk to you. So when Alice-Marie and I went up to our rooms after dinner, I told Alice-Marie I was going to take a long bath, and then I sneaked down the maid's stairs and out the back door."

Pete slapped his forehead. "Libby, you are bound and determined to cause trouble." Catching her hand, he dragged her to the curb. "Well, you're going right back."

"No!" She wriggled loose of his grasp. "Petey, you've got to listen to me. There's something you need to know before you see your parents."

He tapped his peg against the ground, trying to stay patient. "All right, but hurry. You've got to get back before they miss you. What is it?"

"It's about your brother Oscar."

Immediately, a fuzzy picture of a round-cheeked youngster with curling butter-yellow hair appeared in Pete's memory.

"He's in jail, Petey, accused of murder."

The sweet picture of innocence shattered. He grabbed Libby's shoulders again, but this time as a means of supporting himself. Surely he'd misunderstood. "M-murder?"

The empathetic pain in Libby's eyes confirmed he'd heard correctly. "I saw it in the paper and went to investigate. Under the pretext of writing an article for the newspaper, I spent an hour with him today. Petey, he's so young and so scared. And he says he didn't do it—says it was someone else, but the court found him guilty, so . . . he's been sentenced to hang." She pulled in a shuddering breath and clung to his wrists. "Petey, I'm so sorry." The last words choked out, as if carried on tears.

Pete found himself gripping Libby's shoulders so fiercely she winced, but he couldn't seem to let go and she made no move to pull away. The market owner—Keith Branson—had indicated his family needed help, but their needs went far beyond Pete's ability to assist them.

"We have to help your brother, Petey. If he's innocent, we can't let him hang." Libby squeezed his wrists. "I asked for Mr. Daley's help, but being a business owner himself, his sympathies reside with the dead clerk. He isn't willing to listen. Judging by Mr. Daley's reaction, I'm not sure anyone else here will reach out to Oscar. So it's up to us."

The same helplessness he'd felt when talking to Keith struck again, harder than ever. His knees trembled. With staggering steps, he made his way to the stoop and sat. The cold concrete penetrated to his flesh, and he shivered. Libby perched beside him, taking his hands.

His thoughts bounced hither and thither until they were a

muddled mess: Oscar jailed for a heinous crime, his younger brothers practicing thievery to combat their hunger, all of them bearing the marks of Gunter Leidig's drunken rages . . . So many things wrong. How could he possibly change any of it?

Eyes closed, he clung to Libby's hands, seeking strength.

Eventually he looked into her pale, expectant face. Tears blurred her sweet image. "As a preacher, I'll be expected to minister to people—to meet their needs. But I'm helpless against problems like these. I can't fix them. . . . Libby, I don't know what to do."

Her fingers slipped between his, the palm-to-palm contact firm and warm and encouraging. Her breath kissed his cheek when she whispered, "Yes you do, Petey. Pray."

Chapter Twenty-six

When Petey's eyes slid closed, Libby closed hers, too, and she listened to his prayer, repeating each phrase in her heart. He asked for strength for Oscar, wisdom for himself, and justice from the court system. She stumbled over his final request. Justice— did that mean meting out punishment? Sometimes the punishment was more severe than what was warranted. Eyes scrunched closed, her hands holding tight to Petey's, she willed, *Even more than justice, let compassion reign, God.*

Petey ended the prayer on a ragged note of thanksgiving, and Libby opened her eyes. He offered her a weak smile. "You need to go back to Alice-Marie's now. Let's hail a cab."

She rose when he did, but she resisted moving to the curb. "Can't I stay with you?" He would surely go up to his parents' apartment now, and she wanted to be with him.

"No, Libby. I need to do this myself."

"Please? I promise I won't say a word. I won't interfere in

any way, no matter what." If she had to bite on her tongue and sit on her hands the whole time, she'd keep her promise. "After talking to Oscar . . . and hearing everything he said about your father . . ." She swallowed, fear making perspiration form across her back. Could she face this man she envisioned as an unfeeling monster? "I would feel better if I went up with you. I don't think you should see him alone."

"And what are you going to tell Alice-Marie? She won't believe you took a two-hour bath."

Libby hung her head. "It will probably end any hope of them forgiving me or trusting me again, but I'll tell them the truth. That I sneaked over here to tell you about your brother."

Petey cringed. "My brother . . . the convicted murderer." Letting his head drop back, he released a heavy sigh. "Alice-Marie will probably tell everyone on campus about this—you know how she likes to talk. Everyone will find out about Oscar. What if that prevents me from becoming a minister?"

"That won't happen!"

"How can you be so sure?"

"Because . . . because . . ." Libby spluttered for a reason. Her conversation with Petey in the barn on Matt and Lorna's wedding day flitted through her mind. Although he'd crushed her with his words then, she now said them back to him. "Because you've been called to it, and God will make sure it happens."

His smile rewarded her. "Thank you, Libby."

"You're welcome. Now . . ." She clasped her hands and pressed her knuckles to her chin. "Are you going to let me go with you when you see your folks?"

To her surprise, he laughed. "I think it would be easier to give in to you than to keep arguing." He took her hand and turned toward the building. "When we're finished here, I'll go with you to Alice-Marie's and see if I can help smooth any ruffled feathers."

Hand-in-hand, they made their way up a narrow, dark stairway littered with trash. Libby steeled herself against the mingled odors of sweat, overcooked cabbage, and sewer. How could people live this way? Although she'd often thought Mrs. Rowley too meticulous about housekeeping, she now appreciated the clean, fresh-smelling home the woman had provided. She vowed her own home—when she had one—would be a pleasant place for everyone who entered.

"This is it." Petey gestured to a door to the right of the second-floor landing. Murmuring voices came from behind the door. One deep and gruff-sounding, and one high-pitched, almost whiny. Petey sucked in a big breath, lifted his hand, and banged his fist against the scarred wood three times.

"Who is it?" the deeper voice boomed.

Petey cleared his throat and leaned close to the door. The grip on her hand tightened. "It's Pete, Pa. Your son."

A long silence fell. Then someone barked, "I got no son named Pete. Go away."

A woman's voice wailed, a man's voice ordered her to silence, and soft sobbing carried into the hallway.

Petey pressed his palm to the door. "I'm not going anywhere until you talk to me." His voice sounded sure, strong, but his hand within hers trembled. Libby gave it a reassuring squeeze. He glanced at her briefly, thanking her with his eyes, and added, "I can stand out here all night if need be. You'll have to walk past me in the morning, so you might as well open up."

A child's voice cried, "Let 'im in, Pa! He said he'd come back! He promised!"

"Shut up, boy."

Both Pete and Libby cringed when the sound of flesh connecting with flesh filtered through the door and a child cried out in pain. The clomp of feet on the floor followed, and then the door was jerked open. Libby longed to throw herself in front of Petey when a large, scowling man in dirty long johns and faded brown trousers lurched into the hall. But she'd promised not to interfere, so she held tight to Petey's hand and remained rooted in place.

The man's graying hair hung in thin strands across his high forehead. Dark bags underlined his red-rimmed eyes, and deep furrows lined each side of his mouth. He braced one hand on the doorjamb and spent several seconds examining Petey from his head to his feet. He gave a barely discernible jerk when his gaze reached the floor and located Petey's peg leg, but then his eyes took the same lingering journey upward until he looked into his son's face. A sneering half smile curled his lips.

"Look at this! Quite the fancy man." Mr. Leidig laughed—a growling, menacing sound. "Boy, you can't be no son o' mine. Not in duds like that an' a piece o' wood where a foot oughta be. Run, er, stump along now."

Libby gasped at the man's callousness, but Petey didn't even flinch. When Mr. Leidig stepped backward and gave the door a shove to close it, Petey darted forward and stopped it with his good foot. The door bounced against his shoe and flew open again. The man, halfway across the floor, spun around and gaped at Petey in surprise.

Petey stepped over the threshold into the small, dingy room, bringing Libby with him. "I came to see you, Pa, and I'm going to have my say."

Mr. Leidig balled his fists. "You get out o' here."

"I will not."

To the left, a door cracked open and two little boys peeked out. Mr. Leidig waved his fist at them. "Get back in there!" The door closed quickly. He turned to Petey. "I told you, you ain't my son, so—"

"He is our son." From the shadows in the corner, a woman

scuttled forward. Thin, round-shouldered, and with the same haunted eyes Libby had seen on Oscar, the woman sidestepped the glowering man and stopped a mere twelve inches in front of Petey.

"You get away from him, Berta," Gunter ordered, but she acted as though she hadn't heard. Her frail hands hovered in front of Petey's chest as if she longed to touch him but feared she'd be slapped. She tipped her head to the side and peered directly into Petey's eyes, tears pooling in her own eyes. "Look at him. He *is* our Petey, Gunter." Amazement lit her tired voice.

The muscles in Petey's jaw quivered as he looked into his mother's face. "Hello, Ma."

Her hands shot out and cupped Petey's cheeks. The sight of those red, chapped hands with their broken nails against Petey's tanned, healthy, clean-shaven cheeks made Libby's chest ache. She had to turn away when the woman began to croon, "Petey, my boy . . . My firstborn . . . All grown up an' lookin' like such a fine, fine man . . ."

Petey stood straight and unmoving until the woman leaned forward, as if to embrace him. Then he jerked free of her touch. Hurt flickered in his mother's sunken eyes, but she stepped back with an expression of sad acceptance on her face. She seemed to expect rejection.

Gunter stomped forward, stood beside his cowering wife, and glared at Pete. "Why're you here? What do you want from us, boy?"

"I don't want anything except to be heard."

Gunter and Berta glanced at each other. After a moment of surprised silence, Gunter barked out another laugh. He swung his hand in a gesture of welcome. "Talk's cheap an' listenin' is free. So go ahead, boy—speak." He plopped into a sagging chair and smirked at Petey. Berta seemed to have taken root in the middle of the worn rug. Neither invited Petey to sit.

Libby peered into Petey's face, holding her breath as she waited to hear what he would say to these two broken, bitter, beaten-down people. They deserved his wrath, but looking into his eyes, she believed she saw compassion lurking beneath the pain and anger. Her heart skipped a beat. She had prayed for compassion to reign. Had her prayer found its way to God and returned to touch Petey's heart?

Petey licked his lips. "I confess I've been wanting to come here for years. Ever since . . ." He glanced briefly downward, tapping the tip of his peg leg against the faded cabbage-rose carpet covering the wood floor. His gaze sought his parents again. "I've wanted to tell you, face-to-face, that if you hadn't sent me away, I'd still be whole. That trolley would've never rolled over my foot if I hadn't been out on my own."

Berta seemed to shrink into herself, but Gunter sat unmoving, a sullen expression on his face.

"I've practiced the words so many times; I've got a memorized speech in my head. And I've imagined your faces as I recited it. I wanted to see sorrow and shame bring tears to your eyes." Petey paused and swallowed twice, his Adam's apple bobbing in his throat. He still held to Libby's hand, and she suddenly realized the tremble was gone. "But that doesn't matter anymore. I don't need it anymore."

Petey squared his shoulders. He seemed to blossom with peace and strength. "I recognize now that my life wasn't dictated by you. You were only pawns in God's hands. He allowed you to send me away so I could find people who would love and nurture me. People who would teach me to love God and to serve Him. Who knows what kind of occupation I'd have sought if I'd had two good legs to carry me into the future. Maybe something self-serving instead of

God-serving." His head bobbed in a nod, as if he were coming to an agreement about something. "So thank you, Gunter and Berta, for pushing me out that door. I've lived a better life than the one you could have given me."

Berta's chin crumpled, and she pressed her fist to her mouth. Tears poured down her thin cheeks. But anger hardened Gunter's face. He leapt from the chair and jabbed his index finger toward Petey. "You said your piece. We listened. Now you leave. An' don't come back here again."

Petey didn't move a muscle. "I want one more thing before I go. I want to see my brothers and sister."

"No!"

"Then I'm not leaving."

"You'll leave if I throw you out," Gunter growled through clenched teeth.

"And I'll keep coming back. Again and again and again, until you finally let me see them. So if you want to get rid of me, call my brothers and sister out here."

Libby was torn between admiration for her friend's tenacity and fear that Gunter Leidig would shove him down the stairs. The two men faced each other, eye to eye, neither blinking. And finally Gunter whirled and flopped into his chair again.

He waved at his wife, who stared at him in silence. "Get them kids out here so he can look at 'em."

Berta scuttled to the door from where the boys had peeked out earlier. She twisted the knob, and the door's hinges squeaked eerily as the door opened. "Young'uns? C'mon out here an' see your big brother Petey." Pride wavered in the woman's voice.

Barefooted children dressed in threadbare nightshirts spilled from the little room. They lined up from tallest to shortest. All had Petey's blond hair and blue eyes, but none possessed his easy grin. Libby's heart ached just looking into their empty, unsmiling faces.

Berta went down the line, touching each by turn. "This here's Wendell, Petey. Look at him—a fine, big boy. Smart, too—his teachers all say so." She moved to the next boy, half a head shorter than Wendell. "An' this's Orel. He's twelve already. Then Elma . . . not very big, but ain't she a purty girl? She was just a wee babe when you . . ." Berta's lips quivered, and she pressed them tightly together for a moment until she gained control.

She stepped between the last two, pulling them both close. The littlest one rested his head on her ribs, but the other stood stiff and unresponsive within her embrace. "Then the least'uns are Dennis an' Lorenzo—but you already met them. They come home with tales o' how they seen you today, but we didn't believe 'em." She glanced at Gunter, and something akin to hostility flashed in her eyes. "Now we know it's true."

Petey stood looking at his siblings, appearing to memorize them one by one. Libby wished she could push him forward, encourage him to make friends with each of them, maybe even to give them each a hug, but the promise she'd made kept her still and silent. His gaze not leaving his brothers and sister, he asked, "Where are Marta and Oscar?"

"Marta got married less'n a year ago—lives down by the river with her man. We . . . we don't see much o' her anymore. An' Oscar—" Berta's face paled. She looked to Gunter for help, but he stared off to the side, his jaw clamped shut. "Oscar's . . . lost."

Knowing the truth, Libby had to force herself to stay silent. She bit down on the tip of her tongue and waited for Petey to tell his parents he knew full well where Oscar was and why. But he didn't.

"You young'uns get on back to bed now." Berta shooed the children into the bedroom and closed the door behind them.

She leaned her back against the door, her pleading eyes aimed at Petey.

He cleared his throat. "Thank you for letting me see my brothers and sister. I'll go now." Tugging on Libby's hand, he stumped to the door and took hold of the doorknob. "When I leave here, I intend to see a lawyer about changing my name. I won't be a Leidig anymore, so you don't need to worry about me pestering you again."

One bright tear trailed down Berta's pale cheek. Gunter didn't even look at his son.

"Bye, Pa . . . Ma."

Berta's response was a quavering whisper. "G-good-bye, son."

With one giant step, Petey lurched out the door and yanked it shut behind him. In the hallway, he slumped against the grimy wallpaper and blew out a huge breath. "That's the hardest thing I've ever done."

Libby gently touched his arm. "Confronting your parents?"

"Leaving my brothers and sister in there." He shook his head; his eyes slid closed. "For years, I've harbored resentment toward my folks because I blamed them for the loss of my foot. In my mind, they stole it from me by sending me away from their home." Opening his eyes, he met her gaze dead-on. "But when I look at my brothers and sister, I realize what I lost is insignificant to what's been taken from them. My pa stole their souls, Libby." Tears glimmered in his blue eyes, but steely determination stiffened his jaw. "I'm not leaving them here. If I have to fight my pa with my fists, I'll do it, but I'm not leaving those children in this awful place."

Chapter Twenty-seven

B ut what about your classes?" Bennett watched as Pete folded his good suit and placed it carefully in his suitcase.

"I'll catch up with my studies when I get back from Shay's Ford." Pete buckled his suitcase and faced Bennett across the small hotel room.

Bennett shook his head and sat on the edge of his creaky bed. "What makes you think you can take care of five kids on your own?"

"Six." The word barked out, harsh and insistent. "I haven't given up on Oscar." Pete's shoulders sagged. He looked more tired—and worried—than Bennett had ever seen him. "Marta's married. I'll just have to pray her husband is a decent man and she'll be all right. I can't do anything for her now. But as for the others . . ."

Remembering the two boys who'd come to their hotel room that day, Bennett understood Pete's concern. Those kids looked like they could use a helping hand. But Pete didn't seem to realize his hands were already full.

Bennett flopped against the limp pillow and propped his ankle on his opposite knee. "I admire you for your starch, but how do you expect to go to school *and* play papa to a bunch of kids? How're you going to provide for 'em? You don't have the money to support five—"

Pete glared at him.

"Six kids. You take that on, you'll have to forget about becoming a preacher. Did you suddenly decide that's not so important after all?"

Pete flinched.

Bennett hated to throw cold water over his friend's fire, but somebody had to be the voice of reason. No eighteen-year-old ought to be saddled with the responsibility of surrogate parenthood. He sat up, thumping the rough floorboards with his stocking feet. "Think about it, Pete. You can be either a student or a papa, but not both. Which'll do the most good for the most people? Take over with those kids and you reach five . . . six lives; but if you become a preacher . . ."

Pete chewed on his lip, and Bennett knew he'd hit a nerve. Pete had wanted to become a preacher for so long; how could he give it up now? And what made him think he could raise five kids? Five, not six. That oldest one was a goner no matter what Pete wanted to believe.

"Your family's been managing without you all these years. Let 'em go, Pete. They're strangers to you. Strangers. That means they're *nothin'*."

Instead of nodding in agreement, Pete stuck out his chin. Resolve burned in his eyes. "You're wrong. Those kids—they're everything, Bennett. They're my brothers and sister—my flesh and blood. How could I stand in a pulpit and preach about God's love, knowing I'd left my own brothers and sister in a gutter, hurting and broken? I'd be the biggest kind of hypocrite. No"—he snatched up the suitcase and headed for the door—"I'm hopping the first train to Shay's Ford. I need Jackson's help if I'm going to get Oscar's sentence overturned and gain custody of Wendell, Orel, Elma, Dennis, and Lorenzo."

Bennett leapt up, grabbing his shoes as he walked toward Pete. "Then let me come with you."

Pete rolled his eyes. "First Libby, now you. Why does everyone think I'm so helpless they need to come with me?"

Despite the situation, Bennett couldn't help grinning. "Ol' Lib wanted to come, too?"

"Insisted on it. Said she was the one who figured out Oscar was my brother and the one who went with me to see my folks and met my brothers and sister, so she should be with me when I talk to Jackson." He shook his head, then sucked in a big breath and blew it out. "I told her no, and I'm telling you no. This is my fight, and I'll fight it alone."

Bennett wasn't surprised Libby wanted to be in the thick of things. He chuckled as he remembered the way she'd charged into their hotel room like her tail was on fire earlier that evening, spouting that she had to find Petey and quick. Libby got herself in a dither on a regular basis, but he'd never seen so her so wound up.

Pete reached for the door handle, his expression softening. "Don't think I'm not grateful, Bennett. You and Libby are true friends, standing by me when things are tough. I'll always appreciate your willingness to help me."

Bennett squirmed, guilt niggling. He didn't want to go along to help as much as he wanted to be part of the excitement.

Pete continued, "But I have to this do on my own." He paused, an odd look on his face. "There is something you can help me with, though . . ."

Bennett hopped up, eager to be part of this. "Sure."

"Roy Daley . . . Alice-Marie's cousin?"

Hearing the name of his nemesis, Bennett bristled. "What about him?"

"He wants to keep company with Libby, and he asked me to help him out."

Bennett's jaw dropped. "He what?"

Pete nodded, his face flaming red. "He promised he'd hold a place on the Beta Theta Pi pledge list for both of us if I helped him, but that neither of us would be accepted if I didn't."

"He *threatened* you?"

"He was very friendly about it, but it does come down to a threat of sorts. More toward you than me." Pete shook his head. "I don't care about fraternities. Especially now, when I might not even be going back to school." A pained expression creased his brow, but he swept his hand over his face and erased it. "I know how much it means to you, though, and I don't want to stand in the way of you getting what you want. But I can't imagine throwing Libby at him just to secure a spot in a fraternity . . . can you?"

The fraternity was important to Bennett—he wouldn't deny it. Being a Beta Theta Pi would allow him to belong to the most elite group at the college—a big come-up for a homeless, nameless orphan. But could he sacrifice Libby to get in?

Pete must have read his silence as unwillingness. "If you'd rather not talk to him, it's all right. I'll take care of it when—"

Bennett slapped Pete's shoulder. "You've got plenty to think about, so don't worry about Roy and his ol' fraternity. I'll handle it."

Pete seemed to wilt with relief. "Thanks, Bennett. You and the girls have a safe trip to Chambers tomorrow. I'll see you . . . soon, I hope." He headed out the door.

Bennett turned the lock on the door, then crossed to the window. Pushing the curtain aside, he peered out at the night. He'd told Pete he'd take care of the situation with Roy, and he would. A grin climbed his cheeks. Oh yes, he most definitely would take care of Roy. But he'd do it his way.

Pete accepted the glass of milk Maelle offered and took a long drink as Jackson settled into the leather chair behind his desk. After their initial surprise at unexpectedly finding him—disheveled and bleary-eyed from his overnight travels—on their doorstep on a Saturday morning, Jackson and Maelle had welcomed him into their home and behaved as though a weekend visit from him was nothing out of the ordinary.

Maelle leaned in and gave Jackson a peck on the cheek. "You two have a good chat. The girls and I are going to bake bread today." She laughed softly as she headed for the door. "Hopefully *these* loaves will rise!" The door clicked shut behind her.

Jackson rocked in his chair, chuckling. "Maelle has taken to motherhood like a duckling takes to water. She's determined to do everything with Hannah and Hester that she would have done with her own mother, had things been different." His face clouded for a moment. "Makes me almost regret those years she had to wait while I served in the legislature. But . . ." Linking his hands behind his head, he grinned. "We can't go back and change what's been, can we? All we can do is make the most of today."

"I agree." Pete set the empty glass on the edge of Jackson's desk and cupped his knees with his hands. "And that's why I'm here. I need to make the most of today."

Jackson sat in attentive silence while Pete shared the details of his time with his parents and younger siblings. He repeated Keith's observations, then outlined the sad fate awaiting Oscar—the same fate that could very well befall his other brothers someday, if things didn't change. His stomach clenched and his voice quivered, but he laid every ugly detail at Jackson's feet. Then, spent, he said, "I want my name changed—I want to erase every bit of Gunter Leidig's imprint from my life. But more than that, I want to get my brothers and sister away from him before he destroys them. How can I become their guardian?"

Jackson, who had remained sober-faced throughout Pete's entire recitation, now grimaced. He leaned forward, rubbing one hand over his face. "Pete, that's not a battle easily won."

Anger stirred in Pete's middle. "Why not? You heard everything I said—children forced to steal, wearing bruises, skipping school . . . and look where Oscar is right now! Shouldn't that prove Gunter Leidig is an abusive father?"

"I'd say he's far from ideal." Jackson spoke calmly. "But unfortunately the laws are pretty fuzzy on what constitutes abuse. Most courts are very hesitant to remove children from a parent's care. And while I understand your concern and completely support you, I have to be honest with you, Pete. I don't know of any judge who would give an eighteen-year-old university student—"

"I'm dropping out to get a job." During his long night of wakefulness at the depot, sitting on a hard bench waiting for the early-morning train to Shay's Ford, Pete had come to several conclusions. Bennett was right that he couldn't stay in school *and* support his siblings, so he'd have to quit school and find a full-time job. He intended to start looking as soon as he left Jackson's house.

"Aaron and Isabelle will skin you alive."

Pete didn't even blink in response to Jackson's dry comment. "This has nothing to do with Aaron and Isabelle. This is my decision."

Shaking his head, Jackson sighed. "Pete, even if you had a

good-paying job, I can't imagine someone your age being given guardianship of five younger siblings."

Pete grabbed the edge of Jackson's desk with both hands. "Six. Don't forget about Oscar. We've got to get him out of that cell."

Jackson made a face. "I know this is hard for you, Pete, but you may just have to accept—"

"No!" Pete sprang to his feet. His stump tingled wildly, but he ignored it. "I can't just let Oscar be—" He couldn't bring himself to say the word *hanged*.

Jackson shook his head. "A jury found him guilty. A judge passed sentence. The date's been set. Do you know how hard it is to overturn something like that?"

"But it *can* be overturned, can't it? If the jury was wrong about finding him guilty?"

"Is the jury wrong?"

The question, although gently asked, was a knife in Pete's heart. He sank back into the chair. "Libby said Oscar swears he didn't kill anyone—that he was there, intending to rob the store, but someone else shot the clerk. Oscar stayed to try to help the injured man. When the police came, they saw Oscar and arrested him. Even though he told them over and over he didn't shoot anyone, they wouldn't believe him." Pete's chin quivered. "But I do."

Jackson came around the desk and clamped his hand on Pete's left shoulder. Sympathy shone in his eyes. "Pete, as hard as this is for me to say, I have to be honest with you. Nearly every criminal swears he's been wrongly convicted, whether it's true or not. Oscar's bound to be scared, facing . . . what he's facing. Of course he's going to proclaim his innocence."

Pete knocked away Jackson's hand and rose. He paced the length of the thick rug cushioning the wood floor, unable to stand still. "But don't you see? If my father sent the other children out to steal, he probably sent Oscar to that drugstore."

"But Oscar is sixteen—old enough to know right from wrong. So he'll be expected to suffer the consequences of his actions."

Pete came to a halt and glared at Jackson. "I can accept him being punished for trying to steal. But murder? What if he really is innocent of murder, Jackson? Can you live with yourself, knowing he could be facing a hangman's noose for someone else's crime?"

Jackson sat on the edge of the desk, his arms folded and his lips pulled into a deep scowl. The room fell so silent Pete could hear girlish giggles drifting in from the opposite side of the house. He stood, refusing to back down, and waited for Jackson to answer his question.

Finally Jackson sighed. "Did Oscar give the authorities any information about the person who supposedly fired the gun?"

Pete pressed his memory for everything Libby had said. He wished he'd asked for her notes—then he could give the information to Jackson. "I think he said he didn't know the shooter. Why?"

"If he gave a name or a description, they'd be required to investigate his claims. Before I try to overturn a conviction passed down by a judge, I need to know exactly what I'm up against."

Pete's heart leapt with hope. "Then you'll do it? You'll get him freed?"

Jackson held up one hand. "I make no promises. Coming in from a different county, I might not even be allowed to see your brother, let alone investigate. But I'll *try.* That's all I can do."

"And then you'll have me named guardian of Oscar and the others?"

"Pete, please . . ." Jackson shook his head, a sad smile lifting the corners of his mouth. "Let's climb one mountain at a time, huh? And while I'm climbing, you better be praying. What you're asking for is nothing short of a miracle."

CHAPTER TWENTY-EIGHT

Libby flopped open her bag on the bed and removed the dress she'd worn the day before. Shaking it to remove wrinkles, she headed for the wardrobe on the far side of her dormitory room. To Alice-Marie, she said, "I wish Petey would have let me go with him. It's going to be impossible to think of anything else until he returns. I hope he can do something for Oscar."

Alice-Marie wrinkled her nose. "I think he's foolish for trying. As my father said, a jury found him guilty. That should be the end of it."

Alice-Marie's parents had been very upset when Libby and Petey had rung their bell late last night, but after Petey's calm, respectful explanation, they'd reluctantly offered forgiveness. However, they'd informed Libby she was no longer welcome to visit their home. Then they'd taken Alice-Marie into Mr. Daley's den for a long closed-door session. Both girls were put on the train early that morning.

Libby fully expected Alice-Marie to shun her completely after all that had transpired, but to her surprise, Alice-Marie had chatted with her all the way back to school. She turned to her roommate and asked, "If Oscar were your brother, would you be able to let it go?"

Alice-Marie huffed. "*My* brother wouldn't try to rob a drugstore clerk!"

"Because your brother, like you, had a decent upbringing," Libby said softly. "How do children learn right from wrong? From their parents. If their parents teach them to do wrong things, then what can we expect from them? Yes, Oscar was wrong to try to steal from the drugstore, but I think there are other people at fault, too. It isn't right to hold only Oscar responsible."

Alice-Marie let out another little breath, but she didn't argue. The girls worked in silence, emptying their bags and putting away their personal items. When the room was back in order, Libby stretched out on her bed for a nap. Alice-Marie curled up on her bed, too, and closed her eyes. Libby reached over and tapped Alice-Marie's arm. Her eyes flew open. "What?"

"Thank you for still talking to me even after I upset your parents again. Those days when you were so angry weren't very pleasant." Libby smiled, letting Alice-Marie know she wasn't upset.

Alice-Marie grimaced, wriggling against her pillow. "For me, either. It's very hard for me to be quiet."

Libby wisely refrained from laughing.

"My parents did their best to convince me to move into a room by myself. They don't feel you're a very good influence on me, I'm afraid." She sighed. "I finally told them I would consider making the change after Christmas break."

Libby tried to imagine being alone. She'd have more time to write. And often Alice-Marie grated on her nerves with her endless, often senseless, chatter. But Libby didn't relish the thought of sitting in this room by herself every day.

"But," Alice-Marie went on, rolling to her side and scrunching her eyes closed, "I doubt I'll actually do it. Moving is such an inconvenience, and I have no desire to be all alone. Your company, unconventional as it may be, is certainly preferable to loneliness. And where else would I go? All the girls are already paired up for this year. So, we're stuck with each other. At least for now."

Libby let her eyelids droop, but then she remembered something else. She sat up and tapped Alice-Marie again. Alice-Marie snuffled but didn't open her eyes. Libby tapped her harder.

"What?" The cranky tone didn't encourage Libby to continue, but she'd already disturbed Alice-Marie; she might as well share her thoughts.

"Thank you for agreeing to not tell anyone about the situation with Petey's brother. Petey had nothing to do with it, so it wouldn't be fair to have people casting aspersions on his character."

Alice-Marie sat straight up, her eyebrows high. "Elisabet, I would *never* hold Pete accountable for something his brother did. I, of all people, understand the embarrassment of having a relative whose behavior is questionable. Why do you think I didn't tell you that Roy Daley is my cousin?" She shuddered. "He is quite popular on campus, being the star athlete, and I admit I've tried to use our relationship to secure a place in the popular crowd for myself. But I must agree with you—he's completely obnoxious. So of course I wouldn't try to malign Pete's character by discussing his brother's actions."

Reaching across the gap, Alice-Marie gave Libby's wrist a quick pat. "Don't worry. Pete's secret is safe with me."

Libby tried to sleep, but images from the short visit to Clayton replayed behind her closed eyelids, making rest impossible. The picture of Petey as he leaned against the dirty wall of his parents' apartment building, proclaiming he would not leave his brothers and sister in that place, rose above all others and refused to dim.

Had Petey made it safely to Shay's Ford? Had Jackson agreed to help? What would Petey do if Jackson managed to convince a judge to give Petey guardianship of his siblings? And—more importantly—what would he do if Jackson failed?

Don't let Petey's heart be broken. Let Petey be able to save them. Their hopeless, hapless faces floated in her memory until she couldn't lie still.

On tiptoe, she crossed to her desk and picked up the notebook she'd used when questioning Oscar. Although she'd been pretending to be a reporter, she now looked at the pages of scribbled notes and realized she had more than enough information to create an article. Her tongue poking out the corner of her mouth, she grabbed a pencil and began to write, organizing the notes into emotive paragraphs. After an hour of writing, erasing, rewriting, and polishing, she collapsed on the desk with her head on her arms.

Miss Whitford had advised Libby to search for her passion. Was passion the reason she was too exhausted to lift her head? She felt as though she'd bled on the pages while writing Oscar's story. Writing the overly romanticized make-believe stories were work, but also pleasure; writing this article had nearly turned her heart inside-out. She couldn't honestly say she'd enjoyed recording Oscar's life on the page, but she did believe she had created a well-written editorial on the plight of one young man raised in squalor.

But what to do with it?

With effort, she sat up and looked at the article. Surely a lesson was hidden within these pages—a lesson on the importance of family, of teaching morals, of reaching out to those in need. Petey would do everything possible to save Oscar, but as much as Libby hated to admit it, the boy might be lost to them. However, if reading his story might encourage someone, somewhere, to reach out to a troubled youth and, in so doing, change the course of his life, then Oscar didn't have to die in vain.

Libby scrambled to retrieve her shoes from under her bed. She buttoned them as quickly as her clumsy fingers could manage. Then she slipped the article into her leather portfolio. If she had to pay a newspaper editor to print her story, she'd do it. This was one story that must be told.

On Sunday morning, Libby fought through a heavy fog out of which Oscar's voice repeatedly called for help. She sat up in her bed, sweaty and shaking, and forced herself to take several long, deep breaths to bring her erratic pulse under control. A dream, only a dream. Yet the frantic cry had sounded so real.

In the predawn hour, menacing gray shadows shrouded the room. Only a square of paler gray, the curtains backlit by the moon, indicated the location of the window. Alice-Marie slept soundly, her even breathing loud in the still room as Libby sat on the edge of her bed, eyes wide, trying to read the clock on Alice-Marie's bureau. Several seconds passed before her vision adjusted enough to make out the time. Five after five. Releasing a long sigh, she lay back on her pillow and stared into the shadowy room.

In the past few weeks, she had adopted Bennett's habit of sleeping in on Sunday mornings, but today sleep eluded her. Fear that she would revisit the disturbing dream kept her wide-eyed and wakeful. Why was Oscar haunting her? Hadn't she done all she could for him? The article she'd written now sat on the *Boone County Daily Tribune* editor's desk, awaiting his approval. The man hadn't guaranteed he'd print it, but he had promised to read it.

Yes, she'd given her best effort for Oscar.

What about praying for him?

She gasped quietly as the thought captured her mind. First she'd encouraged Petey to pray, and now her heart was telling her to offer a prayer of her own? She sat up so abruptly the bedsprings twanged in protest. She sat very still, holding her breath, until she was sure she hadn't disturbed Alice-Marie. Then she left the room and crept to the bathroom at the end of the hall. Perhaps a long soak in the bathtub, a rare treat, would help her relax. Then she could go back to sleep.

But the bath, while pleasant, only served to awaken her completely. She knew she wouldn't be able to sleep again, but how would she fill her morning?

Go to church and pray for Petey.

She rolled her eyes and muttered, "I don't pray. *Petey* prays." Her words hung heavily in the steamy little room, and sadness struck Libby with such force her nose stung. She wanted to pray. She wanted to trust. But after being discarded so many times by so many people—her parents, her uncle, all sorts of potential adoptive parents, Maelle, Jackson, and even Petey—how would she bear it if God discarded her and her needs, too?

Try. Just try . . .

The persistent voice in her head refused to be silenced. She'd have to distract herself from it. She hurried to her room and dressed as quietly as possible. But Alice-Marie must have heard the slight squeak of the wardrobe hinges, because she yawned and sat up.

"L-Libby?" Her voice sounded croaky.

Libby whispered in reply. "Yes, it's just me. Go back to sleep. I'm going to take a walk." She knew where she wanted to go—no one else would be there.

"In the dark?" Alice-Marie stretched her arms over her head. Her bedsprings groaned softly as she flopped back onto the mattress.

The heavy shadows of earlier had lifted, and the room was cast in a murky pink. Before long, the sun would flood its yellow glow across the campus. "The sun's almost up. I'll be fine." She tiptoed toward the door.

"Where're you going?" came Alice-Marie's sleepy voice.

Libby doubted her roommate would remember this conversation later, but she answered anyway. "Out to the old foundation."

"You mean the burned-down building? So that's real? You've seen it?"

"Yes." Libby turned the doorknob, wincing when it creaked one high note.

"Bennett and I walked to the field one time, but we didn't see the foundation."

Libby opened the door and slipped into the hall. Before closing the door, she whispered, "Maybe you didn't look hard enough. Bye, Alice-Marie." She locked the door behind her and then hurried down the stairs. Miss Banks's desk sat empty, so Libby ran past it and out the double doors. The morning air chilled her, but she ignored the gooseflesh that broke out over her arms and ran all the way to the line of trees that led to the meadow.

She slowed her pace as she walked the tree-lined lane. The trees, once thick and full, now hosted only a few brave russet or brown leaves that waved in the gentle breeze. The ground underneath wore a thick carpet, and she scuffed through the fallen leaves, kicking them in the air and watching them flit back down. A bluejay, apparently disturbed by her crunching progress, scolded from the bare treetops. Its bright blue feathers stood out boldly against the backdrop of plain brown branches and pale sky.

While Libby watched, it flapped its wings and chattered, its bright eyes seeming to look directly at Libby. Such an audacious little creature—did it really think it could frighten her away? Despite herself, she laughed. The bird took wing, zipping between branches. She watched until it disappeared, then put her feet in motion once more.

The meadow waited just ahead, the grass higher than the last time she'd visited. She stepped free of the trees and into the clearing, into the glow of a magnificent sunrise. Bands of pink, yellow, orange, and purple gave the horizon a festive appearance. The sun—a bold white arc—pressed through the center of the ribbons of color, sending beams upward to pierce the sparse clouds and form a giant fan of light.

Libby's eyes involuntarily squinted, the brightness too much to bear wide-eyed, but she faced that glorious sunrise and imagined Petey—always an early riser—in Shay's Ford witnessing the same sight. It bound her to him in a way she couldn't quite grasp.

Then, her senses sated, she sought the stones that had once held a tall, proud building. She pushed the grass aside with her hands, her gaze roving, and finally she located the hidden foundation. With a little cry of triumph, she sat on an oblong stone, pressing her palm to its rough, cool top.

She giggled, remembering how Alice-Marie had sleepily asked if the foundation was real. Just because she'd never seen it herself, she questioned it. But here Libby sat, like a queen on her throne, her weight fully supported by a broad, carved stone the color of pewter. *Oh yes, Alice-Marie, it's real.*

As the sun rose higher, it revealed the entire stretch of the foundation nestled between thick strands of dried brown grass. Libby examined every inch of it, marveling that even though nearly every part of the building had been destroyed by heat and flame, the foundation still remained. Strong, immovable, but only visible to those who took the time to truly seek it.

Sitting there all alone under a rosy sky, a feeling of smallness and vulnerability captured Libby. She wished someone were there to sit beside her and hold her hand. The feeling wasn't new—she'd experienced it many times after coming to the orphans' school, and she'd combated it by running off with Petey and Bennett or begging to spend a weekend with Maelle.

Maelle . . . How long had it been since Libby had indulged in her favorite daydream? Here, all alone, she could close her eyes and imagine being adopted by Maelle. But that fantasy no longer held any appeal. The dream would never come true now.

Her heart ached as she thought about Hannah and Hester calling Maelle Ma and Jackson Pa. Her jealousy toward the two girls went even deeper than her jealousy toward Jackson. At least she'd always known Maelle loved Jackson—Maelle spoke of him every time she and Libby were together.

Once, when Libby had been twelve, she'd asked Maelle how she could still love someone who was so far away. "Why don't you quit waiting for him and just find someone else?" Libby had asked, unaware of the insensitivity of the question.

She could still remember the soft look that had come over Maelle's face before she cupped Libby's cheek and answered, "There's no one else who could replace Jackson. Even though we're far apart, he's close to me—I feel him in every heartbeat."

At the time, Libby had inwardly scoffed at such a romantic notion. But now her heart ached with the desire to be loved that way by someone. To know, even when separated, that she was being held in his every heartbeat. How she longed to be important. To someone. To anyone.

The sun moved ever higher, washing away the bright colors of morning and replacing them with a clear blue that perfectly matched the color of Petey's eyes. The inner prompting to pray for him returned. Tears pricked behind her eyes, surprising her with their presence. She wanted to pray—to support her dear friend, whose world was crumbling.

But she couldn't.

"I'm so sorry, Petey." Lifting her gaze to the blue sky that reminded her so much of Petey's eyes, she said on a ragged whisper, "I can't pray for you. I'm not important enough to warrant God's attention."

CHAPTER TWENTY-NINE

Pete's admiration for Jackson grew by leaps and bounds as the day progressed. Even though the man had gotten little sleep Sunday night, having dozed on the train in lieu of a good rest in his bed, he appeared alert and intelligent Monday as he asked questions, filed papers, and somehow managed to secure a meeting in private chambers with the judge who'd handed down Oscar's sentence. As much as Pete had wanted to speak on his brother's behalf, he clamped his lips tight and allowed Jackson to do all the talking.

Jackson scooted his chair closer to the judge's desk and placed a stack of papers in front of the man. "After reading the report covering the investigation and the trial transcript, there are two questions that were not—in my opinion—adequately addressed by Mr. Leidig's representing attorney." He pointed to something on the top page. "The clerk died of a gunshot wound, yet no weapon was recovered at the scene. No one seemed to inquire about the absence of a gun."

The judge shuffled through the stack of papers as if seeking something. "That does seem unusual. . . ."

"Secondly, although Mr. Leidig repeatedly indicated another man was responsible for the clerk's death, his claims were never pursued. It appears, from reading these reports, they found a boy sitting beside the clerk's body. When he admitted to being in the store for the purpose of stealing money, they simply held him accountable for the murder, as well."

Pete fidgeted as the judge and Jackson discussed the trial transcript at length, line by line, and by the end of the forty-minute session, Jackson had secured permission to talk to Oscar on the guarantee that he would hand any new evidence to the police for investigation.

The judge leaned back in his chair. "Even though I'm granting your request, I find it highly unlikely the boy will offer any information of value. What this transcript doesn't indicate is the boy's attitude during the trial. He was very close-mouthed and uncooperative. But never let it be said retribution took precedence over justice in my courtroom."

Jackson nodded. "Thank you, your honor. I appreciate your willingness to allow a second look at the evidence."

The judge gestured toward a sober-faced man in navy trousers and a matching belted jacket, indicating he should step forward. "The officer will escort you to the jail, where you can visit with Mr. Leidig."

Jackson thanked the judge again and then quirked his fingers at Pete. Pete hop-skipped to catch up to Jackson, and side-by-side they followed the officer down a long hallway to a heavy door. The man opened the door and stepped through without glancing back, and Jackson had to catch it to keep it from slamming shut.

A steep, narrow staircase waited, the steps formed of cement. Moisture clung to the cinder-block walls and concrete floor, leaving the surfaces slick, and Pete held tight to the iron handrail to keep his peg from slipping. Not until they reached the barred door to a cell did the officer turn around. His eyebrows rose when he spotted Pete.

"Judge said the lawyer could go in. He didn't say nothin' about nobody else."

A second officer, portly and with heavy jowls, pried himself out of a straight-backed chair and hustled over with his right hand hovering inches above his sidearm. Pete instinctively drew back.

Jackson put his hand on Pete's back and urged him forward. "This young man is Peter Leidig. He's Oscar's brother. I assume family members are allowed?"

The heavier man nodded. "Well . . . they're allowed. But none of 'em 've bothered. Only person been down here is a little reporter from the newspaper." He puffed up importantly. "She took down my name, too."

The officer who'd escorted Jackson and Pete downstairs made a face of disgust. "You aren't guarding Billy the Kid, Holloway."

The portly man deflated.

"Holloway'll let you in," the officer said, turning back to Jackson. "Judge didn't give a time limit, so just let Holloway know when you're done and he'll let you back out." He strode off without another glance.

Pete's heart doubled its tempo while he waited for Holloway to unlock the door to Oscar's cell. No one besides Libby had come to see Oscar? How frightened and alone the boy must feel. And probably resentful. *Lord, let him be willing to accept our help.*

As he followed Jackson into the cell and the officer clanked the heavy door shut behind them, a chill crept down Pete's spine. The cell was dim, lit by a single bulb hanging from twisted wires in the middle of the ceiling. A narrow cot—the only piece of furniture in the small square space—pressed into the far corner, and a slender blond-haired boy lay curled on the bare mattress. His eyes were open, seeming to look directly at Jackson, but he made no effort to sit up or to speak. Had it not been for his blinking eyes, Pete might have thought he was a mannequin laid out to fool people into believing a person inhabited the cell.

Jackson cleared his throat. "Oscar?"

Oscar sniffed in response.

"My name's Jackson Harders. I'm a lawyer from Shay's Ford, and I'm a friend of your brother, Pete. He brought me to see you." For the second time, Jackson gestured Pete forward. But Pete hesitated. A part of him wanted to rush over and embrace his brother, to assure him he wasn't alone, that someone cared. That *he* cared. But after all their years apart, they were strangers.

With Jackson applying pressure to his back, Pete had no choice but to shuffle forward a step. "H-hello, Oscar." His brother didn't move. "How are you?" Realizing how foolish the question sounded, he wished he could take back the ridiculous query. But, to his surprise, his brother slowly pushed himself into a seated position and examined the floor between his feet.

Head low, Oscar mumbled, "Not so good, if you wanna know the truth."

Despite himself, Pete smiled. He slid his peg leg across the floor, inching closer. Oscar's head shifted, and Pete knew he was looking at the wooden peg leg. Oscar's eyebrows crunched, and his gaze bounced up to meet Pete's.

"You ain't my brother. My brother, he wasn't a cripple. Don't remember much about him, but I do know that."

Jackson slipped in, "This is your brother, Oscar. Pete was in an accident. A trolley car rolled over his leg when he was a little boy. He's used a peg leg ever since."

Oscar peered at Pete, his expression dull. "A trolley run over ya? Prob'ly shoulda killed ya."

Pete nodded. "Prob'ly shoulda." He deliberately slurred his words to match Oscar's speech. "But God saved me. And now He sent me here to try to save you."

Oscar laughed, but the sound held no gaiety. "There's no savin' me. I'm a goner." He scooted over, patting the mattress beside him and waiting until Pete sat. "But it's good ya could come say good-bye. Always wondered what happened to ya."

Pete wished they had endless hours to talk about the lost years. But time was limited. Their catching up would have to come later, after he'd managed to free his brother. Putting his hand on Oscar's knee, he tipped forward to look directly into his face. "Listen, Oscar, last week you talked to a friend of mine—her name is Libby. She asked you lots of questions, remember?"

Oscar nodded. His hair flopped over his eyes, and he pushed it back with the heel of his hand. "I remember. She was real purty, an' she wrote everything down on paper. Said she was gonna write a story about me."

If Pete knew Libby, she'd write a dandy story. "That's right. She told me what you said about there being someone else in the store that night."

Oscar ducked his head.

"She said you told her you didn't kill the clerk, but the other man did."

Oscar's shoulders rose, and he seemed to shrink inside himself. "Yeah . . . I told 'er that."

Jackson stepped forward and crouched in front of Oscar. "Was that the truth, Oscar? Was there someone else there who shot the clerk?"

"What difference does it make?" He sounded confrontational. "Trial's over. Sentencing's done. There's no hope for me now."

"There is hope, Oscar." Pete spoke with as much confidence as he could muster to make up for Oscar's lack. "The judge is willing to look into your claim about another person doing the shooting. You just have to tell us what you know about him." He lowered his voice, grasping his brother's knee. "I know you told Libby you didn't know who the man was, but that wasn't the truth, was it? You wouldn't partner up with a complete stranger to rob a store. That doesn't make sense."

Oscar sat in silence, staring straight ahead.

Pete squeezed his brother's knee. "Go ahead. Tell the truth. Jackson can help you if you tell the truth."

Oscar mumbled something Pete couldn't understand. He leaned in closer. "What did you say?"

He covered his face with his hands. "I can't tell you." The words came out on a snarl.

"Sure you can." Pete gave his brother's knee another reassuring squeeze. "Jackson will find the man and make him tell the authorities that he's the one who shot the clerk, but we need a description . . . a name."

"I said I can't!" Oscar lunged from the bed, pushing past Jackson and cowering in the opposite corner. He hid behind his upraised arms, his body heaving.

Jackson rose and took a step toward Oscar. "Oscar, did the man threaten you? Because I can protect you."

A moan sounded from behind Oscar's arms. He turned his back and hunched into the corner with his arms wrapped around himself. "Ain't me needs protectin'. I can take care of myself. But if I tell, there'll be no one to—" He sank against the cinder-block wall, and for a moment Pete thought he'd collapse into a heap on the floor. Then, drawing in a deep breath, he unfolded to his full height.

He turned slowly and looked at Pete. "It was good of you to

come tell me good-bye, Petey. Glad to know you're doin' good, even if you are a cripple. I'll always remember you came. But you . . . you better go now."

Oscar crossed the floor, passing between Pete and Jackson without looking at them, and dropped onto the cot. Pete stared at the boy, uncertain what to do, until Jackson put his hand on Pete's arm.

"Pete, would you step outside for a few minutes? I'd like to talk to Oscar alone."

Although Pete had so much more he wanted to say to his brother, he didn't argue. Maybe Jackson could use his lawyer skills to pry more information from the boy. He called to the guard to let him out, and Pete paced the small hallway while listening to the low, unintelligible voices behind the door.

Finally Jackson emerged, his face unreadable. He thanked the guard and ushered Pete toward the stairs. "I'm going to stay in Clayton at least another two days. I'd like to put you on a train back to Chambers—Isabelle will have many choice words for me if I don't at least encourage you to return to school."

Pete heaved himself up the final step and folded his arms across his chest. "I'm not going anywhere until my brother is released."

Jackson nodded. "Figured you'd say that. And to be honest, Pete, I could probably use your help."

As they stepped out onto the wide portico that led to the street, Pete swung to face Jackson. His heart beat double time. "So Oscar told you the name of the killer?"

Jackson shook his head. "The judge was right. He's the most tight-lipped boy I've ever met. He wouldn't give me a name. But it doesn't matter. I know who it is."

❧

As soon as her classes ended Monday afternoon, Libby walked to the office of the *Boone County Daily Tribune* to find out whether the editor had read her article. If he didn't plan to print it, she'd take it to the next editor, and then the next, until she found someone who would make Oscar's situation known to the public. She also intended to suggest changing the names to protect Petey's reputation. Surely the editor would be willing to acquiesce to her request when he understood Petey's position as a ministry student.

The receptionist sent her straight to Mr. Houghton's office when she arrived, and Libby's heart pattered hopefully as she slipped into the chair facing the man's messy desk.

"Miss Conley . . ." He snatched up her pages from a stack at his right elbow and tamped them together. "I've read your article. Four times." He peered at her over the top of the papers. His words indicated interest, but he sounded disgruntled.

"Oh?" She couldn't think of anything else to say.

"Yes. I never need to read anything more than once to form an opinion, so congratulate yourself. You've managed to stump me."

She scratched her head. "You mean my writing has confused you?" Had she not been clear in presenting the facts? She reached for her pages, but he held them out of her grasp.

"Not so fast. I want to know what compelled you to make up this tale."

Libby's jaw dropped. "I did no such thing!"

He waved the pages, his lips forming a cynical smirk. "This isn't the fanciful imaginings of a girl who aspires to be a world-renowned reporter?"

Her face flaming, Libby recalled the conversation she'd had with this man shortly after arriving in Chambers. She'd obviously made an impression.

"Because this is the kind of story that can cause an uproar. If printed on the front page, with a big bold headline reading something such as *Wrongly Convicted Youth Faces Gallows*, it would incite public outrage and no doubt inspire some politician to begin saying he wishes to change the laws about capital punishment."

Libby stared at him in amazement. Her writing held that much power?

Mr. Houghton tossed the pages onto his desk. "So it's too bad it's all a bunch of fatuity."

Libby came out of her seat. "Every word of that article is true!" She smacked her palms on his desktop, scattering papers. "Right now, in the jail in Clayton, sixteen-year-old Oscar Leidig is counting down the days until he'll be hanged for a murder he didn't commit. He told me himself he's innocent. But no one is investigating it because the businessmen in town wanted revenge enacted quickly. So this young man must pay the ultimate price for someone else's crime!"

Mr. Houghton stood and began scooping up the pages that had gone flying with Libby's outburst. "I'm well aware that sixteen-year-old Oscar Leidig has been sentenced to hang. Do you think I don't have access to a telephone?" He pushed aside the haphazard stack of collected papers and glared at Libby. "One call is all I needed to confirm you chose a real boy and a real situation to build upon. Clever . . ." He tapped his temple with one finger. "I'll give you that—you're clever. Had me thinking hard enough to check up on you. But the boy was found guilty by a jury in a courtroom. Your claim that he's innocent is unfounded. And that's the part that would incite a riot. Which is why this article won't see publication."

Libby rustled through the stack and withdrew her article. "We'll just see about that, Mr. Houghton. There are two other newspapers in this town, and countless others in the state, so—"

"And every last one of them has been warned about you and

your article." The man settled back into his chair. "You want to be a reporter, young lady? Finish school. Pay your dues. Then stick to the facts. Don't create drama where none exists. We have a word for that: sensationalism. And no journalist worth his salt resorts to it." Rocking in his chair, he added, "You wanna make things up, go write fairy tales. After seeing that"—he jammed his finger at the article she clutched in both hands—"I'd say you'd be good at it."

Libby stared at him in silent fury, biting on the end of her tongue so hard she was surprised she hadn't drawn blood.

"Don't waste any more of my time." He waved his hand at her, shooing her away.

Libby spun and stomped out of the office. As she clomped down the hall, every worker in the place paused to stare after her. She held her head high and refused to give any of them so much as a glance. She burst out onto the sidewalk, blinking rapidly to hold back tears of indignant fury.

Her feet never slowed the entire way back to campus. By the time she reached her dormitory, her chest felt so tight she feared she might explode. Intending to run upstairs and hide under the covers until she regained control, she almost ignored Alice-Marie's cheerful call. But she decided rather than hide, she'd tell Alice-Marie about Mr. Houghton's ridiculous assertions. She needed someone to empathize with her.

Alice-Marie's smile dimmed when she caught up to Libby and got a look at her face. "What's wrong?"

"You wouldn't believe what I just went through!" She opened her mouth to spout the aggravation of the past half hour, but Alice-Marie tittered.

"Oh dear, you are quite in a dither. And of course I want to hear all about it, but I told Bennett I would meet him in the library to do our assignments together before dinner." She hunched her shoulders and giggled again. "Of course, you know I can't keep Bennett waiting. . . . But I collected the mail from our box. Would you like yours?"

Libby held out her hand, and Alice-Marie dropped two envelopes onto her palm. The top letter was from Maelle. Another wave of hurt rolled over Libby. What would she give right now to be able to share all of this frustration with her long-time mentor? Maelle would know all the right things to say to ease away Libby's ache and confusion. But Maelle was busy mothering Hannah and Hester.

With a vicious swipe, Libby flipped Maelle's letter to the back. The return address on the second envelope read *Fiction Editor, Modern Woman's World*. Had they sent her payment for her most recent romance story? She snorted. "At least *fatuity* has its benefits."

Alice-Marie frowned. "Excuse me?"

Libby shook her head. "Never mind. Thanks for getting the mail. I'll talk to you later." But she knew she wouldn't share this frustration with Alice-Marie. Did she truly expect to receive empathy from the daughter of a man who believed to his very soul that Oscar was guilty?

Alice-Marie turned and hurried across the yard toward the library, and Libby slowly trudged up the stairs to their room. Inside, she sat on the edge of her bed and halfheartedly released the flap on the envelope from the magazine. She removed a letter, but no check flitted out. Frowning, she stared into the empty envelope. The last thing she needed today was a rejection for her *fairy tales*! With a sigh, she braced herself and unfolded the letter.

Dear Miss Conley,

It is with great excitement I write concerning your most recent submission to *Modern Woman's World*. Although we've yet to present your stories to our reading audience, our staff has eagerly read the stirring, passionate tales, and all agree your stories far outshine any other author currently writing for us.

Pride filled Libby as she read the words of praise. Miss Catherine Whitford had indicated she would discover a sense of satisfaction and receive acclaim by writing works of fiction. Perhaps this letter arriving right after Mr. Houghton dismissed her attempt at writing a serious editorial was prophetic. Maybe writing romance stories was what she was meant to do, after all. She bent over the letter and resumed reading.

Given the overwhelming response by the avid readers on our staff, I am delighted to offer you a position as romantic serial writer for *Modern Woman's World*. We would ask that you sign a contract guaranteeing to sell your stories only to our publication for the period of one year. As you know, *Modern Woman's World* is published semi-monthly, and beginning January of 1915, we would expect to print one story in each issue, making you accountable for two stories per month. In exchange for your exclusive commitment to our publication, we would offer you a monthly salary of twelve dollars.

Libby dropped the letter; her mind spun. Exclusive contract? Two stories a month? A twelve-dollar salary for less than a week's work? Maybe she could give that money to Petey to help support his siblings. Heaven knew he'd need all the help he could get. As she sat, considering the blessing of this unexpected opportunity, a tap at the door intruded.

"Come in," she called absently.

One of the girls pledging to Kappa Kappa Gamma with Alice-Marie peeked into the room. She held out a newspaper to Libby. "I saw Alice-Marie and Bennett in the library, and they asked me to bring this to you. There's an editorial they thought you would find of interest. The bottom of page three."

Libby took the paper and thanked the girl. Her heart began to pound. Had one of the other newspaper editors chosen to run her article even after Mr. Houghton's warnings? She opened the paper and scanned the bylines on the page the girl had mentioned. But to her surprise, not her name but Petey's leapt from the page.

Petey published? In delightful anticipation, she settled at her desk. But as she read Petey's strongly worded essay, every vestige of gratification inspired by the magazine editor's complimentary words was chiseled away from her heart.

CHAPTER THIRTY

B ennett leaned against the rough exterior of the administration building and chewed a piece of dried grass while keeping his prey in his sights. A long shadow shielded him from view, but the object of his attention waited right where he had directed—in full sun on the lawn outside the library.

Bennett had chosen the spot carefully. Classes dismissed at four o'clock on Wednesday afternoons—an hour earlier than other days. Students always gathered to chat before returning to their rooms or heading to the library to study. There would be enough witnesses to ensure intense and lasting humiliation. Oh yes. The trap was set. And it had all come together with incredible ease.

Smiling, Bennett observed his target's carefree actions, evidence of his complete ignorance of the peril about to befall him. Roy Daley punched a buddy's shoulder then tossed back his head and laughed. He whirled to stick out his foot and trip an underclassman passing by on the sidewalk. The hapless lad went face-first into the dirt, and Roy slapped his knee and laughed uproariously. When the boy tried to rise, Roy gave him a kick in the seat of his pants that sent him scuttling forward several feet. His maniacal laughter reached Bennett from forty feet away.

Bennett tossed the blade of grass aside, chuckling to himself. Oh, what pleasure he'd take in seeing the great and mighty Roy Daley dethroned. When this day was over, Roy would not only turn his attentions away from Libby, he'd be a much more subdued and humble Roy.

He checked his pocket watch. Just a few more minutes . . .

"Hey, Bennett." The whisper came from Bennett's left. He shifted to find one of Beta Theta Pi's most recent pledges peeking out from behind an overgrown evergreen tree. Bennett had been instructed to trim the tree's bushy lower branches a week ago, but he'd put it off. Now he was glad he'd delayed. The spot made a perfect hiding spot.

"You ready?" Bennett whispered, keeping his gaze pinned to Roy.

"We're *all* ready." A muffled guffaw sounded. "We can't wait."

Bennett hadn't been terribly surprised to learn many of the Beta Theta Pi brothers disliked Roy. They went along with him to avoid being one of his targets, but most were counting down the days until his graduation so they'd be rid of him as fraternity leader. Roy's pleasure in hazing new recruits had gone well beyond boyish pranks, and at least eight Beta members professed a desire for revenge. Bennett had found it amazingly easy to recruit help when they were assured Roy would never be able to figure out who was involved. As long as they kept silent, they'd be safe.

He just hoped Libby would forgive him when it was all over.

❧

Libby sat at her desk, a blank sheet of paper in front of her. For as long as she could remember, she'd been able to lose herself in a fantasy world of her own making, but the ability seemed to have fled. No characters whispered to her imagination. No story flowed from her fingertips. Blowing out a breath of irritation, she threw her pencil aside. It rolled across the smooth wooden desktop and came to rest against the newspaper lying on the corner of her desk.

Her gaze fell on the newspaper, folded to reveal Petey's editorial. Pain stabbed. How could she have forgotten Petey's plan to bring an end to the writing of romance stories? If only she'd remembered, the letter to the editor wouldn't have taken her so by surprise. Wouldn't have cut her so deeply . . .

She covered her face with her hands and groaned. Oh, how she wanted to take pride in the magazine editor's comments about her writing ability! How many young women her age had been given the opportunity to be an exclusive writer for a major magazine? Signing a contract with *Modern Woman's World* could give her exactly what she'd longed for—fame, admiration, and financial independence. But instead of pride, shame filled her. She wished she'd never seen Petey's article.

Yanking open her desk drawer, she started to fling the newspaper where she wouldn't have to look at it, but a tap at the door pulled her attention elsewhere. She crossed to the door and opened it quickly. A mousy-looking girl waited in the hallway. Libby pressed her memory for the girl's name and finally retrieved it. "Hello, Caroline. Can I help you?"

"Pardon me for intruding . . ." Caroline offered a shy smile. "But I have a message for you." She hunched her shoulders and glanced furtively up and down the hallway. "Do you know . . . Roy Daley?"

Libby bristled. She wished she didn't know Roy Daley! "Unfortunately, yes."

The girl gave a quick nod. "He said you did. Well, I'm to fetch you for him."

"*Fetch* me?" Libby put her hand on her hip and glared at the girl. Could this week possibly get any worse? "Just what is that supposed to mean?"

Holding up both hands defensively, Caroline shook her head. Fuzzy brown hair bobbed around her thin cheeks. "Haven't you ever heard the saying 'Don't shoot the messenger'? I'm only doing what I'm told."

Libby tapped her foot. "You can just march right back to Roy Daley and tell him I am not one to be *fetched*. Especially not for *him*." She started to close the door.

"Wait!" Caroline sounded frantic.

Libby paused.

"If you don't come, he'll be all upset with me. And . . . and . . ."

Libby rolled her eyes. "All right. I won't put you in the middle of this." She grabbed her coat from the hook beside the door and pulled it on as she followed Caroline down the stairs and out into the yard.

"Roy will be outside the library. He said he'd be waiting." Caroline blurted the final message, then spun and ran around the corner of the dormitory. Her giggles carried on the breeze.

Scowling, Libby headed for the library. With every step, her irritation grew. Who did Roy think he was, summoning her and expecting her to come at his command? She might go to save the piteous Caroline from being tongue-lashed, but he'd regret his decision to "fetch" her as soon as she reached him!

She spotted him waiting on the lawn outside the library with a couple of his buddies, just as Caroline had indicated. Lately, he'd taken to wearing a snug-fitting sweater with a large fraternity emblem embroidered on the chest. He stood with his feet widespread and shoulders back, shamelessly showcasing his physique—an arrogant, self-centered pose. A smug grin creased his face as he watched her approach.

Her footsteps slowed, her frustration mounting. All of the worries and disappointments of the past few days rose up and filled Libby with an indignation that couldn't be corralled. Perhaps Roy had given her a gift by sending for her. She didn't care a whit about Roy Daley, so what would it matter if she used him as a battering ram for her pent-up emotions? Anticipating the sweet release, she charged across the patch of grass like a bull pursuing a waving red flag.

Before she could reach Roy, however, someone let out a whoop akin to an Indian war cry, and Libby came to a startled halt. The fine hairs on her neck prickled when men wearing head coverings made of pillowcases with eyeholes came running from every direction. Libby got a glimpse of Roy's surprised face before someone swooped her off the ground and took off running with her. She held to the man's neck, screeching to be released, but he ignored her until he reached the porch of the library. He set her down, and a gruff voice from behind the pillowcase ordered, "Don't move! Watch the show!" Then he spun to join the others.

From her vantage point, Libby had a perfect view of Roy in the center of a whooping, dancing throng of masked hoodlums. Someone had pulled the hem of his sweater up, the snug-fitting fabric creating a sheath for his head and arms. His hands flapped in the air as he fought to free himself, but to no avail. He staggered in a circle, his muffled voice demanding that someone let him loose. But instead, two men circled him with a length of rope. Libby covered her mouth with her hands, appalled, as the men tied his knees together. He couldn't possibly escape now.

With Roy sufficiently trapped in place, the men's triumphant whoops filled the air. Four others ran up, each carrying a bucket sloshing with foamy white liquid. One stood to the side, using his arm as a lever, and chanted, "One, two, *now!*" On cue, the men flung the contents of their buckets over Roy. White goo ran in thick rivulets down his body to puddle on the ground at his feet. Cheers and applause erupted from the watching crowd, which grew larger and more boisterous by the second.

Libby remained on her perch, repulsed by what was taking place, yet also oddly drawn to watch. She bounced this way and that to peer over the heads of students who spilled across the yard. They pointed, laughed, and called out comments—the gathering more raucous than any sporting event. With Roy caught in the ropes, his arms trapped and face covered, he couldn't retaliate, and everyone seemed ready to make the most of the moment. Even though she'd often called the man despicable, she felt a rush of sympathy for how he must be feeling now—as blind and helpless as a caterpillar in a cocoon.

While Roy bobbled in place, waving his hands and yelling to be released, two more pillowcase-covered men approached. Rather than buckets, they held plump pillows. Libby gasped as she realized what they planned. She clapped her hands over her mouth to muffle her cry when the men slashed the pillows with pocketknives and began shaking out the contents over Roy's head. The yard took on the appearance of a snowstorm with downy feathers filling the air. They stuck in the goo on Roy's body. In school she'd read about people being tarred and feathered and had thought it a terrible way to punish someone. Seeing it played out, with Roy as the victim, proved its capacity for humiliation. Roy howled in protest.

Students—men and women alike—raced forward to grab handfuls of feathers from the ground and slap them onto the gooey mess still dripping from Roy's body. Alice-Marie was in the midst of it, her giggles rising over the cheers and laughter of the crowd. When they'd finished, Roy resembled a half-plucked headless chicken.

A man emerged from behind the library, pushing a wheel-barrow. He forced his way to the center of the crowd and circled Roy three times while taunting him, earning a fresh round of cheers. Then, veering the wheelbarrow in a tight curve, he jammed it against the backs of Roy's knees. Roy let out a startled yelp and tumbled backward, landing on his rump in the wheelbarrow's bed. The wheelbarrow's driver jumped up and down, socking the air with both fists in a sign of victory. He bowed to the cheering crowd, then snatched up the handles to take Roy on a bumpy ride around the yard while students continued to laugh and shout their approval.

Alice-Marie ran up to Libby, tears trailing down her flushed cheeks. "Oh my, have you ever seen anything so funny in all your life?"

"He's your cousin! How can you laugh?"

Alice-Marie's jaw dropped. "You don't think he deserves it?"

Libby couldn't form an honest answer. Yes, Roy deserved to have the tables turned, but this public humiliation seemed beyond justice. It bordered on vengeful. What would Petey do if he were there?

She watched the wheelbarrow driver zigzag across the grass, forcing Roy to roll from side to side. Feathers flew, and Roy's hands continued to flop uselessly above his head. "Whoever planned this has a very sick sense of humor."

Alice-Marie leaned close. "It was Bennett! And he isn't finished yet!" Her eyes sparkled.

Libby caught Alice-Marie's arm. "*Bennett* is responsible for this? What else does he have planned?"

Instead of answering, Alice-Marie pointed. Libby followed the line of her finger to see the wheelbarrow heading straight for the library porch. "Stay here!" Alice-Marie squealed before scampering back to the grass. Students cleared a path, creating a tunnel with their bodies, and the driver careened the wheelbarrow right up to the edge of the porch. The tire banged against the edge of a foot-high concrete slab and the bed flew upward, spilling Roy at Libby's feet. Then the driver bounded onto the porch and gave Roy's sweater a yank, revealing his red, angry face.

Propping his hands on his knees, the driver bent down to Roy's level. "There you are, Daley." From behind his pillowcase mask, his voice rang gleefully, revealing his identity. "Here's Elisabet Conley, just like you wanted."

Libby smoldered as the driver—Bennett in disguise—flung both arms toward her, as if presenting her to the court.

"*Now* ask if she'll go out with you!"

CHAPTER THIRTY-ONE

"Pete, I'm not going to ask you again." Jackson's tone turned stern. He placed his hand against Pete's chest. "Stay here with your mother and the kids. Let me talk to your father alone."

Pete glanced over his shoulder. His mother stood beneath the canopy of Branson's Market. She held Lorenzo close to her side, and the other children crowded around her. Did they huddle near to be close to their ma, or were they merely trying to avoid the chilly rain?

He turned back to Jackson. "I don't think it's wise for you to talk with him alone. If what you suspect is true, he's bound to be defensive and dangerous." Pete swallowed. "A gun was used on that clerk, Jackson. How would I live with myself if—"

"Don't even think that way," Jackson said. "I encountered plenty of unsavory characters in my battle to end child labor. I faced the barrel of a gun on more than one occasion, and I always emerged unscathed. I don't intend to change that now."

"But—"

"Trust me, Pete—I'll stay safe. I've got a wife and two daughters at home who need me. I won't do anything foolish. Now, stay here." Jackson gave Pete a gentle push toward the canopy. Then he hunched his shoulders and trotted across the street, dodging raindrops. Moments later, he disappeared inside the apartment building.

Pete moved closer to his family. His brothers and sister stared up at him with wide, apprehensive eyes. His mother looked as worried as he'd ever seen her. For so many years, Pete had harbored resentful anger toward his parents—both of his parents. But looking into his ma's tired, sad face, he wondered if she was just as much a victim of Pa's apathetic selfishness as he had been. She certainly didn't resemble the monster of his imaginings with her fingers combing gently through Lorenzo's tousled hair.

Pete let his gaze drift from Lorenzo to Dennis to the older boys. What would become of his siblings if their home situation didn't change? Jackson's inquiries to remove the Leidig children from their parents and give Pete guardianship had gone no farther than a snail could race. He supposed he couldn't blame the judge—he was a one-legged eighteen-year-old without a full-time job or a home to call his own. In the judge's eyes, he couldn't offer anything better than they were already receiving.

Yet Pete still wanted them. Desperately.

The market door squeaked open and the owner, Keith Branson, stepped out. "What're you folks doin', all standin' out here?"

Although the question might have been perceived as a challenge, Pete heard no animosity in the man's voice. "We needed a place out of the rain for a few minutes. If we're in the way, we can—"

"Then come inside!" Keith waved his hand, smiling at the children. "Warmer in here. The missus has hot water boilin' on the stove. Wouldja like a cup o' tea? Or maybe some cocoa? My Norma makes the best cocoa in town—everybody says so."

Lorenzo's face lit. He looked up at his mother, his eyes begging. "Can we, Ma? Huh?"

To Pete's surprise, Berta Liedig looked to him, as if seeking approval. A lump filled his throat. He offered a nod, and she ushered the children into the store with gentle nudges and murmured admonitions. Pete followed, and a pleasant shiver wiggled across his frame as warmth from the roaring woodstove in the center of the market reached him.

Mrs. Branson hustled forward, her gently lined face wreathed in a smile of welcome. "Oh my, you all look chilled to the bone! That rain's sure turned our pretty November into a drearsome time, hasn't it? Mrs. Leidig, there's a real nice rockin' chair over in the corner. Why don't you sit a spell—you look plumb tuckered. You children come on over by the stove an' I'll get to pourin' that cocoa. Nothin'll warm you faster than a cup of cocoa with lots of milk. An' cookies? Do you like cookies?"

Lorenzo nodded so hard his hair flopped. "Yes'm!"

Laughing, Mrs. Branson tweaked Lorenzo's nose. "I thought so. Well, I got cookies, too. Oatmeal just overflowin' with plump raisins. Come on over close, now."

Berta sank into the rocking chair and rested her head on the curved back. But she kept her eyes trained on the children, who clustered around the stove while Mrs. Branson busied herself preparing the cocoa. With his family occupied, Pete returned to the front door and peered across the street, focusing on the apartment's entrance. He sure wished Jackson would hustle on out of there.

Keith sidled up beside Pete and nudged him with his elbow. "Ever'thing all right?"

"I hope so . . ."

The man flicked a glance over his shoulder at the others, then inched closer to Pete. "That fancy man I seen out on the sidewalk with you all . . . he here to help?"

Pete nodded. "Yes. He's a lawyer. We're trying to get the children into a better home." *Please let it be with me!*

"That'd be a right good thing." Mr. Branson heaved a sigh. "The missus an' me were talkin' the other night. Feelin' purty guilty, too, I don't mind admittin'."

Pete sent the man a puzzled look. "Guilty? Why?"

"All that time we spent fussin' about how nobody ever raised a hand to help them kids . . . an' we realized we'd done nothin' more'n fuss. We could've helped, too."

Pete gave the man's shoulder a reassuring pat. "I'd say you did plenty. You let them sneak off with fruits and vegetables without ever paying a penny. You made sure they were fed. That's a heap more than others have done." A hard edge crept into his voice.

Keith hung his head, his expression sorrowful. "But it weren't enough. Not hardly enough. We seen that oldest one skulkin' on the street corners, hangin' with riffraff. I'm wishin' now I'd've offered him a job. Idle hands're the devil's workshop, they say. If I'd've kept him busy, maybe—"

"Don't blame yourself." Pete shivered and slipped his hands into his coat pockets. Keith Branson was taking too much responsibility on himself. It was Gunter Leidig's job to keep Oscar out of trouble—a job he'd failed at miserably. The tingling ache in his stump increased as it always did when he stood in one place too long. Yet he wouldn't change this post until Jackson emerged. He tapped the tip of his peg on the floor. "No, sir, it's not your fault. I should've come back long ago. I didn't because I was scared of facing my pa."

Keith's head shot up, and his jaw dropped. "So you *are* a Leidig!"

Shame-faced, Pete nodded. "Yes, sir. I'm sorry I misled you.

But my lawyer friend is helping me change my name. Won't be long and I'll be Peter Rowley."

"How come?"

The childish voice startled Pete. He turned awkwardly to find Lorenzo standing behind him with a steaming mug of cocoa held between his palms. Confusion marred the little boy's face. "Does that mean you won't be my brother no more?"

Pete wished he could go down on one knee before the boy and speak to him at his level. But the best he could do was prop his hand on his good knee and bend forward. "Of course not, Lorenzo. I'll always be your brother."

"But why're you changin' your name, then?"

How could he explain to this boy that the name brought ugly memories? His name made him feel shameful, knowing it was bestowed by a man who cared so little for his family. He detested his tie to Gunter Leidig. He sought words of assurance, but before anything came to mind, a loud *pop!* echoed from somewhere outside.

Lorenzo jumped. Cocoa sloshed over the rim of the mug and dribbled past his hands. "What was that?"

Pete stood up, looking around in puzzlement. Keith stepped closer to the door, his head cocked.

Pop! Pop!

The older man spun to face Pete, his eyes wide. "Those sounded like gunshots!"

"Oh, dear Lord. Jackson . . ." Pete stumbled past Mr. Branson and out the door, clear to the curb. Rain blinded his view, but he cupped his hands above his eyes and squinted through the steady downpour. Across the street, the apartment door burst open and a man leapt off the porch. Without pause, he ran pell-mell down the street and disappeared in the gray curtain of rain. But Pete got enough of a glimpse to recognize him. He quickly looked back at the apartment door. No one came in pursuit. That could only mean one thing.

He whirled toward the market to see Keith standing in the doorway, holding out his arms to keep the children and women inside. Pete hollered, "Mr. Branson, do you have a telephone?"

The man nodded.

"Call the police! And tell them we'll need an ambulance— send them to the Leidigs' apartment. You all stay here. I've got to tend to Jackson!"

Ignoring the stabbing pain in his stump, Pete ran across the rain-slick cobblestones as fast as his peg leg would allow. His soul implored with every clumsy step, *Please, Lord, let Jackson be all right.*

❧

Libby cupped her hands around the steaming mug of coffee and scowled at Bennett. The earlier frivolity that had exploded on the lawn continued in the dining hall. Although the room always buzzed with conversation at mealtimes, this evening students remained long after the dinner hour to chat and sip coffee. Bursts of laughter rang from various corners, giving the room an air of festivity. It seemed everyone had enjoyed seeing Roy get a taste of his own medicine.

"I understand why you'd want to see Roy roundly defeated, but I do not appreciate being the cheese in a mousetrap." Libby used her sternest tone to address Bennett. "If you were going to use me, you should have warned me."

"Yeah, I probably should have." Bennett's voice carried no remorse, and to Libby's increased irritation Alice-Marie released a little giggle at his nonchalant reply. He slipped his arm across the back of Alice-Marie's chair and grinned. "But it would have spoiled the surprise."

Another loud round of laughter burst from the group sitting behind their table. Libby leaned forward and raised her voice. "I nearly forgot to breathe when that masked man picked me up and started running with me!"

Bennett snickered. "Yeah. Half a dozen of 'em volunteered for that part of the plan. I chose Riley because I knew he'd behave himself and actually put you where I wanted you."

She supposed she should thank him for his consideration, but another question filled her mind. "How did you get Roy to come, anyway? I can't imagine him responding to anyone's beck and call."

"That was the beauty of the whole plan." Bennett raised his face and let out a hoot of amusement. "He thought *he* was beckoning *you*, but in reality *we* were beckoning *him*. All it took was a few well-aimed messages sent in someone else's name."

"In other words, lots of falsehoods."

"But look at the end result!" Bennett threw his arms wide and bounced a beaming smile from Alice-Marie to the surrounding tables of jovial students and back to Libby. "Wasn't it worth it?"

Bennett's comment teased at the fringes of Libby's mind. Was an end result more important than the means used to achieve it? "I don't know."

Suddenly Bennett pulled his face into a grimace. "Besides, all you got was the brief scare of being swept off your feet. I'm paying a much higher price."

"What's that?"

Bennett toyed with his napkin, his head low. "To get Caroline to play along, I had to promise to take her to the drugstore for a sundae Saturday afternoon."

Envisioning loud-mouthed Bennett with the meek, mousy

Caroline, Libby hid a smile. "I think that's a fair retribution for being involved in such deception—for Caroline."

Bennett's head bounced up. "Hey! That isn't nice!"

Libby and Alice-Marie shared a laugh at Bennett's expense. While their laughter rolled, someone tapped Libby on the shoulder. She shifted, still giggling, to look into Miss Banks's serious face.

Libby gulped, swallowing her amusement. "Yes, ma'am?"

The dormitory matron handed Libby a folded slip of paper. "This telegram came for you. Sent by Maelle Harders."

A chill inched across Libby's flesh. She took the paper with a shaky hand. "Th-thank you."

Miss Banks gave Libby a quick pat on the back, and Libby was certain she read sympathy in the woman's usually unfriendly face. Spinning to face Bennett, she held the telegram aloft. "I'm afraid to open it."

"Oh, stop with the dramatics, Lib." Bennett rolled his eyes. "Maelle's probably just confirming your travel plans for Thanksgiving—the break's coming up, you know."

Libby shook her head. "No. It's bad. I know it's bad." She shoved the telegram across the table. "You read it."

Releasing a long-suffering sigh, Bennett took the paper. He raised one eyebrow and shot Libby a you're-being-ridiculous look, then he unfolded the telegram. His jaw dropped, and his face drained of color. Somehow Libby knew he wasn't teasing.

She snatched the telegram away from him and read the brief message: *Jackson shot by Pete's father STOP At hospital in Clayton STOP Please pray STOP*

Libby pushed away from the table. Lifting her skirts, she raced for the door.

Chapter Thirty-two

Halfway across the moon-bathed yard, Libby stumbled to a halt. Where was she going? She couldn't outrun her worry and fear. She hugged herself, realizing she'd left her coat in the dining hall. Should she go back? Her chest heaving, she looked frantically right and left. The wind, growing ever chillier as evening turned to night, tugged at her skirt and hair. Shadows lurked in every direction.

In her mind's eye, a parade of faces replaced the eerie landscape. Jackson, Maelle, Petey, even Hannah and Hester. She envisioned them with stricken eyes and trembling lips. Her heart ached for each of them, but mostly for Petey. His father had injured Jackson. Petey would bear a burden of displaced guilt for the rest of his life.

Please pray, Maelle had entreated. Such a short, simple request, but so much agony and pleading behind the words. Libby's eyes flooded with tears, and she pressed her fist to her lips. She thought her chest might collapse, so great was the longing to do as Maelle had bid.

"Libby! Libby, wait!"

Alice-Marie's voice reached Libby's ears. She turned and spotted her roommate and Bennett trotting toward her, but she couldn't talk to them now. She had a mission to complete—she must find God and beg Him to save Jackson. To save Petey. Alice-Marie and Bennett would only distract her. Catching her skirts again, she took off. Unmindful of direction, only aware that she must find the place of solitude where God resided, she ran.

She dashed between rows of towering trees that sent branches like reaching fingers toward the star-sprinkled sky. She emerged in a grassy field, and her race became hindered by knee-high grass. Grunting in frustration—she *must* find God!—she forged forward, and her foot slammed into an immovable object. She fell face-first into the cushion of thick dried grass with her legs draped across something hard and cold. The stone foundation, waiting like an open embrace beneath the moonlit sky.

Her lungs burning, unable to pull herself to standing on her trembling legs, she twisted around and collapsed with her arms and head resting on the length of cold, rough stone. Her fingers curled around the edge of one portion of the foundation, and warm tears washed down her cheeks—the first tears she'd allowed herself to shed since she was a little girl. There, all alone, she pressed her face to the solid, enduring foundation.

As she lay there, chest heaving and heart aching, the opening lines from a hymn they'd sung in the chapel at Shay's Ford winged through her memory. *How firm a foundation, ye saints of the Lord, is laid for your faith in His excellent Word!* She shifted slightly, the stone abrasive against her cheek, as another line echoed through her heart. *Fear not, I am with thee, O be not dismayed, For I am thy God and will still give thee aid.*

One of Maelle's gentle lessons from long ago crept into Libby's mind: *Darling girl, when you ask Jesus to be your Savior, then God becomes your Father. You'll be His and He'll be yours for all eternity.*

"O Jesus, save me, please . . ." The words groaned from her throat. "Please, be *my* God, my Father."

And as another rush of tears poured down her face, Libby finally opened her soul to the One the song proclaimed would be with her. Her worry for Jackson, her concern for Maelle and the twins, her heartache for Petey's burden—everything poured out in a torrent of tearful pleas.

"Please don't take Jackson from Maelle—she loves him so dearly. Please don't let Hannah and Hester lose yet another father—they need him, Lord! And please . . . Please . . . Petey . . ." She gulped, her throat aching so badly she could barely speak. "He's already had to bear so much. He's served You faithfully despite it all. Please save Jackson so Petey won't have to carry the guilt of his death. Please, God. Please . . . Please . . ."

As she prayed, a comforting presence flooded Libby's frame. A feeling of peace and assurance—unlike anything she'd known before—filled her from the inside out. In wonder, she lifted her face to the star-laden sky. "You're here, aren't You, God? That means . . . I've finally found You. Oh Lord, thank You!"

She buried her face again, more tears flowing. Cleansing tears. Grateful tears. She had no idea how long she clung to the stone foundation, inwardly praising the One who held Petey, Maelle, Jackson—and her—in His capable hands, but when the tears finally ceased she pushed herself into a seated position. With her hips pressed securely against the stone, she marveled at the change that had taken place deep inside herself. A new awareness gripped her as surely as the stone foundation now supported her tired body. Just as this stone foundation remained despite the building's destruction, so God remained—immovable, strong, sure—when all else seemed lost. How could she have been so blind as to look past Him? She'd searched so hard . . . and He'd been there all the time, simply waiting for her to stop running and fall into His arms.

The old Libby would have packed a bag and raced to the train station to go to Petey and Maelle. The old Libby wouldn't have been able to rest, not knowing how Jackson fared. But oddly, Libby had no desire to go to her friends. She merely wanted to remain there, in God's embrace, trusting Him to meet the needs of the people she held dear. Sitting there, content and at peace, she pressed her hands to her chest, feeling her strong heartbeat below. A smile curved her lips. "God, I know You're here. I feel You in my every heartbeat." She gulped, fresh tears flooding her eyes and making the stars swim. "Thank you for making me Yours."

When she looked toward the cloudless sky, the moon, round and yellow, smiled down from its perch. Libby sighed, her breath hanging on the night air. A chill shook her body. It was late— Alice-Marie and Bennett would be worried if she didn't return soon. She sent a tremulous smile upward. "We'll talk again, soon." Now that she realized God listened and cared, she would speak to Him often.

Gathering her skirts, she got to her feet and returned to her room. Alice-Marie was pacing the floor like a caged tiger. The moment Libby slipped through the door, she rushed at her and threw her arms around her.

"Oh, Libby! Thank goodness you've come back! Bennett is packing his bag. I've already started packing for you. He said he'd call the train station and find out when the next train for Clayton is due to depart, and—"

"I'm not going."

Alice-Marie pulled back. "W-what?"

Libby gave her roommate a smile and crossed to her bed. She

pushed the open suitcase aside and sat on the mattress. Linking her fingers in her lap, she released a sigh. "I'm staying here."

"But . . . but . . ." Alice-Marie sank onto her bed, staring at Libby mutely.

Libby reached out and took her roommate's hand. "Alice-Marie, there is absolutely nothing I can do for Jackson and Maelle or Petey right now. I'm weak and powerless. But God is strong." The peace that had surrounded her at the base of the stone foundation washed over her again, lifting her heart and bringing a smile to her face. "I've placed my friends into His keeping, and I trust Him to care for them." A little laugh trickled out, joyous and light. How freeing it was to trust God! "*He* is there, and that is enough."

Alice-Marie shook her head, as if confused. "Are you sure?"

Although Libby knew her roommate was asking if she was certain she didn't want to go to Clayton, Libby chose to substantiate her final statement. "I've never been more sure of anything in my life."

Alice-Marie sighed, her shoulders wilting. "Then I'll send a message to Bennett, letting him know you'd rather not go." She rose and headed for the door. But before she left the room, she peeked back at Libby. "You seem . . . different somehow."

Libby tipped her head, curious. Was it possible for Alice-Marie to see, on the surface, what had transpired in her heart? Even though she waited, Alice-Marie didn't explain. With another little shake of her head, her roommate slipped out the door.

❧

What had happened to Libby? Many times during the past two days, Bennett had puzzled over his friend's strange behavior. In his cynical moments, he accused her of walking in her sleep; at other times, he envied her calm acceptance of everything going on in Clayton. Each time they met, she asked if he'd heard anything about Jackson, and with each negative report he expected her to clench her fists, growl in frustration, or declare she simply *had* to go to Clayton. But even though he saw worry flash in her eyes, something indescribable always chased it away.

Libby just wasn't Libby anymore. And he couldn't decide if that pleased or aggravated him.

At noon on Friday, he met Alice-Marie for lunch, always an agreeable diversion. But even Alice-Marie mentioned Libby's change in attitude. "I can't put my finger on it, but she's not acting like herself. I'm really quite concerned for her. I think this situation with Pete and his family has driven her into a kind of madness."

"Madness?"

"Well, how else can you explain it? She's started reading her Bible each day—until this week, I didn't even know she owned one! I've caught her several times on her knees praying, and there's something in her eyes—a kind of dreamy expression that defies description. She's only huffed at me once in the past three days! If that doesn't mean something is amiss, then I don't know what does."

Two people at the table behind Bennett began arguing about who would win the pennant that year, their voices drowning out everything else in the room.

Bennett grabbed Alice-Marie's hand. "C'mon. It's too noisy in here. Let's take a walk."

"In this weather?"

He had to admit, being outdoors had lost much of its appeal. With Thanksgiving only a week away, fall had swooped in with gray skies, chilling winds, and occasional rainstorms. But the walls of the dining hall felt confining—he needed space.

"You can wear my jacket over your sweater, and I'll hold you close." He winked, smiling when she giggled and blushed. "Let's go."

They remained on the paved walkways rather than strolling across the grass. The recent rains had left the ground soggy, and Alice-Marie wanted to protect her shoes from patches of mud. As he'd promised, he tugged her snug against his side, but he admitted the closeness was as much for him as for her—warmth radiated from her body, staving off the cold.

Other students passed them. Everyone—men and women alike—smiled and nodded at him. Bennett found himself strutting. His popularity had doubled since word circulated naming him as the instigator in Roy's humiliation. None of the others involved had openly admitted their part in the prank, but he didn't mind. He'd take full credit, even if Roy plotted revenge. At least Roy had stopped pursuing Libby and stopped bothering other students so much.

Alice-Marie shivered and wriggled even closer to his side. "Are you going home for Thanksgiving, Bennett?"

Bennett had assumed he and Libby would return to Shay's Ford. He hoped Pete would be there, too—and Jackson. "Probably." He smiled down at her. "Why? Were you hopin' I'd come to your house instead?"

Her face flooded with color. He should stop talking like this—he was giving her ideas. Now that he'd won over several of the Beta Theta Pi men, assuring his place in the fraternity despite Roy's objections, he had no need to keep company with her. Besides that, with his increased status around campus, he could snag any girl he wanted. Be a lot more fun to play the field than stick with one. Yet he couldn't seem to separate himself from Alice-Marie.

She bumped him with her elbow and gave him one of her simpering smiles. "I'm sure Caroline would adore showing you off to her mama and papa. Maybe you'd rather spend Thanksgiving with her."

Bennett growled, baring his teeth, which only made Alice-Marie laugh. "You know better than that." Tomorrow he'd endure his promised trip to the drugstore with the plain-faced girl, and then he'd be done with her. Good riddance, too. Her moony looks across the dining hall or from the other side of the lawn tried his patience.

Alice-Marie sighed. Her breath formed a little cloud that hung in front of them for a few seconds. The air was cooler than Bennett had realized. His hands were starting to feel numb. He slipped the one resting on Alice-Marie's waist into the pocket of his jacket, which hung from her shoulders. With a slight push of his torso, he steered her toward the women's dormitory. He'd deposit her in Rhodes Hall so he could reclaim his jacket. He needed it.

She offered him another secretive look, her strides narrowing until he was forced to slow his steps. "I know you can't come for Thanksgiving—it's such a short break and you'll want to go be with your friends at the orphans' school—but might you consider spending a few days of the Christmas holiday in Clayton?" Pink stained her cheeks, and Bennett suspected the color was unrelated to the cold air that brushed their faces. "I truly would like for Mother and Daddy to get to know you. The short minutes you and Pete were at the house last weekend didn't give them sufficient time to become acquainted."

What would Alice-Marie's parents think of him? She hadn't been put off by his orphan status or unknown lineage, but would her parents accept him, just for himself? Uncertain what to say, Bennett chose to tease. "My, my, Miss Daley, aren't you the bold one. I didn't think fine-bred girls were supposed to be so forward."

Her lips pinched into a displeased line. She stepped out from under his arm. "I apologize if I seemed *forward*. I didn't realize a simple invitation would be misconstrued as presumption."

Bennett laughed. Her sassy response reminded him of how Libby used to react to his teasing. How they'd loved to spar. Would that impertinent side of Lib return when they'd finally received word about Jackson's condition?

With her nose in the air, Alice-Marie huffed, "And if you're going to be rude enough to laugh at me, then perhaps I shall withdraw my invitation. There!" She frowned up at him, her eyes snapping. "Now what do you say?"

Bennett didn't say anything. Instead, he tipped his head downward with the full intention to plant a kiss on her saucy lips. Kissing was always better than arguing. But before he could make contact, a cry split the air.

"Bennett!"

He jerked upright, expecting to find Caroline shrieking on the sidewalk. Instead, Libby raced toward them. She waved a telegram. Tears streamed down her face. He stepped away from Alice-Marie. The sight of Lib's tears almost stopped his heart. It must be awful news if Libby was crying.

Holding her shoulders, he peered into her tear-damp face. "Is it Jackson? Is he—"

"He's going to be fine!" A sob choked off her voice. Shaking her head, she gazed at him in wonder. "God saved him, Bennett! He heard our prayers, and He saved him!"

CHAPTER THIRTY-THREE

"God saved him! God saved him!"

Libby's words echoed through Bennett's head so loud and strong they made his ears ring. He released Libby and stepped backward, forcing a reply through clenched teeth. "That's great, Lib." He reached blindly, snagged the sleeve of his jacket, and yanked it from Alice-Marie's shoulders.

Alice-Marie released a displeased yelp, but he ignored her protest and jammed his arms into the sleeves. He turned and strode toward the men's dormitory. An unnamed fury made him pound his feet against the concrete, the solid contact stinging his soles.

"Bennett, wait!" Libby's bewildered cry found his ears right before a hand grabbed the back of his jacket.

He shook loose and marched on, but a persistent *click-click* on the sidewalk let him know she was still pursuing him. He stopped and spun to face her. "What?" The single-word query snapped out, surprising even him with its vehemence.

She drew back momentarily then scurried forward to curl her hands over his arm. "I thought you'd be pleased. I know you've worried about Jackson. So why are you so . . . ?" She seemed to be peering beneath his skin, trying to find the real emotion underneath.

He turned and glared across the yard, his teeth clamped so tightly his jaw hurt. "I'm happy Jackson's fine." His throat ached with the effort it took to speak. "It's good news. Jackson's fine. Pete's fine. You're fine. Everybody's fine!" His hands formed fists, and he jammed them deep into his pockets so he wouldn't be tempted to raise one and use it to do something he'd later regret.

Grabbing his arm again, Libby guided him off the sidewalk and beneath the eaves of the nearest building, where they were somewhat protected from the wind and away from curious eyes. "Tell me what's wrong."

Her tears had dried, leaving shiny paths on her smooth cheeks. The tenderness in her eyes made his chest feel tight. She needed to stop looking at him like that. "Nothin'."

"There *is* something. The last response I expected from you at the news of Jackson's recovery was anger, yet you're angry, Bennett. I can see it." She squeezed his arm, leaning close. "Tell me why."

Bennett jerked free of her grasp. "No."

"Why not?"

"Because it won't change anything!" He wished she'd get mad back—snap at him that he needed to change his attitude or remind him to behave like a human being. She hadn't hesitated to blast him with her opinions in the past. If she'd do it now, he'd have an excuse to shout and rage, too. But she went on looking at him in that soft, sweet way. In a way he didn't deserve. "Leave me alone, Lib."

"I won't. Not until you let loose of what's bothering you."

"What's bothering me is you!" If anything would make her spout in defense, that would do it. He braced himself, prepared for the deluge of furious words sure to spew from her lips.

As he'd expected, her expression hardened. She opened her mouth slightly, her chin lifting into an arrogant angle. But then, to his disappointment, she appeared to shrink into herself. Her eyes slipped closed for a moment, and she drew in a deep breath. When she opened her eyes and looked at him, all of the fury of moments before was gone. That odd calm acceptance he'd witnessed in the past few days returned, and it raised Bennett's irritation another notch.

"Stop making excuses, Bennett. You're hiding from the truth." Her composed speech did nothing to ease his frustration. "You aren't angry at me, but you are angry. What is it?"

He leaned forward until his face was only inches from hers. With his jaw so tight he could barely form words, he snarled, "All right, Lib, you want the truth? You're right. I'm downright, all-fired, purely *mad* right now, and I've got every reason to be. Apparently it's not bad enough that I have to listen to my best friend-turning-preacher spouting God-talk at me every minute— now you're starting to do it!

"I've never fit in anywhere—not at the orphanage, where someone dumped me, not with the Rowleys, where I could never measure up to Pete, not here on this campus with its kids from good families . . . but at least, in a way, I had you. We were alike, you and me—not finding a family like other kids from the orphans' school did, not fitting in anywhere . . . together." He paused. How could Libby understand anything he said? He couldn't even make sense of his own ramblings.

But in spite of his disjointed spillage of words, Libby listened intently. Looking into her open, accepting expression, his anger swelled again. " 'God saved Jackson.' " He mimicked her higher-pitched tone, putting a sarcastic note into his delivery. "Well, doesn't that make Jackson special? God just seems to save everybody—Pete, Jackson, all those kids who got adopted instead of me—" He swallowed, finally acknowledging the source of the change that had come over Libby in the past few days. "Even you." Bennett broke out in a sweat despite the cold temperature. "So where does that leave me? What's God ever done for me?"

Tears glimmered in Libby's eyes. Another change—Libby never cried. He had no idea how to respond to Libby's tears. "Stop that!" He pointed at her face as one tear slipped free and ran toward her chin. "Don't be bawling like a baby. I didn't do anything to you."

She shook her head, her chin quivering. "I'm not crying for me, Bennett. I'm crying for you. Because you just can't see."

"See what?"

"That God's been with you all along."

He snorted. "Oh, yeah. That's just as clear as a brand-new windowpane." Derision laced his words. He turned to storm away.

Libby caught hold of his jacket front. Even though he wanted to pull away, something made him stay put. But he wouldn't look her in the face. Her soft voice reached his ears, though, her warm breath touching his cheek.

"I understand, Bennett. I didn't see Him, either. Not until I tripped and fell into His arms. But He's here, right now, loving both of us just like He always has. Our problem is we've been trying to find Him in the midst of our own selfish wants instead of realizing He's waiting in the middle of where He needs us to be."

Bennett crunched his eyebrows. He blurted, "That doesn't make sense."

"I know. It's hard to comprehend at first, but once you grasp it, it changes everything." She gave his jacket a little tug and he knew she wanted him to look at her, but he kept his face stubbornly angled away. She sighed. "Bennett, you said God never saved you. What makes you think that?"

Hurts carried from long ago rose up. "You know why. My folks threw me away. Gave me to a bunch of people who didn't care about me. When I ran off, nobody came after me." He'd never forgotten the long-ago day when he'd darted out the door of the children's home into the street, hoping—just hoping—someone would follow. He clenched his fists tighter, the remembered fear of that first night alone in an alley bringing a rush of hurt and shame. Why hadn't anyone come? "They just let me go."

So quietly he almost didn't hear her, she asked, "And who found you?"

Bennett swallowed and refused to answer.

"Aaron Rowley found you." She bounced her knuckles against his chest. "Didn't he? And he took you with him. Never once hesitated. He gave you a home, Bennett. Haven't you ever considered that was God's way of reaching down to rescue you?"

"Wanted my *own* home." He sounded childish, foolish, but he couldn't help himself. He did want his own home, and his own folks. God hadn't given him what he'd wanted.

"I wanted a ma and pa . . ." Libby said, her voice turning sad, and despite his determination to stay turned away, Bennett couldn't resist a quick glimpse of her face. Her eyes found his and held him captive. The peaceful acceptance reflected there raised a tide of longing. What must it be like to be as at peace as Libby was right now?

"I still don't understand why God said no to my prayers for Maelle to adopt me. A little part of me will always wish she had, because I love her so much. Maybe . . ." She tipped her head, recognition creeping across her features. "Maybe He said no because

He wanted me to finally accept that I didn't need Maelle's love as much as I needed His. I'll have to think about that."

She tugged his jacket front again. "But for now, there's something I want you to do. Stop trying to see God where you *want* Him to be. Start trusting that He's right where you *need* Him to be. And you'll finally realize . . . He's with you, Bennett, and you're safe with Him."

ɞ

"I'm so glad you're going to be all right," Pete said as he grasped the iron footboard of Jackson's hospital bed. Now that Maelle had finally agreed to leave Jackson's side and get some rest at the hotel, Pete had a chance to spend some time alone with Jackson.

He hadn't begrudged Maelle the privilege of being with her husband, but he'd needed to see for himself that Jackson was recovering from the wound he'd received when he'd wrestled Gunter for control of the gun.

He shook his head sadly. "So much for your promise that nothing would happen when you went to talk to my pa . . ."

Jackson swished his hand through the air, then grimaced and pressed his palm to the bandage that circled his torso. "It's just a flesh wound. Although I regret how much worry it's caused everyone, I'm glad it happened. If it weren't for being shot, the police might not have been as willing to believe me when I told them Gunter confessed to killing the clerk. This crease in my side gave me credibility."

Pete lowered his head. He was the son of a murderer; that fact hung like a boulder around his neck. "I still don't understand why Oscar didn't just tell the police it was Pa who did the shooting. He was ready to die rather than tell the truth."

"Oscar did what he thought was best." Jackson spoke in what

Pete thought of as his lawyer voice. "If your father had been arrested and hanged, who would provide for the family? Oscar knew he couldn't take care of his mother and brothers and sister. He was willing to give himself for them."

Pete marveled at the unselfishness of his little brother's choice. There was good in the boy—he only hoped a judge would recognize it. "What will happen to Oscar now?"

Jackson sighed. "The murder charge has been reversed, thank God, but Oscar admitted to trying to rob the store. He'll have to pay the penalty for that crime."

"But he won't hang."

"No, he won't hang."

Pete hitched his way to a chair in the corner and sat, relief making him weak. They'd managed to rescue Oscar from the hangman's noose, but what of his ma and his other siblings? Gunter Leidig had disappeared. Although the authorities were hunting for him, Pete was certain they wouldn't find him. He'd be a fool to return to Clayton, knowing the gallows awaited. His family was on its own now.

"When Aaron and Isabelle get here tomorrow, I need to talk to them about quitting school." Pete rested his hands on his knees, absently massaging the right one. "Now that Pa's gone for good, somebody's going to have to support Ma and the children. I'm the oldest, so it falls to me."

Jackson shifted slightly on the pillow to frown at Pete. "You're planning to move to Clayton?"

How he hated the idea of being away from everyone he loved. Libby's face flashed in his mind's eye. Leaving her would be the hardest. But it would be good for both of them. They'd be able to release their fruitless emotional bond and move on with their lives. Of course, if he didn't enter the ministry, maybe they could find a way to bridge their differences. Strangely, the thought didn't lift his heart.

Pete held up his hands in a gesture of helplessness. "What else can I do? I can't work full time *and* go to school. Somebody has to pay the rent and buy food and clothes for the kids. My ma sure can't do it. She's never had a job—she always depended on Pa." Was it fear of Pa or her lack of skills that had kept his mother in that house, trapped? "Now she'll be depending on me."

"What kind of job do you think you'll find?"

"Maybe I'll work at the brewery." Pete didn't relish working in such a place, but it offered decent wages. "Or maybe I can find something on the docks."

"You think they'll hire a man with a peg leg?"

Even though Jackson spoke kindly, his words stung. "If they won't, then I'll find a desk job. Maybe in a bank, or as a store accountant."

"Without training?" Jackson shook his head. "You're talking nonsense, Pete. Ever since you were ten years old, you've wanted one thing—to preach. Are you telling me becoming a minister doesn't matter to you now?"

Pete tapped his peg against the floor. He sampled the excuse he intended to present to Aaron and Isabelle. "What if . . . what if I told you I picked preaching because I knew I could stand in a pulpit with only one good leg. Preaching's one job where having a peg leg doesn't matter—it doesn't affect my ability to speak."

"You don't really mean that."

Pete stared at the tip of his wooden peg sticking out from his pant leg. He sighed. No, he didn't mean it, and he hoped God would forgive him for even making such a statement. He'd been called to preach by the God who'd preserved his life all those years ago. Becoming a minister wasn't convenience for him; it was a response to the tug on his heart. He answered honestly. "No. I don't."

"Then don't give up your dream. God has a plan in all of this. Seems to me you're trying to fix everything yourself instead of depending on Him. Aaron and Isabelle have taught you better than that."

Pete swallowed the lump of shame that filled his throat. "Maybe you're right."

"Of course I'm right. I know everything—just ask Hannah and Hester."

Pete chuckled softly. Those girls were lucky to have Jackson Harders as their pa. Even better, Jackson thought he was lucky to have them.

Jackson yawned. "Not trying to chase you off, but I am tired. I'd like to get some sleep before the doc sends me home with Maelle." He grinned. "If I know her, she'll cluck around me like a mother hen and keep me from resting there. Do you mind . . . ?"

Pete pushed off the chair and limped to the bed. "Not at all. You rest. I'll come back and see you tomorrow."

"When are you going back to Chambers?" Jackson nestled his head against the pillow. Pete had never seen his usually neatly combed black hair so mussed. "I intend to meet Oscar at court next Monday and serve as his lawyer when he receives his new sentence. Maelle will look in on your mother and the rest of the family. Why don't you return to school before you're so far behind you can't catch up?"

"Another few days won't hurt." Pete softened the stubborn reply with a smile. "I want to see Aaron and Isabelle." He needed their advice. "And I'd like to be there for Oscar—let him know he's not alone."

Jackson closed his eyes. "All right, all right. But scat now."

"Yes, sir." Pete headed outside and waited on the curb for a passing cab. He'd planned to go to the hotel, but at the last minute he changed his mind. Before he retired for the evening, he needed to make another visit. He waved down a cab and climbed into the narrow back seat. "Driver, take me to Branson's Market."

CHAPTER THIRTY-FOUR

Libby linked arms with Alice-Marie as they walked out of the Sunday morning service. Although Petey had invited her to attend the little rock chapel with him, she'd never accepted his invitation. Not since her weekend in Shay's Ford had she sat in a church service. How had she managed to be away for so long? She smiled, still basking in the glow of meeting with other Christians, singing hymns of praise, and listening to the minister read from the Bible and then offer applications of the words to the congregants' lives.

Looking back, she'd spent a significant amount of time in church. Before they died, her parents had taken her; and then she'd gone with Mr. and Mrs. Rowley to the chapel in Shay's Ford. Libby had spent more Sundays than she could count sitting on a wooden pew. She'd listened, but somehow she'd never accepted the messages. She'd been too busy trying to make God fit her idea of what He should be. Now that she'd realized that God knew best, she found a new joy in attending service. She couldn't wait for Petey to come back so she could tell him everything that had happened while he'd been away.

"Do you suppose Bennett will join us for lunch?" Alice-Marie fastened the top button of her coat and pulled her little felt hat more snugly over her coiled hair.

"Bennett might skip church, but he never misses a meal," Libby answered. "He'll be in the dining hall, ready to be fed, I'm sure." She only wished he would have come to service. The minister's message, taken from the fifth chapter of Matthew, offered assurance that those who hungered for righteousness would be filled. Bennett needed to be filled, and Libby knew the best place to have his deepest hunger met was in God's Word.

She and Alice-Marie stepped to the side to allow another couple to pass them on the sidewalk. The man and woman walked arm-in-arm, slowly, their gazes locked. Libby's heart stirred at their intent focus on one another. She and Petey had looked at each other that way across the barn floor on Matt's wedding day. Would they ever gaze into each other's eyes that way again?

Alice-Marie's giggle disrupted Libby's thoughts, and Libby sent her roommate a puzzled look. "What's funny?"

Alice-Marie pointed at the besotted couple. "Do you see who that is? Caroline and Winston." She giggled again, covering her lips with gloved fingers. "Bennett was supposed to take her to the drugstore for a sundae, but she refused to go. Because she went with Winston instead!" Alice-Marie shook her head. "Can you imagine choosing Winston over Bennett?" She heaved a heavy sigh, her eyelashes fluttering. "But I'm relieved. I didn't like the idea of him spending time with another girl anyway."

A rumble echoed in the distance, and Libby looked up. Gray clouds rolled across the sky, hiding the sun. "We'd better hurry before the clouds decide to let loose. I smell rain." Ducking their heads, they trotted the remaining distance. Just before they stepped into the dining hall, thunder growled overhead and fat raindrops burst from the clouds to pelt the ground.

Alice-Marie grimaced. "I suppose we'll be trapped in here for a while."

Libby shrugged, unconcerned. "It's warm and dry, and there's plenty to eat."

As Libby had expected, Bennett was already seated in the dining hall with a full plate of food in front of him. He barely glanced at them when they approached his table. Alice-Marie planted one fist on her hip and pointed to his plate. "You couldn't wait for us?"

"You couldn't hurry?" Bennett countered. His tone carried a hard edge. For the past few days, he'd been short-tempered and moody with Alice-Marie. Libby wondered why the girl tolerated his boorish behavior. Libby would have cheerfully tossed him to Caroline days ago.

"We were in church." Alice-Marie removed her hat and shook it until drops of water scattered. "Why weren't you?"

Bennett leaned over his plate and spooned up an enormous bite of black-eyed peas. "I don't go to church."

"Maybe you should," Alice-Marie said tartly. "It would do you some good."

He didn't reply.

Alice-Marie took a step toward the serving area. "Let's go get in line, Libby."

"I'll be there in a minute."

After looking from Libby to Bennett and back, Alice-Marie flounced away from the table.

Libby slid out a chair and sat, leaning close to Bennett. "Are you still mad and taking it out on Alice-Marie? Because that really isn't fair. She didn't do anything to deserve it."

Bennett paused with his spoon aimed at his plate and flicked a squinty-eyed look at Libby. "I'm not mad."

"Then why are you so testy? You've hurt Alice-Marie's feelings several times in the past few days. You even made her cry." The protectiveness Libby felt toward Alice-Marie surprised her. When had she decided Alice-Marie was more than an annoying roommate? Somehow, over the past months, they'd become friends.

He shoved another bite into his mouth and spoke around it. "Sorry."

"You don't sound sorry." Libby refused to back down when Bennett frowned at her. "Are you going to be nice when she comes back?"

He grunted.

She smacked his wrist. "Bennett!"

Suddenly he burst out laughing. His eyes twinkled, and he gave her a boyish smirk. "If I'm not nice, are you going to bombard me with dirt clods?"

Her irritation melted away as childhood memories filled her mind. How many times had she gotten even with Bennett for some misdeed, real or imagined, by hiding in the bushes beside the dormitory and assailing him with gathered chunks of dried mud when he least expected it? Many times, Petey had hunkered in the bushes with her, and it had taken all of their self-control to keep from revealing their hiding spot by giggling out loud as Bennett passed by.

"I miss those days," she admitted on an airy sigh.

"Yeah. It was a lot easier then, wasn't it?" Bennett glanced toward Alice-Marie, who stood at the food counter, her finger on her lips in great concentration as she chose what to put on her plate. His brows pulled low. "She wants me to go home with her at Christmas—spend a couple of days getting to know her folks."

Libby's eyes widened. "I knew you were spending quite a bit

of time together—Alice-Marie tells me everything. But I didn't know you'd become so close."

"We haven't. At least I don't think we have. I'm not real sure what to do about her."

Maybe that explained his churlish behavior. He was trying to scare Alice-Marie away. She gave his wrist a squeeze. "Instead of being mean to her, why not be honest with her? Tell her you're uncertain how to proceed."

He frowned. "That would work?"

Libby laughed. "Why wouldn't it?"

"I dunno. She's a girl. Girls are . . . touchy."

She laughed again. "You've never hesitated to tell me what you think."

"Aw, but everyone knows you're not a normal girl, Lib." The teasing tone let her know she hadn't ruined their friendship by scolding him about his behavior. But he was wrong about her not being a normal girl. Even now, she carried the heartache of a girl deeply in love with someone unavailable to her. She wished she could spare Alice-Marie that pain.

"Never mind about me. About Alice-Marie . . . promise me you'll tell her you aren't ready for a relationship beyond friendship. She needs to know before she gives you her heart. It's a lot easier to fall in love than it is—" she swallowed, battling tears—"to climb back out once you've fallen. Don't hurt her that way."

Bennett lowered his spoon and gave her his full attention. "You all right?"

"Not really." She sniffed hard, bringing her emotions under control. "I foolishly let myself fall in love with Petey even though I know we're completely unsuitable for each other. You said it yourself, we just don't . . . fit."

Bennett chewed the corner of his lip. "Yeah, I said that. But you know somethin', Lib? I might've been wrong." He tapped his spoon on the edge of his plate, reminding her of Petey's habit of tapping his peg leg. "Lately you've been different. Calmer. More settled. More like Pete. What you said about finding God? It changed something in you."

He squirmed in his chair, as if the conversation were making him uneasy. But when he continued, his voice was strong. "Now, I'm not saying you should run out and ask Pete to marry you, but . . . in time . . . if you both still love each other and he should ask you . . . I don't think it would be so ludicrous anymore."

"Oh, Bennett." Without thinking, Libby threw her arms around his neck. He didn't hug her back, but he gave her shoulders some half-hearted pats. While she clung to Bennett, an idea seemed to sail through the air and hit on the back of her head. "Oh!" She pulled loose. "I have to go."

"Go? Go where?" He half rose as she jumped from the chair and began buttoning her coat.

Alice-Marie hustled over, a tray in her hands and a frown on her face. "Elisabet Conley, did I just see you hugging my . . . hugging Bennett?"

Libby waved away her roommate's concern. "Yes, but don't worry—Bennett will explain."

"I will?" He looked panicked.

Libby gave him a fierce look and hissed, "Just *talk* to her, Bennett!" She spun and headed for the door.

"Libby?" Alice-Marie's voice called after her. "Aren't you going to eat?"

She didn't even pause. "I'm not hungry!"

"But—"

"I'll talk to you later!" She dashed out the door, ignoring the rain that continued to fall. Eating could wait. This task could not.

❧

"And so Mr. Branson agreed to give Oscar a job when he's finished serving his sentence, whenever that may be." Pete leaned back and beamed across the table at Aaron and Isabelle.

Oscar would be in good hands with the Bransons. The couple reminded him of his own foster grandparents, Ralph and Helen Rowley, who'd been a wonderful influence on his life. He might have entered a life of crime had they not offered him a safe retreat and treated him like their own. He prayed Oscar would now make better choices with the second chance he'd been given.

"We're so happy things have turned out well for Oscar." Isabelle took Pete's hand. Even though they sat in a public restaurant in Clayton, Pete felt no embarrassment. He loved this woman as much as he could have loved his own mother. It seemed good and right that she would hold his hand and offer her support.

He said, "I've been praying for leniency. Justice, yes, but leniency. I trust the judge will be fair in dealing with Oscar."

Aaron leaned his elbows on the table. "I spoke with Jackson last night. He believes the judge will give Oscar a light sentence since it was his first offense and he was only acting in obedience to his father. Besides, he's already served many days in jail."

Pete's chest constricted at the mention of Gunter Leidig. He couldn't wait to become Peter Rowley, erasing his father's imprint on his life. "I think Oscar will be less likely to get into trouble if he's kept busy in appropriate ways, and he'll be able to help contribute to the family income. That will be a big help to me."

Aaron and Isabelle exchanged a look, and then Aaron cleared his throat. "Pete, Oscar isn't the only person Jackson and I discussed. He told me you were considering dropping out of school to take care of your mother and siblings."

Isabelle pulled her hand away, fixing Pete with a dismayed look. "And I must tell you, I am very much in opposition."

Pete groaned. Why hadn't Jackson allowed him to tell Aaron and Isabelle in his own way? "Would you at least talk to me about this? It's important to me."

Isabelle's green eyes flashed fire. "Nothing is more important than you getting your education. Your scholarship was meant—"

Aaron put his hand over hers. "Isabelle, let's at least hear Pete out."

"But—"

Aaron shook his head slightly, and Isabelle drew in a deep breath. She released the breath slowly then faced Pete. "Very well. I'll listen." She pointed at him. "But don't expect me to support any scheme that involves you quitting the university!"

In spite of himself, Pete laughed. Often Libby complained about Isabelle, but they were alike in many ways, including being hard-headed. He decided it might be best to keep that opinion to himself, however. "All right. Let me tell you what I'm thinking. . . ."

For the next few minutes, he shared his deep concern about his mother and his siblings' situation. Without a man providing an income, the children would suffer. His throat tightened as he described his strong desire to take care of his brothers and sister. He finished with, "You took care of me. What would have happened to me if you hadn't? My brothers and sister now need someone to look after them. I just want to do what's right."

During his explanation, Aaron and Isabelle had occasionally exchanged glances, seeming to communicate with their eyes, but they hadn't interrupted. Now Aaron spoke. "First of all, we admire you, Pete, for wanting to be responsible for your family."

Isabelle squeezed his hand again. "You could easily ignore your family's plight, given the way they treated you when you were a little boy." She gave him a warm smile. "Your willingness to meet their needs in deference to holding a grudge shows us what a fine man you've grown to be." Tears glittered in her eyes. "We're both very proud of you."

Pete felt his chest puff at their approval. "Then you agree that I should quit school?"

Isabelle raised her chin. "Absolutely not."

"But you just said—"

"We said we admired your desire. We did not say we agreed it was the best thing for you to do."

Pete looked in confusion from Isabelle to Aaron. "Isn't it the same thing?"

Aaron chuckled. "Not quite. All right, Pete. We listened to you. Now will you listen to us?"

Pete suspected he was going to hear the same arguments he'd already endured from Jackson. But he wouldn't be disrespectful to the people who'd raised him. He nodded.

Aaron propped one arm on the table and his expression turned serious. "You see, Pete, Isabelle and I have been praying about a situation at home. We knew when Matt and Lorna got married, Lorna wouldn't want to keep working at the orphans' school forever. She agreed to continue cleaning and helping with the cooking until she and Matt started their family, but . . ." He grinned, gesturing toward Isabelle.

Isabelle clapped her hands together, joy lighting her face. "Lorna is in a family way. Already! She and Mattie will welcome a baby into their home midsummer. They are so delighted, as are we. Isn't it exciting?"

"I'm very happy for them." Pete had no idea how Matt and Lorna's coming baby affected him or his family.

Aaron continued. "Now that's she's expecting a child, she wants to spend her days in her own home, preparing it. So she asked to be released from working at the orphans' school."

Isabelle cut in. "Of course, that has left us dreadfully short-handed. Poor Cookie Ramona has been run ragged doing all the cooking and the cleaning and the laundry. I help as much as I can, but between my teaching duties and caring for the children, I don't have nearly enough time to spare. So . . ." She once again deferred to Aaron.

"We've been praying for someone to come along and replace Lorna. It takes a special person to be willing to move into the school and dedicate so many hours to the job." Aaron lifted one shoulder, as if hesitant to continue. "After talking to Jackson last night, we got to thinking that maybe your mother would be interested in moving into the school and taking over those chores."

Pete's eyebrows shot up. "My mother?"

"Why not?" Isabelle's face shone with enthusiasm. "We know she has the ability to be a housekeeper. She's been caring for your father's home and her own children for many years. And of course, if she comes, the children are welcome, too." At that, her face pinched into a delicate grimace. "I am aware it wouldn't be the same as sharing their own private apartment, but at least they'd all be under the same roof."

Pete nodded slowly, liking the idea more and more. If his mother agreed, then he wouldn't have to worry about the children going hungry, being cold, or going unsupervised. Aaron and Isabelle would see that they were educated and attended church. He'd had a wonderful upbringing at the Reginald Standler Home for Orphaned and Destitute Children, and he possessed no reservations about seeing his brothers and Elma settled there.

Having his mother live in the place that had become home to him, however, gave him pause. He'd spent so many years resenting her, wanting to erase all memories of her. Each time he visited

Aaron and Isabelle, he'd be forced to see his mother in his place of refuge and security. Could he allow the two halves of his life—one half bearing unhappy memories and one half bringing peace—to blend?

He asked, "Have you mentioned any of this to my mother?"

Isabelle shook her head. "No." Once again, she cupped her hand over his. "We thought perhaps you would like to pray about it first. Then, if you believe it's in the best interest of your mother and your siblings, we feel you should be the one to suggest it. After all, you are the man of the family now."

CHAPTER THIRTY-FIVE

Libby dropped her pencil and rubbed her aching knuckles. A glance at the clock confirmed she'd been writing for four straight hours. In privacy. Alice-Marie hadn't returned yet, and Libby hoped she and Bennett had worked out their differences and were sharing a pleasant afternoon together.

She rose and stretched, unkinking the knots in her back, then picked up the sheets of paper containing her newest story. She smiled. Her best yet. Raising her face to the ceiling, she said, "Thank You, Lord." In her hands she held a love story full of romance with a hero destined to melt the heart of any woman. Yet this was a story that would also meet Petey's approval.

Looking at her work, she prayed it would also please the magazine editor. Her face filled with embarrassed heat as she recalled deliberately penning scenes of physical arousal in previous stories. As much as she wanted the opportunity to write for *Modern Woman's World*, she knew she couldn't send more stories of the kind she'd already submitted. In fact, she intended to ask to have her work withdrawn. She'd have to pay back the money they'd paid her, and she hoped they'd be patient about it, but she could no longer in good conscience allow those stories to be published. They didn't honor God, and from now on, she must honor God with every part of her being.

Returning to the desk, she opened her Bible and flipped to the chapter the minister had used as a reference at Matt and Lorna's wedding. The beautiful words from First Corinthians 13, outlining the meaning of love, stirred a sweet ache in the center of Libby's chest. Verses four through six spoke so eloquently of God's love for man as well as His expectation of how His children should love one another.

She glanced again at the story she'd created that afternoon. "This story reflects Your love, God. I want so much to be able to help Petey take care of his brothers and sister. If it's Your will for me, let this story find acceptance so I can continue to use the writing abilities You gave me."

ఆ

On the Tuesday before Thanksgiving, Pete sat in the back of the courtroom with his mother. Beside Jackson, Oscar stood straight and proud in a new shirt and trousers, his hair freshly cut. He looked nothing like the bedraggled boy who'd curled on the cot in the basement cell.

The judge, sober and stern in his black robe, peered down from his seat behind the bench. "Young man, since you have pled guilty to attempted robbery, I sentence you to six months of hard labor, which will be served at the Missouri Penitentiary in Jefferson City."

Oscar flicked a glance over his shoulder. Pete sent him a re-assuring nod, and he faced the judge again.

"I must also express my gratitude that the truth concerning the murder charge made against you has been brought to light. You are a fortunate young man to have so many people fighting for you. It is my hope that you will emerge from this experience with the determination to be a law-abiding citizen, and will therefore prove that the trust offered by those who have given assistance is not ill placed."

"Yes, sir. Thank you, sir."

The judge rose, and Pete and Berta scrambled to their feet, as well. As the judge left, two officers approached from their post beside the bench, reaching for Oscar. Oscar drew back and threw a frantic look over his shoulder. Pete stumped forward as quickly as his peg leg would allow.

"Could we have a moment of time . . . to say good-bye?"

The officers glanced at each other and then one nodded. "Five minutes."

Berta rushed up and stretched her arms across the wooden bar to embrace Oscar. Copious tears rained down her thin face. "Oh, Oscar . . ."

Oscar clung, burying his face in the curve of her shoulder. "I'll be all right, Ma. Only six months. Won't be so long."

"Me an' the young'uns'll write to you every day." Berta shot a hesitant look at the closest officer. "He'll be allowed letters from his family?"

The officer nodded. "Yes, ma'am. His lawyer here can give you the address."

Pulling loose, Berta cupped Oscar's face in her hands. "See there? That'll give ya somethin' to look forward to each day—a letter from us. An' you write, too—keep up your writin' an' readin'.

Who knows, maybe you'll get to go to a university one day, too, like your brother Petey."

Pete stepped close and reached past his mother to clamp his hand over Oscar's shoulder. "Mind your manners and do what you're told."

Oscar nodded. "I will."

"I'll write, too, and I'll be counting down the days until you're free. Then we'll do something special together—just you and me. Sound good?"

"Sounds real good, Pete." Oscar ducked his head for a moment, then his gaze bounced back up to meet Pete's. "Thank you for comin' to the jail. Thanks . . . for comin' back."

Pete curled his hand around Oscar's neck and pulled him against his chest as tight as he could with the bar separating them. Oscar's temple connected with Pete's chin, his thick hair tickling his neck. Pete didn't want to let go, but the nearest officer cleared his throat and said, "It's time."

Pete handed Oscar to Berta for one more hug, and then they watched the officers escort Oscar through a door at the front of the room. Berta pressed her clenched hand to her mouth, and her body convulsed in silent sobs. Hesitantly, Pete lifted his arm and wrapped it around her thin shoulders. She didn't lean into him, but her face tipped upward, gratitude in her tired eyes.

"We'd better go." Jackson picked up his briefcase and turned stiffly toward the door. With one hand bracing his ribs, he gestured for Pete and Berta to precede him. Their footsteps echoed on the marble floor as they headed down the hallway together.

Outside, Jackson turned to Pete. "Since your train to Chambers leaves three hours earlier than ours to Shay's Ford, I'll say my good-byes here." He stuck out his hand, and Pete gave it a firm shake. "Have a safe trip back."

"I will. Thanks for . . ." How could Pete possible encapsulate all Jackson had done for his family in the past week? He shook his head. "For *everything*, Jackson."

Jackson grinned. "My pleasure. I'm just glad it all turned out as well as it did."

"Me too."

"Will you come to Shay's Ford at the end of the week for Thanksgiving?"

Berta sent a hopeful look in Pete's direction when Jackson posed the question. As much as Pete wanted to go home for Thanksgiving—to make sure his siblings had settled in and spend time with Matt and Lorna and all the others—he'd been away from school too long. He'd need many days to catch up.

Reluctantly, he shook his head. "I'm afraid not. One of my professors, Pastor Hines, said I could stay at his home if I ever needed a place, so I'll probably take him up on his offer and use the break to catch up on the classes I missed while I've been here." The disappointment sagging his mother's face pricked his heart, so he added in a cheerful tone, "But I'll be there for Christmas—you can count on it."

"I think that's wise," Jackson replied. "Well . . ." He bounced his leather satchel against his leg and looked at Berta. "Maelle is probably still at your apartment, helping the children pack for your move. Let's go there and finish up. That train will leave before we know it."

But Berta remained rooted in place, her pleading eyes aimed at Pete's face. Pete knew what she wanted. What she needed. And he wished he could give it. But it was too soon. Maybe one day he'd find the ability to put his arms around his mother, to hold her close, but God needed to do a little more work on him before he was ready.

Giving her a smile, he said, "You'll be in good hands with Aaron and Isabelle—they're some of the best people God ever planted on this earth." He raised his hand in a wave. "Bye now."

Berta's lips trembled. "Bye, Petey." She turned and followed Jackson to the curb, where he flagged a cab. Pete waited until they climbed in and the cab clattered away before he turned toward the hotel. He'd retrieve his bag and then catch a cab to the train station. By this evening, he'd be back in Chambers. He'd only been gone a week, but it seemed like a year, so much had transpired in such a short amount of time.

Pausing on the busy sidewalk, Pete bowed his head and offered a silent, heartfelt prayer of thanks to God for His redeeming intervention. So many broken threads had been woven into place. Pete had emerged stronger, more determined to seek and follow God's will in every aspect of his life.

He opened his eyes and hitched forward, eager to return to Chambers and share with his two best friends all the miracles of the past week. Then his steps slowed, his enthusiasm waning. In order to share truthfully, he'd have to give God the glory. Would Bennett mockingly call the events happenstance? Would Libby's defensive ire flare—was she still annoyed that he'd sent her away? For a moment, he considered keeping all that had happened to himself rather than face their scorn.

But then he straightened his shoulders and hop-skipped to put himself in motion again. Whether they wanted to hear it or not, he'd tell them all that had happened. And he would give praise where praise was due.

The following morning Pete arose early, dressed, and met with Pastor Hines before breakfast. The man cheerfully agreed to host Pete for the Thanksgiving weekend and even offered to assist him with his missed assignments.

"I'm glad to see you back, Mr. Leidig. I was half afraid you'd decided the work was too hard."

Pete shook his head. "No, sir. I'm determined to complete my divinity degree. God's called me to this task, and He's given me everything I need to see it through. So I aim to please Him with my efforts."

"Good man." The professor smacked Pete on the back. "And I look forward to working with you. Head on to breakfast now—I'll see you in class later."

On his way to the dining hall, he stopped by Franklin Hall to retrieve Bennett, but to his surprise Bennett was already gone. His roommate was in the room, however. Winston blinked at Pete behind round, thick spectacles.

"I'm afraid you won't locate Bennett on the campus today. He left last night after packing a bag. When I questioned him, he said he had an imperative obligation to complete and he would return shortly."

Pete doubted Bennett had used the words *imperative obligation*, but he thanked the skinny kid and went on to the dining hall. Maybe Bennett had talked to Libby. He hoped she'd be able to tell him where Bennett had gone.

He'd almost finished eating by the time Libby, accompanied by Alice-Marie, came in. His heart leapt when he spotted her, dressed in the soft brown two-piece suit Isabelle had chosen as her college outfit. He couldn't understand how a plain brown dress made her cheeks look so rosy and bright, but somehow it did. With her long dark hair tumbling across her shoulders and her sweet lips tipped into a soft smile, she was the prettiest woman on campus. Maybe on earth.

Pressing his hands on the tabletop, he rose. "Libby!" Her head turned, seeking his voice, and when she spotted him her face broke into a smile of jubilation. She glided toward him, both hands reaching, and he took hold. The simple contact set his heart to banging around in his chest like a moth trying to escape a jar. He laughed just for the sheer joy of it.

"You're back!" She beamed at him. "I didn't think I'd see you again before Thanksgiving. Is Jackson on his way to Shay's Ford? Did the police capture your father? Did Jackson manage to convince the judge of Oscar's innocence? How was Maelle—did you spend time with her?" Then she laughed, shaking her head. "And if I don't stop yammering, you'll never get a chance to talk."

Pulling loose, she waved her hands at him. "Sit back down. Finish eating. I'll go get my own breakfast, and then—"

Pete glanced at the clock on the wall and groaned. "I have a class, Libby. Our talk will have to wait until lunchtime."

Her face fell in disappointment. "Oh, but I agreed to meet with Alice-Marie and several girls who serve on the Women's Pan-Hellenic Council. They need two freshman representatives, and Alice-Marie is determined we'll both be selected. I'm so sorry."

He forced a grin when he would've rather groaned. "That's fine. Maybe dinner?"

"Oh yes. Definitely dinner." Her smile returned, and to his amazement she rose up on tiptoe and planted a kiss on his cheek before backing up two steps. "Dinner at six, Petey. I'll see you then!"

He watched her skip back to Alice-Marie, her steps light. He had so much to share with her, but he also had much to ask. Something had transpired in the past few days, igniting an even more attractive side to her. What could it be?

He limped to the dish bins to discard his tray, his gaze lingering on Libby. How would he last until six o'clock, when he could see her again?

CHAPTER THIRTY-SIX

Humming joyously, Libby ran the brush through her hair, smoothing the strands away from her face. Then with deft twists, she formed a braid and tied the end with a piece of ribbon. She smiled at her reflection, pleased with the results.

Trailing her fingers down the length of her thick black braid, she remembered the times Maelle had allowed her to brush her flowing auburn tresses. She'd always wanted to be like Maelle—strong, independent, full of confidence. And now, looking into her own peaceful face, she believed she'd accomplished the goal. But it had nothing to do with long hair or steeling herself against tears or even being self-confident.

Maelle was a woman of faith. She viewed God as her Father—her ever-present companion and helper. Libby pressed her hand to her heart, gratitude filling her at the assurance that she, too, knew God. He was with her and would never let her go.

She turned from the mirror and glanced at the clock. Five

forty-five. Her heart skipped a beat. She reached eagerly for her coat, but her fingers trembled as she struggled to fasten the buttons. Laughing at herself, she said aloud, "One would think I was going to see the Prince of England rather than meeting Petey Leidig in the dining hall!" But even the prince couldn't be as important as Petey—not to her.

Bowing her head, she clasped her hands together and closed her eyes. "God, You know how much I love Petey. But even more than I love him, I want to please You. If I must say . . ." The word she never said quivered on her lips. In her memory, her childish voice rang, calling out that word cheerfully to her parents as they headed down the lane. For so many years, *good-bye* had meant never seeing the person again. Could she trust God enough to give Him control of that word?

"Good-bye . . ." It rushed out, and her chest ached, but her lungs still drew breath. She flung her gaze to the ceiling, imagining God's smile of approval. "If I must say good-bye to Petey, I shall bear it, because I know I rest in Your every heartbeat." Blissful contentment swept over her. Surely something broken deep inside of herself had discovered healing with that long-denied utterance.

She retrieved her leather portfolio, which she'd filled with pages to share with Petey, and reached for the doorknob. She was ready.

She tried to walk, but her feet refused to cooperate. After a few sedate steps, they skipped. And then ran. Drawing herself up, she enforced slow, measured progress. But after only a few yards, she began skipping again. Propelled forward on a bubble of eagerness, she finally gave her feet freedom, and she ran the final distance to the dining hall. And there stood Petey, already waiting on the porch in his finest suit, his hair neatly combed and a smile of welcome lighting his face.

Libby stopped so suddenly she slid on the concrete floor. Their gazes met, and she couldn't prevent a grin from climbing her cheeks. "You're early."

"So are you."

Then they stood awkwardly, saying nothing. Several students pushed between them and filed through the door. Libby had to joggle her head to keep Petey in her sights; his smile never dimmed. Was he even aware of the interruption? She scampered forward, close enough that no one else could creep between them, so close she had to tip her face back to look into his dear blue eyes.

His eyes crinkled, and her heart fired straight into her throat. He stuck out his elbow. "Shall we go in?"

With a giggle, she took hold. They walked in together, his elbow pressing her hand tight against his ribs. The line was long, but she felt no sense of urgency. She didn't mind waiting. Not while she was with Petey. They didn't talk, even though people around them engaged in conversation. She discovered no need to talk. Looking up and seeing his familiar smile and the contentedness in his eyes was enough. When they finally had trays in hand, he gestured her to a table in the far corner. She reached it first, but for some reason she didn't quite fathom, she didn't immediately sit.

Petey limped up beside her. Something sparked in his eyes—understanding? approval?—and he set down his tray. With a slight bow, he took her tray and placed it next to his, then pulled out her chair. She slid into it as if they'd followed this routine dozens of times before. Their actions were seemingly by rote, but the quivering awareness of him in the center of her being was far beyond the ordinary.

God, I told you I could tell him good-bye. If You deem it best for me, I'll do it, but please give me strength.

"Shall I pray?" Petey held out his hand, and she slipped hers into it. His fingers closed, warm and firm, as he offered God thanks and asked a blessing for the food. His eyes opened, but he didn't let loose. Just sat there, his penetrating gaze pinned to her face, while he continued to hold her hand gently.

For a moment, Libby felt she was one of her storybook heroines come to life. Fluttering heartbeats and the blissful sensation of floating somewhere in clouds left her shaky and uncertain how to proceed. Someone would have to restore normalcy, and clearly it wouldn't be him.

With a little giggle, she pulled loose and reached for her fork. "So catch me up on everything that happened." Her voice squeaked out unnaturally high, but her casual actions seemed to bring Petey back to reality.

He jolted, looked at his plate as if surprised to have food in front of him, and picked up his own fork. After the first jerky stab with his fork, he relaxed, and while they ate he regaled her with the details of his time in Clayton.

Libby listened in amazement. In her mind, she envisioned puzzle pieces sliding effortlessly into place, completing a picture of God's own choosing. When he'd finished, she touched his wrist. "Petey, if Aaron and Isabelle hadn't invited your mother and siblings to reside in the orphans' school, would you really have quit school to take care of them?"

His forehead puckered. "I believe I would have. I don't think God could have blessed the decision—I left Him out of the planning—but I would have done it. And, as much as I wanted to help them . . ." He heaved a sigh, as if recognizing something for the first time. "I probably would have been miserable. I'm supposed to preach, Libby. That's my God-designed purpose. Anything else—even something well-intentioned that resulted in good—would have been less than satisfying. I'm more determined than ever to stay within God's will, no matter what it costs me."

As a pained expression took over his features, he set down his fork beside his half-empty plate. "Even if it costs me you."

Tears sprang into Libby's eyes. She clutched his wrist. "Oh, Petey . . . me too."

He sent her a puzzled look.

"Petey, may I share what happened while you were away?"

He turned his chair slightly to peer directly into her face. Transfixed, he listened as she explained her pell-mell race to find God. As she shared the revelations of her moments at the old stone foundations, tears winked in his eyes, and a sweet smile grew on his face.

"I was foolish for so long, trying to make God be what I wanted Him to be—some kind of wish-bestower." She chuckled ruefully, shaking her head. "As if He could ever be that small . . . Now that I've discovered my value in His eyes, being known and admired by thousands is so insignificant. His love has filled all the empty places in my hungering, needy soul."

Petey flipped his hand around to capture hers, squeezing hard, letting her know he approved. Then he gave a little start. "Libby, does this mean you've given up becoming a writer?"

She sucked in a breath. Biting down on her lower lip, she reached for the portfolio. Her fingers fumbled with the catch, but she finally managed to open it and pull out the newspaper bearing Petey's article.

"Petey, when I read this . . ." Head low, shame teasing her heart, she forced herself to continue. "I wanted to crawl in a hole and never come out. I've written stories just like the ones you're describing—stories glorifying the physical aspect of love but ignoring everything else. They were so easy to compose. My endless imagination . . . it served me well." She risked a glance at him. No recrimination showed in his face. Swallowing, she continued. "A magazine even purchased some of those stories from me and recently asked me to write for them exclusively. They offered me a contract."

She pulled out the letter from Mr. Price. Petey took it with a solemn nod and examined it as she went on. "I could think of a dozen ways to use that money, but what I wanted most was to give it to you." His head shot up, his eyebrows high. "For your family," she clarified. "I knew you could use it."

"Oh, but—"

"But after reading your article in the paper, and listening to my own heart, I couldn't agree to their request. I couldn't continue writing those kinds of stories—not even to help you."

His shoulders collapsed as relief flooded his face.

"I've already written to Mr. Price, asking him to withdraw my stories from their publishing schedule, and . . ." Her hands shook anew as she reached once more for the portfolio. "I'd like to offer him this instead." She placed six written pages in Petey's waiting hands. "It's a story. An allegory. Do you know what that is?"

His eyes on the pages, he shook his head.

"An allegory is a metaphorical story. It tells the tale of one thing while representing another."

His expression didn't clear.

She laughed softly. "Jesus told parables."

He tipped his head, his expression attentive.

"They were stories about people or events, but they held a deeper meaning. An allegory is similar in that the tale carries a moral or religious meaning outside of the story itself." She tapped the pages. "I used a reference from First Corinthians 13 when crafting this one. It's a love story, Petey, between a man and woman, but the deeper message reflects the love God holds for all of us." She smiled. "It occurs to me that God is the maker of romance. Is there any greater love story than the one in Luke that tells of Jesus' sacrifice for mankind?"

Petey blew out a soft breath. "I'd never thought of it that way."

Her hands shook as she made her next request. "I want you to read my story. And then, afterward, if you believe it's appropriate, I'll send it to Mr. Price."

"Why do you need me to read it first? It's your story. You should do what you want to with it."

"But your opinion is important to me. That day you caught me on the lawn and told me you were going to wage a battle against love stories, I—" She cringed, remembering her fierce reaction. "I felt guilty. It made it hard for me to look you in the face." Sighing, she admitted, "I never want anything like that coming between us again. So read it, Petey, please? And be honest with me." She shrugged. "Of course, even if you approve it, Mr. Price may tell me it's not what he's looking for. But that's all right. At least I'll know I followed my conscience and didn't proceed with something that I believed would displease God. That's much more important."

Petey lowered the pages to the table. For long moments he seemed to examine them, his mouth set in a serious line. Then he looked at Libby. Something in his expression made her hold her breath.

"Libby, what you said about following your conscience and not doing things that would displease God . . ."

"*There* you two are!" The voice came from behind Libby's head. She whirled around and found Alice-Marie, hands on her hips and fury blazing in her eyes. "Come with me *right now*. You must see what Bennett has done this time!"

CHAPTER THIRTY-SEVEN

Students clustered on the lawn beneath a bare oak tree, jabbering excitedly. The glow from a nearby streetlamp highlighted Bennett's unruly mane of red hair in the center of the group. Pete took hold of Libby's arm. "C'mon." With Alice-Marie stomping along behind them, they pushed through the crowd to reach Bennett. When Pete got a good look at his buddy, he jerked so hard in surprise he almost knocked himself down.

Libby clapped her hands to her cheeks. "Bennett! What have you done?"

Bennett smoothed his hand down the front of a grayish-green army uniform. "Signed up." He smirked at Libby. "Didn't I tell you I would?"

"But—" She shook her head, her focus bouncing from his head to his toes and up again. "Now? When you're in school?"

Bennett laughed. He smacked the arm of the closest student

and bobbed his head toward the dining hall. "You all go on in and get a seat. I'll join you in a minute."

The others wandered off, still chattering. Pete stood in stunned silence between Libby and Alice-Marie. Both girls stared at Bennett, and they seemed to have lost their ability to speak. Bennett grinned widely, fingering the metal buttons on the trim-fitting blouse. "Pretty sharp, huh? No gun yet—that'll come after I've been through training—but they let me wear the uniform anyway." He tugged a little hat free of his back pocket and plopped it on his head, setting it at a jaunty angle. Then he threw his arms wide. "So whadd'ya think?"

Alice-Marie sprang to life. "I think you've completely lost your mind!" She turned to Libby. "Look at him, all ready for war! All ready to . . . to . . ." She burst into tears and took off running toward the women's dormitory.

Libby advanced on Bennett. "What in the world compelled you to do this now? The United States isn't in the war. There's no reason for you to take up a gun." She sounded more hurt than angry. She looked to Pete, and he stepped forward, placing a comforting hand on her shoulder.

"Did you really join the army, Bennett, or did you just borrow this uniform?" Knowing Bennett's penchant for attention-getting, he wouldn't put such a stunt past his friend.

Bennett's jaw tightened. "It's real." He shrugged, tugging at the hem of the blouse. "Only the reserves, though. 'Course, if we go to war, that won't matter—they'll still send me. But with the reserves, I can stay in school. School's paid for, so I might as well stick with it."

Pete felt Libby wilt beside him, and he understood her relief. At least Bennett wasn't planning to take off immediately. "So why not wait until you've finished school?"

Bennett set his chin at a belligerent angle. "Wanna know the truth? When I first started thinking about it, I wanted to do it because of you, Pete."

Pete jolted. "Me?"

"Yeah. I'm just so tired of never measuring up." A derisive note crept into Bennett's voice. "At the orphans' school, the Rowleys were always holding you up as an example of how I should behave. Any games we ever played, Lib chose you before she'd choose me. Here at the college, people seemed to take to you better than me—giving you a nickname and talking about how you could do so much even with that blasted peg . . ."

He drew in a deep breath and blew it out. A cloud formed around his head and then drifted away. "But you could never be a soldier. You could never show up here"—he held out his hands, indicating the surroundings—"in a uniform."

"So you did it to spite me?" Pete really didn't want to know the answer. If Bennett had joined the army simply to one-up him and was one day killed on a battlefield because of it, it would destroy him.

"Maybe at first, but . . ." Bennett dug his boot toe in the grass, his head low. "Got to thinking about it. I don't have a family—not like you have. Nobody waitin' for me. No place to really go when I get out of school. Figured if I'm in the army, then I'll always have a place . . . to belong."

Bennett's words pierced Pete's heart. He'd done a poor job of helping his friend see that he could secure a place of belonging if he would only accept God's love. He hung his head, forcing down the knot of sadness in his throat.

"Guess that's why I wanted to be in Beta Theta Pi so bad. Best fraternity on campus. It'd make me feel special—like I fit some-where." He snorted. "Pretty dumb. Now that they said I can join, I told 'em no. Just doesn't seem all that important anymore. Not sure why . . ." Bennett glanced over his shoulder toward Rhodes Hall. "Guess I really upset Alice-Marie, huh?"

Libby nodded. "You certainly did."

Bennett pulled his lips to the side. "Think I should go . . . talk to her?"

"I think you should."

She spoke matter-of-factly, making Pete smile. He'd always been amused by Libby's feisty side, but this even-tempered angle was nice, too.

"Well, guess I'll . . ." He flapped his hand in the direction of the dormitory.

"Go talk to Alice-Marie," Pete said, "and when you're done, come see me. There's something I need to tell you. Something I want you to *hear*."

Bennett stood for a moment, looking directly in Pete's face. A crooked grin tugged at the corner of his lips. "Yeah, I think I know what." He gave a brusque nod. "I'll try to hear you out." He ambled off, his feet scuffing at the grass.

Pete turned back to Libby. "Now, we were in the middle of—"

Her mouth dropped open. "My portfolio!" She spun and raced back into the dining hall. Moments later she emerged carrying the black leather folder. She held it up, her smile bright. "I didn't want to lose this."

"And I was about to say . . ." Pete swallowed. She'd been so supportive in Clayton, offering encouragement and fighting hard to keep Oscar from the hangman's noose. When given the opportunity to earn money with her writing, her first thoughts had been to use it to help him.

He knew she cared for him—she wanted his support in submitting a different kind of story to the magazine. And now God was important to her. She'd openly admitted she wanted to follow

God's will for her life. That change made his heart sing. But did all of that mean she loved him?

She swung her portfolio, the leather creating a soft swish as it brushed her skirt, while she waited for him to speak. But he couldn't seem to make his tongue form the sentences. He'd heard that actions spoke more loudly than words. So Pete decided to let actions speak. Taking one step forward, he caught Libby in his embrace and pressed his lips to her surprised mouth.

❧

Libby dropped her portfolio in the grass.

At that moment, a group of students exited the dining hall, their presence an untimely intrusion. Petey backed away from her, looking toward the sidewalk. Libby quickly bent over and picked up her portfolio. The moment she straightened, Petey took hold of her elbow and propelled her across the dark yard. At first she thought he was returning her to the women's dormitory, but he hop-skipped past the building and headed for the far edge of the campus.

Her breath came in little bursts as he led her farther and farther from Rhodes Hall, and they finally reached the tree-lined path that led to the stone foundation. But instead of taking her to the meadow, he tugged her beneath a tree and leaned against the trunk, his chest rising and falling with the heaviness of his breathing.

Libby's chest also heaved, but she couldn't be certain which bore responsibility—the brisk walk or the wonderment of what he'd done. "P-Petey?" Her voice rasped out. "You kissed me!"

Petey caught her braid and let it slide through his fingers until he reached the end. He held the tip, playfully swishing the long plait to and fro. "I've wanted to kiss you since your sixteenth birthday. I've loved you that long. Maybe longer." His features, tinged by moonlight creeping between the bare branches over-head, were pinched with remorse. "But I shouldn't have chosen that moment. I—"

"You should do it again."

He jerked upright and gawked at her for one startled second. Then a soft laugh—a joyous sound—escaped his throat. He released her braid and brought up his hands to cup her cheeks. He leaned in slowly, torturing her with the delay, and at last brushed her lips with his.

Her eyes slid closed. *So the storybook tales are right. One's heart does take wing.* She let the portfolio slip through her fingers. It landed with a light crunch in the leaves beneath their feet. She curled her arms around his waist and rested her cheek against his chest.

"Libby?" He held her tight, proving that his heart was as affected as hers. She felt it beating even through his jacket. "You said you wanted to please God with your life . . . with your talents. Is that right?"

"Yes." She couldn't be certain how God would have her use her writing abilities—whether in allegorical stories meant to paint a picture of His love and grace, or in articles that would inform and inspire. But she trusted He would reveal His will to her if she continually sought Him in prayer.

"I want to follow Him, too, with every decision I make, including . . ." His fingers splayed on her back momentarily and then very gently he set her aside. He collapsed against the tree's trunk. "I can't think when I'm holding you."

She swallowed a knowing chuckle. So the storybook tales were right on that, too. She wouldn't tempt him. She inched backward, allowing him plenty of space. Then linking her hands in front of her, she admired the sight of Petey bathed in starlight. Alice-Marie was right—his hair was the color of moonlight. And hers matched the dark sky behind the stars. A perfect fit.

"Petey, you don't have to think right now. There's time for thinking. We're still very young. God has much more to teach us, I'm sure. Right now, it's enough to know He brought us together and He gave us the opportunity to become friends."

"Good friends," he added.

"Best friends," she corrected. She reached out, and he responded in kind. Their fingers met and wove together—a simple touch, yet heartfelt. "I love you, and it makes me so happy to know you love me. But what's even better is we both love God. With both of us seeking His will, we'll discover what He wants for us . . . in time . . . and it will be perfect."

For long moments they stood, her fingers linked with his, her senses thrumming. It seemed to Libby they were the only two people in the world.

Her gaze drifted to the edge of the trees, to the meadow where the stone foundation lay, unobtrusive but available to any who would seek. Petey's thumb caressed hers, and she looked up as he looked down. They smiled in unison.

His voice husky, he said, "I should walk you back to Rhodes Hall. I don't want you to miss curfew."

She nodded. If she came in late, Miss Banks would surely reprimand her. Again.

"I also need to talk to Bennett tonight."

Libby knew what Petey would address—Bennett's overwhelming need for belonging and where he could find it if only he would release his stubborn will and submit to God. It was difficult to relinquish one's pride, but she'd experienced the joy that followed when one finally surrendered. She prayed that Bennett would listen to Petey's words, and believe.

Hand-in-hand, they ambled up the tree-lined path. When they reached the dormitory porch, she started to head inside, but he held her back with a gentle tug on her hand.

"I won't be going to Shay's Ford for Thanksgiving. I need to catch up on my schoolwork. But I promised my ma—"

Libby marveled at how easily the title *ma* slipped from Petey's lips. No resentment colored his tone or hardened his features.

"—I'd be there for Christmas. Please greet everyone for me when you go, and make sure my brothers and sister are settling in all right, will you?"

Libby squeezed his hand, touched by his concern for these people—these strangers—who bore his name. "Of course I will. And I'll pray, every day, for their peace and happiness."

His lips curved into his familiar endearing smile. Then he looked quickly right and left before leaning forward and brushing a sweet chaste kiss on her cheek. "Night, Libby. Sweet dreams."

She had no doubt his parting words would find fulfillment.

CHAPTER THIRTY-EIGHT

"Libby, I've missed you. It's so good to have you home—and for three whole weeks!"

Libby leaned into the lumpy cushions of the well-worn parlor settee and grinned at Maelle. "You might change your mind before our Christmas break is over. After all, you aren't used to having *three* girls underfoot. I might become an intrusion."

Maelle had insisted Libby stay in her home rather than at the orphans' school for the lengthy break, but every day they'd driven out to the school for time with Isabelle, Aaron, and the children. Even though Isabelle had put them to work decorating the orphans' school, wrapping gifts sent by area churches for the children, and helping Cookie Ramona prepare goodies for the upcoming holiday celebration, Libby hadn't minded. It felt so good to be *home* again, surrounded by people she loved.

She glanced across the orphanage's parlor at Hannah and Hester, who sat cross-legged on the woven wool rug with Petey's little sister Elma engrossed in dressing paper dolls. Their faces looked so content, and an occasional giggle rang from the small circle. Such a change in a short of amount of time—the difference love made, Libby realized. She also realized, with a start, that no animosity twisted her heart. She and Petey had begun praying together each evening, and they'd asked God to help her release her resentment toward Maelle and Jackson. Apparently the prayers had been answered.

Maelle lazily bumped Libby's shoulder. "Since when have I seen you as an intrusion?" She offered a mock scowl that disappeared on a brief laugh. "Just because I'm a mother now doesn't mean I don't have time for my favorite hand-picked little sister. And I suspect—" her expression softened as she gazed at the blond-haired girls—"Hannah and Hester will benefit from having you as an aunt. Attending college, becoming a published author . . ." Maelle's eyes glittered. "I'm so proud of you, Libby."

Libby contemplated Maelle's words. If she couldn't have Maelle as her adopted mother, having her as a big sister was the next best thing. She also liked the idea of being a positive influence for Hannah and Hester—much the way Maelle had influenced her. She smiled, nodding. "I'd love to be Hannah and Hester's aunt . . . as long as they don't call me Aunt Libby." She pretended to shudder. "Makes me feel old!"

Maelle slung her arm around Libby's shoulder, and the two shared a laugh. Libby leaned in close, relishing the comfortable camaraderie. How wonderful to set aside hostility and be at ease with her dear mentor and friend.

Isabelle Rowley bustled into the room, wiping her hands on a full, ruffled apron. She flapped the apron's skirt at the girls and scolded mildly, "Get your mess picked up quickly now—Mr. Rowley, Pete, and Wendell are coming up the front steps with the Christmas tree. They'll stumble over you if you don't move."

Giggling, the girls gathered their things and scuttled around the corner. Their feet clattered on the stairs as the front door burst open, bringing in a chill breeze and the scent of snow and pine. Maelle caught Libby's hand, and they dashed to the wide doorway leading to the dormitory's foyer in time to witness Aaron trying to wrestle a giant pine tree through the opening. Needles flew in every direction as Aaron yanked on the rough trunk.

Isabelle stood on the first stair riser, wringing her hands. "Oh, Aaron, be careful! I think this one's too big. You might need to go back and cut a smaller one."

He shook his head. Sweat beaded across his brow. "Nope. This is the one Wendell chose, and we're gonna get it into the parlor if I have to cut a bigger door opening!" He gave another mighty yank. The large bottom branches folded inward, allowing the tree to pop through the doorway with another shower of needles. Aaron fell *kerplop!* onto his backside, and Petey and Wendell stumbled in behind the tree, nearly falling onto their cold-reddened noses.

Isabelle gasped, Maelle burst out laughing, and Libby stared at the tree. She clapped her hands in delight. "Look at it! The biggest tree ever!" She dashed past Petey and Wendell to slam the door closed, then shifted up beside Petey. Cold radiated from his jacket. She shivered and hugged herself. "It's perfect!"

"I think so, too," Petey said, clapping his brother on the shoulder. The boy beamed.

The thunder of footsteps sounded overhead, and children spilled down the stairway. Apparently the twins and Elma had spread the news that the tree had arrived. Eagerness lit every face, and their happy chatter filled the crowded space.

Isabelle raised her hands, holding them back. "Yes, we'll decorate the tree after supper, just as we'd planned, but for now you must stay out of the way. While Mr. Rowley and Pete secure the tree in its holder, you go upstairs and round up all the ornaments."

With cheerful shouts, the children wheeled and bounded up the stairs, disappearing around the bend at the top. Isabelle turned to examine the tree. "I hope we'll have enough ornaments to decorate this tree. Goodness, but it's monstrous!" Then she laughed, shaking her head and winking at Wendell. "It's also the loveliest one we've ever had—so full and well shaped. Even without ornaments, it's beautiful."

Wendell hunched into his jacket, red streaking across his face. "Thank you, ma'am."

Maelle stepped around the tree, heading for the staircase. "I'll go help the children find all the boxes of ornaments. I might even put them to work making paper chains. That should keep them out of the way until you're ready for them." She dashed up the stairs.

Isabelle shook her head, looking after Maelle with fondness lighting her green eyes. "I'll never be convinced she didn't offer to oversee the children to avoid helping with the supper preparations." She shrugged. "Oh well. She'll keep the children out from underfoot, which is a tremendous help. And Libby can set the table for supper. Come along, dear." Isabelle swept down the hallway.

Libby preferred to stay and watch Petey and Aaron stand the tree in its wooden holder in front of the parlor's largest window, but she trailed after Isabelle as directed.

Promptly at six, everyone gathered around the trestle table in the school's massive dining room and crowded onto the benches with no small amount of giggling and good-natured elbow bumping. As always, Isabelle and Aaron sat at opposite ends, and the children filled the benches that stretched along the table's sides. Aaron offered grace and began passing bowls.

It never failed to surprise Libby how the Rowleys managed to fit everyone around the table. Over the years, the faces had changed, with some children going to adoptive homes and new ones arriving, but regardless of how many children resided under the school's roof, there was a place for everyone.

It was an especially tight fit this evening. Since it was Christmas Eve, Matt and Lorna had joined the family for supper, and even Cookie Ramona and Petey's mother sat at the table instead of bustling back and forth between kitchen and dining room. With the other additional guests—Petey and Libby, Maelle and Jackson and their daughters—everyone was forced to squeeze together. But no one complained. However, Libby decided it was best Bennett had gone to Alice-Marie's for the first week of break. There wasn't a spare inch of space on either of the benches to accommodate his bulk.

Libby looked across the table at Petey, who scrunched between his youngest brothers. Despite having to press his elbows to his sides to keep from jostling either of the boys, he appeared relaxed and assured. Finding peace with his mother had erased the worry from his brow, and each time he leaned across little Lorenzo to share a few words with Berta Leidig, Libby's heart thrilled.

God, so many prayers have been answered. Petey is at peace with his family; I'm at peace with Maelle. . . . Christmas is a time for peace—thank You that we can celebrate without even a hint of unrest.

The moment they finished eating, the children began clamoring to decorate the tree. Isabelle raised her hands, commanding silence, and after several boisterous seconds their voices finally stilled. "Everyone, carry your own plate and cutlery to the kitchen to help Cookie Ramona. Then *walk*—no running, or someone might be trampled—to the parlor and we'll—"

Whoops erupted, covering her final directions. Wild scuffling filled the air as the youngsters scrambled from the benches, snatched up their plates, and dashed for the kitchen. Spoons and forks bounced onto the floor. Giggles and squeals rang. Feet thudded as children ignored Isabelle's instruction to walk. Libby placed her hands over her ears to block the raucous noise, but even then the joyous clamor threatened to deafen her.

Isabelle looked across the table to Aaron and laughed, holding her hands out in surrender. He added his laughter, then plucked their little son, Reggie, from his high chair. "I'll direct in the kitchen. You head to the parlor and monitor from that end," he said as he strode after the children.

Maelle and Lorna rose and began helping Mrs. Leidig clear the table, but Matt curled his hand around Lorna's elbow. "No work for you, soon-to-be mama. You go on to the parlor and supervise the decoratin'. I'll help with the clearin' off." Lorna offered a mild protest, but Matt hushed her with a kiss.

Although Libby knew she shouldn't watch their display of affection, she couldn't seem to look away. Love spilled from every corner—between Maelle and Jackson, Matt and Lorna, Aaron and Isabelle, and even Petey and his family. Her heart expanded, happiness filling her so completely she thought her chest might burst. What joy to be in the midst of this wonderful throng!

Eager to join the others in decorating the tree, she reached for her plate. But she felt a warm hand rest on her shoulder, stopping her. She glanced up to find Petey standing behind her, grinning. Her pulse immediately quickened just having him near. She started to ask what he wanted, but he lifted his finger to his lips, and she held the question inside.

Without a word, he slid his hand down her arm until he found her fingers. Linking hands with her, he led her around the corner and down the hallway, drawing her into the small cubby beneath the stairs, out of everyone's sight.

He leaned into the corner, ducking slightly to avoid the sloping ceiling above. "Ah, quiet . . ."

Libby could have argued with him. Varying sounds carried from other parts of the school—children's voices from the parlor, dishes clanking together in the kitchen, Isabelle's confident voice offering directions on placing ornaments on the tree. But then she looked into Petey's dear blue eyes, and those sounds faded into the background. The shadowy niche, even though far from idyllic, became a refuge of intimacy.

He still held her hand, and she curled her fingers more snugly around his. He offered a slight squeeze in return before releasing her to reach into his pocket. "I have something for you."

His voice, low and husky, sent a tremor of delight down Libby's spine. An eager giggle escaped her throat. Although he'd been a perfect gentleman for the past weeks, not stealing so much as a kiss on her cheek, she hoped he might take advantage of their solitude and gift her with a kiss on her lips. Tipping her head, she offered a teasing smile. "But Christmas isn't until tomorrow."

"But tomorrow others will be around. And this gift is . . ." He crinkled his brow for a moment, seeming to search for an appropriate word. With a sigh, he ended with, "Personal."

Perhaps he did intend to kiss her. Unconsciously, she swayed toward him. His hand lifted from his pocket, and he held a small box on his open palm. Libby jolted back slightly to peer at the box. Formed of wood with a hinged top, it appeared scarred, as if the finish had been rubbed away over years of use.

"Merry Christmas, Libby."

Something sweet and yearning wound around Libby's heart at his tender tone. Her gaze lifted to meet his. "What is it?"

He gave his palm a slight bounce, enticing her to reach for it. "Look and see."

With slow, deliberate movements, allowing anticipation to build within her breast, she reached for the box. Her fingers trembled as she popped the lid, and she released a gasp of surprise. Who would have expected such a worn-looking box to contain such a bright treasure?

Pressing her hands to her wildly beating heart, she gaped at Petey. "Oh! It . . . it's beautiful!"

He lifted the brooch from its nest of threadbare black silk. The scant light reaching from the hallway lamps glinted on the red-faceted stones, casting a rosy glow on the inside edge of the pearls that circled the center cluster. He slipped the empty box into his pocket and reached for the rounded collar of her dress. His knuckles brushed her collarbone, sending a prickle of awareness down her spine as he fastened the brooch into place. Libby automatically shifted her hand, fingering the stones by turn. With the brooch pinned almost beneath her chin, she couldn't see it, but she easily distinguished the pearls from the red gemstones.

He stood gazing down at the brooch. "It looks perfect there. I knew it would."

Libby took in a deep breath, willing her galloping heart to slow. "Petey, I've never seen anything more lovely. But where . . . ? What . . . ?" Her tongue seemed incapable of forming sentences. Never would she have imagined receiving such an elaborate gift.

He leaned against the wall and smiled at her, his peg leg softly *tap-tapping* against the planked floor. "The brooch is made of pearls and rubies. Ma told me my grandfather gave it to my grandmother on their wedding day. Then my grandmother gave it to Ma when she married my father. And now . . ."

Libby touched the brooch lightly with her fingertips, imagining the generations of women who'd worn this brooch before her. She shook her head slightly. "Petey, you should keep this. It belongs in your family."

He shifted, his body angling toward hers until his face was mere inches away. "If you have it, it will be in my family. Because I'm asking you to accept it as an engagement brooch."

Might she be dreaming? She pinched her wrist. The sharp pain let her know she was very much awake. She met his unblinking, serious gaze. "Engagement brooch?"

He offered a slow nod. "Yes. We shouldn't marry yet. Not until we're finished with school. But I know I love you. I know I want you to be a part of the rest of my life—a part of my ministry, a part of my heart . . ." Suddenly he paused, his brow furrowing. "Am I assuming? This past month . . . meeting every day to pray together, and to talk. My love for you has grown deeper. I can't imagine myself without you. But if you—"

She grabbed his hands and clung hard. Sweet memories of past moments—when laughter rang, when tears pricked, when their hearts united in prayer for Bennett—rose up and swirled through her mind, almost making her dizzy. She'd shared so much with Petey. She couldn't imagine herself without him. "I feel the same way. I love you. And I'd like nothing more than to pledge myself to you."

She rose up on tiptoe as his arms slipped around her waist, drawing her near. Their lips met, and she was surprised by the salty taste. She hadn't even realized she was crying—joyous tears of homecoming. Nestling close to Petey, she felt as though a little puzzle piece slid into its place in the picture of her life.

From the parlor, a melody wafted—children's voices joining in song. Libby tipped her head toward the sound, a smile tugging at the corners of her lips. Ever since Libby had come to the orphanage, Isabelle had led the children in Christmas hymns before sending them to bed on Christmas Eve. Although she wanted nothing more than to remain in Petey's arms forever, she knew they should join the others.

He must have had the same thought, because he gently removed her from his embrace. "They're singing. We need to go."

She nodded, and he took her hand. Together they moved down the hallway to the parlor, where they paused in the wide doorway.

The children sat on the floor, clustered around the towering tree weighted with glimmering glass balls, paper chains, and childish cutouts of stars and gingerbread men. The tip of the tree brushed the ceiling, its bent top branch seeming to peer down at the gathered singers.

Libby stood in silence, listening to the children sing, with her hand secure within Petey's grasp. Her gaze drifted slowly around the room, the images burning into her mind: Isabelle and Aaron at the fireplace, little Reggie drowsing on Aaron's shoulder, and Rebecca and Constance leaning against Isabelle's skirts; Maelle and Jackson scrunched on the settee with Hannah and Hester pressed between them; Matt and Lorna sharing the old rocker, Matt's arms encircling Lorna's waist and Lorna's arm crooked behind his neck, her fingers in his hair; Petey's mother perched on a straight-backed chair with Lorenzo and Dennis at her knees and Elma, Wendell, and Orel surrounding her. Peaceful expressions on every face.

A lump formed in her throat, bringing a fresh rush of happy tears. She loved every person gathered here. Her fingers tightened, and Petey's pressed hers in response. Warmth and contentedness filled her so thoroughly she wondered how she could contain the feelings without bursting.

Maelle's face shifted, her gaze meeting Libby's from across the room. Libby touched the brooch, and Maelle's eyes followed the movement of her hand. A knowing smile lifted the corners of her lips, and she winked at Libby. Libby smiled in reply, their communication complete although absent of words.

Eager to see whether Petey had glimpsed the blessing in Maelle's eyes, she looked up at him. The glimmer in his eyes told her he'd seen and was as touched as she by Maelle's approval. Without a word, he slipped his arms around her waist, drawing her against his length. She folded her arms over the tops of his, discovering they fit perfectly together. He dipped his head to rest his chin on her hair and sighed contentedly.

Libby closed her eyes and allowed her other senses to soak up every detail of the moment—the warmth of Petey's embrace, the gentle pressure of his chin at her temple, the sweet voices of the children singing "Silent Night," the mingled scent of pine from the freshly cut tree and smoke from the fireplace. Later, she would want to recall the unique serenade that heralded her heart finding its place of peace and belonging. Perhaps she would write of it so it was captured forever. But for now, it was enough to rest blissfully in Petey's arms.

ACKNOWLEDGMENTS

To my family: *Mom and Daddy, Don, my sweet girls*—this writing life has taken me in directions none of us could have foreseen, but you walk alongside me, sharing in this ministry. Thank you for your support and for being proud of me.

To my critiquers: *Eileen, Connie, Margie, Judy, Ramona, and Donna*—thank you for your suggestions, but mostly for your prayers and friendship. I'm glad we're in this together!

To *Grant Bumgarner*—thank you for openly sharing your experiences as a "one-legged man" with me. Your honesty helped me delve deep into Petey's character and feel as though I truly knew him.

To *Deena Sawyer*, my sister-in-law but also my friend—your encouragement is always perfectly timed. Sure do love you!

To *Charlene and the staff at Bethany House*—I'm so blessed to work with people who share my passion for creating stories of God's love and grace. Thank you for everything you do.

Finally, and most importantly, to *God*—You have proved the truth of Jeremiah 29:11–13 to me. You are found by all who seek You, and Your plans are always better than our own. Thank You for blessing me abundantly, exceedingly, and beyond all I could have hoped or imagined. May any praise or glory be reflected directly back to You.

KIM VOGEL SAWYER is the author of sixteen novels, including many CBA and ECPA bestsellers. Her books have won the ACFW Book of the Year Award, the Gayle Wilson Award of Excellence, and the Inspirational Readers Choice Award. Kim is active in her church, where she leads women's fellowship and participates in both voice and bell choirs. In her spare time, she enjoys drama, quilting, and calligraphy. Kim and her husband, Don, reside in Kansas, and have three daughters and six grandchildren. She invites you to visit her Web site at *www.kimvogelsawyer.com* for more information.

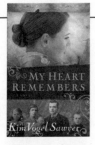

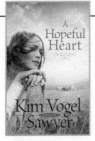